"Sey's prose sparkles with energy and heart . . . A delightful debut novel packed with strong, intelligent characters and a plot that truly satisfies!"

—Jane Porter, bestselling author of *Flirting with Forty*

Killer Kiss

Patrick moved faster than Liz imagined was possible. Before she could even work up a good sneer, he was there in front of her, his big, hard hands cupping her elbows and lifting her right off her feet and into his body. Then his mouth was on hers, hot, seeking, hungry.

A thousand fragmented thoughts flitted through her brain, none of which were any help. Should she jam a pencil in his ear? Ram a knee into his crotch? Throw her arms around his neck and start participating with some enthusiasm?

Then his tongue traced the seam of her lips, a request, a demand, an invitation . . .

"*Money, Honey* is laugh-out-loud funny and fantastically hot! Susan Sey is a fantastic new voice on the romance scene."

—Victoria Dahl, author of *Lead Me On*

"*Money, Honey* is fast, hot, fresh, and outright fun. Just go read it. You'll love it!"

—Susan Kay Law, author of *The Paper Marriage*

Money, Honey

SUSAN SEY

BERKLEY SENSATION, NEW YORK

THE BERKLEY PUBLISHING GROUP
Published by the Penguin Group
Penguin Group (USA) Inc.
375 Hudson Street, New York, New York 10014, USA
Penguin Group (Canada), 90 Eglinton Avenue East, Suite 700, Toronto, Ontario M4P 2Y3, Canada
(a division of Pearson Penguin Canada Inc.)
Penguin Books Ltd., 80 Strand, London WC2R 0RL, England
Penguin Group Ireland, 25 St. Stephen's Green, Dublin 2, Ireland (a division of Penguin Books Ltd.)
Penguin Group (Australia), 250 Camberwell Road, Camberwell, Victoria 3124, Australia
(a division of Pearson Australia Group Pty. Ltd.)
Penguin Books India Pvt. Ltd., 11 Community Centre, Panchsheel Park, New Delhi—110 017, India
Penguin Group (NZ), 67 Apollo Drive, Rosedale, North Shore 0632, New Zealand
(a division of Pearson New Zealand Ltd.)
Penguin Books (South Africa) (Pty.) Ltd., 24 Sturdee Avenue, Rosebank, Johannesburg 2196,
South Africa

Penguin Books Ltd., Registered Offices: 80 Strand, London WC2R 0RL, England

MONEY, HONEY

A Berkley Sensation Book / published by arrangement with the author

PRINTING HISTORY
Berkley Sensation mass-market edition / July 2010

ISBN: 978-0-425-23548-5

BERKLEY® SENSATION
Berkley Sensation Books are published by The Berkley Publishing Group,
a division of Penguin Group (USA) Inc.,
375 Hudson Street, New York, New York 10014.
BERKLEY® SENSATION and the "B" design are trademarks of Penguin Group (USA) Inc.

PRINTED IN THE UNITED STATES OF AMERICA

10 9 8 7 6 5 4 3 2 1

Acknowledgments

First, to my mom, Dorothy, who taught me to love books and to think I could do anything. And to my dad, Bob, who taught me the day's not over until the work is done. Between them, they gave me the courage to start and the grit to finish. I love you both.

To my mother-in-law, Linda, and my father-in-law, John, both of whom love me and don't hesitate to claim me in public in spite of the fact that I write books with s-e-x in them. I know it's not exactly what you signed up for, and your support means more to me than I can say.

To Claudia and Greta, who fill me with pride and wonder every single day because they are amazing little people. And also because they can and do occupy themselves during the hours I spend hunched over the keyboard. Thanks, chickens. Mommy loves you.

To my agent, Susannah Taylor, who always finds a way to make my work *more* rather than *different*. Thank you.

To the Romance Bandits—a girl couldn't have better friends. Here's to potted plants, the arsenal and true love with lots of boom.

To my wonderful critique partner and dear friend Inara Scott, without whom I would be a long-winded (okay, *longer*-winded) disaster. I'm so grateful our husbands have exquisite taste.

And finally, to my husband, Bryan, whose faith in me is a force of nature. You are, without a doubt, the best thing in my life. If this writing thing actually takes off, I'm totally going to buy you that ridiculously huge TV your heart desires. And if you want to watch Husker football on it all weekend, I won't say a thing except Go Big Red. I love you that much. xoxoxoxo

Chapter

I

Patrick O'Connor strolled into the FBI's Grief Creek office with a sangfroid not normally seen in the average felon. Patrick, however, was no ordinary felon. He was a *superior* felon. At least he had been. And had it not been for a woman—*two* women, actually—he might still be one today.

He didn't necessarily regret reforming. The straight world had been ridiculously good to him. But having his hand forced, and by a couple of women? That was a trick he didn't care to repeat. He'd spent the past three years shunning them both with a bloodless and very satisfying precision.

So he was mildly astonished to find himself on the verge of paying a visit to one of those very women at the behest of the other. He was a rich man, but loyalty had already cost him more than he could afford. He really ought to give it up.

Not that he hadn't tried on occasion. Thieves didn't achieve Patrick's level of success without a certain moral flexibility on the concepts of loyalty and ownership, after all. So he'd been startled to run up against this stubborn and unexpected streak of possessiveness in his character. What was his was, apparently, his. Troublesome women included.

And while he'd been more than happy to allow them to weather life's storms these past years without his supervision or influence, this was different. This particular storm was his fault and Patrick wasn't one to shirk responsibility. No matter how uncomfortable that responsibility might be.

He paused outside a cubicle, checked the nameplate stuck to the cheap fabric partition: FBI Special Agent Elizabeth Brynn. He hesitated next to an evil-smelling coffee station, amused by an unexpected tingle of nerves. Liz Brynn. The law-enforcement half of his own personal Waterloo and the last person to ever arrest him. The *only* person to ever arrest him, actually.

He put his usual mental asterisk next to the word *arrest*. After all, did it really count as an arrest if a man voluntarily surrendered himself to the authorities? If he was never booked, formally charged or incarcerated?

Not that he hadn't done his time. Three years weaseling for Liz Brynn in exchange for his sister's get-out-of-jail-free card had been a particularly punishing sentence, and not just because he wasn't accustomed to the leash.

It was more because Liz Brynn wasn't just a cop. She also had the unfortunate distinction of being the only woman Patrick had ever wanted but never had. Fate's idea of a laugh, he supposed. Cosmic justice, maybe. His cross to bear in return for all those years of unrepentant thievery. Who knew? The universe was a mystery, and he'd given up trying to work it out.

The urge to smooth his shirt was unbearable, but he didn't give in. He shook his head at his own foolishness, sank deeper into the indolent slouch he knew she hated and stepped into her world.

Her back was to him. She had the desk phone tucked into that old-gold spill of hair at her shoulder while she typed with one hand and punched buttons on a cell phone with the other. Even from the doorway, Patrick could see that her black pantsuit was off the rack and not the best choice for that interesting little figure of hers. Certainly not the best choice for concealing the shoulder holster she wore.

Even so, the usual shot of pure adrenaline rocketed through his system at the sight of her, and he had to reach for a properly lazy tone when he said, "Hello, Liz."

He had the pleasure of watching that capable hand falter over the keyboard, clench briefly into a fist, then slap down on the arm of her chair as if she needed to put it somewhere safe. Maybe she didn't want him the way he wanted her, but at least she wasn't unaffected by him. That was something.

She snapped shut her cell phone, hung up the landline and spun her chair around to glare at him.

"Patrick O'Connor," she said. "Our security must be slipping."

Patrick only smiled at her, uncomfortably aware that words were quite beyond him for the moment. God, that face of hers. It had always packed a punch, but now that she'd grown into it, he could hardly breathe for drinking it in.

She wasn't pretty. Liz would never be pretty. The cheekbones were too strong, the chin too sharp, the eyes too big and not nearly guileless enough. But all those precise, determined edges framing that soft, baby-doll mouth commanded his attention just like it always had, God help him.

"It's nice to see you, too," Patrick finally said, when he was certain he could speak again. "You're looking well." He allowed himself a brief glance at the sleek sweep of gold that brushed her shoulders and made his palms itch to touch. "You've grown your hair a bit. A little girlie for you, but it works surprisingly well."

She ignored him. "What are you doing here, Patrick?" she asked.

He lifted his brows, all innocence. "You don't know?"

"If I did, would I have asked?" Her cornflower eyes went narrow.

"Well, no. You're not one for idle chitchat, if I recall."

"You do, and I haven't changed. Now what are you doing here?"

He shrugged. If the FBI didn't already know, he wasn't going to tell them. "Mara called me."

"You haven't spoken to your sister in three years."

"Not on purpose, no. But Mara stays in touch, whether people cooperate or not. She has an unfortunate command of voice mail and e-mail technologies." He gave her a faint smile. "Which is how I've come to understand that her restaurant has fallen victim to some criminal bedevilment."

"You're here because of that?"

"Yes." Which was the truth. Just not all of it.

"It's my case, Patrick. I'm taking care of it."

"Yes, she mentioned you were involved. Let's just say she's unsatisfied with your progress."

"And you're, what, the cavalry?"

"In a manner of speaking."

Liz closed her eyes and pinched the bridge of her nose. "You haven't had any sort of relationship with Mara for three years, Patrick. Why the hell would you start riding to the rescue now?"

"She said she needed me." More than she probably knew, actually, if Patrick's instincts were correct. And unfortunately for all parties concerned, Patrick's instincts had proven themselves exceptional.

"Uh-huh." Her mouth tightened into a skeptical rosebud that Patrick didn't allow himself to look at. "So you just hopped on the next flight out of LA and rushed to her aid?"

"It was Palm Springs, but yes." He lifted his shoulders in a lazy shrug. "She's an O'Connor. We protect our own."

"I do, too," she said. She stood up and moved closer, her blue eyes steady and assessing. "And I consider anybody who comes to the FBI with a legitimate complaint *my own*. So there's really no need for you to be here."

The clean, no-nonsense scent of her drifted under his nose as she moved toward him, and a familiar desire uncurled in his gut. He squashed it with the ease of long practice and sent her a bland look.

"I'll have to hear that from my sister, I'm afraid."

"Fine." Liz spun away and stomped over to a filing cabinet. "What does she think you're going to do, anyway?"

"I have no idea," he said, watching her yank open a drawer to retrieve an ugly satchel-like bag she probably thought passed for a purse. She tossed it over her shoulder, pocketed her cell phone and marched past him into the hallway.

"Well?" she said, poking her head back into the cubical to glare at him. "Do you want to come?"

"Come do what?"

"Come straighten Mara out."

Patrick considered this. Did he want to witness the two women, who between them had turned his life upside down, go after each other like a couple of feral dogs?

"Why, yes," he said, a smile spreading over his face. "Yes, I do."

FIFTEEN MINUTES later, Liz blew through the doors of Brightwater's Casino and Restaurant like she had a SWAT team at her back. Patrick, however, saw no point in charging about when walking sufficed quite nicely. Besides, he wanted a look around. It never failed to amuse him that his baby sister had fallen in love with a guy who owned a casino. Not that it had been much of a casino when Jonas Brightwater had inherited it from his deadbeat father, but still.

After the unfortunate incident in which Mara had escaped jail time by the skin of her brother's teeth, she'd vowed with religious solemnity to never come within one hundred yards of a gambling establishment again. Jonas, however, wasn't the sort of guy who took no for an answer.

Patrick had always admired his brother-in-law's business acumen—the guy had worked some serious magic transforming the broken-down casino his father had left him into this sleek showpiece of a gaming hall, after all. But now, with the scent of Mara's culinary magic hanging in the air like a cozy invitation to sit down and eat, his respect for the guy grew. Investing in an on-site restaurant had been a master stroke, second only to pursuing Mara with a single-minded intensity until she agreed to run the place.

Giving her a wedding ring and half his assets in return for a job well done seemed a bit excessive to Patrick, but so far he hadn't heard any complaints. And given his sister's stubborn penchant for leaving chatty, endless messages on his voice mail that he never returned, he figured he'd have heard a few if there had been any.

He strolled after Liz, taking a moment to admire the rear view she presented. She never walked when she could jog, and jogging gave a very compelling bounce to everything she'd packed into that ugly black suit.

Perhaps *too* compelling a bounce. There were appearances to be maintained after all. Patrick tore his eyes from her backside long enough to slide the woman at the hostess stand a warm smile. She smiled back, and Patrick shifted course.

"Can I help you?" the woman asked, her voice as husky as a brand-new smoking habit. She leaned over the reservations book, treating him to an outstanding view of her cleavage.

"Absolutely," Patrick said, just as Liz looked over her shoulder and snapped, "No." She flashed the woman her badge and said, "We have a meeting with Mara."

"Oh, of course." The hostess sent Patrick a more guarded look and straightened until her cleavage was more suggestion than invitation. Patrick sighed. "Let me just show you in."

"We know the way," Liz said, then drilled Patrick with a

stern look. "Are you coming, or was there something more pressing you had to do?"

Patrick gave the hostess a wry smile. "Forgive her. She's nasty when she drinks her own coffee."

The hostess nodded solemnly. "I'll bring some of the good stuff to Mara's office, then."

He took up her hand, pressed a lavish kiss to her wrist. "You're an angel."

Her mouth formed a silent *oh* as she gazed at him, coloring prettily. Liz made an impatient noise and stomped toward the kitchen. Patrick suppressed a smirk and followed her.

IF ANYBODY knew the value of a second chance, it was Liz Brynn. She'd gotten hers when she was ten, and she'd worked like hell to make herself worthy of the badge that allowed her to grant a few herself. Six years ago, she'd given one to both Mara and her brother. And while she and Mara hadn't exactly become fast friends as a result, Liz did like and respect the woman for everything she'd done with the opportunity.

Putting herself through culinary school, starting a little catering business, then transforming Brightwater's from a casino that happened to also serve dinner into a destination restaurant for foodies all over the country—an admirable resume for anybody, let alone a woman who'd grown up in one of the country's most fabled criminal families.

Patrick, however, was another story.

It had been three years since she'd last seen him, since he'd fulfilled their contract to the letter and disappeared. Three years of servitude as Liz's personal weasel in exchange for Mara's clean slate, then poof. Into the wind like the shadow she knew he was.

Maybe he was straight now, but he hadn't changed otherwise. He was still all razor-sharp intellect, startling beauty and dizzying charm. He still set her nerves on edge in a way she'd have sworn she outgrew years ago. And he was still about as easy to read as hieroglyphics.

Liz punched through the kitchen doors into the steaming, shouting heart of Mara's restaurant. The grill shot an enormous flame toward the range hood, and Liz's hand twitched toward the weapon concealed under her suit jacket. She shook her head impatiently and relaxed her stiff muscles. Jesus, she was tight.

She glared at Patrick over her shoulder. His fault. She didn't normally find thieves—allegedly ex-thieves—disturbing, but there was nothing normal about this man or what he stirred up in her.

But this wasn't about her. This was about him. And while she didn't doubt the power of love or family, she *did* doubt that either could command the likes of Patrick O'Connor. Which begged the question, what could command him?

Only a few answers came to mind, none of them any more reassuring than the last. Because while Patrick himself had been strictly nonviolent as a criminal, the same couldn't be said of his colleagues. And if the same sense of familial responsibility that had prompted him to trade his own freedom for his sister's was still at work, Liz had to wonder what—or who—he was protecting Mara from this time.

She plowed through the chaos of Mara's kitchen to the open door of her tiny office. A vast desk filled the space, making Mara look even more fairy-sized than she actually was. With a pile of crumpled receipts at one elbow, a mug of coffee at the other and a pencil clamped between her teeth, Mara punched buttons on an adding machine and muttered curses at the ensuing spill of paper. Liz cleared a pile of kitchen catalogues off one of a pair of folding chairs across from the desk and plunked herself down. She glared hard at the meticulous part running dead center down the top of Mara's bent head.

Mara's tapping and cursing continued without pause, so Liz said, "I brought you something."

"Is it an incarcerated counterfeiter?" Mara asked around the pencil.

"No."

"Then go away. I don't need presents. I need—"

But what she needed was lost when Patrick appeared in the doorway with his usual sense of timing and style. No, Liz thought, watching Mara jump to her feet with a little cry. *Appear* was the wrong word. Patrick didn't *appear*; he made an entrance. Debutantes could take lessons from this guy, and Liz ought to know. Her grandmother had paraded her around the debut circuit like a prize heifer until she could hit her mark like Miss America.

Which was saying something considering that she hadn't known Miss America even existed until she was well into her teens. Hell, she hadn't even seen a TV until she'd turned eleven.

She crossed her legs and watched Mara fling herself at her brother. It amazed her, as always, to think that these two people had been fished from the same gene pool. Maybe they had matching heads of thick, spilled-ink hair, but that was where anything remotely approaching a family resemblance ended.

Where Patrick was long and lean and wore three-thousand-dollar suits the way other people wore skin, Mara was small and curvy and, at least in Liz's experience, wore nothing but jeans, T-shirts and huge, stained aprons. And where Mara buzzed with a constant, irresistible energy, Patrick walked around in an impenetrable bubble of mannered, moneyed calm. Such a waste, Liz thought now. All that jaw-dropping male beauty, lavished on a guy people were afraid to touch.

At least most people. Mara, she noticed with interest, squeezed her brother with a delighted relish that had Liz's brows heading for her hairline. She waited for him to reclaim his personal space with the sort of pithy, faintly condescending remark he was famous for, but he just patted Mara's back with oddly helpless hands until she was finished with him.

"I can't believe you actually came!" Mara said, drawing back to beam at him.

"I can hardly believe it myself," he said, frowning down at the wrinkle Mara's embrace had left on the sleeve of his undoubtedly expensive shirt.

Mara rolled her eyes. "Your shirt's fine, Sheila. Have a seat."

Patrick glanced at the chair next to Liz. She could almost hear him consulting an imaginary dry cleaner. "I think I'll stand," he said.

"Don't be a crybaby," Mara said. "Look, Liz managed to sit down without incident."

Patrick cast an expert eye over Liz's black jacket and pants. "Liz buys her suits at Target," he said. "She has far less at stake." He sent Liz a charming smile. She didn't smile back. She was too busy battling down a ridiculous wave of feminine embarrassment. She was FBI, for God's sake. She was dressed for the job, not a freaking cocktail party. What did he think she was going to wear? Armani?

Mara snorted. "You've been spending too much time in California," she told Patrick. "It's not a healthy environment, you know. All those pampered celebrities and their designer noses. You're going native."

Patrick lifted a lazy brow. "I'm well compensated for the risk. Though I doubt that continued exposure to the celebrity element will somehow tempt me into plastic surgery. As it turns out, I have a very good nose."

Liz sighed. "Does anybody mind if we skip the chitchat and get to the point? I have other cases, you know."

Patrick waved an expansive hand. "By all means," he said. "Fire away, Agent Brynn."

Liz turned a pointed look on Mara, who had the grace to look faintly sheepish. "You have something you want to run by me, Mara?" she asked. "A plan of some sort? Involving your brother?"

"Yes, Mara. Do tell," Patrick said. "I confess, I'm curious. The last time the three of us had anything to discuss, it was which of us was going to jail."

Mara glared at him. "Are you going to hold that over me for the rest of my life?"

Patrick gave her a pleasant smile. "Yes."

"It's not like I asked you to sacrifice yourself on the altar of my freedom, Mr. Christ Complex," Mara said. "It's entirely possible that I'd have managed the situation on my own, you know."

Patrick inclined his head. "If you say so."

She gave him a narrow look. "Did you come back here to help me, or are you just here to be condescending and arrogant?"

"Do I have to choose?"

Mara opened her mouth but Liz jumped in before she could peel another chunk off her brother's hide. Not that he looked at all disturbed at the prospect.

"Okay, so Patrick informed me of your concern regarding the counterfeiting case," she said in her best Joe Friday monotone. Because when life went haywire—and today certainly seemed to qualify—Liz liked to fall back on procedure. It was, in her opinion, what procedure was there for in the first place. So people didn't have to rely on their own flawed and subjective judgment to figure out the right thing to do. They could memorize it ahead of time.

Mara stopped glaring at her brother long enough to say, "Yes. This is about the damn counterfeiter."

"You sent your brother an SOS because you have some joker running a few fake bills through your restaurant?" she asked.

"And the casino," Mara added, frowning darkly. "Mostly the casino, really."

"And this pertains to me how?" Patrick asked. "For God's sake, Mara. Casinos *expect* to get taken on a certain percentage of their cash business. It's just how things are done."

Mara's frown deepened. "Not on my watch it isn't."

Liz had seen that look before. Determined. Stubborn. Mara had a plan and she was digging in. Patrick seemed to recognize the futility of arguing because he sighed and shook his head. "Where's your husband, Mara?"

Mara plunked down into the ancient chair behind her desk and scrubbed weary hands over her face. "South Carolina. He's been overseeing renovations on a suite of cottages we picked up last summer, and until he gets home, I'm in charge. And I'll be damned if some asshole counterfeiter's going to skim off the profits while I am. The FBI's spinning its wheels on this—no offense, Liz—and sitting around wringing my hands just isn't a viable option for me."

Patrick sighed again. "No, I know. Inaction has never been your problem. You have a plan, don't you?"

"Bet your ass."

Chapter
2

"WHAT DID you tell me about our guy that last time you were here, Liz?" Mara asked, rolling her hands in the air as if trying to pluck out the words. "His psychological profile, or whatever?"

No capacity for true stillness, Patrick thought as he watched his sister. It was a typically female problem, and it was exactly why so very few women became elite gamblers or thieves. He wondered if Mara even noticed her hands in motion.

"Our profiler tells us that we're most likely looking at a white male, between the ages of eighteen and thirty-five," Liz said, and Patrick turned his attention to her, unwillingly fascinated.

Every rule had its exception, and in this case, it was Liz. She was absolutely, utterly still. If there was anything on her mind but FBI business, it was securely locked away or else vaporized by the force of her training. Her voice was cool, her eyes steady as she spoke.

"Highly intelligent, highly egocentric, driven by a need

for excellence and acknowledgment. As with all criminals, there's an element of the sociopath—a conviction that rules are for others, that his exceptional brainpower exempts him from the moral boundaries confining lesser mortals." She didn't look at Patrick, didn't acknowledge him in any way, but he knew she was speaking to him, about him.

"Sounds like Dad, doesn't it?" he asked Mara, letting a fond smile play around the edges of his mouth.

Liz spared him a cool glance. "Sounds like a lot of common criminals."

Patrick showed his teeth in what passed for a smile. "Nothing common about Seamus O'Connor."

Mara sighed. "Believe me, if Dad were still alive, I'd be taking a hard look at him. Be almost a relief."

Liz blinked at that, but Patrick inclined his head in complete understanding. "Better the devil you know," he murmured, watching Liz's brows arch in rare surprise. Devils went to jail in her world, and he doubted she'd ever been grateful for tangling with one that was familiar and predictable.

Mara blew out a breath. "But in the absence of anything that simple, I think the prudent thing to do here is to focus on our felon's Achilles' heel."

Liz sharpened that laser-beam focus of hers on Mara. "And that would be . . . ?"

Mara smiled. "The ego. Don't forget, I grew up surrounded by criminal-minded men in the eighteen to thirty-five age range, all with exceptional brain power—"

"Thank you," Patrick murmured.

"—and enormous egos," Mara finished, with a sweet smile for him. "If this guy is anything like you or Dad, all it'll take to bring him out of hiding is a little challenge to the ego."

Liz tipped her head, considering this. "And you think our suspect is going to jump up and reveal himself because you brought a retired jewel thief and ex-poker king to town?"

"Patrick's been a busy boy since he was in Grief Creek

last," Mara said patiently. "His history helps, but it's his current career that's going to bring our boy out of the woodwork."

Patrick thought he knew what Mara wanted but decided to let her spell it out. He'd never been one to lay down his cards without knowing for certain what the other guy held. Besides, Mara wasn't exactly the close-to-the-vest type. If she, too, suspected that Patrick's past and present were on a collision course—and that she and her family could easily end up as collateral damage—he wouldn't have to wait much longer to find out.

"I'm just a writer now, Mara," he said, spreading his hands. "Trashy little crime novels, the occasional script. Some ghost writing. I do fairly well at it, but I'm with Liz on this one. I fail to see how I would be of any interest to your counterfeiter."

Mara smiled back at him. "You sell yourself short, Patrick. You're famous. That gorgeous face of yours is all over the media every time you put out a new book. Everybody's desperate to know how much of all that crime drama is fact and how much is fiction. Everybody wants to know what you made up and what you actually did."

Patrick leaned back against the door frame. "Everything I pulled has been fully confessed and duly recorded by the FBI years ago. I'm sure Liz has the whole thing in her archives somewhere. My writing is all fiction, Mara. You know that. You both do."

Liz continued with the stone-faced cop routine, but Mara nodded.

"Of course I do," Mara said impatiently. "I was there when you were pulling it all, wasn't I?"

Most of it, anyway, Patrick thought, but he nodded in return and Mara went on.

"But the rest of the world wonders, you know? You've got a new book out, don't you?"

Patrick narrowed his eyes at her. "Released last Tuesday. As you well know."

"There's always a nice little spike of publicity when you

release a book." Mara leaned back in her chair, satisfied. "All you have to do is spend a few days here in Grief Creek, do the club scene. Be high-profile, be decadent, be Hollywood." She smirked at him. "Be yourself, in other words."

Liz gazed at him, a speculative light growing in those shrewd blue eyes of hers. "He'll ask a few questions about counterfeiting," she said to Mara, picking up the thread of her thought. "Tell people it's research for his next script. Maybe imply that he's in the market for a script consultant, a real expert in the art of forgery."

Mara grinned companionably at Liz and nodded. "No flies on you, honey. Yeah, he'd be looking for a real, live counterfeiter. Might even need the guy on location when the movie goes into production."

Liz tapped a finger to her lips and squinted into the middle distance. Patrick could practically see her reducing the idea to individual components in her brain, weighing, labeling, measuring. It was a process with which he was extremely and unfortunately familiar.

"It's a decent angle," she said finally to Mara. "If our profile is accurate, the suspect will be highly unlikely to resist the opportunity for attention and adulation on that scale. It's not ideal"—she cut her eyes at Patrick at that— "but I can work with it."

Patrick folded his arms and sank deeper into his slouch against the doorjamb. It didn't hurt, he told himself. Why should it? Liz stomached all kinds of ugly things in the pursuit of justice. Why should it hurt to be counted among them?

"What makes either of you think I'd care to work for the FBI again?" he asked, but it wasn't really a question.

He'd paid for his sins over the years, of course. Liz had seen to that. But he'd never made the mistake of thinking he'd balanced the scales. Good thing, too, because it looked like fate was serving him up another big old plateful of comeuppance. A comeuppance that would require nothing less than subjecting himself to Liz's authority— and the strange temptation she presented—one last time.

Fate, he decided, was a stone-cold bitch.

His question hung there until the silence vibrated like a struck piano wire. Then Mara broke it.

"Nothing makes me think you want this," she said, her voice low and quiet. She came to him, put a hand on his sleeve. "This is a favor, one I have no right to ask. God knows you don't owe me. Not me, and certainly not the FBI. But I'm asking anyway. You're my brother, and I need your help. I want you to stay."

Patrick shifted his gaze to hers and she didn't blink.

"Even if you don't do this, I want you to stay," she said. "Give me a week. Just your time, if nothing else. I've missed you."

Oh, hell, he thought, swamped by an uncomfortable surge of love and reluctance. He was going to have to do this thing.

He'd always been so careful with Mara, so meticulous about treating her with a casual mix of indulgence and obligation. Nobody who wanted to hurt him could possibly know she was the one thing in this world he loved.

Except one guy. The guy who'd born witness, up close and personal, to Patrick's one and only display of public affection. The guy who, on the night Mara's inept thievery had landed her ass in jail thereby forcing Patrick to prioritize his loyalties, had been screwed over without remorse. Because when it came down to choosing between his mentor or his sister, his partner or his family, Patrick hadn't hesitated. He'd chosen Mara and left Jorge Villanueva holding the proverbial bag.

But it had been, what, six years since Villanueva had posed any immediate threat? The guy had disappeared into sunny Central America within minutes of Patrick's betrayal and, for all Patrick knew, was waiting out the statute of limitations in some warlord's mansion with a bottle of rum in one hand and a pretty senorita in the other. Patrick kept him on radar more as an exercise in vigilance than out of any real concern.

All of which changed when multiple sources—and yes,

Patrick still had a few—placed Villanueva back on U.S. soil these past few months. A fact which took on new urgency when those sightings had drifted closer and closer to Grief Creek. Mara's call for help had been just the excuse he'd needed to drop in for a brotherly visit without arousing suspicion. Sticking close to Mara while tracking down his old mentor's ghost wasn't the problem.

The problem was Liz. Because the plan as it stood had him living in her back pocket for the foreseeable future, and, unfortunately for Patrick, the years apart had done nothing to tone down the odd and uncomfortable threat she posed to his self-control. He could keep her at arm's length with the usual truckload of sexual innuendo and the occasional barbed comment, but he couldn't convince himself it was for her own protection. She'd made a career out of living in the same world Patrick did. She was no innocent to be sheltered.

The distance was for Patrick's protection. It always had been. But what the hell. It worked. It would again.

"Two weeks," he finally said. "I can give you two weeks."

LIZ CHECKED her watch as she barreled down Main Street toward the FBI's Resident Agency in Grief Creek. It had been twenty-two minutes since she'd said a tense goodbye to Patrick at his sister's restaurant; she had another two to make this meeting.

She briefly considered canceling due to the O'Connor family's impromptu destruction of her carefully constructed game plan. But she wouldn't. She wouldn't beg off and she wouldn't be late. The new plan she'd hastily sketched out to her boss over the phone a few minutes ago was a bit unorthodox but it had merit. Now it was just a matter of selling it face-to-face.

Which she would do in precisely—she checked her watch—one minute. No tardies, no excused absences. Because Special Agent in Charge Grayson Bernard believed firmly that punctuality and discipline were the foundations of the civilized world. Some agents muttered words like *rigid* and *tight-assed* behind his back, but Liz wasn't among them. Using nothing but strict procedure, dogged effort and the unflagging strength of his convictions, Bernard faced down the chaos and wrenched order from it. Liz respected that. Hell, she aspired to it.

Patrick O'Connor's devil-on-holiday smile raced unbidden through her mind, hot and fast as a prairie fire. Liz scowled. *Chaos personified,* she thought, and clamped down on the frisson of awareness that smile always sent skittering over her skin. For that reason alone, Patrick O'Connor would always be the enemy in Liz's mind, no matter how reformed he claimed to be.

She skidded her government-issue sedan into a parking spot, nearly kissing her neighbor's paint job. She refused to let herself be late on account of Patrick O'Connor and his fallen-angel face. Not now.

Snatching up her briefcase, she bolted out of the car and into the building at a dead run. She had her butt planted in the single chair outside SAC Bernard's office with thirty seconds to spare and gave his admin a smile that rode the line between pleasant greeting and teeth-baring menace.

The woman blinked, murmured into her headset, then said, "SAC Bernard will be with you in a moment."

Liz nodded and ran a quick hand over her hair. It had suffered considerably on the ride in from the reservation. Her car had air-conditioning but she'd needed the slap of fresh air that only a seventy-five-mile-an-hour breeze could provide.

She yanked impatient fingers through her snarls and scowled. She was a cop, damn it. The badge meant everything to her, and she'd be damned if she'd let a criminal—no matter how slick, how potent, how *reformed*—knock her off her stride. And she'd be double damned before she'd give her SAC a reason to wonder if such a thing could even be done.

Bernard's office door opened a moment later. "Agent Brynn," he said. "Right on time."

Liz rose to her feet. "Sir."

She stepped past him into his office. He swept a hand toward the small of her back without making contact or even coming close. Observing the courtesies without opening himself to a harassment suit, she realized. And she thought *she'd* achieved a level of automatic deference to the rules. Compared to Bernard, she was a rank amateur.

She stopped beside a straight-backed chair in front of his desk. She didn't consider sitting in it and Bernard didn't invite her to do so. He settled himself into the position of authority behind the desk, steepled his fingers and pressed them against his lips while he considered her. His suit and his eyes were the same color—a cool, flinty gray that discouraged bullshit of any variety.

Liz pushed back against jumping nerves. Her proposal was solid, her players lined up. The only weak link was her.

Ten years of her father's so-called care had taught Liz that survival depended on granting instant obedience to powerfully charismatic and dangerously intelligent men. Particularly those who viewed the U.S. legal system as a trifling inconvenience rather than a public service. She'd spent the past twenty years trying to scrape that axiom out of her subconscious. Trying to transform herself into somebody powerful enough to protect the innocent from men like her father.

But then along came Patrick O'Connor. Granted, he'd shown none of her father's inclination to exploit women or children, but he was enough like her father in style if not substance that he should disgust her. Enrage her. Anything but light up this firestorm of shameful want inside her. Which meant she hadn't come quite as far as she'd thought, transformation-wise.

But she *had* come a long way. Long enough that she wasn't defenseless anymore. Long enough that she now had a badge and a gun and the law on her side. Long enough that she could handle this. Could handle him. She had to. She needed to walk through the fire of her fear and come out the other side triumphant. It was the only way to heal herself completely, and she knew she could do it.

The trick was in convincing SAC Bernard to let her try.

"I received your request to approve an inter-agency counterfeiting task force," Bernard began, brows drawing down in his smooth, even face. "I'm curious as to why you're not handing this matter over to the Secret Service. Counterfeiting falls under their jurisdiction, you know."

Liz nodded, met his gaze directly. "Yes, sir. But enforcing federal law on Indian reservations falls under ours. My territory includes the Grief Creek Ojibwe reservation, which has given me cause to develop and maintain working relationships with many of the reservation businesses. That includes Brightwater's Casino and Restaurant, from which this particular complaint originated. When I made contact with the offer to turn the complaint over, the Secret Service stated a preference for working in tandem with the FBI on this."

"Who are you looking at over there?"

"Maria di Guzman, sir. This matter falls within both her territory and her area of expertise."

He nodded once, though whether in approval or assent Liz couldn't tell. "She's good. Does the job." He rose and walked to the window and watched scanty traffic trickle by on Grief Creek's main drag. "Frankly, Brynn, I have no problem with an inter-agency task force. A show of solidarity across the agencies, rising above politics to get the job done. It's good for business, but it's also the right call. I don't fault your instincts on this."

The silence held an unfinished quality that had Liz's nerves buzzing. "But you question my instincts in other areas," she said, her voice carefully neutral. "Sir."

Bernard clasped his hands behind his back, his face impassive. "You're a good agent, Brynn. Among my best. Ordinarily, I'd have no problem with you cultivating an informant. But I have serious doubts about the wisdom of bringing Patrick O'Connor into this matter."

"I do, too," Liz said tightly. "But he's in it now, with

or without us. I'm just taking an unfortunate situation and working it to the FBI's advantage."

"I have yet to determine whether or not the FBI will be served by allowing O'Connor an official role in this investigation. Your performance in previous cases to which he was attached was less than I've come to expect from you. It makes me loath to approve your use of him again."

Liz refused to flinch. "I've closed every case to which O'Connor was attached, without exception."

"The record shows that you closed the cases. But it also shows that, in at least one case and potentially more, O'Connor fulfilled only the bare minimum of his obligations to the FBI while using his undercover status to pursue his own agenda." Bernard angled his head and watched her shrewdly. "You were dancing with the devil, Brynn. If you didn't get burned it's because you got lucky."

Liz's stomach churned with an uneasy mixture of nerves and shame that she kept cleanly off her face. "To the best of my knowledge, O'Connor neither participated in nor facilitated criminal activity of any sort during his tenure as a confidential informant." She met the SAC's gaze directly, forced her own not to waver. "Do you suspect otherwise?"

Bernard lifted one eyebrow and said, "Brynn, please don't waste my time. Three years ago, you employed the man to gain access to Brightwater's Casino as part of a drug trafficking investigation. He did as he was asked, yes. But he also staged a three-ring circus under your nose that involved a poker tournament, his felonious parents and a jewelry heist."

"An *attempted* jewelry heist," Liz said stiffly. The last case she'd worked with Patrick had not been her finest moment. "And it wasn't *his* attempt. It was his parents'." Bernard gave her a level look. "Plus the relationship he developed with his brother-in-law during that time was crucial to securing the man's eventual cooperation with the investigation. Cooperation which, as you know, allowed us to close the case."

Bernard maintained a meaningful silence, then said, "Your lack of perception disturbs me nonetheless."

Liz clasped her hands behind her back. "It's been three years since I last worked with O'Connor. I would argue that my instincts have sharpened, as has my confidence as an agent." The words were solid, her voice steady and sure. But it cost her. The hands behind her back were slippery with sweat, and her knees felt like water. But it wasn't because her SAC's scathing assessment of her skills was so accurate. It was because he was so miserably off the mark.

She'd never made the mistake of thinking she'd tamed the mighty Patrick O'Connor, that he worked exclusively for her or at her command. No, he was dangerous to her on a whole different level. A more personal level. A level her SAC knew nothing about, and if Liz had her way, never would.

She said it again, for herself, for her SAC, this time putting all the steel in her spine into her voice. "I can handle O'Connor."

Bernard held her gaze for a long, searching moment, then exhaled what, in a softer man, might have been termed a sigh. "I'm afraid that will have to be good enough."

"Sir?"

"Sit down, Brynn." He flicked that broad hand toward the chair she'd forgotten was at her hip. "Your case just got more complicated."

Chapter
3

LIZ SAT, automatically reaching into her bag for a notepad and pen while Bernard took his seat behind the massive desk. Not a single mote of dust clung to either the desk or to the picture of his pretty wife and their pretty kids angled at its corner. *Good housekeeping?* she wondered. *Or dust with a healthy sense of self-preservation?*

"O'Connor's old mentor is back in town," Bernard said.

Liz narrowed her eyes as several missing pieces clicked into place. "Jorge Villanueva," she murmured. "Fled the country the night I busted Mara O'Connor, what, six years ago now?"

"Yes, well, his passport photo was identified by agents working at LAX last month."

"This certainly clarifies a few things."

"Indeed." Bernard angled his head and the afternoon light picked out the first strands of silver streaking across his temples. "You were with the Jewelry and Gem squad at that time, yes?"

"Yes, sir," Liz said. "In Vegas. We'd been tracking the

O'Connor family for some time, Mara in particular. The weak link. We figured we'd bust her, and mommy and daddy would come running, ready to cut a deal."

"How did you wind up with Patrick O'Connor instead?"

"I have no idea. I didn't even know he was pulling anything that night. He just waltzed into my office and started giving terms like he owned the place." Her lips twisted into a wry smile at the memory. "They were good terms so I took them."

"And the parents?"

"Already en route to Monte Carlo."

"They abandoned their daughter?"

"Without a second thought."

A small smile curved Bernard's lips. "So much for honor among thieves."

"Patrick flaked on Villanueva midheist that night," Liz said. "Saving his sister meant giving up his partner and his half of the haul without a flinch."

"It also meant forcing Villanueva to slice his way to freedom through a very young, courageous agent."

Liz fell silent. She hated what Villanueva had done—and the violence with which he'd done it—but she couldn't help wincing at the choice Patrick had faced. Circumstances had demanded that he screw somebody. Would he abandon his sister or betray his partner? Neither option was particularly appealing.

She shook off the weakness of sympathy and forced her mind back to the implications of Villanueva's unexpected return to the country. "Villanueva wasn't exactly taken by surprise, though. He'd skipped the country before O'Connor even finished giving his statement. Why's he back now? What's he after? Revenge?"

Bernard shook his head. "Unlikely. Villanueva's a pro. For that matter, so is O'Connor. Neither of them probably expected much from the other in terms of loyalty. No, these guys worship a different god." Those flat gray eyes of his went one degree flatter. "Money."

Liz felt her brows creeping toward the ceiling. So much

for Patrick's supposed retirement. "You think Villanueva's in town to hook up with O'Connor for a job?"

"I don't know. Intelligence speculates that Villanueva's been living like a king in Central America these past six years. Dealing arms to warlords with deep pockets. But it's not what he chose. It's not his home. It's exile. And the guy who put him there is living the high life in Hollywood."

"Palm Springs," Liz said automatically.

"Whatever. The point is, everything O'Connor touches turns to gold, and if Villanueva's in the market for a triumphant return to the U.S., he probably wants some of that magic at his disposal. O'Connor owes him and they both know it."

Bernard leaned back and frowned as he went on. "A reunion's going to happen, Brynn. And it looks like it's going to happen on my turf. The only question is whether O'Connor's open to resuming the relationship. Bringing him onto your case as an informant allows us to keep an eye on that matter without tipping our hand, so I'll approve it."

"Thank you, sir."

He pushed back and from the desk, rose with his fingers splayed across its shiny surface. Liz rose as well. "You've got your team," he said. "And you've got O'Connor as well. But I'd better see *you* playing *him* this time around. If he doesn't know Villanueva's in town yet, he's not going to hear it from the FBI. Understood?"

"Yes, sir."

"Dismissed."

Liz waited for Bernard's office door to click shut before she allowed herself to push a thumb into the headache brewing between her brows. She'd gotten what she'd wanted,. she reminded herself. So why the hell was her stomach in knots?

She threaded her way back to the ugly little cubicle she called her office, and since she had the dubious pleasure of working directly next to the communal coffeepot, she poured herself a thick, vile cup. The caffeine surged into her system with a satisfying kick.

She savored the boost. She'd need it. She was about to attach herself to Patrick O'Connor for the foreseeable future.

Maybe she should make more coffee.

PATRICK REGARDED the pile of potatoes on his sister's kitchen counter with suspicion. "I'm sorry," he said. "You want me to what?"

Mara smiled at him. "Peel 'em."

"That's what I thought you said."

"Hey, you want to eat, you help cook."

"What I want," Patrick said, for what felt like the hundredth time that afternoon, "is to check into a hotel."

Mara's smile broadened. "This *is* a hotel, in case it escaped your notice. Restaurant on the first floor, casino on the second, guest suites on the third. Brightwater's is a full-service establishment."

"This is *not* a hotel. This is your private residence, which just happens to occupy the same floor as your guest suites." Patrick gave her a sorrowful look. "I was looking forward to room service."

"You're living with the damn chef. What more do you want?"

"Any number of things spring to mind," Patrick told her grimly.

The doorbell rang and Mara shouted, "It's open!"

"You don't lock your doors?" he asked, dismayed. "Did we even grow up in the same family?"

"People come and go in this place like Grand Central Station," she said. "I'd spend half my life answering the door if I locked it."

"Still." Patrick frowned. "This is a casino and God only knows what kind of people might—"

"Oh, please. You expect me to believe you're worried about my mixing with gamblers? I could stack a deck before I could spell, Patrick. And so could you."

"Which is why I know exactly how important it is to lock the damn doors."

"Why are you so worried about my doors all of a sudden?" she asked, her eyes direct and shrewd.

"What, a brother can't watch out for his sister?"

"Of course he can," Mara said quietly. "You did it our whole lives, right up until I figured out that's what you were doing. Then you disappeared and I've been trying like hell to get you to come home ever since. This isn't the first business blip I've cooked into an emergency to try to get you here and you know it. So I have to ask myself what's different this time? What has the unflappable Patrick O'Connor riding to my rescue like some kind of white knight?"

He smiled at her, though truthfully, he rather missed his naïve baby sister. This beautiful, steady-eyed woman who'd taken her place wouldn't be so easy to mislead. "Your imagination is as charming as ever, Mara."

She shook her head. "I may not have your talent for the criminal life, Patrick, but I'm not an idiot either. Until I figure out why you're really here, I'm not letting you out of my sight. Or out of my house."

Tiny footsteps approached the kitchen at a gallop, and Patrick's heart rate kicked up to match the pace. "Look, you have a kid," he said, seizing desperately on the idea. "I'll be in the way."

"For God's sake, Patrick, get a grip. Evie's a two-year-old, not a piranha. You're staying here. Deal with it."

A tiny scrap of humanity burst into the kitchen, all sticky hands and shining green eyes, her chubby legs chugging, her black ringlets flying. The kid launched herself off impossibly small tennis shoes and vaulted straight into her mother's waiting arms.

Oh shit, Patrick thought as Mara covered the round little face with noisy kisses. The kid—Evie, he reminded himself—beamed up at her mother with a love so brilliant, so intense, that his heart stopped dead in its tracks. This was purity, he thought dully. This was innocence. This was love. Capital *L*. The form Plato had waxed poetic about. Truth, Beauty, Justice.

Love.

How the fuck was he supposed to bunk down with this and not screw it up?

"Here," Mara said, and Patrick bolted out of his frozen panic to catch the child she all but tossed at him. He might not know much about babies, but he was pretty sure you weren't supposed to drop them. "Evie, this is your uncle Patrick. He's your godfather, and though in general a very smart and capable man, he's a little phobic about family. Little girls in particular. You're going to have to help him out."

She and Evie exchanged some kind of innately feminine look, which did nothing for the terror chugging around in Patrick's gut. He carefully shifted until his hands were hooked in the child's armpits, then he lifted her away from his body. She dangled there at arm's length, grinning at him and waving her sneakers dangerously close to his crotch.

"Hi, Unca Padwitt."

"Mara." It was as close to a plea as he'd ever heard from his own voice. "Please. Let me get a hotel."

"No." Mara turned and spoke to the young woman who'd followed Evie into the kitchen. "Hey, Jessica. How was she today?"

"Oh, monstrous," Jessica said, giving Evie a broad wink and rolling her eyes. Evie wriggled with delight and Patrick shifted his grip somewhat desperately. "Same time tomorrow?"

"That'd be great. Thanks."

"No problem. See you, kiddo."

The doorbell rang while Patrick stared helplessly at the child dangling from his hands.

"I'll get it," Jessica called from the foyer.

Patrick was still contemplating this new wrinkle in his living situation when Liz appeared in the kitchen, all sober eyes and ugly suit.

God, how he hated that suit, he thought, grateful for the distraction. It was so *black*, and any fool could see that Liz had been made for color. Not that what she wore was any of his business, he reminded himself. He should be thrilled that she wanted to hide that interesting little body inside gender-neutral cop clothes. But somehow her efforts to downplay her femininity didn't make it any easier to ignore. It only made him more desperate to see it all on display. Hell of a thing.

"Hello, Liz," he said. "You're looking . . . professional."

Mara shoved an elbow into his ribs. She smiled at Liz while Patrick nearly bobbled his niece.

"I'm so glad you dropped by," Mara said to Liz. "Are you here in a professional capacity?"

Liz's brow wrinkled slightly, as if the concept of any capacity besides professional were new and utterly foreign. Or maybe she was just struck stupid by the sight of Patrick O'Connor with a toddler in his arms.

"Um, yes," she said. "Is this a bad time?"

Mara dismissed the noise and the chaos with an airy wave. "Not at all."

Patrick rolled his eyes.

"I wanted to let you know that my supervisor officially approved Patrick's attachment to the counterfeiting case this afternoon," she said. "I was going to call, but I thought it would be good to confirm in person."

Patrick lowered the child carefully until her feet hit the ground. She took off like a shot. Mara beamed, first at Evie, then at Liz. Patrick just stared. The kid was a miniature wrecking ball.

"That's great news," Mara said to Liz. "We should celebrate. You're just in time for dinner."

"Oh, no." Liz blinked. "I have to get home. I just wanted to talk to Patrick about something before I—"

"Nonsense." Mara took her by the elbow and dragged her farther into the kitchen. "I was just getting ready to hop downstairs to the restaurant for a minute and Patrick was going to peel these potatoes for me."

Damn it. He'd been hoping she'd forget about the potatoes. "I was?" he asked.

Liz eyed him skeptically. "He was?"

Mara deposited Liz on a long-legged stool and gave

Patrick the sort of good, hard stare he hadn't seen since their mother had been alive. He shrugged and sat on the stool across from Liz's.

"He was," Mara said firmly. "And now that you're here, I feel like it might actually get done."

She rummaged in a drawer and produced two peelers. She slapped one in Liz's palm and tossed the other to Patrick. He caught it automatically, gauging the weight and the balance of it without conscious thought. It felt good in his hand. Solid. Purposeful.

He watched while Liz gave her peeler the same meticulous inspection she'd have afforded a loaded gun. For one weak moment, he actually envied the peeler. What must it be like to be the subject of attention that intense? To wait patiently under it while she worked out how to use what she saw to the best advantage?

Christ. He shoved the thought aside and tore his gaze away from those long, graceful fingers. It was just a *peeler*. What was wrong with him?

Mara gave him a knowing smirk. "I'll be back in a few. I want those potatoes peeled and chopped into one-inch cubes. There's a pot on the stove for them when you're done."

She included them both in a cheery grin and headed for the door. Patrick smiled back, a smile that said *you are so dead*. Mara blew him a kiss as the door swung shut.

Liz shrugged out of her jacket and hung it neatly over the back of a kitchen chair, then started rolling up her sleeves. Patrick made a point of *not* noticing the way he could almost see the outline of a lacy bra through her plain white blouse. He didn't want to know if she balanced out the cop clothes with decent underwear. Seriously didn't want to know.

"So," he said, twirling the peeler through his fingers but making no effort to actually peel anything. Good tools were always worth using, he supposed. Still, there were appearances to maintain. He gave her an intimate little smile. "What's on your mind, Liz?"

She selected a potato and began methodically stripping it of its skin. "Before this case goes any further," she said, her face small and serious, "before you do any work for me in an official capacity, I need to know something."

Patrick held her gaze, let his brows lift with casual inquiry. "And that would be . . . ?"

"What you're doing here."

"Me?" He gave the peeler a jaunty little toss and picked up a potato. "I'm just being a good brother." The blade was viciously sharp and it pared the skin away from the potato practically by itself. Patrick was impressed in spite of himself. Maybe his favored tools ran more toward laptops and lock picks, but quality was quality.

"And that's it?" Liz didn't look away, didn't smile. "You're here simply because Mara called you for help. There's nothing else on your agenda, nothing else on the radar screen? No ulterior motive that's going to make me look like a fool when it comes out?"

Better a live fool than a dead cop. Not that he didn't trust her to do her job. Liz was all about the job, much to his eternal regret. But he only said, "Liz. Darling. Would I do such a thing to you?"

She frowned at him. "The last time I placed you undercover somewhere your parents tried to rob the place."

He gave her an indulgent shrug and said, "Family, huh?"

"I'd have helped you if you'd trusted me, Patrick."

He pretended to consider that for a moment. "I don't believe incarcerating one's parents is generally considered helpful."

Liz didn't answer—what could she say, after all?—but Patrick didn't have time to savor the victory. He was too busy watching in horrified fascination as the kid emerged from the cupboard at his knees. She wrapped herself around his shins like poison ivy and beamed up at him, her smile full of what looked like half-chewed graham cracker. "Hey, Unca Padwitt."

He stared at Liz in equal parts bafflement and horror.

This time she smiled back with every appearance of spontaneous amusement. She bent and peered around the edge of the counter. "Hey, Evie," she said.

"I'll make you a deal," Patrick said. "I'll answer all your questions. Just as soon as you pull her off my pants and direct me to the nearest dry cleaner."

"Serves you right for bringing haute couture into the kid's house."

Liz turned back to the kid on Patrick's shin. "Come on, Evie. Want to play in the sink till your mommy gets back?"

"Yeah!" Evie pulled her hands off Patrick's trousers with a sound like Velcro separating, and bounced merrily away on the twinkling lights of her shoes. "Sink, sink, sink!" He didn't even bother to inspect the handprints, just reapplied himself to the potatoes. He suddenly felt the intense need to shred something.

"So you're just being a good brother, huh?" Liz tossed him a skeptical look over her shoulder while she supervised Evie at the sink. "Nothing going on that I should know about."

"That's right," he said with perfect sincerity. Because Liz definitely should *not* know about his plans to run his old mentor to ground. She was so . . . rules oriented. She'd only complicate what should be a very simple conversation. "Hard as it is for you to believe, I'm clean. Have been since the night I let you arrest me. The only stuff I pull now is in my imagination."

There was a long pause, then she said, "Okay."

Nothing more, just *okay*. Any other woman would have pushed for elaboration, for details, but not Liz. She'd asked, he'd answered. End of story.

The silence that stretched between them now was almost companionable, and Patrick let himself fall into it. The monotonous hiss of the peeler, the slap of potato peel hitting the counter, the clink and splash of Evie playing at the sink. The evening sun pouring through the French doors at his back was lazy and warm, and something deep in the core of him, something he hadn't even been aware of, loosened just the tiniest bit.

It was such a novel and unexpected sensation that it threw off his rhythm, and he fumbled the potato. Nearly peeled his knuckle before he could recover.

"Fu—"

Liz cut him off. "Language," she said primly.

Patrick stuck his knuckle into his mouth. "I nearly sliced off my thumb."

Liz rolled her eyes and Patrick sighed. Had he expected sympathy? He slid open the knife drawer and paused, arrested.

"Wow."

"What?" Liz came to look over his shoulder. "Knives? Since when are you into knives?"

"Since never. Violence is the last resort of the terminally unskilled, as my dad always said. But opinions vary on such matters, and I know when to be impressed. I've worked with knife men before."

Patrick broke off as he heard his own thoughtless words. Then he closed his eyes and waited for Liz to pounce. *Knife man? Who was that again? Whatever happened to him?*

But she didn't say anything. She just turned away from the glittering drawer full of blades and left him alone with the knowledge that the most dangerous guy he'd ever met was still out there. Somewhere, Jorge Villanueva was sharpening his knife and dreaming of the day he'd plunge it into Patrick O'Connor's black, betraying soul.

He let that go with a mental shrug. Nothing else to be done on that front. He'd already made his move. The next move belonged to Villanueva. If the guy was even out there. In the meantime, Patrick would focus his energy on keeping the amateurish mistakes to a minimum.

He selected a knife from the drawer and began reducing potatoes to efficient little cubes. When he was done, he slid the cutting board and knife into the sink, then frowned at Evie who grinned up at him from her perch on a stool. She was bellied up to the sink, soaking wet, and even Patrick knew that knives and children didn't mix.

Liz caught his look and hiked Evie into her arms. "Hey, you want to show me your room?" she asked. "I heard you have Legos."

They disappeared down the hall, Evie chattering a million miles an hour about something, Liz nodding wisely. Patrick moved to the French doors opening onto a pretty balcony as the sun sank low over the prairie. That novel sense of ease still cruised around in his gut and he wasn't at all sure he liked it. Especially not if it was contentment, or something like it. Loyalty was expensive, but doable. Contentment was downright dangerous.

A COPSE of red oaks capped a gentle rise behind the casino, and from within its shadows, Jorge Villanueva watched. He lay on the ground silent and motionless, a high-powered spotting scope focused on the bright kitchen window.

O'Connor had come.

Satisfaction flowed thick and hot in Villanueva's veins. Not because of O'Connor's cooperation, of course. The man was incredibly predictable when it came to his precious sister. No, it was more the relief of acting after the endless waiting. The meticulous planning. The silent, impotent watching.

He'd stalked Patrick O'Connor for six years now, his thirst for revenge so deep, so elemental, it was like pain. He'd slipped into the country undetected dozens of times over those years, spent countless nights watching, planning, while O'Connor pecked at his keyboard, while he paced that cavernous museum of a house in the desert all alone.

He'd watched, too, on the rarer occasions when O'Connor got all slicked up in a designer suit and walked the red carpet with some overly endowed starlet on his arm, smiled his movie-star smile for the popping flashbulbs and lapped up the good life.

It had stung to watch from the shadows. Of course it had. It stung now, watching the man who'd stolen everything from him welcomed home by a loving family. By that ridiculous, impulsive sister of his and her gap-toothed toddler.

Villanueva had had a family once. He didn't anymore. Soon Patrick wouldn't either.

A woman for a woman. A child for a child. Betrayal repaid in kind.

But which woman? He'd assumed the sister, but that was before he'd seen O'Connor and the curvy blond cop together. Before he'd watched the careful distance they gave each other while performing the casual dance of everyday tasks. Before he'd seen his nimble-fingered former protégé nearly maim himself with a potato peeler because he was too busy watching a woman to pay attention to the task at hand.

Which woman indeed?

Chapter
4

TWENTY-FOUR HOURS later, Liz was curled comfortably in the corner of the couch cleaning her gun when Patrick O'Connor strolled into her living room as if he owned the place. She blinked at him, frozen. The highlight of her typical Saturday night ran more toward a trip to Home Depot, but there he was between her and the TV in all his preternatural gorgeousness. It was as if the wasteland of her social life had finally prompted the Ralph Lauren ad people to drop off an extra in her living room.

She was starting to wonder if he was a stress-related mirage when he smiled at her with that wicked mouth of his. Then she wondered if this fantasy was more rooted in libido issues.

"Do come in," she said.

"Don't mind if I do," he said, his grin broadening at her sour tone. "Security systems only work if you turn them on, Liz. And it helps a ton when you actually close and lock the door. Doesn't anybody in this town know that?"

Not a mirage, she thought with a sigh. She took a

moment to wish with great fervency that she were wearing more than the bathrobe her grandmother had given her the Christmas before she'd died.

"Guess you caught me," she said, shifting smoothly to pull the robe over the expanse of thigh that hadn't mattered so much when it was just her, the gun and *Return of the Jedi* on cable.

She swept a hand toward the disassembled Glock 9mm on the table between them and said, "Give me a second to get my backup system online. It's really effective."

He flicked a glance at the glistening pieces of oiled weaponry and said, "I imagine so, though it might be more effective as a backup system if it was actually online while the primary was disabled."

For one weak moment, she considered shooting him. Not fatally, of course. She wouldn't even draw blood, probably. Maybe she could just shoot his sleeve or something. She smiled, imagining the look on his perfect face when she smoked a bullet hole through that fancy summer-weight cashmere sweater of his.

He smiled back at her, as if he could read her mind. "A backup system doesn't give the bad guys pause if it's in pieces on the coffee table, Liz. And I'd know, wouldn't I?"

He looked like an upscale frat boy, all good breeding, excessive privilege and no remorse. Anger surged through her, a sharp, black wave of it, as shocking for its suddenness as for its intensity. Her mouth was engaged before she gave it a decent thought.

"It's all just a joke to you, isn't it?" she snapped. "Stealing."

"A joke?" He considered that. "No, more of a vocation, I'd say. A gift, if you will. One the FBI—and you, Liz— appreciated very much when I exercised it on your behalf."

She ignored that. "You spent twenty-some years of your life taking things from people, breaking into their homes, their apartments, their hotel rooms, and just *taking* things. Things that didn't belong to you, things that were important to them. Heirlooms, investments, wedding rings.

And it didn't matter to you—still doesn't matter to you, apparently—that you hurt people along the way."

She shot off the couch and stalked to him, close enough to poke a finger into that gorgeous sweater of his though she didn't do it. Didn't trust herself to. Something cold and dangerous leapt in the clear blue of his eyes, but she didn't back up. She leaned in instead, that choking, unexpected rage backing up in her chest.

She couldn't fix the world. She couldn't protect every victim. Judging by the way Patrick's mere presence sent her nerve endings into overdrive, she couldn't even fix herself. But stealing—whether an heirloom diamond or a little girl's self-respect—had consequences. Her father had died in prison without ever comprehending them. Liz refused to let Patrick do the same.

"You didn't just take people's things, Patrick. You stole their security. You stole their safety, their peace of mind. You stole their *trust*. How can you stand there and smirk about it, as if it was all one great big lark? You *hurt* people."

Liz broke off, horrified at the hitch in her voice there at the end, but Patrick didn't move. He didn't blink, he didn't shift. She wasn't entirely certain he was breathing. Even his eyes were still. Whatever she'd seen move in those frigid depths was well and truly buried now, and she wondered for a split second if it had been remorse.

Then he reached out and trailed a finger down the curve of her cheek, and her rage spontaneously morphed into something else altogether. His touch was whisper light, but it sent a wave of heat over her entire body that had her knees going to butter. He tapped his finger lightly on the very tip of her chin and it gave her such a jolt that she slapped his hand away. He gave her that crooked smile that never failed to send her pulse into the stratosphere.

"Ah, Liz. I love it when you do that avenging-angel thing. Righteous and impassioned is gorgeous on you." He ran an expert eye over her from damp hair to bare feet. "Although the robe helps. Is that Burberry?"

He reached out as if to finger her lapel and Liz slapped that hand away, too. She shoved her fingers through her damp hair, frustration and embarrassment at war in her gut.

"Christ." She turned from him. "I don't know why I even try."

He caught her shoulder lightly and pulled her back into his side in a casual, one-armed hug. The kind Liz figured men gave women when they wanted to smooth ruffled feathers without spilling their martinis.

"Now, Liz, don't say that. People like you have to try. It balances out the people like me, and Lord knows the universe demands its balance." He gave her a final squeeze and then nudged her toward the couch. If she'd been a little quicker, or if he'd been a little less agile, she could have landed her elbow in his gut and they both knew it. He was, Liz thought bitterly, half a step ahead of her. As usual.

She plunked herself back into the corner of the couch and tucked her bare feet up under the robe. The Burberry robe. She made a mental note to set the security system the next time she wore it. Most FBI agents couldn't afford Burberry, didn't even know anybody who could. She didn't like calling attention to the fact that she both could and did.

"What are you doing here, Patrick?" she asked, frowning at him.

He sent her a charming grin and gave his pant legs a little hitch as he seated himself at the other end of the curvy antique sofa she'd had reupholstered as a housewarming present to herself. The setting was patently female, but it only made him look more vibrantly male. She felt her frown deepen and tried to smooth it out.

"You might like this," he said. "It seems the universe has dealt out a bit of my own back to me."

"What do you mean?"

"Somebody broke into Mara's apartment today while we were up in Minneapolis."

"Minneapolis?" Suspicion flowed cold into her chest. "What were you doing up there?"

"Shopping."

"You were *shopping*? Here in fly-over country?"

He gave her a mildly chagrined look. "I didn't say I bought anything. But, you know, it was something to do."

She maintained a skeptical silence and he lifted his shoulders in a minute shrug. "My theory is overly enthusiastic paparazzi," he said.

Liz cocked an eyebrow. "Paparazzi."

"Sure. Opportunity presented itself so some ambitious photographer had himself a little unauthorized sneak and peek into my new living situation."

"Patrick, please. This is Grief Creek, not LA."

"A fact that has not escaped me." He gave her a grim smile. "But my latest book came out last week, and some heightened attention from the press is par for the course. Plus all that's missing is a stuffed bunny."

"A stuffed bunny?"

Patrick lifted a shoulder. "Mara can't say for sure, but the baby was making an unholy racket over it and it didn't seem to be in any of the usual locations. So either Grief Creek has an evil bunny thief at large or there's an ambitious photographer out there with exclusive pictures of my luggage and a new cuddle bunny. You pick."

Liz treated him to a cool-eyed stare. Paparazzi, her ass. She was ordering surveillance for Mara and the kid the second Patrick walked out her door. She didn't care what he knew or didn't know, what he thought he was doing here. When it came to Villanueva, Liz wasn't taking any chances.

"Either way," Patrick said, "Mara's spooked. She's worried that my less-than-law-abiding past is coming back to haunt me."

"That can happen when we don't fully put the past away," she said. And she ought to know. She'd given two decades of dedicated effort to the cause of leaving her own past behind.

"For goodness' sake, Liz. I've been clean for years now." Patrick spread his hands, all innocence with just a whiff of ironic amusement. "I recognize that there's a certain poetic justice to my reporting a break-in, and if it were just me, I doubt I'd even be here. But then it's not just me, is it?" The amusement died out of his eyes as he leaned forward, that beautiful face of his going hard and cool. "It's Mara and her child, too. And I'll be damned if I let you and your lofty ideals put their safety on the back burner because you don't approve of what I am."

Liz held his gaze for a long, stony moment, then said, "Was."

"Excuse me?"

"Was," Liz said again. "You said 'what I am,' but I believe you meant to say 'what I was.' Being so squeaky clean these past years and all, surely you didn't mean to imply that you haven't changed."

He went still for an instant, as if struck, then a flicker of amusement softened the harsh lines of his face. He draped an arm over the back of the couch between them and turned to face her more squarely. It put him just a touch farther into Liz's personal space than she found comfortable, though she'd be damned if she'd give him the satisfaction of seeing her edge away. His fingers danced over her shoulder and skimmed the ends of her damp hair, sending a jolt of electricity over every inch of skin she possessed.

"I didn't steal my girlfriend's car to go for a joyride over state lines, Liz," he said. "I was a thief." His eyes were cold as ice, but they burned as they traced the edges of her face, her hair, her body. "I was designed for theft the way thoroughbreds are designed for speed. It's in my bones, my flesh. It's what I am. And a few years on your side of the law doesn't erase that."

Liz felt his words thud into the vulnerable center of her being, prayed they didn't take root in the fertile soil she knew they'd find there. She'd worked her entire life to prove that a person *could* change, and she hated that he could so easily accept—hell, *embrace*—that his tendencies defined him. She shifted away from his touch, from the oddly gentle fingers playing havoc with her nerves.

"You were a career criminal," she said simply. "An accomplished one. Some might even say brilliant." Patrick inclined his head humbly and Liz narrowed her eyes at him. "You say you aren't anymore, and there's no evidence to make me suspect that you've backslid to any significant degree. But you're also a virtuoso liar, and that gives me pause. Makes me wonder if you know more than you're telling me about this little break-in of Mara's."

He lifted a brow. "Why would I lie to you about this?"

"I don't know, but that doesn't mean you aren't."

"I could be, I suppose." He smiled. "But I'm not."

She wondered if that was true. Did he really not know that Villanueva was back in the States, that he was a likely suspect in today's little break-in? If he knew Villanueva was back, she couldn't tell from looking at him. Then again, he'd once been a world-class poker player. He'd made his living—the legitimate part of it anyway—keeping the truth of his intentions off his face.

So she couldn't afford to give him the benefit of the doubt. Particularly not when she was still vibrating from his touch like a plucked guitar string. Her objectivity was already perilously close to compromised where he was concerned, and she'd need every trump card available to keep the reins of this case firmly in her hands.

"I've watched you these past couple of years," she said slowly. "I've seen the life you live. The mansion, the women, the cars, the clothes. Everything's gorgeous, but from what I can see, you don't own a single thing you couldn't walk away from in a pinch. If you're not planning to chuck it all for the life of crime that's apparently in your DNA, why do you live like that?"

He drew back from her slowly. It was satisfying to finally score a point, but Liz felt his retreat more keenly than she'd have liked. Or admitted to.

"Why, Liz," he drawled. "You've been spying on me?"

She rolled her eyes. "What, you thought you could agree to reform and we'd just take your word on it? We're the FBI. If we didn't take a second to figure out where a guy with your background was coming up with the buckets of money you're making, we wouldn't deserve the badge."

He lifted a single brow, mocking, ironic. "I don't even use a pen name."

"I didn't say we had to look very hard."

He sighed and patted her knee. "Just keep an eye on Mara and the kid, will you?"

Then he rose to his feet with a feline grace that even a Swiss finishing school had been unable to instill in Liz, and left without another word. Liz blinked. The gun was still disassembled on the coffee table, *Return of the Jedi* still murmuring along on the TV, her hair still damp from the shower. If it wasn't for the hum in her blood, the vital, thrumming awareness of her entire body, she might have thought she imagined the whole episode.

She jumped violently when a shrill *beep* ripped through the stillness of her empty house, then cursed under her breath when she realized it was only Patrick.

The bastard had set her security system for her on his way out. She didn't even want to know how he'd figured out her pass code, and she wanted even less to dwell on the little kernel of warmth that glowed in her belly at this small act—however subversive—of protection.

She'd devoted her entire adult life to protecting the world at large. How long had it been since somebody had tried to protect her?

Chapter
5

POOR LIZ, Patrick thought with reluctant fondness. She just wasn't good at relaxing. Even the other night, when he'd caught her all wrapped up in that delicious indulgence of a bathrobe, soft, damp, clean, smelling like soap and heaven, she hadn't been sprawled on the couch, watching her TV, letting her brain go to hell after a tough week. No, even then she'd been cleaning her gun with an efficient, meticulous grace, the way another woman might touch up her nails.

Waiting to find out why she and her pet felon had been called into her boss's office first thing Monday morning had to be killing her.

She wriggled in the chair beside him and tried to look like she wasn't checking her watch for the fifth time in as many minutes. He gave her no more than thirty seconds before she opened her mouth to take charge.

At ten seconds, she spoke. He grinned into his lap.

"SAC Bernard," she said, her voice earnest and sober,

"respectfully, we've been waiting for Agent di Guzman for nearly ten minutes. I suggest we begin—"

"We'll wait," Bernard said, and his tone made it perfectly clear that the point was nonnegotiable. As far as Patrick could tell, there wasn't much about SAC Bernard that *was* negotiable. Everything about him—words, suit, hair—was precisely correct, properly colorless and utterly lacking in imagination. Patrick could see how a cop like Liz had flourished under the supervision of such a man.

He wondered about the woman in her, though. She'd channeled her boundless energy and passion into her work, but she could hardly keep it clamped down and properly behaved all the time. Not an idealist like Liz. A couple of clashes with an unreasonable bureaucracy and it was bound to come unleashed. What happened to the cop when it did?

She pressed her lips together and folded her hands into her lap in a semblance of patience. Patrick sent her a winning smile, which she ignored entirely. *Another two minutes before she tries again,* he thought. *Tops.*

Barely thirty seconds had passed and Patrick was thinking of revising his estimate downward when Bernard's admin knocked discreetly. "Agent di Guzman," she murmured and ushered nearly six feet of glorious, sun-kissed Latina into the room.

Agent di Guzman, Secret Service, strode across the office on yard-long legs helped out by a couple inches of skinny heel. Her hair was a swinging bob of black silk, her skin a smooth expanse of café au lait. A conservatively cut suit the exact color of a good cabernet sauvignon nodded at good taste while doing nothing to conceal some impressive curves. *Liz could learn a thing or two about living the good life within the rules from this woman,* Patrick thought.

"SAC Bernard," she said, her voice low, smooth and warm as she shook the man's hand. Her dark eyes swept the room, lingered briefly on Patrick, then homed back in on her target.

"Agent di Guzman," Bernard said. "Thank you for agreeing to meet at such short notice."

She gave him a dazzling smile. "The FBI isn't obligated to reach out on this, and we're grateful for the help. I was glad to work it in. Would have liked to have been on time, but . . ." She broke off, let an elegant little shrug fill in the gap.

A pained looked ghosted across Bernard's face and Liz rose to her feet. Not impatiently, but without an instant of delay. Patrick's grin tried to widen, but he clamped down on it.

"Liz Brynn," she said briskly, shaking the woman's hand. "Good to finally meet you in person, Agent di Guzman."

The woman treated Liz to the same dimples she'd tossed at Bernard. "Please," she said. "Call me Maria." Then she turned that dark gaze on Patrick. He felt it, certainly. He'd have to be dead not to. Those eyes were a force of nature— warm, interested, frankly sexual—but running alongside the invitation was something cool and analytical. Something that promised both sweaty sheets and an empty bed by morning.

"Maria di Guzman," she said, the words jumbling together into a beautiful rush of syllables. "Secret Service." She lingered over the handshake just a shade longer than was strictly polite.

"Patrick O'Connor," he said, and had the pleasure of watching her eyes flare with what might have been anything from surprise to interest to appreciation. To his dismay, he didn't feel any particular motivation to find out which it was. He slid Liz a bad-tempered glare. She smiled at him sweetly, then transferred it to di Guzman.

"Patrick's the weasel I told you about," she supplied helpfully.

"Ah." The woman turned her attention back to Patrick. He smiled at her, slow and warm. Liz clapped her hands together with one businesslike smack, turned to Bernard and said, "So, are we ready to get started?"

"Actually, we've been ready for a good fifteen minutes now," he said, and Patrick watched him exhale with relief at finally having been afforded an opportunity to remark on the lateness of the hour. He seated himself with a practiced economy of motion that Patrick found vaguely irritating and said, "Mr. O'Connor? You have something to discuss?"

"*You* called this meeting?" Liz swung around in her chair to stare at Patrick, her eyes blazing. He gave her a small shrug. Knowing when to raise was mostly a matter of instinct, after all. You couldn't learn it, you just had to know it. And after the little chat he and Liz had had on Saturday night, Patrick's gut had been screaming for higher stakes. So he'd dialed up Liz's boss and raised them.

He turned now to Bernard with a serious, professional look.

"I'm concerned about my ability to function effectively on this case as a confidential informant," he said.

"You weren't concerned two days ago," Liz said, an angry flush burning at her cheekbones. Patrick smiled. She could chain down that passionate temperament all she liked, but skin that pale and perfect was going to betray her every time.

"I gave it a great deal of thought over the weekend," he said with an easy smile he knew would ratchet her blood pressure a few points higher. "It's just not going to work." He turned back to Bernard and said, "If you want my help, you'll have to elevate my status to that of civilian consultant, a third—and equal—party in this investigation."

Patrick leaned back into the suddenly tense silence and waited while everybody chewed on his unorthodox request for an even playing field for this, his last dance with the FBI. With Liz.

Not that he begrudged her the moral high ground, of course. She'd earned it, God knew. But judging from Saturday night's tirade, she was a little too certain of her superiority. And with certainty came smugness. And with smugness came carelessness. And carelessness was something neither of them could afford, not with this ravening beast of want still crouching inside him, just waiting for him to loosen his grip on the leash.

Then Liz was out of her chair, a magnificent fury blazing in her eyes. "With respect, sir," she said, "I object to such a change in status."

Bernard leaned back in his seat thoughtfully. "I imagined you would," he said. "Speak."

She stood at rigid attention, her golden hair smooth as rain, her profile a study in outrage, and she began to do just that.

FURY BUZZED in her ears like a swarm of killer bees and Liz sucked in a breath through her nose, trying to grasp the threads of her previous calm. She should have expected this, she told herself. This was Patrick O'Connor she was dealing with, after all, not some junkie snitch. She should have seen the power grab coming a mile away.

But she hadn't. She'd been blindsided by him, by the meeting, by the request. And why? Because on some stupid, unconscious level, she'd already given him a measure of trust.

Self-disgust dripped cold and slippery into her gut but she focused on the anger. On the bright, cleansing purity of her rage.

She said, "Mr. O'Connor has been a valuable source in the past but has also proven himself willing and able to break the law for little more than entertainment. Raising him to the level of private consultant gives him access to privileged and confidential information on the counterfeiting process that would be dangerous in the hands of a common criminal. In O'Connor's, it could be devastating."

Bernard turned his gaze to Patrick, who sat neatly in his uncomfortable chair. Just like the meek and upstanding citizen he pretended to be, Liz thought in disgust. "How long have you been, ah, reformed now, Mr. O'Connor?" he asked.

"Six years, I believe," Patrick said. "I've been determined to use the second chance Agent Brynn afforded me to build a legitimate career. I felt I owed her that much."

Liz folded her lips down tight and ignored him, directing her words instead to Bernard. "That sounds good, I know, but you have to understand. Nothing is sacred to this man. Not loyalty, not the law, not justice and certainly not a debt to me. He has no moral center, and if you remove my authority over him, he has no motivation to cooperate within the confines of the law as interpreted by the FBI and the Secret Service."

"Mr. O'Connor?" Bernard turned to him, one brow lifted, waiting for his response.

"The record also shows that I have a long-standing and well-documented desire to see my sister safe from harm, one that's prompted me to cooperate readily with FBI demands over the past six years. At great personal cost, if I may be so bold. At this point, I believe the FBI owes me the courtesy of acknowledging that. My participation in this case hinges on it, in fact."

Her breath died in her throat, evaporated by the heat of her fury as the balance of power tipped his way again. She glared at Patrick, who simply looked back at her, one eyebrow cocked while those pale eyes of his laughed. A bolt of white-hot fury lanced through her, bubbled up and erupted.

"I won't allow this," she said, her words clipped and controlled, the terrible desire to inflict injury where she herself was bleeding giving her a cold focus. "I've worked my entire life for this badge. I paid for it with my own sweat and blood. I earned it and I honor it. Accepting Patrick O'Connor as my equal diminishes not only my badge, but everything I've worked for." She watched him rather than SAC Bernard as her words dropped into the still, tense air of the office, had the bitter pleasure of seeing that perfect face go smooth and remote.

"Your objection is noted," Bernard said. "And overruled. As of today, Patrick O'Connor will be accorded the status of an independent consultant to the FBI and will be compensated with hourly wages accorded to such. He will also be expected to sign an agreement as to his knowledge of the moral and ethical responsibilities of such a position and the penalties involved in violating any of them." The look he gave Patrick was hard and penetrating. Liz watched through a haze of fury as Patrick nodded his understanding humbly. "Now get to work."

TWO HOURS, one punishing run and a cool shower later, Liz was ready to admit that she owed Patrick an apology. She didn't like it and she certainly wasn't looking forward to it, but she hadn't ever lied to herself and didn't plan to start now. Keeping whatever twisted tendencies she had leftover from childhood in check required a brutal, uncomfortable honesty. About everything.

So she felt more for Patrick O'Connor than she wanted to. Okay, fine. She admitted it. Some women, she knew, would simply have told themselves that they weren't attracted, that there was no admiration there, no warmth, no . . . friendship, or kinship, or whatever you wanted to call that weird and electric connection to him that struck her on occasion like a lightning bolt from a clear blue sky. But because she couldn't control what she didn't acknowledge, she made herself acknowledge it. It was there. Fine.

But she hadn't been in control today. He'd pushed her buttons and she'd given him what must have been a very satisfying show. And as a result, she'd said things that should never have seen the light of day, much less been splattered all over her boss's office.

Not that she had a problem with the content of her little tirade. If pressed, she'd stand behind it, one hundred percent. Her boss had just put a man who treated the law like a minor inconvenience on equal footing with two women who'd devoted their entire professional careers to protecting the general public from men exactly like him. And that wasn't right.

But the fact was that Patrick was helping her. Whatever his motivations, he was doing her and her agency a favor. Taking a few shots at Liz along the way was probably just a little bonus in his mind. If she'd been thinking straight, she'd have seen that.

But she hadn't been thinking. She'd been feeling to the exclusion of all else, and she'd let an old fear take control. And though the FBI field agent's manual didn't cover personal manners, Liz knew better than to believe that blabbing her private opinion of another person's character in front of not only that person but a room full of interested spectators qualified as exemplary conduct. Not even if the words were true.

She stuffed her running clothes into the hamper and buttoned herself into her sternest black suit, gave her hair one last swipe with the brush and slipped back into her sturdy leather flats. She didn't bother with makeup, wouldn't allow herself the girly pleasure. She'd face Patrick O'Connor, king of the beautiful people, with the face God gave her. Maybe Agent di Guzman would be with him so Liz could suffer by comparison. Let it be a penance of sorts.

She took a deep, calming breath, flipped open her cell phone and dialed his number. "Patrick?" She turned away from the mirror over her dresser. She didn't want to watch herself do this. "It's Liz. Where are you? We need to talk."

Chapter
6

"IT'S ALL in the paper," Agent di Guzman was saying. Her lipstick left a lush red imprint on the china coffee cup she sipped from and Patrick enjoyed the sight. It was so essentially female. "You get the right paper, you're more than halfway to a good fake bill. Two sheets, smooth application of adhesive—one motion, you see?" She swept her hand through a smooth and delicate arc. "Press them together, and you're there."

Patrick gave her an answering smile that stayed carefully shy of the invitation he saw in hers. "You make it sound so simple."

She shrugged. "It is. But there's an art to it as well. Counterfeiting isn't for dummies."

"I didn't imagine it was," Patrick murmured, then watched as Liz stepped through the doors of his sister's restaurant and spotted them. He'd been expecting her, of course. She'd called to say she was coming, and he'd been appropriately cool and noncommittal. He'd heard quite enough of her opinion of him today and had very little interest in a private replay of her public declaration.

He glanced over at di Guzman. They were seated at a café table in a cozy corner, beside rather than across from each other as di Guzman had about as much interest in putting her back to the door as he did. He watched her well-shaped brows elevate at the way Liz scanned the room, spotted her target and locked in on it. On him.

"Oh, my," Maria said. "She's . . . direct, isn't she?"

"That's one word for it," Patrick agreed grimly.

Amusement curved her coral lips, and her air of casual invitation melted into something more like understanding. "You'd pick another?"

He lifted his shoulders at the flicker of compassion he saw in her dark eyes. "She's honest," he said. "Terrifyingly so."

"That's what I've heard," Maria said. "Passionate, too. Dedicated. More committed to her convictions than her reputation." She patted his knee under the table, but it was brisk rather than suggestive. "Looks like you two are going to go a round or two."

Patrick sipped his lukewarm coffee. "Looks like."

"I'll let you get at it, then." She rose just as Liz arrived at the edge of their table. "I need to lay in some supplies before we get started with Counterfeiting 101," she said when neither of them spoke. "I should be ready in, say, an hour? Why don't we meet at the Rapid Copy on Barrel Street, and I'll run you through the basics."

"Fine." Liz looked like a small, blond thunder cloud.

"Sure," Patrick said, unable to resist giving di Guzman another slow, warm smile. It warmed another several degrees when she bent to retrieve her briefcase and rolled her eyes at him where Liz couldn't see. Patrick made a point of watching her saunter to the door. Liz remained standing.

"I need to speak with you," she said, her voice as stony as her face. "In private."

Patrick lifted his coffee. "Mind if I ask why?"

She looked like a woman about to swallow bleach. "I want to apologize."

The cup froze halfway to Patrick's lips. He set it back down with a tiny, startled chink. "Excuse me?"

"Apologize." Liz gritted the word through her teeth. "You're familiar with the concept?"

"In connection with you? Not precisely."

She sighed and some of the starch left her spine. "Listen, you deserve to be mad at me. I was a raving bitch to you earlier, and you have every right to be pissed. But I'm going to apologize, and I'd consider it a personal favor if you didn't make me do it in front of all these people."

She waited a beat. Patrick just studied her.

"Well?" she asked.

"I'm thinking."

"Oh, for God's sake," she snapped.

"All right, all right," he said, pushing away from the table and taking her elbow. "Let's use one of the meeting rooms on the third floor. I hope you're planning to make this worth my while."

She glared at him, but he just ushered her politely to the stairwell.

Patrick picked a meeting room at random and waved Liz in ahead of him. No excuse for bad manners, after all. A long conference table filled the room, polished to a high gloss and surrounded by square chairs and dreamy watercolors. Liz stalked in, ignoring the chairs in favor of pacing the carpet like a caged animal. Patrick selected a seat at the head of the table for himself—the seat of authority. He figured that when Liz finally finished debasing herself by apologizing to a known felon, she'd be good and pissed to find she then had to sit at his elbow like a supplicant.

He considered her for a moment, this fierce little woman the universe kept flinging at his head. She was like an avenging angel, raging through the world with her ruthless sword, cutting down the guilty with a certainty that Patrick envied with all his heart.

She'd slapped at him today but had done so with nothing

more than the truth, and he found his anger fading with each turn she took around the long room. Maybe he should let her off the hook, he thought. What more fitting way to pay for his sins than to willingly accept her judgment of him? He didn't disagree, after all. But his pride wouldn't allow it.

He could accept her leash, her authority. He had in the past. He'd protected her, helped her, *wanted* her, knowing the whole while that she simply endured him. But he hadn't known that she'd felt stained by his very presence, and he'd been unexpectedly hurt to find out. But he'd be damned to hell and back before he'd let her see that. So he kept his mouth shut and let her pace.

Finally, she swung around and faced him from the far end of the room. Without twitching a muscle, Patrick braced himself for more of the truth, disguised as apology.

She opened her mouth, shut it again, then sighed. She shook her head and walked back to him. She ignored the subservient seat at his elbow, instead leaning back against the edge of the table next to his knees, her arms banded over her stomach.

"I said some ugly things to you today," she said, her gaze direct and very, very blue. "I had no cause to say them, not in private, and certainly not in front of others. I apologize."

Her eyes had always been a problem for him. The color of bruised forget-me-nots, they should have been limpid pools of innocence, but they weren't. At first glance, she was all blond sweetness, but Patrick saw more. He saw the knowledge, the awareness, the darkness that swirled around in the depths, and he'd always wondered what had put it there. He'd never asked. He wouldn't now.

"You believed it," he said with a shrug. "Why shouldn't you say it?"

"Truth isn't always synonymous with right."

"Sometimes it is. For example, this suit is just an insult to your figure. Why do you tolerate it?"

"My clothes are fine," she said, rolling her eyes. "For the work I do."

"If you're undercover as a small-town sheriff with an allergy to natural fibers, sure." He reached out to finger the fabric of her lapel. "But I thought we closed that particular case three years ago."

She slapped his hand away with an automatic motion that nearly had him smiling at her again.

"*I* closed it," she said. "No thanks to you."

He smiled at her. "Then why are you still wearing this . . . thing?"

She glared at him. "Can we please get back to the subject at hand?"

"By all means." He leaned back and stretched out his legs. "Just trying to help."

"I know."

He blinked. "You do?"

"Sure. I mean, any idiot can see that you really buy into this whole better living through fashion thing. And I get that. I don't understand it, but I get it. You think nice clothes equal happiness and you think I could be happier."

"A *lot* happier."

She ignored that. "My behavior today wasn't nearly as well intentioned."

"No?"

"No." She looked so miserable that Patrick wanted to wrap her up in his arms and soothe her in spite of himself. But he didn't. She wouldn't appreciate the gesture, and he wasn't looking for another insult to his raw ego this afternoon. "I wanted to hurt you."

"Liz. Darling. Whatever for?" He injected just the right note of lazy amusement into the question.

"You know damn well what for," she snapped. "I've worked my ass off for my badge. It *means* something, to me and to everybody I admire. And to you it means nothing. Less than. How can you be my equal behind it, under it?"

"I can't," Patrick said flatly. "God knows I don't want to be."

"Then why the hell did you ask to be?" The words exploded out of her with a gratifying lack of control. Another little push, Patrick thought, and he might finally see behind that damn badge of hers. He knew he shouldn't, knew she was balancing on an unfamiliar edge, but God help him, he desperately wanted to see her. The real her.

"Why are you here, Liz?" He slouched down in his seat and shot her a lazy smirk.

"To apologize," she said. Through her teeth.

Patrick laughed softly. "Are you? Or are you just worried that I'm going to take my ball and go home?"

"What do you mean?" she asked, though he suspected she knew quite well.

"Come on, Liz. We're all grown-ups here. We've been pretty honest so far today, let's just keep it rolling. You spoke the truth as you see it; don't back off it now. You're a badge, I'm a criminal. You're the handler, I'm the weasel. You'll tolerate me in the name of justice, but at your discretion and on your terms. But I'm Joe Average now, at least in the eyes of the law, and that changes things between us. Levels them out a bit." He leaned toward her on one elbow, propped his chin in his hand and considered her with narrowed eyes. "I'd give good odds that you thought long and hard after our little meeting today. Came up against the bitter truth."

Liz held his gaze, unflinching. "And that would be?"

He rose slowly, flattened one hand on the table to the left of her hip and leaned in. He was close now, close enough to catch the scent of her rising with the heat of her skin. "I'm not your lapdog anymore, Liz," he said, his mouth a breath away from the lovely pink shell of her ear.

"I never thought you were a lapdog," she said. Her voice was wary, but Patrick noticed that she didn't move away from him. Fear and courage, certainty and doubt. She was such a paradox, his fierce little angel.

"Liz. Darling." He drew back just far enough to look

into those wide, troubled eyes. "You're a wretched liar. But it hardly matters. I'm not pulling out of the investigation."

She stared at him, suspicious. "Why not? I was horrible to you today."

"Fate, I suppose," he said, and turned to hitch a companionable hip onto the table beside her.

"Fate?" She frowned up at him.

"Mmmm," he said, pleasing himself by flicking at one of the tasteful gold hoops in her ear. "Fate. That's why I went to work for you in the first place all those years ago."

"I thought you were trying to spring your sister."

"That too." He smiled at her. "But nothing in life is free, is it, Liz? The universe demands balance, and even thieves have to pay sometime. When you dropped into my life, I figured my bill had finally come due. So I paid. For years. But fate's still throwing you in my path, Liz, and I have to wonder why."

"Fate doesn't throw me anywhere." She screwed that curvy mouth of hers into a humorless line. "I make my own decisions and I decided a long time ago that fate's nothing but a handy place to put the blame when you don't like your life."

That startled a laugh out of him. "Right," he said and reached out to stroke his thumb down the pretty column of her throat to the pulse point at its base. She lifted a hand to slap his away, but he gave his head a single, warning shake and put the barest pressure against the hollow of her throat, just enough to remind her of the vulnerability of her current position. Her hand froze midswipe and he released the pressure almost before he'd applied it.

He shifted his hand to comb his fingers through her lovely, heavy hair instead, lifting it away from her scalp and letting it drift away from his hand like so much spun gold. "I don't suppose the word *hubris* means anything to you?"

Her eyes went hot and narrow as she shook off his hand and glared at him. "You're so full of shit, Patrick. Why can't you just admit that you were pissed about working for me again and took a dig?"

He was on his feet in one smooth motion, had her caged between his arms, his fingers gripping the table on either side of her hips, his gut twisting with frustration and useless want. But he didn't touch her. He could smell her, could feel the heat of her against his skin, but he didn't touch her.

"I wish it were that simple." He was a breath from her lips, his voice gone to a silky whisper. "But I'm going to spell it out for you, so you don't do either of us the injustice of underestimating the situation."

Her eyes went suddenly wide and wary. "What situation?"

He struggled for cool control, dragged in a breath, but it was full of her, of her awareness, of her heat, and it coursed through his veins like fire.

"I want you, Liz," he heard himself say, a hungry edge on his voice. "More than I should. More than I want to."

"You *what*?"

He ignored that, and allowed himself the exquisite torture of brushing his cheek against her hair. "Up until now, I've been very, very good," he said. "The image of self-control. I've wanted, but I haven't taken. Haven't touched. Haven't tasted. But I realized something just now, something strangely liberating."

He nuzzled her hair aside, pressed his lips to the lovely line of her neck. Gloried in the quick, shaky breath she drew. "No matter how good I try to be, I'll never hold a candle to you," he said. "You with your badge, your morals, your pristine soul."

She made some kind of distressed noise, but he was too far gone to stop now. He just sucked in a lungful of her and plowed ahead. "It's just occurred to me that maybe fate's on my side this time. What if it's the universe that owes *me*?"

"Owes you what?" Her voice was thin and wary, but she didn't move away from him. She stayed perfectly still, and renewed desire clutched at his gut.

"Oh, I don't know. A little something for my trouble."

He lowered his face deliberately into the crook of her neck and let it wash over him in one huge sensory moment—the incredible softness of her skin, the slippery coolness of her hair, the way her head automatically dropped ever so slightly to the side to accommodate him.

"I'll work for you, Liz." He pulled back just far enough to smile into her eyes. "*With* you, I mean. One last time. But it'll cost you."

She lifted her hand slowly, rested it against his chest and applied a questioning pressure. The touch of her hand burned through the light cotton of his shirt, but Patrick seized the threads of his control and dropped back a step. Obediently.

"Cost me what, exactly?" Her eyes were clouded, though with what he couldn't tell. Unhappiness? Fear? An answering desire?

"Nothing you don't want to give." He took a second to pull it together, to breathe, to make sure that what he wanted to say would come out in one coherent piece. He tucked his hands into his pockets, nice and nonthreatening. "I'm done taking the high road, that's all. I want you, and I can be damn persuasive when I try."

Her eyes went narrow with comprehension. "What does that have to do with forcing my boss to promote you?"

"Nothing. That was just for fun." He smiled at her, though it cost him an effort to keep it smooth. "But it came with an unforeseen bonus."

"What's that?"

"You're an ethical soul, Liz. You would never sleep with an informant. An independent consultant, however, an equal . . ." He let the words trail off into suggestion.

She rolled her eyes. "For God's sake."

"Hey, if I'm not good for you, if you don't want me, all you have to say is no. I won't take anything you don't willingly give." He let years of suppressed want loose in his smile, felt it shift from warm to carnal. "But I swear to God I can make you want to give me things you don't even know exist yet."

She stared at him, her lips parted just slightly in shock, eyes maybe a little glazed. An insane rush of anticipation had an unexpected laugh bubbling up in his throat. Why hadn't he thought of this approach years ago? Either she'd resist him to the bitter end or they'd set his sheets on fire. Either way, he'd get what he wanted—a resolution to the Villanueva issue without going stark, raving mad from suppressed lust.

He summoned up a level look for Liz. "You still want me on the team, you've got me," he said. "But those are the new ground rules. Take it or leave it."

Chapter

7

LIZ NODDED slowly, watching him. He gazed back, cool and utterly contained. As if he hadn't just caged her between his arms and practically incinerated her with the heat of his desire. But even then, Liz realized, he hadn't been out of control. Not really. It was pure, vintage Patrick. The guy could stage a class-one seduction without ever losing his cool. Good Lord.

"Listen, I *get* it, all right?" She eased off the edge of the conference table where she'd almost let him do any number of ill-advised things to her person and crossed her limp arms to keep them from flailing around like beached fish. "I know you're pissed about this. About cooperating with an FBI investigation, especially now that you're no longer obligated to even be civil to us, let alone work for us. And then I was a colossal bitch to you in front of God and everybody. I'm sorry about those things, Patrick. I really am."

"Mmmm-hmmm."

"I know you want to punish me, to keep me off balance, but purposely injecting a"—she groped for a word; it was hard with her hands tucked safely into her elbows—"a *sexual* note into our relationship is not only stupid, it's bad business. No matter what you think of me personally, we're colleagues of a sort, okay? We can work this out like grown-ups, so knock it off, will you?"

He took a step toward her, and she took a hasty step back only to meet up with the edge of the table again. He reached for her, and everything in her entire being went hot and liquid with delicious anticipation. Good Lord, was he going to kiss her? She closed her eyes briefly, whether for strength or just to enjoy it, she wasn't sure. But he only smoothed her lapels, laid his hands on her shoulders and was looking right into her eyes when she opened them.

"I'm not doing anything, Liz," he said. She snorted and tried to shove past him, but he held her with an easy strength that had her eyes widening and her knees weakening again. He put his mouth very near her ear and she tried hard not to breathe because she didn't want the smell of him hanging around her brain doing stupid things. "I've always been attracted to you," he said. "A feeling you've returned, whether you knew it or not. I just clued you in, that's all."

He stepped back while she gaped at him, then smiled at her as if he hadn't just kicked the shit out of her reality. He flicked her hair back over her shoulder and said, "Don't look so surprised, darling. Everything evolves. You'll learn. Just keep that badge nice and close."

"I don't believe you," she said, but Patrick only gazed at her with fond amusement. She shrugged, as if he hadn't just tapped in to her most private fear and weakness. "But whatever. If this is what it takes to make you feel better, fine. I'll . . . deal with it."

His mouth curved slightly at that. "You have your agenda, I have mine." He tucked his fingers into the pockets of khakis that looked as comfortable as bare feet in the summer. And they probably were, since she suspected they were custom-made.

"I can take care of myself," she said, but in all honesty,

she had her doubts. Because, God, her pulse was still jumping, and she could feel those wicked lips against the sensitive skin of her neck like a brand.

"I can take care of you, too." A smile spread across his face like warm honey and she felt it all the way to her toes. "If you'll let me."

"No." She eyed him, then checked her watch. "We have to meet Agent di Guzman in a few minutes. Are we square here?"

He considered. "Yes. Yes, I believe we are." He gifted her with a beaming smile.

"Great," Liz muttered, and pressed a hand to her stomach. "Fabulous."

TWENTY MINUTES later, Liz was back in her element. A giant whiteboard at her back, a squeaky dry erase marker in hand, a case file open in her head, her team assembled in front of her. The air smelled like burnt coffee and hot copy paper, which made her feel right at home.

The only sour note was O'Connor, but she was prepared to work around him. Work being the operative word. She would just focus on work to the exclusion of all else, and maybe she'd manage to forget that the world's most beautiful man had targeted her for revenge via seduction. Hey, it could happen. She was good at work. And she was good at focus. Extremely goal oriented. All her performance reviews said so.

She could only hope that she reached her goal before Patrick reached his.

"All right," she said briskly. "An overview of our cover story. After some research, we've decided that Patrick will be preparing to write a movie script about the counterfeiter who cracked the 1996 one-hundred-dollar note."

"Why the 1996 one-hundred-dollar note?" Patrick asked.

"It's without a doubt the biggest single leap the U.S. Treasury ever made, in terms of anticounterfeiting," di Guzman told him. "It's all got to do with the—"

Liz cut her off. "We'll get there in a minute, Agent di Guzman," she said. "Let's get the cover story established, then you can get your hands dirty."

"Sure," she said. "But enough of this Agent di Guzman business. If you can't wrap your mind around Maria, you can go with Goose."

"Goose?" Patrick turned to her, his brows arched in amused surprise. "Please tell me I get to call Liz 'Maverick.'"

She laughed, a rich, lusty chuckle that had Patrick's smile widening with appreciation and Liz gritting her teeth. Liz didn't, as a rule, pay much attention to other women's looks, but God help her, she hated watching Patrick admire this woman. Which was stupid. She should be encouraging the attraction, but she'd come too far in the personal honesty department to pretend a spade wasn't a spade. Patrick watched this woman with a patently male appreciation. He looked at Liz with something completely different, and to her thinking, it wasn't nearly as flattering.

"Not Goose as in *Top Gun*," the woman was saying, laughing. "Goose as in di Guzman. It happened in middle school, kind of stuck." She widened her eyes charmingly, as if imparting a grave secret. "I was, ah, tall. And awkward with it."

"I can't imagine such a thing," Patrick said nobly, and di Guzman chuckled again. Liz breathed through her teeth.

"If we could get back to the little matter of our criminal investigation?" she asked evenly. At the obedient silence that followed, Liz continued. "You'll be basing the movie loosely on the life of Art Williams, Jr., a Midwestern counterfeiter who's been rumored to have printed more than ten million dollars' worth of the bills in question before he was eventually caught in 2001. He did three years. Here in Minnesota, actually. Waseca."

Liz took a slug of her cooling coffee, relished the full-body jolt of caffeine. "You'll want to know the details of how he did it, and Agent di Guzman—Goose"—she'd rather go with the ridiculous nickname than the musical blur of syllables the woman made of her first name—"will take care of that. But as a screenwriter—reputedly a good one—you'll want to go deeper. You'll want the hands-on experience."

Patrick watched her thoughtfully. "Of course I would," he said finally. "In order to write it, I'd want to know how it feels, not only to create the notes with my own hands but to pass them. The rush of actually pulling it off, of turning nothing into money."

"Exactly," Liz said. "And with Goose's help, you'll have a few to pass. Not of the best quality, however."

Goose smiled, and it spread across her perfect face like spilled syrup. "Not that I couldn't produce excellent bills, of course. But our goal isn't to pass good quality fakes. It's to get our counterfeiter's attention."

"Exactly," Liz said again. "We're coming at this from two angles. First of all, we're assuming that the counterfeiter views himself as a businessman with an eye on the bottom line. This is a small community, and word spreads fast. His money is very good, but it's not perfect. Maybe a seven or an eight on the Treasury's ten-point scale. He lets you run tame in his territory passing fours and fives, every cashier in the tri-county area is going to be looking more closely at anybody passing a hundred."

Patrick nodded. "Puts too much heat on his operation. He offers to help me out, he keeps us both under the radar."

"Right." Liz finished off her coffee, pitched the crumpled cup into the trash for a solid two points. "The second thing working in our favor is his ego. You're a big name, a big face. You make it known that you admire his work, that you maybe have a position for somebody with his kind of talent on your writing staff. The profile we have suggests he'll be extremely tempted to step forward to provide your hands-on experience."

"And when he does?"

"We wire you up, record the meet. Then your work is done and you're a private citizen again with a meager paycheck and the thanks of your government."

"And a working knowledge of making fake money," Goose put in. "That's the bonus. Though if you ever put it into practice, I'll arrest your ass myself."

Patrick grinned at her. "Is that supposed to be a deterrent?"

"Oh, for crying out loud," Liz said, scrubbing her hands over her face. "I never thought I'd say this, but can we please get on with it? Just teach the guy to make fake money?"

FOUR HOURS later, Patrick held one of Goose's bills in one hand and one of the U.S. Treasury's notes in the other. He had more than a passing acquaintance with the crispness of a brand-new hundred-dollar bill, but when he closed his eyes and rubbed each bill between a thumb and forefinger, he couldn't tell the difference.

"That's impressive," he said to Goose, who stood by the makeshift clothesline where a small line of fakes was drying. She handed over a yellow felt-tipped pen.

"It's a Dri Mark," she said. "Real currency is starch free, but most of the papers that have the right feel aren't. Any starch in your bill and the marker turns a nice dark brown."

Patrick scored a bold line from end to end of both bills. The lines stayed yellow. Goose beamed.

"Now check the color shift," she urged, and Patrick held the bill up to the light, looked at it from an angle. Sure enough, the ink appeared black. He put it back on the table between them and it went back to green.

"Damn," he said. He sounded impressed, and he was. "You're an artist, Goose."

She shook her head. "Nah. That's probably nothing more than a four or five on the scale. I didn't have time to fiddle much with the microprinting."

"So this was, what, a quick scribble, then?"

"Something like that."

"I stand corrected. You're not an artist." He clapped

her on the shoulder. "You're a freaking genius. My father would have *loved* you."

Goose laughed and Liz spoke for the first time since Patrick had started putting bills together under Goose's supervision. "Imagine," she said sourly. "She could be a criminal mastermind and yet she uses her powers for good rather than evil."

Patrick threw Liz a laughing look over his shoulder. "I'm using my powers for good," he said. "Now."

Liz made some kind of adorable huffing noise, and Patrick tossed a friendly arm around her shoulders. But he made sure to snug her up against his side so that he could feel every soft curve and angle hidden by that very ugly black suit. He would burn it someday, he promised himself. Very soon. Getting her out of her suit would be a reward in and of itself, of course. But he was a greedy man. He'd get her out of the suit and he'd burn it, too.

"Liz. Darling. Do you know what this means?" She didn't answer, just frowned up at him from very close proximity. "It means that you and I are going out on the town. We have a counterfeiter to bait." He released her and snapped the fake bill, delighted in the crisp, new, *authentic* sound of it. "And we've got money to burn."

THE LIGHT was going to liquid gold by the time Patrick pulled into Liz's drive Thursday evening in a sleek little sports car that reeked of Hollywood. Liz watched from the window as he unfolded that long, lean frame of his with the sort of assured masculine grace that probably had women two blocks over freshening up their lip gloss. Even the sun worshipped him. It poured reverently down that perfectly carved profile and put a supernatural gleam on hair that was already black as midnight, curving onto his forehead with the kind of mannerly obedience that only a two-hundred-dollar haircut could buy.

She caught herself staring and turned abruptly away

from the window. Beauty was a dangerous thing, she reminded herself. Especially a beauty as mesmerizing and outlandish as Patrick's. Did she really need a refresher course in that particular lesson?

She snatched up her suit coat and shoved one arm into it while she bumped open her front door with her hip. "I'm coming," she called to him, her voice brisk and business-like. It was the perfect tone to dispel any notions he had about fetching her at the door like a prom date. Because she wasn't his damn date. She was on the job. They both were. "Just let me lock up."

Then he was on the porch beside her, his hand—always bigger, warmer and more *solid* than she ever anticipated—over hers. Then her key was gone, as if he'd simply poofed it into the next dimension.

"Hey!" She glared at him. "You have a problem with me locking up my house?"

"No," he said calmly, pushing the door back open and dragging her inside by the hand he still held. "I have a problem with your outfit."

Liz looked down at herself. Suit was still there, same as always. She looked back up, eyes narrowed. "What kind of problem?"

He sighed. "Let me count the ways. No, that would take too long. Let me summarize. It's inappropriate."

"A black pantsuit is always appropriate. Ask Hillary Clinton."

He rolled his eyes and renewed his grip on her hand. He dragged her down the back hall, opening doors as he went. "Not for what I have in mind," he told her.

Liz dug in her heels and yanked her hand free. "What, exactly, do you have in mind?" Then he found her bed-room.

"Ah," he said, heading in. "Here we go."

Liz bolted after him, alarmed. "Patrick, what are you doing?"

She found him in the little shoe box of space that passed

for a walk-in closet, hands on hips, the light from the single bulb hanging from the ceiling illuminating his expression of pure, unadulterated surprise. And then the smirk rolled in and Liz could feel the blush crawling from her toes all the way up to her ears.

"Well, well, well," he said, wandering deeper into the closet. He reached out to finger a puffed bit of candy pink taffeta, then a delicate curve of deep green chiffon. "Isn't this interesting?"

Liz banded her arms over her stomach and yanked on the chain connected to the lightbulb. The little closet plunged into the half-light of early evening. "Yes, it's fascinating that I own clothes that aren't the suits you hate so much. I realize it comes as an enormous shock. Now will you please get out of my closet? We have work to do."

Patrick reached out and snapped the light back on. "Not dressed like that we don't." He turned back to study the row of vintage cocktail dresses that marched along an entire wall of Liz's closet like a very elegant army. Her cheeks burned and she spun on her heel with a noise of disgust and stalked out. He followed her a moment later with the green chiffon. He removed it from its hanger with a reverence Liz appreciated even as it pissed her off.

"Now this little beauty, this is more like what I had in mind."

"No." She didn't bother glancing at the dress. She knew what it looked like, and more to the point, she knew what she looked like when she wore it. Curvy, retro and flat-out hot. At least that was how she *felt*, and judging by the number of men who looked twice, she wasn't wrong. But putting a nice big spotlight on her femininity in front of a predator like Patrick was like waving a red flag in front of a bull. She was working hard enough to keep her libido in check where he was concerned and wasn't about to sabotage herself by shimmying into a dress that all but crooked a finger his way.

Patrick gave her a reproachful look. "Liz, let's not make this personal, hmmm?"

She stared at him. "I'm not the one trying to stuff my colleague into a cocktail dress."

He shook his head. "I realize you don't think much of my judgment, but if this little partnership is going to work, you're going to have to accept that I have an expertise in certain areas, limited though they may be." He shot her a charming, roguish grin. "And when it comes to club hopping—rural, urban and in between—let's just acknowledge that I have a superior knowledge of what's going to blend."

"Fine, but I seriously doubt that a dress like that"—she eyed the billowing mound of crinoline and chiffon on her bed—"is going to *blend* anywhere in Grief Creek."

He went on as if she hadn't spoken. "So let me just assure you that while I have all the regard in the world for such a charming little dress and what your figure can do for it, my interest in getting you into it is solely based on my professional goal."

"Which is?"

"Making sure that everything about your entire person stops shrieking *cop* at the top of its lungs."

She glared at him. "I *am* a cop."

"So I understand." He spread his hands innocently. "But not tonight. Tonight, you're my date."

"I am *so* not your date—" she began hotly.

Patrick cut her off. "Yes, my date," he said calmly. "My accessory. A tasty little bit of arm candy I've picked up for the duration of my stay in the Midwest to alleviate the terrible dullness of it all. And if you can't leave your badge at home long enough to make that happen, we might as well just wait until Goose clears enough of her caseload to take your place."

Liz opened her mouth. Shut it again. Considered. He was right. She hated it that he was right, but he was. If she was going to keep this case on schedule, she needed to be Patrick's source of on-site local information. As his date, she could murmur a steady stream of who's who and what's what into his ear without anybody looking twice. And if she wanted to look even remotely like the kind of woman Patrick would pick up as arm candy, she was going to have to wear that dress.

She hissed out a breath through her teeth and said, "That dress shoves my boobs practically into the stratosphere."

He smiled, silkily. "I'd wondered. Matching shoes?"

She closed her eyes, prayed for strength. "In the closet."

"Excellent."

Chapter

8

IT WAS an intimate thing, dressing a woman. Patrick reflected on it while he listened to Liz stalk around her bedroom, presumably shoving herself into the dress and shoes he'd laid out for her. He hoped she wasn't too angry to take proper care of that gorgeous dress. Harming it would be nearly a criminal act in his mind. And he was far more impatient to see that soft, pale green chiffon laid over that creamy, milkmaid skin of hers than he'd like to admit.

He'd been knocked nearly to his knees when he'd walked into her closet and found a veritable treasure trove of vintage cocktail dresses. He'd recognized some of the designers immediately, others he'd never heard of. The colors had spanned the spectrum, as did the styles, but the one thing they all had in common was an exquisite sense of fabric and line. How could a woman who bought her suits off the discount rack at God knows where have possibly put together such an amazing and frivolous collection of dresses?

She was such a paradox, his Liz. And a lovely diversion. One he felt he deserved after spending the past three days diligently pumping his sources for anything they could provide on Villanueva while concealing that activity from his sharp-eyed sister. Neither endeavor was going particularly well. Not that he'd expected to whistle and have Villanueva appear on his doorstep like a well-trained dog. But his lack of anything even resembling progress had put him in a foul mood. As had the *family time* Mara seemed determined he enjoy. Forcing his sensible cop to put on a party dress had cheered him considerably.

He was still grinning over it when the door to her bedroom shot open and she stalked through, an emerald green clutch purse dangling from her fingers, a filmy wrap of some sort lying over her arm. The smile died on his lips and his mouth went dry as he simply stared.

She stood there, framed in the dying light, one impatient hand propped on the crinoline of her skirt. "Well?" she asked. "Everything you'd hoped for?"

He forced himself to rise, to walk over to her with a deliberate air of inspection. He spun a finger in the air, a silent command to revolve. She rolled her eyes but complied.

God, he thought, was there anything sexier than a woman's naked throat and shoulders? The dress was perfection on her, the pale, sea-foam green chiffon crisscrossed over her chest and angled over each shoulder. The neckline was far from revealing, but framed the full upper curves of her breasts in a way that made his palms go damp. A more daring V of that smooth skin was displayed in the back, the delicate wings of her shoulder blades limned in the golden light.

Just under the bodice, the entire dress went a deep, rich emerald green. It banded in to highlight an impossibly tiny waist, then billowed out into an extravagantly full skirt that swirled around her knees in a frothy, feminine indulgence. He followed the silky line of her legs to the sky-high heels he'd picked out in a matching green. He had to swallow hard at the things her well-toned legs did for the vintage, ankle-strapped shoes.

She stood there, one eyebrow cocked, that fist still jammed into the hollow at her waist. "Well?" she asked again. "You're the expert on arm candy. Are you satisfied?"

He smiled at her, let it spread like warm chocolate. She'd expect that, he knew. And he couldn't let her see that all he wanted to do was stare for a few more minutes, then start at her feet and work his way up her entire body, lingering at all the most interesting points until he'd put his lips on every single square inch of her skin and she was begging him, *begging* him, to take her right back out of the dress he'd insisted on putting her in.

But all he said was, "Satisfied? What an interesting word."

She rolled her eyes again but didn't back away when he reached for the wrap lying over her arm. He held it out for her, giving her his most dazzling smile. She blinked, then turned and allowed him to drape it over her bare shoulders. She pulled it briskly to her and murmured a very business-like thanks over that gorgeous shoulder.

But he didn't remove his hands as she so clearly expected. Instead, he smoothed the delicate fabric over her shoulders, enjoying the warmth of her skin under his hands. He felt her jolt but didn't step back. He stepped closer instead, left barely an inch or two between their bodies, and slid his fingers into her hair, against the sensitive skin at her nape.

He gloried in the sharp breath she sucked in at his touch, and he took his time freeing her hair from the wrap. When he was finished, he smoothed the fabric back into place against her shoulders and turned her to face him.

"Lovely," he said, and took an immense amount of pleasure in the fact that she looked about as flushed and distracted as he felt. "Ready to get to work?"

"There's something you should know," she blurted.

Patrick lifted a quizzical eyebrow. "Yes?"

"I have a gun in my purse." Those wide blue eyes he admired so much were suddenly very clear and snapping with temper. "You get fresh, I'm using it."

"Right," he said. "Good to know."

He put a hand in the small of her back and let her precede him out the door.

LIZ GLANCED around as Patrick linked his fingers casually through hers and led her through the dark, hot crush of bodies. Even that minimal contact sent a jolt through her system, but she'd gotten used to it. Patrick had been touching her all night, in hundreds of tiny ways. If she let them all get to her, she'd have been in cardiac arrest four clubs ago.

"I saved the best for last," he murmured in her ear as he deposited her on a curved, red velvet settee. It was one of several scattered throughout the room up on little pedestals with spotlights trained on them. Patrick brushed a hand over the ends of her hair as he spoke, and Liz, intensely aware of being all but onstage, leaned into the caress like a cat. She'd fallen easily into her role over the course of the evening—too easily for her peace of mind, if she was being honest—but she consoled herself with the fact that she was probably convincing as a result.

"I think you'll like this place," he said, trailing a lazy fingertip down the exposed line of her neck.

"I already do," she purred, canting her body intimately into his space for the benefit of the watching crowd. "I'm not sitting on or in front of a two-story speaker, my shoes aren't stuck to the floor, and if the volume level in here stays put, my hearing will probably be back to normal by morning."

Patrick's gaze dropped somewhere south of her face and Liz winced inwardly at the amount of cleavage she was exposing. A gentleman—hell, even another agent—wouldn't look, but this was Patrick O'Connor she was dealing with.

"I'll get us a drink," he said, and followed his gaze with a fingertip, trailing it along the vulnerable skin along the edge of her bodice before he pulled his hand back. Just in time, too, because she was thinking about snapping it off for him. Or she should have been. He shot her a look of wicked amusement, then turned and melted into the crowd.

Liz was careful to keep her eyes half lidded and faintly amused as she glanced around the cavernous space and filed away a mental image. The club was called Cargo, and given its location in the warehouse district and the correspondingly boxy exterior, Liz had been unprepared for all the red velvet and black lacquer she was seeing. It was art deco, but not quite. Lots of angles and edges, silver accents and indirect lighting. F. Scott Fitzgerald meets *Rent*, she decided.

The crowd was a mixed bag, too—plenty of club kids, but plenty of professionals as well. Hers was not the only vintage dress in the place, either. Score one for Patrick. There was a pale blue halter pantsuit swirling around the dance floor that caused Liz a sharp pang of envy. Halston, if she wasn't mistaken. She didn't have the figure for it herself, but that didn't mean she couldn't admire the sleek, heroin chic of it. Very Studio 54.

The music—thanks be to God—wasn't the crushing physical presence it had been at most of the other clubs Patrick had dragged her through. The speakers were hidden inside shiny black panels that extended from ceiling to floor, and what pulsed through them was some oddly appealing combination of techno and big band. And the floor, though just a cement slab, hadn't sucked at her shoes like double-sided tape.

She had no trouble spotting Patrick as he wended his way through the crowd to the raised black-lacquer bar in the center of the soaring room. The masses simply melted away in front of him in unconscious deference to his wealth, his power, his wardrobe and his utter disregard for their opinion. Liz gave her head a tiny shake. An identical scene had unfolded at each of the clubs they'd already hit this evening, so she couldn't claim to be surprised. Just incredulous.

Was she truly the only person in the world who gave Patrick O'Connor shit? The thought made her smile, a small, feline smirk that turned up just the sharp edges of her mouth. Her first ten years had been distinctly lacking in privilege, but she'd spent the second ten trapped inside ancient, ivy-covered buildings being educated alongside the heiresses to some of the world's most impressive fortunes. She'd spent enough time in the company of the ultra-wealthy to have developed an immunity to the overwhelming air of social privilege that dripped from them like heavy perfume. Enough time so that the sight of their poster boy in motion didn't strike her dumb with awe, anyway.

Which was a good thing, because it certainly filled her with lust.

Her smile faded at that lowering thought, and she watched him hand a counterfeit hundred over the counter in return for their drinks. The bartender never blinked, never even looked away from Patrick's face as she made change. Liz refrained—barely—from rolling her eyes in disgust.

A few moments later, Patrick strolled up, drinks in hand, not a drop spilled. He handed her a glass of something cool and golden, then slid onto the couch next to her, the long line of his thigh pressed firmly to hers from hip to knee.

"No problem with the pass," he said, brushing her hair away and leaning into her ear.

She swept her lashes down and peeked sideways at him, shooting for coquettish. "That's because you keep ordering drinks from women."

He smiled at her, slow and warm. "Hey, I just present myself at the bar. Is it my fault that women feel compelled to serve me?"

She did roll her eyes this time. "We're not here for you to pick up women, Patrick. We're trying to get caught passing fake hundreds, but nobody's looking at the money because they're too busy being dazzled by your stupid face. For God's sake, order from the men next time, will you? Give them a fighting chance."

Patrick slipped an arm around her shoulders and gave

her an intimate little squeeze. "Did you bury a compliment in there somewhere?"

Liz suppressed a hot shiver with all the willpower left in her body, and took a fortifying slug of her drink. It burned a path of lemony fire straight to her stomach. "What the hell is this?" she asked.

"It's called a Between the Sheets." He grinned at her. "Or a Maiden's Prayer, depending who you ask. Apparently, it was quite popular in the Roaring Twenties."

Liz tried very hard to turn her frown into something more adoring in case anybody was watching. Which they probably were, because men like Patrick didn't need a damn spotlight to attract attention. "Which explains why this tastes like something my West Virginia cousins brew up in the barn."

He leaned in, feathered his lips along her cheekbone all the way to her ear. A shock wave rolled over every inch of her skin and detonated in parts best left unconsidered. "Let's dance," he said.

"What?" She blinked at him. Techno/big band still pumped out of the speakers. "To this?"

He plucked the drink from her hand, set it aside and rose to his feet. She automatically went with him, as he'd somehow availed himself of her hand. "Trust me," he said over his shoulder and led her into the chaos.

She didn't trust him. Far from it, but Liz was no fool. She held on. She had no idea where he was going or what he was going to do once he got there, but she'd rather stick with him than be abandoned to the sweaty tangle of elbows and hips he was currently parting like the Red Sea.

When he finally stopped, she managed a glance over his shoulder and found they had arrived at the DJ station. A young guy was manning the turntables, working an elaborate array of slides and switches with one hand while holding an enormous set of headphones against his ear with the other. His head bobbed to whatever rhythm he heard there, though how he heard anything over the spill of music coming from the speakers at his back, Liz hadn't a clue.

The cop in her automatically noted his description and filed it: Caucasian, brown hair, brown eyes, an inch or two past six feet. Fashionably scruffy, hair straight and just this side of greasy, wrinkled retro bowling shirt, expensive sneakers. No visible scars or tattoos. Hard to get an age in the poor light, but she'd put him anywhere between sixteen and twenty-six. Probably closer to twenty-six if she was any judge of stubble, though.

She concentrated on keeping the cop off her face while he and Patrick held a conversation that she could neither hear nor lip-read. She had to concentrate even harder when she saw Patrick slip him one of the fake hundreds.

"WHAT ARE you doing?" Liz yelled over the music, murder in her eyes.

Patrick turned into her and grinned. He slid both hands over the sweet curve of her hips and pulled her right up against him, savoring the way she was both lush and lean, round and toned, distant and absolutely, completely touchable. It was like playing a grown-up version of red light/green light, and damn if he wasn't just a little bit dazzled.

"I want to dance with you," he told her, as if it were the most reasonable thing in the world. "So I'm bribing the DJ to play better music."

"You bribed him with a counterfeit note," she pointed out. Her tone was even, but she was pushing the words through her teeth, Patrick noticed. She was also stiff as a ramrod in his arms. He trailed a hand up the pretty line of her spine, felt the tiny shudder run through her. "And this music isn't worth even that."

"Patience, darling," he said, watching those wide, blue eyes of hers narrow with suspicion and something like trepidation as the thumping disco beat suddenly morphed into something slower. Something smokier. Something achingly hot and frankly sexual. He swayed into it with her, splayed his hands lower over her hips and held her steady against him as the music rolled over them, into them,

through them. He wondered briefly if she was going to stab
him to death with one of the heels he'd put her in for the
night, then decided it didn't matter if she did.

It would totally be worth it.

He slid his thigh into the froth of her skirt, nestled it
exactly where he wanted it and, leaving one hand splayed
across the swell of her bottom, swept the other up the warm
expanse of her bare back and into the silky mass of hair at
her nape. He pressed her firmly into his body as he moved
to the beat, deliberately keeping them in intimate contact
from knees to chin.

"Patrick." He heard her say his name, or maybe she just
breathed it. But he heard it nonetheless, and it went straight
to his belly like fire, ignited his blood and raced through
his entire body. He nudged her head into the curve of his
shoulder and felt his entire world come into focus at the
sweetness of the fit.

"Just one dance," he whispered into her hair.

LIZ COULD feel him everywhere. The crowd pressed
against her back, her sides, hemming her in, but she didn't
care. All she cared about was the hot friction of Patrick's
long, firm body, aligned as intimately with hers as was possible when they were both standing up and fully clothed.
Some small voice in the back of her brain pleaded for reason, for restraint, for caution, but she wasn't listening. She
was dancing. With Patrick.

Just one dance, right? How much trouble could she get
into wearing sixteen yards of crinoline anyway? She gave
in to the gentle pressure of his hand at the base of her skull
and let her head fall into the curve of his shoulder. It fit
as if the space had been custom-made for her. She nestled
her cheek into the really superior linen of his shirt and
pulled in a deep lungful of the warm, spicy air at the base
of his throat. She had enough self-control left not to sink
her teeth lightly into the solid rise of muscle that pillowed
her cheek, but it was a near thing. She settled for lifting her

arms instead and winding them lazily around his neck, blatantly flattening her breasts against his chest and running her nails through the crisp smooth hair at his nape.

A distant alarm clanged in her head, warning her that she was well into the danger zone, but she really couldn't hear it over the throbbing of the music. Or the throbbing of her pulse, for that matter. Her daring was rewarded when he slid a warm palm from her raised elbow down to the wildly sensitive skin of her ribs. It skimmed over her waist and settled heavily, possessively in the hollow at the small of her back.

She smiled to herself and let him hold her there, intimately, against him. Let him roll her hips easily with his in time to the pulsing beat of the music, let her body slide against his in the hotly erotic rhythm he'd chosen. Her blood turned to warmed honey. It buzzed and spread languidly through her entire body, every nerve exquisitely sensitive to his touch, his scent, his direction. She danced with him, moving without thought or conscious volition, simply anticipating him in the wordless harmony of a woman who recognizes a man on the most primitive of levels.

The music thudded heavy and alive inside her chest, the crowd surged and swirled around them, Patrick slid and pulsed against her and Liz simply surrendered.

VILLANUEVA LET the writhing mix of people carry him toward his target. The dance floor was dark, hot and sweaty under a thick blanket of collective lust. Strangers made free with their hands and Villanueva had the good fortune to encounter a friendly redhead in a silky dress not two feet from O'Connor and the blond cop.

He smiled into her heavy-lidded eyes and slid his hands around a set of ripe hips. She purred her approval and pressed her lush bottom into his groin. His body responded appropriately and automatically.

But he wasn't paying attention. Not to her. Every cell in his body was attuned to O'Connor and Special Agent

Elizabeth Brynn, lost in their own private dance two feet away.

He was so close. Anticipation jittered through him, pure adrenaline boosting his knee-jerk appreciation of the redhead into something more potent. Arousal burned through him, inseparable from an awareness of the blade he kept strapped to the small of his back. Hunger howled inside him—for revenge, for blood, for satisfaction.

It would be quick, he knew. A simple turn, a step, two practiced, efficient motions. They would crumple to the floor like a pair of drunks or overeager lovers while he melted into the crowd, wiped his prints off the blade and reclaimed his life.

But no. Not yet. He rubbed himself against the accommodating redhead, channeling his energy away from vengeance and into her warm, willing body. Killing them now, together, without warning, would be a travesty of justice.

Because even here in this sexually charged atmosphere, he could smell the lust on them. Could see a miasma of raw want radiating off their bodies. Off O'Connor, especially. Anybody who cared to look could see he wanted the cop with an urgency that blew his customary cool all the way to hell and back. Which interested Villanueva a great deal.

Astonishing as it seemed, this woman—this *cop*—had a hold on O'Connor. Something strong, deep and unprecedented. And as much joy as it would give him to spill their blood on this dirty concrete floor, Villanueva was too disciplined to veer from the plan. Too disciplined to even consider not using the weapon O'Connor had just handed him.

Maybe fucking the redhead would take the edge off his hunger. He smiled into her willing eyes, took her hand and drew her into the darkness.

THE HEAT gathered inside Liz as she and Patrick danced. It tightened, focused, until it became a heavy, yearning gravity at the very center of her. She wanted him there, she realized with a dull shock. And it could hardly be a secret, not with the way she was unabashedly riding his thigh.

This wasn't a dance, she realized, heeding her shrieking brain far, far too late. This was seduction. God damn, the man was determined. And good.

She snapped back to reality with an ugly shock to find herself wrapped around Patrick like a climbing vine, hot, hungry and aching for him with a violence that shook her all the way to her foundation. She snatched her arms away from him as if he'd burned her and cursed her body for the way it mourned the loss of his fire.

Patrick didn't try to hold her. He just tucked his hands into his pockets, his shirt now deliciously wrinkled. She'd done that, she realized with a sick twist of her stomach. Her greedy hands had put those wrinkles there. He gazed at her, his crystalline eyes heavy lidded and hot, his mouth faintly curved. Liz just shook her head. She was beyond words anyway, not that he'd have heard her over the music. He lifted his shoulders in good-natured defeat, as if to say, *hell, I had to try.* She spun on her heel and started fighting her way through the roiling crowd.

Patrick caught at her hand, and Liz made a valiant effort to yank free. Furious tears were stinging her eyes, though she'd be damned if she'd let him see her cry. She doubted very seriously that she'd allow herself the luxury of tears even in private. The terror she was experiencing was too primal, went too deep.

But Patrick wasn't to be shaken off. He held firmly to her hand and somehow had her tucked behind him before she could renew her efforts to free herself. And then he was using that bizarre ability of his to dissolve crowds at will, leading her past their drinks and directly to the door.

Liz could feel his eyes on her as the steel door swung shut behind them, reducing the music to a deep, grinding rumble. Her ears felt queerly hollow in the stillness of the packed parking lot, and her heart felt about the same, God help her. He squeezed her hand once, and she pulled hers away.

"I'll take you home," was all he said.

"SET IT up," Villanueva said into the phone when the kid finally picked up. It was several hours later than he'd intended to call, but the redhead had been more energetic and diverting than he'd anticipated. American women always tried harder in their forties. He'd forgotten that pleasant fact.

"Yeah, sure." The kid yawned enormously into the phone. "But what the hell, right? I mean, you were *right next to them*! I saw you! Why didn't you do anything?"

"Improvisation is for amateurs."

"Dude, you got distracted by the cougar, didn't you? The redhead."

Villanueva shrugged off a shimmer of impatience. The kid had his talents, useful ones, but knowing when to shut up was, sadly, not among them. "Can I count on you to perform the task as assigned?"

There was a sullen silence, then, "Yeah, sure."

"Excellent. I'll be waiting."

Chapter

9

LIZ STOOD back and gazed critically at the whiteboard she'd just filled with her small, blocky printing. It was a terse recap of last night's events and she wanted it that way. Objective and analytical. Succinct. Neither the raw desire she'd been blindsided by nor the eventual and shaky triumph of her self-control had any bearing on the case, and she wanted no trace of either in her report.

She refilled her coffee mug for the fourth time since beating dawn to the office and took a brutally hot gulp. In spite of her burning gut, her fingers were cold as she pressed them to the bags under her eyes. She'd be facing her team in moments and didn't care to do it with the evidence of her sleepless night all over her face.

She was still frowning at the board when Goose sailed in, this time in a suit of deep periwinkle. The jacket was buttoned over a silky camisole of a paler blue, the trousers expertly tailored to show off her yards and yards of leg, all that shiny black hair pulled back into some kind of artful knot at the base of her skull. Chunky silver earrings winked in the fluorescent lighting. Liz suppressed a twinge of envy. Did this woman *never* have to roll in garbage in the course of a day's work? Jump in a Dumpster? Liz liked good clothes too much to subject them to the kind of work she did, and she had no idea how Goose could possibly reconcile the two.

"Morning," Goose said, smiling easily. "That smells sort of like coffee."

Liz eyed what was left in her cup. "It's in the same zip code, but I wouldn't actually classify it as such. More like boiling hot rocket fuel. Does the job, though. Nice little caffeine bump."

"Ah." Goose surveyed the little conference room Liz had secured for their morning recap, zeroed in on the coffeepot and the two chipped mugs beside it. "As long as I know what I'm getting into." She crossed to the coffeepot, threw Liz a glance over her shoulder. "How did it go last night?"

Liz shrugged, though it felt more like a bad-tempered jerk of her shoulders than the casual little gesture she'd intended. "Nobody looked twice at the bills."

"No?" Goose filled her mug and quirked an eyebrow through the rising steam.

"No." Liz plopped down in a chair that squeaked remorsefully. "They didn't get past his damn face."

"Ah." There was a wealth of understanding in the single syllable. Goose seated herself at the scarred conference table with the air of a queen ascending her throne and lifted the mug to deep red lips. "He *is* rather dazzling."

Liz snorted. "And don't think he doesn't know it."

Goose swallowed her coffee, blinked. She stared down into her mug, then back at Liz. "How much of this have you had this morning?"

Liz frowned at her. "I don't know. A couple cups maybe."

"Hmmmm." Goose raised the mug again, this time with careful respect. "Hard night?"

Liz brought her attention back to Goose, gave her a dark look. "What do you mean?"

Goose laughed, a lovely twinkle of sound. Liz tried not to grit her teeth. "Just that you don't look like a woman who got to go clubbing last night with a devastatingly handsome man on the government's dime."

"What do I look like then?"

"Like you've been thrown, hard." Goose set aside her mug, tapped a nicely manicured nail against the table. "Forgive the bluntness, Liz, but this team isn't going to work if all the cards aren't on the table. There's more happening between you and the delicious Mr. O'Connor than either of you is saying."

Liz leaned back in the chair, studied her. "Nothing's going on."

Goose shook her head. "Maybe nothing's *happened*. Not yet. But that doesn't mean nothing's there."

"Nothing's happened," Liz said. "Nothing's going to happen, either. It's out of the question."

"What, he doesn't do it for you?" Goose asked, a wicked grin tipping up the corners of her mouth.

Liz rolled her eyes. "He *does it* for just about everybody on the planet," she said. "It's hardly personal."

"See, that's where you're wrong. I think he's taking it very personally indeed."

Liz shoved away from the table and shot to her feet. "Why would he? He can have any woman he wants. I'm sure he'll find a way to comfort himself in the wake of my stunning rejection."

Goose took another cautious sip of coffee. "No, you misunderstand. He's not taking your rejection personally. Surely someone somewhere has said no to him before. Hard to imagine, but odds are. No, it isn't so much that you want him and won't have him." She waved a dismissive hand over Liz's protesting noise. "And please don't insult me by denying that basic truth."

Liz shut her mouth and shrugged tightly. "Fine."

"It's more that he wants you just as desperately, and can't talk himself out of it. That, he's not used to. And he's taking it damn personally."

Liz goggled at her. Then she laughed. "That may very well be the nicest thing anybody's ever said to me." She wiped her eyes and sighed. The laugh had felt good. A tension breaker. She ought to try that more often. "No, see, there's a revenge thing at work here. He's pissed because I keep roping him into weaseling for me. I'm sure there's some male ego tangled up in it somewhere."

"Mysterious thing, the male ego," Goose murmured.

"Exactly." Liz nodded, finally in harmony with the other agent. "And when Bernard promoted him from weasel to independent consultant, I dinged his ego a nice fat one, right in front of you."

"You did."

"So I cornered him to apologize, but he was still riding the mad, I guess, because there was this little, uh, scene."

"Really?" Goose's dark eyes sparkled. "What kind of scene? Don't spare the details."

Liz squirmed. "Turns out, he needed more than an apology. He's got to ding me back before we're straight—ego again, I guess—and he pretty much declared war on me."

"War?"

"Yeah." Liz cleared her throat. Felt the blush creeping up her neck and cursed her pale complexion. "Of a sexual nature. He doesn't win until he's screwed me six ways from Sunday and left me weeping and brokenhearted, the abandoned notch on his proverbial bedpost."

Goose considered this. "Worse ways to go, you know."

Liz sighed and closed her eyes. "You're not being helpful."

"I'm not trying to be. I'm just sizing up the situation. If I have to work with you both, I need to know where the land mines are buried."

Liz tightened her mouth. "I'll keep you posted."

Goose smiled brightly. "I'll look forward to that."

They both turned at the sound of approaching footfalls,

and Patrick appeared in the doorway in all his obscene gorgeousness. He leaned against the doorjamb, a paper tray of Starbucks coffees balanced in one hand, his dark trousers breaking just so over supple leather loafers, his button-down shirt untucked and rolled casually back at the cuff.

Didn't look like he'd lost a wink of sleep himself, Liz thought sourly. He grinned at her.

"I could smell that god-awful coffee all the way to the parking lot," he said, strolling into the room and distributing the steaming to-go cups. Liz pointedly ignored hers and took another gulp from her mug. "Until further notice, Liz is hereby banned from having contact of any nature with a coffee machine."

Goose sipped gratefully at the paper cup and sighed. "Amen."

"If I have gourmet coffee catered in every morning, will you show up somewhere in the vicinity of on time?" Liz asked, wincing inwardly at the shrewish snap in her voice.

Patrick said, "Oh, I started work somewhat before my arrival this morning."

"Oh?" Goose leaned her chin onto her hand and blinked up at him. Charmingly. "Do tell."

Patrick treated her to a blinding smile. "By the way, you look particularly lovely this morning, Goose. That's an incredible color on you."

"Thanks." She smoothed a pleased hand over her lapel.

Liz ground her teeth. "Would you care, Consultant O'Connor, to report on what kept you so busy this morning? Besides patronizing overpriced coffeehouses?"

He turned that grin on her, though it cooled a few degrees. "The target made contact this morning via my cell phone," he said simply. "Asked for a meet on Friday night. At Cargo."

Liz blinked. "Today is Friday."

Patrick lifted one shoulder easily. "Yep. He must have seen us there last night, because he specifically told me to, and I quote, 'lose the skirt.' "

Liz closed her eyes. She'd been reduced to a skirt. For God's sake.

Patrick patted her hand and Liz tried not to let the jolt show. "You did look particularly *Guys and Dolls* last night. I thought it was lovely on you."

"Fuck it," Liz said wearily. "Give me details. We don't have much time to get something set up."

A DOZEN hours later, Liz stood in a cramped office over-looking the bottling line of the abandoned brewery that adjoined Cargo.

Lucky break, she knew, that they'd been able to come up with an effective surveillance location on such short notice. Even luckier that the property manager had been coopera-tive, because Liz hadn't had the time or the patience to follow the paper trail all the way to the owner. Not that she cared who actually owned the building. All she cared about was getting a legal signature on the waiver and a key to the front door. Which she had.

But that was where Liz's luck had ended. Because Goose had disappeared ten minutes earlier, muttering something about reception and secondary locations, leaving Liz alone with Patrick and the handful of wires, microphones and receivers that needed to be affixed to his chest. His bare chest.

Liz found she didn't have the wherewithal for light con-versation, so she simply stabbed a finger in Patrick's gen-eral direction and said, "Shirt. Off."

Patrick smiled at her. "Liz. Darling. You have only to ask." He began unbuttoning his shirt, and she tried like hell not to watch. She didn't want to notice the crescent of firm skin that appeared in the widening V of his shirt. Didn't want to know that his chest was broad, smooth and sprin-kled lightly with dark hair. Didn't want to wonder what it would feel like under her curious fingers. Certainly didn't want her mouth going absurdly dry. She reminded herself that she was a professional. She'd wired up countless informants over the years, and this would be no different.

Except that the informant in this case wasn't just an informant. He was technically a consultant and therefore her equal. And beyond that, he was the man who'd pledged to avenge his pride by seducing her. The man who, through a series of unfortunate coincidences and plain old rotten luck, was custom-designed to appeal to her on any number of subconscious and self-destructive levels.

She'd been programmed from birth, courtesy of her late, unlamented father to serve a man just like Patrick O'Connor. By the time she'd landed in her grandmother's blue-blooded custody at the ripe old age of ten, the damage had been done. Her psyche was already permanently bent. So of course she'd feel the attraction, she told herself. She'd feel the power and the temptation of him. She'd feel it so she could acknowledge it. Then she'd rise above it. She'd free herself to choose a different way. A just way. Her own way.

She looked up at the whisper of expensive fabric drifting to the desktop and her heart stuttered to an uncertain halt in her chest. Her thoughts slid loose, spun around her head in a desperate search for traction.

Where on earth had all this lean golden muscle come from? She'd been prepared for him to be beautiful, but more the kind of perfectly proportioned beautiful that made artists want to draw. Not the kind of leanly powerful beautiful that made women the world over want to reproduce.

He held his arms out to his sides in a gesture of submission. "I'm at your mercy, Agent Brynn," he said. His expression was meek but his eyes danced with unholy glee. The light poured down from overhead, the harsh fluorescent bulbs throwing those hard and surprisingly well-defined muscles into sharp relief.

Liz swallowed, hard. There was nothing romantic, she reminded herself sternly, about shaving a bald spot into a guy's chest hair and gluing a tiny microphone to it. She dug

deep for a neutral expression, then picked up the shaving
cream.

FIFTEEN ENDLESS minutes later, Patrick was safely back
in his shirt, but the damage was done. The feel of all that
gorgeous, smooth skin sliding under her fingertips was in
her brain now, permanently burned there, ready to haunt
her dreams. She was pretty sure her cheeks were beacons
of color but resisted the urge to press her fingers to them in
case he'd somehow failed to notice that the fairly innocu-
ous act of fitting him with a wire and transmitter had her
this close to spontaneously combusting.

She didn't trust her voice, so she just twirled a finger
in the air. He rolled his eyes but revolved obediently. He'd
left the shirt untucked, and even her critical eye couldn't
detect the minute bulge of the transmitter taped to the
small of his back.

"Well?" He tucked one hand into his pocket and struck
an elaborately casual pose. "Will I do?"

She shrugged. "The wire's secure. He pats you down,
he'll find it, but I don't see how that would happen in a
public meet. Just don't ask him to dance and you're probably good."

"Liz. Darling." His lips curved in lazy amusement. "I'm
always good, but I'm at my best when dancing."

Memories of his body moving with hers in a sexy, edgy
rhythm rolled over her like a slow, hot wave. She turned
half away from him and picked up the two-way radio.
"Goose? You in place?"

Goose's voice crackled back. "Loud and clear," she
said, a driving bass beat thumping under her words. "I
have a nice little couch staked out in the back and the
two-way fits into my purse pretty nicely. Let's just hope
the music doesn't get any louder, or we won't have squat
to record."

Liz turned back to Patrick. "Try to get him somewhere

quieter. You're wired both to transmit and to record, so don't worry about staying in range. We'll just work with tapes if it comes to it." She frowned at the wall of the office. "We might have to anyway. There are about eight inches of solid concrete between us and the club and that itty-bitty transmitter of yours isn't as powerful as the two-way Goose has. Unless the ventilation systems are connected, we're probably not going to get much in real time."

Patrick glanced at the open ductwork hovering over the desk. "Want me to boost you up before I go?"

"No." Liz thought about his surprisingly solid chest and arms. "No, I don't."

He smiled at her, slow and easy. She didn't smile back. "What I want is for you to tell me again exactly what you're going to do in there."

"Such a mother hen. If I didn't know better, I'd think you were worried about me." At Liz's pointed silence, he just folded his arms and sighed. "Okay, fine. I'm going to do exactly what the guy on the phone said to do. I'm going to plant myself next to the DJ booth and wait for a guy to identify himself as the Wizard, the Great and Powerful Oz. And when he does, I'm going to suggest that he get a better code name."

Liz shook her head. "Doesn't need one. He picked perfectly. He's nothing but smoke and lights. And in the end, he's going to trip over his own ego." She leaned back on the desk, checked her watch and folded her arms over her waist. "Are you ready to get started?"

"At your service, Liz. As always. Just one thing first."

He moved faster than she'd imagined was possible. Before she could even work up a good sneer, he was there in front of her, his big, hard hands cupping her elbows and lifting her right off her feet and into his body. Then his mouth was on hers, hot, seeking, hungry.

A thousand fragmented thoughts flitted through her brain, none of which were any help. Should she jam a pencil in his ear? Ram a knee into his crotch? Throw her arms around his neck and start participating with some enthusiasm?

Then his tongue traced the seam of her lips, a request, a demand, an invitation. Her last coherent thought was *oh shit*. Then she just burst into flame.

She opened for him, and he slid into her, slowly, deliberately, like a man who knew how these things were done and didn't care to rush the good stuff. A shudder ran through her, and she made some desperate noise in the back of her throat. She didn't know what she wanted but thought it probably involved the use of her hands and her turn at the wheel of this kiss.

But Patrick drew back instead and the rush of cool air between their bodies sent her eyelids fluttering open. Rational thought returned a beat later when her feet touched the ground again, though the power of speech seemed beyond her still.

He stepped back a cautious foot as he set her down, those cool blue eyes sparkling with evil good humor. "For luck," he said simply, and let himself out of the office while she just stood there dumbly and watched him. The radio in her hand crackled and she fumbled it, jerking back to her senses in time to catch it before it bounced off the concrete floor.

"Was that half as good as it sounded?" Goose breathed reverently through the static.

God, yes, she thought. She keyed the radio and said, "Shut up, Goose."

"Roger that." There was a pause. "So, was it?"

Liz sighed and crawled up onto the desk. "I'm not talking about this," she said as she boosted herself into the open ductwork. Hopefully the signal from Patrick would strengthen up here. She could hear Goose's radio fine, but the miniature transmitter she'd taped to Patrick's chest wasn't nearly as powerful.

"That good?" Goose asked, her tone wistful.

Liz was starting to wish the other agent's signal wasn't quite so strong. "Shut up."

"Wow. I mean, I'd figured, but still. Wow."

"Will you *please* shut up?"

"Roger."

SEVERAL HOURS later, Patrick ushered Goose back into the darkened brewery office. Liz sat cross-legged on top of the desk, all expectation.

"So?" Liz asked, as she unfolded herself and slid to the ground. "What the hell happened in there? The transmitters were useless over the music."

"I know. I spent the entire night next to the DJ booth. Right under the speakers." He poked a finger gingerly into his buzzing ear. "The guy never showed."

Liz's eyes flew to Goose, who shrugged her corroboration, because what he'd said was exactly what she'd seen. Several deafening hours of nothing going on. What Patrick didn't mention was what he suspected all that nothing meant.

Because unless his criminal instincts had gone horribly wrong, he'd spent the last several hours looking Oz right in the face. And that face belonged to the kid spinning the discs. A face that, upon closer inspection, probably hadn't seen seventeen yet. What the hell would somebody as black-and-white as Liz do with information like that? Probably toss his ass into reform school where he'd learn to perfect his trade and more than likely pick up the finer points of grand theft auto while he was at it.

"I'm guessing he was there," Patrick offered. "Somewhere. He was probably checking me out, waiting for me to bust somebody or hook up with somebody of the federal persuasion. So I didn't." He sent Goose a warm smile. "Not that I wasn't tempted. You look marvelous, Goose."

She pinked up prettily, and not for the first time, Patrick wished his life could be so uncomplicated. He turned his attention back to Liz and her frown.

"Fine," she said. "Even so, I think I'll bring in the DJ first thing tomorrow morning. See what I can shake loose from him."

Patrick tucked his hands into his pockets and pursed his lips, as if considering. As if panic hadn't just set up camp in his stomach. He couldn't let Liz put this case to bed so quickly. Not when he had yet to draw a bead on Villanueva.

"What?" she snapped. "You have a better idea?"

He gave her his easiest shrug. "Why not just play it out? The guy wanted a look at me, he got one. Chances are, he satisfied himself that I'm not a cop and will make contact in the next day or so to go forward. Why blow the good-will we've earned by sweating the DJ? What'll a day or two cost us?"

She stared at him with a speculation in her face that did nothing for the uneasiness in his stomach. Goose looked back and forth between them, then lifted her shoulders. "Fine by me," she said. They both looked to Liz.

"I want an ass to kick by next week," she said.

"If Oz doesn't turn up by then, you can have the DJ with my blessing."

"Fine."

Chapter

10

PATRICK PADDED across his sister's kitchen in the early morning to pour himself a cup of coffee. He didn't sleep much as a rule, but even he was dragging under the strain of being a loving brother/FBI weasel by day while covertly tracking a revenge-seeking maniac by night. Or attempting to track, anyway. Because while everybody he talked to agreed that Villanueva *was* local, nobody had any idea where exactly he'd holed himself up.

So Patrick had done all he could do. He'd made sure Villanueva knew where to find him when he was ready. All that was left now was the waiting. Lucky for Patrick, patience was a strong suit.

He picked a pretty blue earthenware mug and turned from the cupboard, only to find his niece had magically appeared and taken hold of his pant leg. Nice. He pressed a knuckle to his eyebrow. Just what he needed.

She was dressed in something soft, floppy and admittedly adorable, gazing up at him with a sleepy, pink-cheeked expectation that filled him with dread. Weren't babies supposed to sleep in cribs or something? Seemed to him like people would want to limit a kid's ability to just . . . appear.

He looked around the kitchen for her mother but came up empty. He sighed and filled his cup right up to the top. Figured he'd need the kick to get through this.

He looked down at Evie. She looked up at him, all angelic black curls, perfectly round cheeks, enormous green eyes and a mouth that had stubborn written all over it.

"Wan' some," she said.

"Excuse me?" He stepped carefully aside, but there was a grubby little hand fisted into the crease of his favorite khakis, and Evie just followed along. She gazed up at him, all earnest cuteness, then stuck her free hand into her mouth.

"Wan' some," she said around wet fingers.

Patrick took a fortifying slug of coffee. It was strong enough to power a nuclear submarine. He looked down at the kid, who was rubbing the material of his khakis between damp fingers with a concentration that concerned him.

He should have made stronger coffee.

"Where's your mommy?" he asked finally. This, Patrick saw immediately, was the wrong question. Evie looked up at him, and there was a certain tightening around the eyes that Patrick hadn't seen since his days as a professional poker player. It was an expression that said, *You are perilously close to my bad side. One more stupid move, and there's an ass kicking in it for you.* Patrick blinked, strangely comforted by this unexpected development. Maybe there was more O'Connor blood in this kid than he'd thought.

Evie didn't remove the fingers from her mouth, but she managed to invest her next words with a grave clarity anyway. *"Wan'. Some. Tawfee."*

Patrick frowned. "I'm sorry, you want *coffee*?"

Magic words. The kid beamed up at him and grabbed for the other pant leg with a slimy hand. "Yeah, yeah, yeah!"

she chanted, using her grip on Patrick's pants for leverage while she bounced herself into paroxysms of joy.

"Jesus!" Patrick shoved his mug toward the counter, scalding hot coffee slopping over the sides and onto his skin. He fumbled for a dish towel to mop up his hands, then reached down and pried the kid off his pants. It was time to take control of this situation.

"Okay," he said, holding two grubby little fists at arm's length and drilling a no-nonsense glare into those enormous eyes. "Let's get a few things straight. First, no touching. These pants are off-limits to anybody whose pajamas come with the feet attached, all right? And second, babies don't drink coffee. So forget it."

He set the child a safe distance away and retrieved his mug from the counter. He belted back another decent gulp and watched with suspicious eyes as Evie slunk under the overhang of the island counter, head down, gaze mournful, the picture of dejection. Scam, Patrick thought with a quick surge of pride. This kid was good.

He fully appreciated just how good a moment later when Evie drew in a deep, shuddering breath, flung back her head and howled like a heartbroken hound dog. Or an opera singer on crack. Patrick stared in wide-eyed, ear-ringing disbelief.

He was still staring a minute later when Mara staggered into the kitchen, shoving at the tangled black curtain of her hair, an ancient bathrobe thrown crookedly over what looked like one of her husband's T-shirts.

"Good Lord," she muttered, glaring at Patrick. "What are you two doing in here? What time is it, anyway?" She lifted her head, sniffed at the air. "Is that coffee? Please let that be coffee."

Patrick silently poured her a cup and handed it over, watching in mild disbelief as Mara competently ignored the shrieking child and slugged back a good half of the mug.

"Okay," she said, relaxing into a slouch on one of the stools near the island counter. "Okay, the caffeine's hitting my bloodstream. I feel prepared to deal with this."

She reached under the counter and scooped up her wailing child.

"Wan'! Some! Tawwwwfeeeeee!" Evie howled, melting into her mother's arms with a red-cheeked fury. Mara deposited a quick kiss on her hair and gave Patrick an eye roll.

"I know, babe," she said, shifting the kid onto her hip. She crossed to the fridge and jerked it open. "Here." She shoved a cup under the kid's nose, the kind with two handles and a lid with a spout. "Here's your coffee."

Patrick frowned. "You give your baby coffee?"

"You bet," she said, flicking a loving finger over her child's flushed and remarkably placid cheek. "Evie loves her coffee."

Evie bounced on her mother's arm, completely restored to sanity as she guzzled at the cup. Mara glanced over her head at Patrick. "It's just juice," she told him. "But in a special cup. She doesn't like feeling left out when Jonas and I have coffee in the mornings. So we give her a *coffee*"—she put the word into exaggerated finger quotes—"of her own and let her tear up the classifieds while we read the paper." She shrugged lightly. "It works for us."

Patrick poked a testing finger into his ear. "Glad to hear it."

The phone on the wall burbled and Mara's black brows shot up. "This can't be good," she muttered. "Not this early." She tucked the receiver into the tangle of hair at her ear and moved around the kitchen, absently setting to rights a few small bits of clutter while she made soothing noises into the phone. Patrick eyed his niece warily, but she seemed perfectly content to ride along.

Mara set the receiver back onto the cradle with a decisive click. "God da—" She broke off, glancing at her child. "Well, darn," she said feelingly. "Just darn it all to heck."

Patrick felt his brows creeping up in reluctant amusement. "Bad news?"

"The shipment of organic field greens I ordered for today's menu isn't in yet, and neither is the free-range farm chicken. Some kind of scheduling snafu. Thank God you're here," she said. "The babysitter's off on Saturdays and it looks like I'm going to work this morning."

"Wait, what?" He broke off to catch the kid she all but tossed to him, shifted so he could evade those grimy little hands and swinging feet. The kid was a damn howler monkey.

But Mara had disappeared down the hall, shedding the robe as she went. Patrick wasn't about to follow her into her room to argue. He assumed she'd be out when she was dressed, which was soon enough to argue in his book. Evie beamed up at him around the cup she was devouring, then grabbed a handful of his favorite virgin wool sweater.

He dumped her on the counter as if she were on fire, then pried her sticky little fist out of his sweater. "Okay, what did I tell you about touching?" he asked as he reached for a damp cloth.

"No, no, no!" she sang, bouncing on the counter. Patrick knew instinctively that the squishy noise coming from the vicinity of her diaper probably wasn't good, nor was the vague sensation of wetness on his forearm.

The kid had peed on his sweater.

"Christ," he yelped as the kid polished off her juice and held it out to him. "What *are* you, a sieve?"

She laughed and threw the cup at him. It bounced off his shoulder, but only because Patrick's reflexes were still damn sharp. She'd been aiming for his chin. "More," she said and there it was again. That look. The one that said, *I know where you sleep, pal.*

Patrick narrowed his eyes at her. "Listen up, you little terrorist. I don't know what you get away with in this household, but look at my face and understand me. You are not getting more juice while the stuff you just drank is still draining out of you. Especially not since it just drained all over my arm and the chances of my finding a decent dry cleaner in this godforsaken state are somewhere south of zero."

The kid tightened her mouth and glared at him. Patrick

glared back. "And even if you *were* getting more juice, it wouldn't be coming from me. Got it?"

She gave him a considering look, the kind that said, *On your head be it*. Then she opened her mouth and unleashed The Howl. Opera singer on crack again, heading for high C. Patrick was prepared this time. He grinned at her.

"That all you got, kid?" He crossed over to the breakfast nook with his steaming cup of coffee and settled in for the show. It was bound to be a good one. This kid was determined, and she was already turning a violent shade of red. "I've got all day, but smart money says you'll be out cold in two minutes or less."

"For God's sake." Mara sighed, marching back into the kitchen in a well-worn pair of jeans and a fleece pullover. She scooped up her child again. "Why was Evie on the counter?"

Patrick shrugged. "I put her there."

"It's not the ideal place for babies, you know."

He shrugged again. "We were doing fine until she peed on my sleeve."

The kid had ratcheted the noise back to pathetic, snuffling little moans, and Mara leaned down to nuzzle at her curls. "She's two, Patrick. They do that. For crying out loud, you're her uncle. Her blood relative. Surely you can find a way to survive each other for a couple of hours while I keep my livelihood afloat for another day?"

Patrick thought for a minute. "There's some O'Connor in that kid," he said finally.

Mara sighed. "Tell me about it." She glanced at her own empty mug on the counter, then grabbed for Patrick's. He let her have it. She drained it, then set it on the counter and Evie safely on the floor. "You guys will be all right?"

Patrick and Evie eyed each other. "You bet," Patrick said. "Go on. We'll figure something out."

Then she was gone in a swish of fleece, boots and flying braids, leaving him with a toddler, her wet diaper and her amazing lung capacity.

"Unca Padwit?" The voice was small, penitent.

"Yeah?"

"I need a fwesh diaper."

He pressed a fist to one eye. "Oh hell."

He picked up the phone and dialed.

LIZ HAMMERED at Patrick's door while the cell phone at her ear continued to ring. She'd been dialing and redialing him for the last fifteen minutes, ever since *he'd* called *her*, demanded her presence, and then abruptly hung up on her. She could hear his phone ringing through the door and it only intensified the ball of dread gathering in her belly. Nobody answered. Not the door, not the phone.

Christ, what if she'd been wrong to keep Villanueva's presence in town to herself? What if he wasn't in town to lure Patrick into a new score? What if he was really some psychotic, revenge-seeking killer who was even now selecting a nice Chianti to go with Patrick's liver?

"Patrick!" She pounded on the door again and kicked it once for good measure. "I'm armed and I'm pissed, and if you don't answer this door in five seconds, I'm kicking it in and leaving you to explain it to your sister!"

She had one hand on her weapon when Patrick flung the door open and glared down at her. "What, did you stroll here? How the hell long does it take you to get across town?"

Liz felt her mouth drop open, and she stared at him in complete amazement. He was rumpled. Wrinkled. Disheveled, even. The meticulously dressed and pressed Patrick O'Connor had fallen apart. She groped for something to say, then settled on the obvious. "You have . . . um, a naked kid on your shoulders."

He glared. "Say hello to Agent Brynn, Evie." He turned and stalked down the hallway. Liz stepped into the apartment and followed him into the sunny kitchen.

"Hi!" The little girl sang more than said it, and Liz couldn't help smiling at her. There she was, naked as the day she was born, bouncing on the shoulders of the world's best-groomed man, both her sticky hands twisted ruthlessly into one of the more expensive haircuts Liz had ever seen in person. One of Patrick's sleeves was suspiciously damp, and there were two distinct handprints on those custom-made khakis, about knee high. Liz couldn't help it. She laughed. Nice and long and loud.

He turned and drilled her with another ice-cold glare. "Something funny?"

"This is your emergency?" she asked finally, swiping at a tear. "I hauled ass across town, thinking you were being kidnapped or maimed or God knows, and here you are, completely undone by a toddler." She laughed again. "Christ. How the mighty have fallen."

"You don't believe in fate, remember? So don't try to blame this . . . this . . . *incident* on me." He sneered at her, though the punch was somewhat diminished by Evie's beaming grin about six inches above his head. All was right in that kid's world. Liz smiled back at her, in perfect charity.

"That's right. Fate's a bunch of bull," Liz said cheerfully. "This is more like cosmic justice. Your talent for getting attractive women naked just turned around and bit you on the ass, didn't it?"

Evie bounced enthusiastically. "Ass!" she sang.

Patrick closed his eyes and grabbed at Evie's flailing feet. "Nice going, Liz."

"Sorry." Liz smiled evilly. "Clearly, I'm not fit company for little kids. I'll just be going now so you can get back to . . . whatever it is you two were doing."

"Liz, please."

She stopped, arrested by the unexpected note of desperation in his voice. "What?"

"Don't leave me alone with her." Even Evie seemed struck by the switch in tone, and she laid her cheek on the top of Patrick's head and wrapped both little arms around his throat. He wedged a hand under her arms and opened his airway a little. "You owe me that much."

Liz folded her arms and cocked a hip. "I do?"

"Somebody sure as hell does," he said quietly. "And Christ knows I've done you enough favors."

"I've done you a couple myself." Liz watched him closely. He always kept his true self so meticulously hidden behind those immaculate clothes, that sophisticated veneer. But for a moment, she thought she'd heard something more. Something honest, intense, revealing, and she was irresistibly drawn by the idea of widening that crack, of seeing more of what he really was.

He gazed at her, silent, impassive, as if he'd never lowered himself to plead. She sighed.

"You owe me," she said. "Big-time."

Chapter

11

AN HOUR later, Liz handed Patrick a steaming disposable cup of coffee and a plastic stir stick. She plunked herself on the sticky yellow bench beside him and watched him wrap those long, elegant hands around the coffee.

He watched Evie with the concentration of a new parent, his eyes following every move as she scampered joyfully through the maze of molded plastic tunnels and slides that made up the McDonald's play land. Liz was pretty content to watch for a while herself. Freshly diapered and bundled into a little romper covered with daisies that Liz privately thought was absolutely charming, Evie was clean, full, happy and energetic, thanks in no small part to Liz's determination to make her so. Patrick had mostly just hovered in the doorway and taken directions.

And it was fascinating to Liz that a task as mundane as diapering a two-year-old could drive a man so patently self-assured to his knees.

She sucked contemplatively on her straw, then said, "Why am I here?"

He shook his head, never taking his eyes off Evie. "Beats the hell out of me. I'd never have thought to take her to McDonald's, though it looks like it's working out great. How did you know to bring her here?"

"I've had some experience with kids." She didn't let herself think about all the kids she'd diapered, walked, rocked. Kids who shared her blood—her father's blood—whom she'd never see again. She—and they—were a hell of a lot better off than when they'd been together, so nostalgia was nothing but stupid.

Instead, she drilled a finger into his shoulder, gave a satisfied sniff when he winced and gave her his full attention. "I mean why do you need me here? Why does a grown man need supervision to watch his own niece?"

He slid her a sideways look, full of self-deprecating humor. "Surely I don't have to explain this to a woman who already feels that her very badge is tainted by my presence?"

"Unless you're planning to come out of retirement to pull a couple of jobs in front of her little eyes, I don't see the connection."

He turned his attention back to the tunnels. "I have all the money I could want, a mansion in Palm Springs, and a little black book full of starlets." The smile that touched his lips was rich with irony. "What kind of fool would throw it all away to shinny in and out of other people's windows in the black of the night?"

A nonanswer, Liz realized, but she didn't push. She'd file that away and chew on it later. "So you were afraid that, what, you'd lose your mind and teach her how to bust into a safe or disarm security systems? Pick a lock maybe? Cheat at cards?"

He chuckled. "Liz. Darling. Cheating at cards is a life skill. But no, I wasn't planning on it. Child care just isn't a strong suit, I'm afraid. So I outsourced. Simple as that."

She frowned at him a moment, thinking. "Oh my God," she said suddenly. "You're afraid." She thumped him on the shoulder and ignored his theatrical wince. "I can't believe I didn't see it before. You're terrified." She let her eyes round dramatically. "Of a toddler."

He waved this away. "Oh, please. She has some impressive lung power, sure, but in the end, I've got her by nearly thirty years and four feet. If it came down to fisticuffs—and Lord help us both if it did—I could take her." He watched Evie tumble willy-nilly through a clear plastic tunnel and land in what looked like a hamster bubble. "Probably."

Liz looked up to see Evie squishing her face against the curved plastic and laughing down at them. She sealed her open mouth against the plastic and blew until her entire face inflated like a puffer fish. Her maniacal laughter came floating through the tubes as she shouted, "Dat's a fishy kiss fo' you, Unca Padwit!"

Patrick hunched his shoulders and said, "Jesus. Fishy kisses."

"You *are* afraid of her," Liz said. "For God's sake, look at yourself! The kid blows you a kiss and you act like she just peppered you with buckshot or something. You're her uncle. She loves you. Why is that so damned frightening that you need somebody running interference?"

"First Mara, now you," he said, sifting a distracted hand through his hair. "Why is it so difficult for otherwise intelligent women to understand that she's an impressionable child and I'm not a good influence?"

"Bullshit." Liz flapped a dismissive hand. "You already promised not to tutor her in the dark arts. So what do you think could happen over the course of a couple hours? Unless we believe you to be so inherently evil that normal, law-abiding folk are endangered by your mere presence, I don't see how spending a morning alone with your niece is a 911 emergency."

"I don't need you to understand it," he said, watching her with something sad and knowledgeable in those lightning blue eyes. "I just needed you to come."

He turned back to Evie, carefully tracking her progress through the maze of molded plastic.

Liz blinked, her heart breaking just a little. Holy Christ.

It had been a total shot in the dark. She'd never expected to hit the target so accurately. Or to wound him with the shot. "And what about your sister?" she asked slowly. "She's a decent person. Does she get to love you, or is she frozen out, too?"

"God, Liz, everything is so black-and-white for you. It's more complicated than that." Liz watched as he remembered his coffee, paid great attention to peeling back the plastic tab, then took his time over the first sip. She wanted to yell at him for some reason, but she didn't know what to say. How could she tell him he was wrong when she herself thought he was the most dangerous man she'd met since her father?

Patrick was silent for a long moment; then he spoke. "She did this thing with her face this morning, Evie did." He smiled into the half distance. "It was like seeing inside my dad's head." He gave a tiny shrug and said, "There's more O'Connor in this kid than I realized."

Liz touched his shoulder, unable to stop herself from giving that much comfort at least. "What does that mean?"

"It means," he said, "that she's like me. What's in my blood is in hers and I don't know if just being around me is going to encourage it. What if she has a chance to be different? To be better?"

"To use her powers for good, not evil?"

He glanced at her, his smile wry. "Something like that. If she has that chance, we shouldn't even be sharing a zip code. I mean, God, look at her. This child is precious and innocent and pure. I can't leave my fingerprints on that. I've done a lot of evil things in my life and I can live with most of it, but not this. It's too much. Even for me."

MARA WAS chopping what looked like grass clippings with some wicked looking kitchen shears when Patrick and Evie sauntered in.

"I hope that's not lunch," Patrick said, depositing Evie into his sister's arms and flinging himself into a kitchen chair with great drama. "Because I deserve better. I've earned it."

Mara made a clucking noise that Patrick assumed women learned when they gave birth. "Poor baby," she murmured, though it was unclear to Patrick whether she was speaking to him or Evie. "Tough morning?"

"Hell, yes," he said before Evie could volunteer anything about McDonald's.

Evie bounced on her mother's hip and said, "Hell."

Mara shot Patrick a killing look. He shrugged. "Liz taught her to say ass."

"Ass!" Evie sang.

Mara pressed green-tinged fingertips to the line between her brows. "For crying out loud."

"Is now a good time to discuss my compensation?"

Mara's eyes went to glittering black slits. "You want me to pay you for teaching my child to curse?"

"Oh, please. You have the foulest mouth I've heard this side of a Mexican prison. Do *not* try to imply that I'm the first person to curse in front of your child." He watched her bite her tongue, could almost hear her grinding her teeth. So he smiled at her, smug and superior, because he knew she hated it. "I did you a nice big favor today, Mara. And that puts me in position to demand a nice big favor in return."

She folded her lips into a thin line and her eyes went dangerously hot. "May I remind you that this child—who does, by the way, have a perfectly decent name you seem unwilling to use—is your niece? Your blood relative? She *loves* you, for God's sake. We both do. We shouldn't have to pay you to love us back."

Patrick felt her words all the way to the bottom of his irredeemable heart. And, God, they stung. But what else could he let her believe? He'd already slipped up with Liz today, let her see too much, know too much. He couldn't risk it with Mara, too. She'd only insist that he was wrong, that he wasn't dangerous, that he wasn't contagious, that he should chuck it all and move back to the Midwest to spend the rest of his life in the loving bosom of her family. Or some senseless bullshit like that.

Bullshit he could scotch in one easy step by simply telling her Villanueva was back in town and most likely looking for some homegrown justice. Loving Patrick was a dangerous endeavor, one he couldn't in good conscience allow a decent person to pursue. Especially a person with an innocent and precious child.

Because even if he managed to neutralize Villanueva—and he would—it hardly changed the fact that he couldn't ever settle down and be Mara's ever-loving brother. He'd stolen too much, broken too much, enjoyed it too much to ever have the kind of blissful happy ending she wanted for him. The happy ending that in his most pathetic moments he wanted for himself.

He pulled haughtiness around him like a familiar coat and drifted over to pat Mara on the cheek. "I *have* missed you, Mara." She backed away from his touch and he tucked his hand back into his pocket. "Nobody does high drama quite like you do." He turned from her and chuckled, though it sounded a bit hollow even to his own ears. "You're too much an O'Connor not to understand the rules, though. Love has nothing to do with it. I did you a favor, and now you're in my debt. But take heart. I don't want you to cook up any fake gemstones or anything."

Mara watched him warily. "I should hope not. I'd hate to call the FBI on your ass." She jerked a shoulder at Patrick's lifted eyebrow. "What? She already knows the word, thanks to you."

"Thanks to Liz," he said. "*Hell* was mine. *Ass* was hers. Which brings me around to my favor."

"What do you want?"

"I want a gourmet meal, the kind that put Brightwater's on the Michelin map, catered into one of the private guest suites here on the third floor."

Mara blinked. "For how many?"

"Two. Me and Liz."

"Ah." The anger in her eyes died into something more

speculative, more—God help him—amused. "So it's like that, is it?"

Patrick sighed gustily. "It's like nothing you need to be concerned about." After this morning, he needed Liz back off balance, needed the reins of power firmly in his own hands again. And nothing seemed to throw her off balance more effectively than the prospect of romance. Especially romance with him. It was a tool, and he'd use it. God help them both.

"I like Liz," Mara began.

Patrick smiled. "So do I. She's a big girl, Mara. She doesn't need you playing mother hen."

"You bet she does. I'm married to a guy like you. I ought to know what a girl needs when confronted with"— she waved a hand up and down his person—"this."

"I don't think Jonas would appreciate the comparison, and at any rate, I really don't want to hear about your sex life."

"I don't need to facilitate yours," she shot back.

"But you will," Patrick said, smiling serenely. "You have a soft spot for me. Besides, this isn't the only favor I'm doing you. I wouldn't even be in the same state as Liz if you hadn't called me here."

Mara's brows shot up. "You must really want this," she said softly. "Because that's a damn big card to play for a favor this small."

You have no idea, Patrick thought. He only smiled.

IT WAS almost sunset as Liz mounted the steps to Brightwater's Restaurant and Casino that night. It was a lovely old Victorian, three rambling stories of wraparound porch and gingerbread trim. Little paper lanterns had been strung under the eaves, and they bobbed playfully in the late spring breeze. Her hair bounced a bit, too, and Liz touched a rueful hand to the curled ends as she clipped across the porch to the red lacquered screen doors.

She'd probably gone too far with the hair, she thought.

But it had gone so well with the dress that she hadn't been able to resist. She had no idea which clubs Patrick was planning to drag her to tonight, but he'd suggested in that cool, supercilious way of his that she dress for the occasion. So she had. If he didn't like it, tough.

But what if he liked it too much? And what if she *liked* it that he liked it too much? She shoved that possibility out of her mind and yanked open the screen door with a calculated effort at businesslike purpose.

The homey clink of silverware on plates drifted over her on a rush of warm, delicious air. It was nearly a tangible thing, this cozy invitation to sit down and eat that Mara seemed to produce wherever she went. Liz took a moment to close her eyes, breathe it in and wish she'd had more than a spoonful of peanut butter for dinner. She was about to slip down the oak-paneled corridor to the stairs when a smiling young waitress appeared.

"Agent Brynn? Mr. O'Connor's asked me to put you in the River Suite."

Liz blinked at the girl. "I'm sorry?"

The waitress didn't break stride, just put a professional hand under Liz's elbow and said, "The River Suite. Mr. O'Connor asked that you wait for him there."

"Oh." Liz frowned but allowed herself to be towed to the elevator in the lobby. "All right."

The door swished shut with a competent little *bing*, and the waitress slid a surreptitious look at Liz's shoes. Liz angled one foot so she could get a better look. They were great shoes, after all. Mocha satin, three-inch heels, tied onto her feet with big floppy bows over each instep. Who wouldn't look?

The girl flushed prettily. "I'm staring," she said on a little laugh. "Sorry. They're just so . . . cool."

Liz smiled. "I know. They were ridiculously expensive, but I fell in love."

The girl sighed wistfully as the elevator slid past the casino level and came to a well-mannered halt at the guest suite level. "Who wouldn't? They look like they belong on a forties call girl." Her hand flew to her mouth, her eyes wide with dismay. "Oh my God. I didn't just say that. I didn't mean it the way it sounded."

Liz laughed and stepped onto the comfortably faded carpet of the hallway. "No, that's perfect," she said. "You're absolutely right. Put a nice demure dress like this with some vintage hooker shoes, and it's an interesting picture isn't it?"

The picture got more interesting when you put a 9mm in the handbag, but Liz didn't mention that little fact.

The girl's eyes stayed round, but she gave another sigh. "I'm totally going to remember this if I ever get asked to the prom." She led Liz to the door at the end of the hallway and said, "You're going to knock Mr. O'Connor's eyeballs out."

Liz shook her head. "He's not my target audience, but thanks."

The waitress shook her head in return but didn't say anything. She just removed a key card from her apron pocket and swiped it through the reader. The door swung open and Liz stepped into the River Suite, named obviously for the majestic sweep of the Mississippi that curved away under the purple sky. From this height, it was a ribbon of night black satin dropped carelessly between the red-oak bluffs, framed by a wide, three-paned window. Liz had lived most of her life within driving distance of the river and yet was drawn to the view like she'd never seen it before.

It pulled her across the deep green carpet until she could lay a hand against the polished oak window frame. She was vaguely aware of the waitress withdrawing and the door clicking shut behind her, but she still spoke out loud. "God, that's just gorgeous, isn't it?"

"It is," Patrick said. She turned to face him, not entirely surprised by his sudden appearance. She rarely heard him approach unless he wanted her to, she knew that. And he hadn't wanted her to hear him. Because tonight was, judging from the intensity with which he was watching her, all about keeping her off balance.

"Well, well," she said, keeping her voice light, "look at you."

And she did. How could she help it? His hair was a black spill of raw silk over his forehead, his fallen-angel face all stark planes and hollows in the fading light. He wore an open-collared shirt of off-white, the cuffs rolled easily back, the tails untucked and flowing the way that only truly expensive fabric can. His trousers were nearly the same mocha color as her dress and broke beautifully over his long and somehow elegant bare feet. She arched a brow. "Forget something?"

He smiled at her, and in the half-light it was both wicked and remote. "I don't believe so." He strolled across the carpet toward her, and the hair at the nape of her neck rose in delicious anticipation. He picked up one of the hands she'd buried in the froth of her skirt and brought it to his lips. "Though I can't guarantee my memory in the face of such beauty."

Liz hissed at the fire of his lips against her skin, hoped she sounded angry rather than singed. It was an effort, but she kept her hand easy in his and said briskly, "Well, I suppose you'll remember as soon as you set foot in any one of the number of clubs you're dragging me to this evening. Those floors are disgusting."

He looked down at his bare feet ruefully. "Now there's a mental image I may never be free of. Thankfully, it's an experience I can skip. We're not going anywhere." He reached out his other hand and traced a palm over the smooth curve of her hair, his eyes going dangerously hot and intimate. "I'm not sharing you with anybody tonight."

Chapter

12

"WHAT?" LIZ did yank her hand away now. She gaped at him in astonishment. "Do you know how long it takes to get *into* a getup like this?" She flapped a hand in front of her, indicating the dress, the shoes, the hair.

"I have no idea," he said, his eyes warm and smoky as they traveled leisurely from head to toe. "I'm rather more interested in the other side of the coin."

She glared at him. "Could you cut it out with the innuendo for just a minute here? I'm trying to work."

He lifted his shoulders and reached for her hand again. Held it this time when she tried to yank it back. "This isn't about work, Liz."

"Then what the hell is it about? And if you hand me one more tired line, I swear on all that's holy, I'll shoot you."

"Understood." He cast a respectful glance at her evening bag. "Come with me," he said, drawing her toward the door that presumably led to either a sitting room or, God help them both, a bedroom. "I want to give you something."

Liz grudgingly allowed herself to be led, curiosity warring with good sense. "What is it?"

He tossed a smile over his shoulder that did nothing to calm her jumping nerves, pushed open the door and pulled her through.

PATRICK STOPPED when Liz's fingers slid from his, turned to find her still and staring, those incredibly sexy shoes of hers frozen to the floor.

"Liz?"

"What is this?" she asked, staring at the white-draped table for two as if he'd pulled a gun on her instead of surprised her with a lovely dinner.

He let his lips curve into an indulgent smile. She was so suspicious of gifts. She had every right to be, of course. His motives were hardly pure. But still, it was charming. "It's dinner," he said simply. "The meal people generally eat between lunch today and breakfast tomorrow?"

"I know what dinner is," she snapped. "I'm more concerned with the *why*." She shifted her gaze to him, and he felt the punch of it all the way through to his soul. This was dangerous, he knew. *She* was dangerous. But the rising sweep of excitement and pursuit pushed any caution underground. Maybe it was foolish, dancing this close to the edge of his control, but he'd been half dead for years and hadn't even known it. Not until he'd kissed Liz.

Now he was vividly, painfully alive again, and he'd be damned if he'd let her go before he'd had the chance to slake whatever crazy thirst she'd awakened in him.

He put on his best placating smile but added just a touch of condescension. It would put her at ease, he knew, to think that he was amused by her, perhaps exercising just the tiniest bit of patience. The raw hunger churning in his gut for her was best left undiscovered. For the time being.

"Why are we eating dinner?" he asked. "Together?"

"Yes."

"Because you did me a favor today. Quite a large one, as it turns out. I wanted to return it."

She stared at him. "I put *curlers* in my hair. How is that a favor to me?"

He couldn't help himself; he reached out and threaded a finger through one of the fat curls framing her face. "Soldiers went off to fight the Nazis with pictures of girls like you in their helmets."

She slapped his hand away. "And it wasn't just soldiers making the sacrifice, believe me. This is not an easy look. I thought we were *working* tonight. If you wanted to do something nice for me, you could have dropped off a pint of Ben and Jerry's."

"You misunderstand." He smiled and handed her a chilled glass of wine. She took it automatically and he sipped his own, approving the fruity tones and the hint of bubble in the texture. Mara knew what she was doing, he thought. "Dinner is my favor to you. Seeing you in that dress is my favor to myself."

Her blue eyes went steely, and damn if he didn't want her just a bit more. "Did you owe yourself a favor?"

"No, but I'm the self-indulgent sort. Try your wine."

She narrowed her eyes but lifted the glass to her lips. He saw the moment the wine hit her tongue. Those bluebell eyes of hers widened just slightly, then drifted half closed to savor. He'd give anything to get that reaction the next time he kissed her.

"Sit," he said, taking advantage of her preoccupation. Who'd have guessed that Liz was such a sensualist? That his ever-practical cop could enjoy so profoundly the flavors, the textures, the scents of beautiful things? His entire system revved at the idea of all the sensations he could introduce her to, but he kept his hands impersonal as he slid her into a pretty, curved chair. She sat without argument in a puddle of crinoline and café au lait silk that he found indescribably feminine and unbearably hot.

"What is it?" she managed, and Patrick laughed, pleased with her.

"It's a Vin de Savoie. From Domaine Marc Portaz."

"Oh my Lord," Liz said faintly. "It's heavenly."

"You're incredibly rewarding to indulge, Liz," he said, watching her take another slow sip, prepared this time for the pleasure of it. It was wickedly arousing, so he set his own wine aside and selected a candied walnut from the platter between them. He brushed it against her lips and to his surprise, she opened for him. He slid it between her lips and was gratified by her small sigh of utter delight.

A single candle burned on the table, slim and elegant in a silver holder, and it turned her skin the smooth gold of early peaches. Patrick watched his hand tremble—actually tremble, for God's sake—with the force of his desire to touch all of it.

"What is that?" he asked blandly, and watched as her eyes fluttered open and then focused. "The dress, I mean. This part here." He reached out with a now-steady hand to finger the sheer material in the tender hollow under her collarbone. It was warm and he gritted his teeth against the overwhelming urge to keep touching.

"Oh." Liz laid a protective hand over the demure scoop of her bosom. "The underdress is just a strapless cocktail dress in silk. The overlay is marquisette, though. Don't you love the corded trim and all those swirly patterns over the shoulders? They totally make the dress."

He smiled and handed her a green grape. "No, that would be your skin."

"Excuse me?"

"Your skin," he said again. He didn't smile this time. This time he meant it and he'd let her see it. "That's what sells a dress like this. It's all clean, sober lines—no cleavage, no cling, just all that smooth, warm skin under a transparent layer of gauze. It's an invitation to touch, Liz. Your shoulders, your arms, your throat, God, just here." He touched the very tip of his finger to the crazy beat of her pulse. "It's sexier than hell and would make any man worth the title want to put his hands on you." He gave her a crooked smile. "God knows I do."

Liz stared at him, still and shocked. Patrick let the silence draw out, wondering what she would say once she wrapped that agile mind of hers around his words. A discreet knock at the door had her whipping around before he was nearly done watching her.

The door eased open and the waitress rolled a silver cart into the room bearing two covered plates. "Are you ready for your salads?" she asked politely.

Patrick leaned back in his seat and watched Liz. She wanted to run; this was her chance. She glanced at him, found him watching her. He tipped his palms up, let his brows raise in challenge.

"Where's your courage, Liz?" he asked softly.

For a moment, he thought she would shove away from the table and stalk out of the room on those amazing shoes of hers. But she just drew in a sharp breath and lifted her chin as she turned from him to smile benevolently at the waitress.

"Yes, thanks," she said. "Salad would be wonderful."

"YOU REALLY speak German?" Patrick asked.

Liz leaned back and sipped at her wine. It was lovely and made her feel loose and light. Or maybe that was Patrick. She couldn't remember the last time she'd had dinner with a man who'd actually asked her questions, let alone listened to the answers.

"I do," she said. "And French. And a little bit of Portuguese. Curses mostly." She smiled at the memory, selected a wafer-thin cookie from the plate between them and bit in. "One of my roommates had a Portuguese mother and a foul temper."

"Were you an international studies major?" He studied her over the rim of his own wineglass, and Liz shook her head.

"No, criminal justice. I picked up the languages during high school."

"Just picked them up?" He quirked a brow. "Must have been some high school."

She raised her glass in sarcastic salute. "The finest Swiss boarding school money could buy."

"I never would have guessed you grew up with money, Liz."

She smiled over her wineglass. "That might be the nicest thing you've ever said to me."

"You have something against money?"

She took another sip of that lovely, fruity wine. "No offense to you or your buckets of money, but rich people aren't really my cup of tea."

He leaned forward, his blue eyes laughing in the flickering light. "Liz. Darling. How can you say that? Unless I miss my guess, you're very much one of us."

She frowned at him. "Hardly. Money and education do not a rich person make."

He made some noise she couldn't interpret, but it made her feel petty for complaining. "What about you?" she asked suddenly. "Where did you go to school?"

His eyes danced. "I, ah, squandered my college years pursuing ill-gotten gains."

She sighed. "I know that, Patrick. I've practically memorized your case file by now. I meant high school."

"Oh." He waved a dismissive hand. "I didn't go to high school."

"Didn't go?" Liz tipped her head and studied him. "Your folks homeschooled you, then?"

"Ah, no." He gave her that devastatingly crooked smile again. "I didn't go to school at all."

She set her wine down with a click. "Ever?"

"No." He shrugged. "We were on the road a great deal. It wasn't feasible."

She frowned. "So, what, your parents just let you order room service and watch TV?"

"They provided an education of sorts. I read, after all. My math skills aren't lacking."

"A photographic memory doesn't make up for that kind of neglect." She frowned darkly, her heart breaking for the child he'd been. She shoved that aside, let a welcome anger surge in to take its place. "Somebody should have arrested your parents."

"Believe me, people tried." He leaned forward to prop one elegant elbow on the table and study her. "I don't believe it was ever on my account, though."

"They should have. Your parents robbed you."

"They robbed a lot of people," Patrick said blandly. "But they also exposed me to a side of life most kids don't ever see."

"You weren't most kids," Liz shot back with a vehemence that startled even her. "You were brilliant, damn it. Gifted beyond what most people can even imagine, and curious along with it. You could have been anything, and they chose profitable." She pressed a hand to her pounding temple because it was easier, less revealing than pressing it to her heart. "It was beyond criminal, Patrick. It was cruel. And I ought to know."

She broke off abruptly. She hadn't meant to talk about herself. Her own childhood. The reasons she recognized, instantly, what a brilliantly selfish parent could do to a child. Would do, given the chance.

A beat of silence passed, and Liz was intensely aware of his eyes on her, pale, sharp, discerning. He'd noticed her stumble, she had no doubt. He didn't miss a thing, but he let it go.

"It stung to miss college, I'll admit that," he said, smoothly picking up the conversation. "But by then, it was my choice. Money is a powerful incentive. And it buys a lot of books." He set aside his wine, leaned forward and took her hand. "But it's lovely, Liz, truly lovely, to see all that outrage of yours from this perspective."

"What do you mean?" she asked, stupidly. Because she felt stupid. Slow. Drugged. All because he'd taken her hand.

He rose, drew her to her feet as well. Then she was in

his arms, one warm hand spread smoothly over her hips, the other lightly clasping hers, and she responded without thought to his movements. She swayed in the circle of his arms to the whisper of music that had been in the background all night like the scent of unseen flowers.

"Up until now I've only seen you outraged *with* me. I hadn't even thought what it might be like to have you outraged *for* me. All righteous and defiant and valiant. I'll admit, it's going to my head a bit."

"That's the wine." She smiled at him, unable, unwilling to resist giving him that much. *Somebody ought to love this man,* she thought. Not her. But somebody. Surely he deserved that much. Somebody at least to smile at him without expecting something in return.

"Oh, no. I gave you most of the wine. It's definitely you."

She tried to stiffen, to glare, but she felt so loose and light still, and his hands felt so wonderfully at home on her body. "That's a shame, because the wine was very nice."

He shifted her fractionally closer, until she could feel the heat of his body through the layers of her dress. Everything in her yearned to move closer, to close the gap he'd left between them. She wanted to snuggle her cheek right into that gorgeous shirt of his, twine her arms around his neck and be the woman who loved him. Who gave him whatever it took to fill up the sad, empty spaces she could feel inside him.

She had enough to share, she thought drowsily. Enough heat, enough energy, enough passion, enough strength. She could give him what he needed and never feel the loss. Because he'd return it, in spades. And she knew he would. With Patrick O'Connor in her bed, she'd never be cold.

But then cold wasn't exactly the issue, was it? It was more what he'd ask of her once she was warm and loose and *his.* Because a soul like Patrick's had empty spaces in it she'd never be able to fill. Men with supercomputer brains, beautiful faces and this raw, powerful charisma had appetites and needs far beyond anything the law and polite society generally sanctioned. Far beyond anything Liz was capable to providing, anyway. And she refused to wreck herself on those rocks. Not again.

After escaping her father's grip, she'd worked herself bloody to find something approximating true north on her own moral compass. Hell, it had taken her a couple years after landing in her grandmother's care to even *locate* her moral compass. She couldn't afford to take a flier on Patrick.

But even as the thought wandered through her mind, she allowed him to pull her in. Allowed him to brush his lips against her hair. Even with doubt whispering through her veins, she pressed her cheek to his shoulder, greedily soaked up the heat and vitality of him. Even as some part of her brain hung back, waiting for him to trip up and expose some connection to Villanueva, she wanted him.

God, what was wrong with her? Even if he wasn't in league with Villanueva, he was still the bait in her trap. She was *using* him, and she wanted to let him run tame in her bed? In her house? Damn it, in her heart? She was no fool, but that's where she was headed. And it wasn't a path she meant to take.

"Liz." His voice was a rumble against her cheek, warm, intimate. "Are you ready to move along with our evening?"

She stumbled to a halt, pushed herself out of his arms, snapped out of the sensual haze he'd woven around her. "I'm not going to sleep with you," she said flatly. She shook the hair out of her eyes, the wine out of her blood, the feel of him off her skin. God, she hated to do it.

His eyes widened, then warmed with silent laughter. "Liz, darling. I had no idea you were considering capping the evening off so . . . personally."

"Don't screw around with me," she said tightly. It was more painful than she'd imagined, letting go of something she'd never even admitted she wanted. "We both know that's where you were heading, and you need to know right now that it's not happening. Not now, not ever."

He lifted his palms in a gesture of surrender. "Fair enough. But the next item on my agenda wasn't sex."

She propped a hand in the froth of her skirt and cocked a hip. She let her skeptical gaze rest on the intimate little table for two, the lush suite, the empty bottle of hand-chosen wine. "No?"

"Not the next one, no." He smiled at her benignly. "I thought we'd play poker."

Chapter

13

"YOU WANT to play poker." She stared at him, with all that narrow-eyed skepticism he found so unaccountably enchanting. Suspicious, law-abiding women weren't his usual fare, but there was no arguing with the fact that Liz in cop mode really turned him on. Maybe it was the juxtaposition with the soft, yielding woman he'd held in his arms two minutes ago, he thought. He never knew exactly who she was going to be next.

He shrugged. Life was unpredictable. God knew he'd learned that lesson the hard way often enough. He had a weakness for this woman that apparently wasn't going away. He'd just have to go with it. What he couldn't change, after all, he felt honor bound to enjoy. Life wasn't exactly easier that way, but it was certainly more fun.

The fact that indulging himself kept Liz disgruntled and off balance was just a bonus.

He rocked back on his heels and studied her, from the top of her coiffed head—no other word for that kind of careful, old-fashioned style—to the bows on her provocative shoes. God, he wanted to muss her all over.

"Poker wasn't my first choice, no." He let his gaze linger, just a moment, on her mouth. "But it'll do. I thought a small wager would liven up the evening."

"Patrick, you won the World Series of Poker like eight times running. Why on earth would I play poker against you, let alone bet?"

He pursed his lips, considered her. "Tell you what. If you can win even one hand before midnight, you can name your prize."

She gazed at him suspiciously and Patrick tried not to think about the lake-sized bed in the next room. "One hand?"

"One hand." He shrugged. "It could happen. Poker can be just as much luck as skill. The question you need to ask yourself is, what do you want to win that's worth the risk of losing?"

"I can name my prize?"

"Anything you like."

"Even a halt to this ridiculous sexual thing you're doing?"

He let his gaze touch on her mouth again. "There's nothing ridiculous about wanting to get you out of that dress, but yes. Even that."

"Fine," she said. "Deal 'em."

"Aren't you even interested in what I want if you don't win a hand?" At her flat, challenging gaze, he simply smiled and said, "A kiss, Liz."

"A kiss," she repeated warily. "That's it?"

"I'm a very good kisser." He smiled at her, hot and intimate. "I'll make it worth your while."

"Right." She rolled her eyes. "Deal."

LIZ STALKED to her own car, allowed Patrick to open the door for her and plopped into the passenger seat. "You cheated," she muttered, just before he clicked the door shut on her. She could see him chuckling as he rounded the hood, and she shoved irritably at the mountains of crinoline rising up from her lap.

"I don't cheat," he said once he was ensconced in the driver's seat—her driver's seat—and had adjusted it and all the mirrors to his liking. "The cards just weren't running your way, that's all."

She folded her arms over her chest. "Not my lucky night?" she asked acidly.

"It could be very lucky for both of us," he returned, sliding her a sideways look. "Unless you're thinking of crying off?"

She glared straight out the windshield at the inky night. "I don't renege on a bet. But I'd rather have just gotten it out of the way and driven myself home."

He tsked. "A gentleman always sees a lady home, especially after she's indulged in alcoholic refreshment."

"The wine was hours ago, and I ate like a farmhand. I'm fine to drive."

"Even so," he said, lips twitching. He didn't deny the farmhand analogy, she noticed. Some gentleman. "I won't rest easy until I've seen you to your door."

"And my door is all you'll be seeing," she muttered.

He pretended not to have heard. Fine. She tucked her arms more firmly across her bosom and turned her face resolutely out the window.

ALONE IN the darkened house, Villanueva slid a sheaf of bank statements back into the filing cabinet in Agent Brynn's home office and closed the drawer. Now what, he wondered, was an FBI agent doing with that kind of money? And what was she doing with that dazzling collection of party dresses he'd found in her closet?

It seemed the lovely Agent Brynn wasn't who she presented herself to be. Or maybe she was running from something. Who knew? Either way, O'Connor was falling in love with a mirage and Villanueva couldn't have been more pleased.

Because, as any connoisseur knew, pain was a complex and layered experience. Villanueva intimately understood and appreciated each facet—loss, grief, terror, heartbreak, humiliation, rage. He fully planned to enjoy the hell out of walking O'Connor through each and every one before he killed him. Agent Brynn was shaping up to be an enormous help.

His cell phone vibrated in his pocket. He tapped his earbud and said, "Yes."

"Hey, it's Oz. They're coming. O'Connor and the girl."

He moved swiftly out of the office and toward the front hall. "ETA?" he said.

"What?"

Villanueva squelched a sigh. "When did they leave, Oz?"

"About ten minutes ago?" Oz paused. "So they should be there, like, any minute."

He shifted course to the back door. "Thank you, Oz."

"Dude, sorry. But there's, like, this waitress, see? She's totally into me, I think she's trying to get me to take her to her prom or something and I had a hard time getting away to make a private call."

Villanueva let the silence play out, stretch into an uncomfortable blank.

"But I'm passing bills left and right here, no problem. I told you Brightwater's was easy," Oz said. "So, there's, uh, that."

Patience, he told himself. Chanted it in his head like a mantra. Patience was a virtue, knowledge a weapon. Research relentlessly, plan precisely. Set up the endgame, then put it in motion. "We'll go forward tomorrow as planned," he said.

Gravel crunched in the driveway. Villanueva hung up without waiting for an answer, killed his red-tinted penlight and slipped out the back door.

PATRICK SHIFTED into park, and Liz turned to find him watching her, one hand draped over the steering wheel, the other on the gearshift between them, his eyes hooded and unreadable.

"Liz," he said, and she couldn't tell if it was a question or a command.

"Oh, hell," she said, "just get it over with, will you?" She leaned over the gearshift, closed her eyes and offered him her mouth.

She'd become almost accustomed to it, she thought in that suspended moment of anticipation, the way this man could hijack her good sense and liberate her sexuality with the most careless touch. And this touch wouldn't be careless. It would be an assault. He'd be laying siege to her castle, so to speak. And she had no idea whether her defenses could withstand such a thing.

Even so, she steeled herself against it, but he hesitated. At first she thought he meant to take his time, use the delay to let her nerves do some of the legwork for him, but then she heard him sigh and open the car door. Her eyes fluttered open in time to see him step out and click the door shut behind him. Shame and relief waged a silent war inside her—relief that she'd been spared what would surely have been a vicious assault to her self-control, shame that she was so undeniably disappointed at it.

She half expected him to just walk off into the night, but he only rounded the hood of the car and opened her door with a flourish. "Liz, darling," he said, a quick smirk lighting that perfect face of his. "If you think I'm going to be satisfied with a quick peck over the gearshift, you've been dating entirely the wrong sort of man."

She scowled at the hand he offered her and stalked out of the car without aid. She'd nearly forgotten that men were supposed to do things like this—open your door, help you to your feet, see you to your door. It made her feel small, cherished, valuable. And while the cop in her wanted to snort at the idea that she needed help getting to her feet, for God's sake, the female in her stretched and purred like a cat under the attention. It was purely mind over matter that she managed not to arch into the warm hand he laid at the small of her back as she led him up the walk at a march.

"Thank you for a lovely evening," she said primly at the front door, her purse clutched in front of her body like armor. He wanted old-fashioned manners, she could perform with the best of them. But old-fashioned girls didn't kiss like hookers, so he'd get a chaste little peck on the cheek for his trouble and see how he liked it.

He smiled at her, slow and warm. Her entire scalp prickled at the lazy intent she saw in it. But he only said, "Keys?"

She goggled at him. "Now you're going to open my door for me?"

He laid out his hand. "Yes. That's how it's done. What kind of cretin have you been dating, anyway?"

She blinked, perplexed, but dug into her purse for the keys. "The kind who assumes I'm capable of working a dead bolt all by my little old self, I guess."

"It's not a question of capability, but of courtesy," he said, smoothly dispatching all her locks and pushing the door open. He gestured her through with a gallant sweep of his arm. She stepped into the foyer and turned, reached for the keys he held out. He dropped them in her hand and before she could even formulate her next move, he'd backed her up against the far wall of her tiny foyer where, apparently quite finished with being a gentleman, he kissed her with a burning ferocity that incinerated every rational thought kicking around in her brain.

Her entire world focused, constricted, and nothing existed except his big, hard body pressing hers hotly into the wall and the primitive surge of want that weakened her knees and had her arching mindlessly into him. Her eyes drifted shut as his lips moved over hers in a silent demand she had no thought of resisting. She opened to him, giving him everything he asked and blindly offering more. Her wrists were in his hands, pinned to the wall on either side of her head, and the solid heat of him against her from breasts to thighs had the keys sliding to the floor. Her fingers twitched restlessly with the urge to touch, to caress, to possess, but he held her relentlessly still.

He surrounded her, invaded her, dominated her in every possible sense. The seeking thrust of his tongue, the subtle rasp of his whiskers against her lips, the hot, clean scent of him on every gasp she managed, it all rolled into a dizzying wave of desire, and even as it pulsed through her, she wanted more. Wanted him closer. Wanted him deeper. In her, over her, under her. Whatever it took to slake this aching *need* he'd created in her.

He answered the arch of her body with a noise she didn't know how to interpret except that it stroked every nerve she had to a quivering awareness. She slid one knee up the outside of his thigh, drew him deeper into the cradle of her hips. He pressed into her with a slow deliberation that had shock waves rippling through her entire body. He rocked against her, and even through the froth of her dress, she could feel the hardness, the heat of him. She squirmed against the layers of clothing between them, made a desperate noise when he dragged his hot mouth down the side of her neck to nip at her collarbone.

"Liz," he said, and he sounded as ragged as she felt. She slid her wrist free from the manacles of his hands, laid it against the hard plane of his cheek and tilted his face toward hers until she could look into his eyes. They glowed like blue fire, passion weighting his lids, his mouth. He had her caged between his arms, her back to the wall, her dress rucked up where one of his thighs had insinuated itself between hers.

Every point where he touched her throbbed and ached for him—her wrists, the tips of her breasts, the V between her thighs. He was stunningly, potently male. Aroused, dominant, unapologetic. And it damn near set her on fire to see it all in his face, in every line of his beautiful body, in the exquisite care he took when he brushed back a stray lock of her hair, then cradled the curve of her jaw in his big, warm palm.

"Liz," he said again. This time it was undeniably a question, one she didn't want to answer. She wanted him to just tumble her to the floor, toss up her skirt and keep ravishing her. No responsibilities, no questions asked, no time to answer anyway. She wanted to lose herself in satisfying the urgent, visceral demands of her body, the demands that only he seemed to provoke.

She shook her head, trying to clear it. But he took a sudden step back, frowned and said, "Liz. How long was I kissing you?"

She shoved a hand through her hair, found it as rumpled as she felt. "God, I don't know. A few minutes?" Whole lifetimes could have slipped by while he was kissing her and she wouldn't have noticed, but now that cold reason was reasserting itself, she didn't feel that was an appropriate thought to share.

"Why isn't your security system going off?" he asked, searching out the blinking red light that would indicate an armed system awaiting the access code. "Please don't tell me you didn't set it."

She frowned, tried to focus. "Of course I set it. It should have been beeping from the minute you opened the door."

"It didn't," he said.

"Yeah, I realize that now. I might have realized it sooner if you hadn't been mauling me."

He quirked an eyebrow. "Guy's got to make his move." She ignored him, because Lord knew she'd been making a few moves of her own and didn't want to discuss it. "Is it in silent mode? Are the cops going to pile into the driveway any second and haul me off to jail for kissing you?"

"I wish," she snapped. "But, no. It should have been making a god-awful racket by now."

Patrick frowned at the serene green glow of the light beaming from the box, indicating a manually disarmed system. He took her by the arm and shoved her through the open door onto the front porch. "Stay here," he said shortly. "And call the cops, will you? Tell them you've had a little unauthorized company."

Liz stared in disbelief as he turned on his heel and slid into the darkness of the living room like the shadow she knew he was. Then she snapped her mouth shut and said, "Fuck that. I *am* the cops."

She yanked open her little evening bag, pulled out her gun and followed him in.

FIFTEEN MINUTES later, Liz leaned against the doorjamb of the kitchen and watched Patrick putter. The guy moved with such a fluid, masculine grace that he made putting on a pot of coffee look like some kind of high-class performance art.

"Anything missing?" he asked without turning to her. She jumped guiltily, lost in the poetry of watching him, then pulled herself together.

"No. Some tampering with the alarm system, of course, and a pro tossed the place, but nothing's missing." She moved into the room, sank onto a stool at the high counter that constituted the eat-in portion of the kitchen.

He poured water into the top of the coffee machine with a steady, methodical flow. "This kind of thing happen often?"

"Nope. I've been with the Bureau eight years now and this is a first." He hadn't yet met her eyes, but Liz folded her arms on the counter and leaned forward to give his back a searching look. She wished he would look at her, damn it. She wanted to see his eyes. "Doesn't surprise me, though."

"Why's that?" he asked as the first fragrant drips of coffee sizzled into the carafe.

"Don't screw with me on this, Patrick," she said wearily. God, she was sick of pretending. Villanueva had been inside her *house*, for God's sake. She knew it, and Patrick most likely did, too. The difference was she was under orders to keep her secrets. He wasn't. "First your sister's place gets broken into, then mine. Not a robbery, though, just a search. A thorough, methodical, *professional* search.

Both occur in the two weeks since you got here, both victims are known to be your relatives or acquaintances."

He still hadn't looked at her, and she desperately wanted him to. If he looked at her, maybe she could see what he was thinking. What this meant to him. What she meant to him.

"As of this moment, I'm officially done politely accepting lame excuses about paparazzi. Somebody followed you to Grief Creek, Patrick, and the only questions I have are who and why."

He spread his hands on either side of the coffee machine, bowed his head and leaned in. *Talk to me,* she pleaded silently. *Just trust me with this. Tell me what's going on and I can help you.* She was practically leaning over the counter with the effort to reach him on some level, but when he finally turned to her, there was such rage twisting his face that she jerked abruptly back.

"Why do you do this?" he snarled, with nothing like his usual upper-crust drawl. This was fury, raw and primitive, and it hammered at Liz along with a vicious slap of self-disgust. God, she thought, there she went again, trying to pull thorns out of lions' paws. As if she didn't know by now to steer clear of wounded predators.

"Do what?" she asked, careful to keep her voice cool and neutral.

"This *job.*" He spat the word like it was toxic, and a fresh wave of unwelcome hurt rolled through her at his contempt for the work that meant everything to her. "For Christ's sake, Liz, there could have been a killer in here tonight. And you just traipse right in with your high heels and your gorgeous dress and your gun and all that beautiful, fragile skin. Skin that isn't fucking bulletproof, no matter what Quantico's told you. Why the hell do you *do* it?"

"You're concerned about my *job*? Being too *dangerous*?" She stared at him in wonder. "Remember the time Lenny Andrusco tried to take me apart like a Barbie doll? Guy had to weigh a good three bells. Charged like a bull once he finally figured out we were wired."

Patrick nodded tightly. "I remember, Liz."

"Then you should also remember how you *stepped aside* while I took his ass down." She leaned in, gave him a good, hard stare. "You weren't overly concerned about the dangers of my job then. So why now?"

He shoved an impatient hand through all that rumpled black hair. "Andrusco was about as bright as your average second grader, Liz. He was big and pissed but he wasn't dangerous. This is different. This is—" He broke off, shook his head.

"This is what?" Liz asked softly. "Tell me what this is, Patrick." *Please.*

He shook his head. "You should have stayed on the porch."

Disappointment pooled heavy in her chest, but Liz folded her arms and cocked a hip. "Some jerk breaks into my house and I should let *you* kick his ass?"

"*Yes.*"

She frowned at him, an unwanted warmth stealing in to mix uneasily with the confusion. All this fury, simply because she hadn't let him protect her? "I'm good at my job, Patrick. Nobody needs to shield me, not ever."

He shoved the other hand into his hair now, frustration in every line of his face. "I'm not saying you aren't good at your job, Liz. But why the hell do *you* have to do it?"

She frowned at him, taken aback. "What do you mean, why do *I* have to do it?"

He turned back to the counter, propped his elbows on it and leaned on them, dropping his head. "I grew up surrounded by violence and crime because that's all that was available," he said quietly. "And I think we're both clear on how that worked out for me."

She closed her eyes briefly. "I don't think you're a malformed human being, Patrick. I know I said as much the other day, but I didn't mean it that way. You've made some wrong choices with your life, but I don't think you're an evil influence on the world." She hated herself for taking the chance, but she couldn't stop herself from rising, from going to him. She laid a light hand on his shoulder. "There's good in you, too."

His shoulder was tight under her hand, but when he glanced up at her, his eyes were wry, self-mocking. Normal again. Or what passed for normal. And she hated herself for wondering with such a violent curiosity which man was really Patrick O'Connor.

He said, "Let's just say that by now, I am what I am. Any choice I had about it is long in the past. But you, you're different. You had prep schools and debutante balls and I'd bet you're still sitting on one hell of a trust fund. You have a closet full of vintage cocktail dresses for God's sake. Why do you insist on rolling around in the gutter with the absolute worst the world has to offer day after day?"

Because somebody had dirtied his hands pulling her out of that gutter twenty years ago. But Patrick didn't need to know that. He could just keep right on believing in her silver spoon.

Liz shrugged. "When you have all those things," she said slowly, "it's never clear what you've earned and what you've been given. But this job doesn't care who my people are or where I went to school. I earn my way through each day with nerve and courage and strength, and I need that kind of clarity. But I'm also obligated. Just by virtue of my family connections, I've had opportunities lavished on me that other people won't see in ten lifetimes. Maybe because I have more than most people, I owe more, too."

"Bullshit."

Liz stared at him, eyes round, heart suddenly pounding. She'd given that speech dozens of times. Nobody had ever questioned it. It was exactly the kind of sound bite the FBI loved.

"Excuse me?" she asked warily.

"I said bullshit. Come on, Liz. Noblesse oblige?" Patrick shook his head and gave her a half chuckle. "We're both too familiar with the breed to believe that growing up rich invests you with a sense of obligation. Entitlement, yes. But obligation? I don't think so. If that's the story you tell your parents, fine, but don't lie to me. Why do you do this really?"

She glared at him as the ground crumbled underneath her feet. What the hell did he want her to say? That she'd been not only a victim, but the most famous victim of a generation? That she'd dedicated herself to protecting the vulnerable as a way to reassure herself every day of her own invulnerability? That carrying a badge was the one thing in her life she was proud of? The one thing she knew she'd earned all by herself? The proof of exactly how far she'd come?

He just waited, watched. Finally, she said, "I wasn't born rich, Patrick. That came later." Let him make what he would of that because she wasn't adding a word.

Patrick blinked, clearly surprised. Then he said, "Ah," but nothing else. Liz refused to look away, just stared back, daring him to push. But he didn't. When he did speak, it was only to ask, "Will you call the cops now about the break-in?"

Liz sighed and pushed both thumbs into the headache brewing at her temples. "How many times do I have to tell you? I *am* the cops."

"If you don't call them, I'm sleeping on your couch tonight."

She pushed harder against the headache. "Fine. I'll call. Maybe they can give you a ride home."

She could hear the smile in his voice when he said, "That would be lovely, thanks."

Chapter

14

TWO NIGHTS later, Liz tracked Mara down in the kitchen of Brightwater's. The usual mélange of chaos, steam and cursing slapped at Liz's innate sense of order the instant she pushed through the swinging doors, but she spotted Mara almost at once. Dishes crashed, flames leapt and lethally sharp knives flashed, but Mara was happily, serenely at home in it. She had a pimply kid hanging on her every word as she demonstrated some intricate knife work that had Liz tucking her own fingers safely into her pockets and wincing in anticipation. She waited for a plate-laden waitress to sail past, then barreled into the gap and headed for Mara.

"Let the knife do the work for you, Sam," Mara was saying to the kid, who gazed at her as if she were the second coming. "It's a tool, like any other. Picking the right one for the right job's half the battle." She glanced up to see if the kid was getting it and caught sight of Liz.

"Agent Brynn," she said. "I've been wondering when you'd drop by."

Liz felt her brows lifting. "You have?"

Mara handed the knife off to the kid, who accepted it reverently, then nudged Liz toward her office. "Of course I have." She clicked the door shut behind them and waved Liz toward one of the folding chairs while she dumped herself into the creaky office chair behind the desk. "Oh Lord, it feels good to be off my feet." She flipped off her plastic clogs and dug her thumbs into one stockinged foot. "I'm getting too old to work double shifts."

Liz watched her warily. "Why were you were expecting me?" she asked.

"Aside from the fact that I got stung for a couple thousand in counterfeit hundreds on Saturday night?"

Liz winced. "I'm working on that."

Mara tipped her head and gave her a long, deliberate look. "I heard about your break-in," she said. "One for you, one for me. You're not a moron, Liz. You think this is connected to Patrick."

Liz leaned forward, elbows on knees. "What do *you* think?"

"I think it's a damn good possibility."

"What does Patrick say?"

"To me?" Mara chuckled wearily. "About what he's said to you, I'd imagine."

"That would be nothing," Liz said.

"Exactly." Mara looked at her, and that sharp, mobile face reflected everything Liz herself was feeling: frustration, worry, determination and a good dose of honest irritation. It was enough, Liz thought, to justify the risk of sharing some information.

"What do you know about Jorge Villanueva?" she asked.

Mara closed her eyes. "Ah, crap," she said. "That's a name I'd hoped never to hear again."

"And yet you don't look surprised to hear me say it."

"I'm not."

"Why not?"

Mara's eyes flicked open, and there was both irritation

and fear in them. "Listen, I don't know how normal families work, but mine wasn't big on affection, okay? My parents sure as hell didn't love us kids, and until I heard about the deal Patrick cut with you to keep my ass out of jail, I'd have said the same about him."

"You'd have been wrong," Liz said quietly.

"Yeah, I know." Mara lifted her hands, let them fall. "I love him, too. I always have, and I wish he'd just . . . let me."

"Let you love him?"

"Yeah. I mean our folks are gone, right? So Jonas, Evie and Patrick, they're all the family I have. And had it not been for Patrick, I wouldn't have even that much. My happiness, my marriage, my kid, my career? I owe it all to him." She shot Liz a wry smile. "And to you, too, I suppose."

Liz shifted, uncomfortable. "Hardly. Patrick bought you a second chance. You earned your own way after that."

"Regardless, he deserves a little more than a quick thank-you note. He deserves to be part of the family he allowed me to create. A family that wants him, understands him and loves him. *My* family. He should be *here*, with me, not sequestered in that sterile McMansion of his out in California."

Liz lifted a skeptical brow. "Any luck with that?"

"Do you see him visiting at Christmas?"

"Uh, no. But maybe this thing with the counterfeiter—"

"Oh, please. You think this is the first time I've trumped up a minor business issue into a major drama to see if he'd come running?"

"No?"

"Damn straight. I've been crying wolf at least once a quarter for the past three years, and he ignores that the same way he ignores any and all invitations, pleas, threats and bribes. So when he suddenly turns up in town and hops into bed with the FBI, you think I'm not waiting for the other boot to drop?" She rubbed her pinched brows. "I just wish like hell that boot didn't have Villanueva's name on it."

Liz shoved aside the mental image that popped into her head at the words *into bed with the FBI*. "But it does. Looks like, anyway. So is there anything you can tell me—about Villanueva, about Patrick's relationship with him, about the night Patrick ditched him to save you—that might explain what the hell's going on here?"

Liz leaned forward, desperate for Mara to give her something, anything that would put her feet on a path. She'd spent the day poring over case files, everything connected to Villanueva, everything connected to Patrick. She'd read until her eyes had begged for mercy, then she'd read for another hour. She had to close this case. It was the only way to get Patrick the hell out of Grief Creek before she did something stupid. Like sleep with him. Or, worse, fall utterly and irretrievably in love. Because, God help her, she might do either at any moment.

"I don't know," Mara said with a helpless shrug. "We were doing what we'd been trained to do from the cradle that night. Stealing. Patrick was pulling something with Villanueva, and from what I'd managed to overhear, it was something complicated, but I'd never met the guy. I was very minor league in comparison. Still taking my marching orders from Daddy." She smiled crookedly and looked so much like Patrick that Liz had to avert her eyes. "Unlike my brother, who doesn't take orders from anybody."

"Not even from your father?"

"Not for years," Mara said. "He was flying solo by then but stuck close to the family. Mostly to keep tabs on me, which I don't mind telling you burned my toast when I was a kid. Saved my ass, though, didn't he?"

Liz smiled at that. "I hadn't had you in custody more than twenty minutes when he came waltzing through my door like he owned the place and started offering me terms."

"Yeah, I've been thinking about that," Mara said, a frown puckering her brow. "Can I ask you something? Something that might be protected under those terms?"

Liz shrugged. "I'll tell you what I can."

Mara leaned her elbows on the desk and gave Liz a very direct look. "Was it Patrick who turned me in that night?"

Liz blinked, fascinated. "What? Why on earth would he do that?"

Mara returned her attention to the arch of her foot, rubbed thoughtfully. "I wasn't what you'd call a natural-born thief. Oh, I have my skills, but Patrick was just gifted, you know? Every time I would master something really impressive, Patrick would effortlessly top me and there was no standing ovation from Daddy. It pissed me off like you wouldn't believe, but I've wondered over the years if he did it on purpose. If he was trying to save me from a life he knew I wasn't suited to. He certainly kept our dad from looking to me for his legacy."

She gave Liz a self-deprecating smile and said, "And the funny thing was that Patrick never even *wanted* to take over the family business, such as it was. That would have been me. I'd have done anything to be the heir apparent, to have my father look at me the way he looked at Patrick." Her lips twisted bitterly. "Even go to jail, I suppose."

Liz's stomach rolled and she braced against her own memories of being just such a child. A child so desperate for security that she'd have debased herself in any conceivable way to win the love of a sick and selfish parent. Liz pushed back against the past though it howled for release. She'd banished that girl years ago and didn't dare speak of her now. But she wondered.

Who would Liz be now if somebody hadn't rescued her? Who might she be if her father had had a lifetime rather than just ten years to work on her? There'd been no rescue for either Mara or Patrick, and yet they had both managed to find their way to a decent, respectable life. Not without scars, not without detours, but they'd managed. Would Liz have had the courage or the strength to do the same? From this new vantage point, the O'Connor children seemed exorbitantly valiant, and Liz's easy condemnation of them, simplistic and naïve.

Mara didn't seem to notice or be offended by Liz's

silence, just continued talking almost to herself. "Patrick can be ruthless when it suits him, and he's willing to deal with the consequences."

"I've noticed," Liz murmured, her throat raw from the words she kept trapped there.

"It wouldn't surprise me if he turned me in himself. I was going to get myself arrested at some point, that much was inevitable given the limitations of my talent. Not much room in the game for a mediocre jewel thief. I can totally see him orchestrating my arrest himself if he thought he had the right cards to keep me out of jail. He had to inform for the FBI for a couple years to pay for my sins, but he got me out of the life, free and clear."

Liz frowned, considered this. "We don't know who turned you in," she said finally. "It was an anonymous tip."

Mara shook her head, smiled fondly. "I'll have to ask him about it someday."

Liz would like to know the answer to that herself. She'd always given Patrick credit—reluctantly but sincerely—for strength of character. He'd been, what, all of twenty-four years old and at the pinnacle of his dubious profession when he'd faced an unthinkable choice. Either turn his back on his newly arrested sister, or screw his partner by abandoning him midheist. Liz knew the time line of that night better than she knew her own face. Patrick hadn't hesitated. He'd chosen Mara, had given up both himself and Villanueva in exchange for her freedom.

Villanueva had evaded arrest, but Patrick had paid. Not with jail time, though. He'd simply been forced to reform himself and to inform on his former colleagues, thereby making himself persona non grata in the world where he used to be crown prince. And he'd taken it all with that fatalistic acceptance Liz had come to expect from him.

But this thread Mara had tugged loose was one Liz hadn't previously considered. One she didn't really want to consider. Was it possible that Patrick had not only accepted an inevitable fall from grace, but had actually instigated it? Sacrificed everything he'd earned to protect somebody he loved?

She squirmed, uncomfortable with this new idea that Patrick not only had a bit of moral fiber, but that it might be tougher than her own.

"Do you really think he'd *do* that?" she asked, a little desperately. "I mean, for God's sake, he had everything your parents taught him to want. Do you really think he'd just give it up on the off chance that it might buy you a second chance you didn't even know you wanted yet?"

Mara tipped her head. "Might have."

"Did somebody appoint him savior of the world when we weren't looking?"

Mara laughed. "He seems to think so. He has some pretty wild ideas about fate and justice. I think that's why you appeal to him so much. You're like the other side of his coin, the photo negative that balances him out."

Liz blinked. "Excuse me?"

"He thinks there's something in him, something sinister and wrong but predetermined. As if it were the universe and not our father that made him a criminal. Which means that the things normal people take for granted—a nice neighborhood where you don't have to lock your doors at night, police to stand between you and the bad guys, a wife, a few kids—are beyond his reach."

She paused to smile at Liz's skeptical expression. "He was a damn good criminal, and he's comfortable with that identity. But he doesn't know how good a *man* he is, or could be. And he's afraid to even try, because if he fails, it'll just mean he was right about himself all along."

Liz rolled her eyes and dug deep for a flip tone. "Oh, please. He'd be the damn president by now if he felt like it. If he hasn't embraced the suburban life, it isn't because he's afraid to try. The man's not afraid of anything."

"He's afraid of showing you his heart," Mara said gently. "He's not invulnerable, just scared. You're his ideal, Liz. And look where he's been, what he's done. Can you blame him for thinking you're out of his reach?"

Liz shook her head, instinctively denying. She didn't want this new conception of Patrick in her head. The old Patrick had been dangerous enough, and now this? She refused to think of him this way. Cast out and stoic, longing for the acceptance of a society that both reviled and revered him, aching for the love of a woman who upheld that society with everything in her.

Mara smiled. "You're in love with him, aren't you?"

Not yet, she wasn't. And if she had her way, she never would be. But all she said was, "That would be a remarkably bad decision."

"No risk, no reward."

Liz glared. "Life isn't a poker game."

Mara shrugged serenely. "A game of chance, then. You play the odds every day in your line of work, Liz. Love's just another decision you have to make with imperfect information. So what's it going to be? Bet or fold?"

Liz had her mouth open to retort, but a smooth male voice interrupted. "God, I love it when she talks gambling." Liz jumped like a cat and spun to find Mara's husband Jonas leaning against the doorway, six-plus feet of muscle, cheekbones and sun-bronzed skin. Liz wondered if all the men in Mara's life moved like shadows and looked like movie stars. "Say something else, babe. I've missed hearing your voice."

Mara leapt up on an inarticulate cry of joy and launched herself into Jonas's arms. He was laughing when he caught her, was still laughing when she speared her fingers into all that inky black hair and fused her mouth to his. Liz looked away. There was too much in that kiss for her to watch. It was all need and passion, an aching stretch of loneliness abruptly broken by the recognition of the heart's other half.

It was too intimate, she told herself. None of her business. And she tried like hell to squash the sharp thrust of envy that raced through her when Jonas reached up to cradle the curve of his wife's cheek in his big, work-roughened hand. Patrick had done just the same thing to her, not forty-

eight hours before. Kissed her with that same sort of passionate recognition, laced it with that sweet little gesture of
honest affection.

She shoved the thought back. She wouldn't love him.
Couldn't. He wasn't safe, and no amount of risk could
make him so.

"I'll just, um, see myself out," Liz murmured, slipping
past them through the doorway. She doubted they even heard
her, let alone noticed her exit. But Mara called after her.

"Liz."

She turned to find Mara still wrapped loosely in her
husband's arms. "Think about what I said, will you?"

"You, too. You come up with anything, call me." Liz
pushed back through the swinging doors to the normal
world with an overwhelming sense of relief. Out here, chaos
didn't rule, risk wasn't the norm and husbands and wives
didn't expect or even want what she'd just seen between
Mara and Jonas.

She wished like hell she didn't want it herself.

She buzzed down the car windows on the drive home.
The sky was soft and purple, just fading into twilight, the
breeze heavy with the promise of summer. She angled into
her driveway, then braked abruptly when she saw Patrick's
sporty little bullet of a car parked there in front of her
garage.

She gave herself a moment. Pressed her thumbs into her
eyebrows, tried to head off the mounting pressure there.
God, all she wanted to do was curl up somewhere safe and
regroup. She felt raw, assaulted and too damn tired to shore
herself up for another round with Patrick. She wanted her
couch, some mindless TV and an enormous quantity of
premium ice cream, and what did she get instead?

A Hollywood playboy and reformed jewel thief standing in her open doorway, uninvited, unwelcome and glowering like she'd stood him up for the prom.

She shoved out of the car and mounted the steps, didn't
stop until she was toe to toe with him. He didn't budge. She
glared into those crystalline eyes, found them snapping

with temper. Well, good for him. She'd been rolling in guilt and fear and lust for days, and she was good and ready to let it all morph into a raging tantrum.

"What are you doing at my house, Patrick?" she snapped, stalking past him through the open door into her foyer. She turned on her heel, planted both hands on his chest and gave him a good, solid shove that knocked him back a step. Not quite far enough to slam the door in his pretty face, but it was a start. "More to the point, what are you doing *in* my house? I believe I set the alarm system before I left, and I've got to say, it used to be relatively effective before you came to town."

He didn't flinch, though she must have been radiating rage like the desert radiated heat. He just stepped right back into her face. "This alarm system hasn't been effective since 1986, Liz. I've bypassed it six ways from Sunday in the last two hours, and I haven't even broken a sweat yet."

"Are you *trying* to get arrested?" Liz asked, incredulous. "Or is this one of those high-adrenaline hobbies? Regular old breaking and entering just doesn't have enough kick, so you've moved up to cop houses?"

He took another step toward her, his hands flexing as if it were willpower alone that kept him from seizing her. She didn't back up, and it brought him close enough that she could smell him, feel the heat and temper rising off him, mingling with her own. "You work with violent criminals every day, Liz," he said, spacing the words carefully, evenly. She could see that it cost him an effort. "You had a break-in not two days ago, and yet you continue to walk around as if that badge of yours is a bulletproof vest. Leaving yourself this deliberately vulnerable goes beyond stupidity and into willful ignorance. If I didn't know better, I'd think you were trying to make me insane on purpose."

She stared at him. "I've been working sixteen hour shifts trying to nail a counterfeiter who makes contact only via your cell phone, and even then it's only to set up fake meetings and give himself grandiose nicknames. I've got about a dozen other cases screaming for my attention, but then some joker starts systematically breaking into and searching all the houses you've set foot in since you got to town. You're no help—I'm bringing in that stupid DJ whether you like it or not, by the way—and now I come home to find that you've been breaking into my house all afternoon?" She gave him another shot to the shoulder. "And *I'm* making *you* insane? How do you figure that?"

He took her chin in one hard hand, forced her gaze to his and held it. "I don't know what's going on here, Liz. Not yet. There are any number of dangerous people out there who'd love to take a shot at me. Who deserve the shot if they can line one up." He shrugged. "I can handle myself, but—"

"But nothing," Liz snapped. "I can handle myself, too. You think there aren't a shitload of dangerous people gunning for me, too? I'm not going to live in a goddamn fortress because I put a bunch of skeevy sociopaths in jail."

He closed his eyes, as if pained. "I know that. I don't like it, but I know it. I accept it. You kick ass for a living. Good for you. But you're not doing it on my account."

She frowned. "What do you mean?"

"This one's on me. You're not a target because of the badge. You're a target because you're important to me, and I wasn't careful enough to hide it. I should have protected you better." He shoved his hands into his pockets and watched her. "I don't know what's going on," he said again. "Not yet. But I will. And I'll figure it out a hell of a lot faster if I'm not worried half out of my head about you."

She stared at him, her anger draining abruptly away with a simple realization. "You spent two hours breaking into my house just to test my security system?" she asked slowly. He was—in his own screwy, illegal way—protecting her.

"Yes." He glowered at her. "And I'm here to tell you, it didn't make me feel any better."

"Oh Christ," she said, and felt it happen. The slow, ill-advised tumble of her heart as it slid right into love. She tipped her head and took him in, the grease beneath his manicured nails, the streak of dust across his white T-shirt, the dirty jeans that had seen better days. She'd never seen him like this before. Angry, disheveled, direct. And under it all, fiercely protective. Somebody had threatened her, and he had placed himself as directly as possible between her and a threat he couldn't see.

Or wouldn't admit to seeing, a voice whispered in her head.

But she ignored it. It was done. She'd done the inevitable, the ridiculous, the impossible. She'd fallen in love with Patrick O'Connor. Reformed criminal, ex-poker king, FBI weasel and erstwhile crime novelist.

This was an utter disaster.

But Liz was nothing if not pragmatic. Love didn't last. Everybody knew it. If she was in love—and she was too scrupulously honest to even think about denying it—the only smart thing to do was embrace it. Accept it. Accelerate it toward the inevitable messy end. And in Liz's experience, nothing propelled a romance toward a crash-landing faster than sex.

She'd have to sleep with him.

Soon.

Like, now.

Chapter
15

PATRICK FROWNED and took his first step backward since Liz had stepped out of her car. Those bluebell eyes of hers had gone all calculating, and he had to squash the heady little zip of adrenaline that look always sent racing through his veins. God, he loved a woman with a plan. Liz's plans had never gone well for him, but that didn't mean he couldn't appreciate a woman with guileless eyes, a china-doll face and a crafty, devious mind.

"What now?" he asked warily.

She blinked, as if she'd just realized he was standing in her doorway, as if they hadn't spent the last ten minutes toe to toe, hissing at each other. Then a smile curved her lips, a smile so packed with carnal promise that his mouth went dry. "Come inside, Patrick."

He obeyed, his brain in high-analysis mode while his body was just hopeful. He fell back on the habits of a lifetime and slouched easily against the foyer wall. Act like you know what you're doing, like you have every right in the world to be exactly where you are, and people believed you. His ability to exude superiority had bought him considerable time in many a sticky situation over the years, and he was counting on it now. Because Liz had a new angle here, something he couldn't quite figure out.

He gave her a lazy grin, something slow and easy and somehow southern despite the fact that he'd been born in Iowa and had never spent more than a few weeks at a pop below the Mason-Dixon. "What now? Are you going to offer me some sweet tea? Because busting into your house all afternoon surely was a thirsty job."

His breath backed up in his chest when she laid her small, cool palm against his jaw and smoothed her thumb over his cheekbone.

"You had a little something," she said. "Just there."

His entire system surged to attention, making the space between their bodies suddenly supercharged and electric. But a part of his brain hung back, wondered. She'd sounded like the Liz he knew, all brisk and direct, so why was she touching him like the Liz of his dreams? Something was off.

His body didn't much care. It was still hung up on the part where Liz was six inches from his mouth and looking suggestible. He forced himself to speak, had to really dig for an appropriately amused tone. "Liz. Darling. What are you doing?"

She leaned in, eyes wide, the faintest hint of calculation still swirling in the deep, deep blue. "I'm saying yes," she breathed.

Then she kissed him. If he hadn't already been leaning up against the wall, he'd have sagged there for sure. He'd kissed Liz enough lately to anticipate the punch of it, to know that it would be sweet, sharp and addictively hot, that it would have him dancing perilously close to the edge of control. How could he have possibly known she'd been holding back all this time?

But she had been. Must have. Because this kiss was like nothing he'd ever experienced. It was like being there for the birth of a star. Blinding light, incinerating heat and a merciless gravity that had him helplessly circling her like a planet in orbit. He felt his arms band around her, his mouth open to the demand of hers. The edges of reality blurred, and his entire world narrowed to her. Just her. A curvy little angel with a gun and a badge who was pressed up against him and kissing him like the fate of the free world depended on making him happy.

And she was doing a damn good job, because he was extremely happy. He tried to loosen his grip on her, show a little finesse, but she wriggled against him and said it again. *"Yes."*

He lost track of his thinking. He didn't know exactly which of them had opened the buttons of her ugly suit coat, but he slid his hand inside to find her breast. She made a hot little noise against his mouth and arched into his hand until he could feel the jut of her nipple through her shirt. Lust pounded through his veins in a steady, accelerating pulse, and he brushed his thumb over her nipple until her head lolled forward and her breathing went ragged.

Which was nice, because his own wasn't so steady, come to think of it.

"Yes," she said, her forehead against his shoulder, both hands fisted in his shirt. Patrick glanced toward the living room, dismissed the curvy lady couch and the hardwood floor. That wouldn't do. He wanted a bed. A big one. He slid his hand from her shirt, vaguely disturbed at how difficult it was for his body to process the command from his mind to let her go.

"God, Liz," he said, shaken. "I want—" He broke off. He couldn't define exactly what he wanted. Her body, yes. And Lord, that mouth. Everywhere. But more. There was something primal and possessive racing through his system. Something that made him want to mark her, own her, claim her.

"Yes," she said again. "Yes, yes, yes." She chanted it like a mantra, her eyes closed, her pulse beating like mad in the delicate hollow of her throat. And it pierced the fog of desire just enough for a chilling note of doubt to creep in.

It was all she'd been saying, *yes*. It was all he'd wanted to hear from her for years. So why did it feel wrong?

He turned her slowly, put her back to the wall, watched her eyes flutter open. They were heavy, hot and dazed with passion. But not lost. Patrick knew what lost looked like. He knew what it felt like to spin beyond reason's reach, carried helplessly away by lust or desire or greed. He hadn't stolen for a living without learning a thing or two about *lost*. It chilled him to his very core that he could still see the remnants of calculation there.

Liz had a plan. Screwing him was part of it.

"What is this, Liz?" he asked, very carefully.

"What does it look like?" she asked, her lips damp and well kissed. Looking at them did unnerving things to his resolve, so he watched her hands instead. But then they went to the hem of her blouse, starting at the bottom, slowly freeing buttons as she worked her way upward. A strip of pale, smooth flesh appeared in the V of her shirt and Patrick swallowed hard. He reached out, put his hand over hers. For an instant, he didn't know if he was trying to stop her or trying to take over the work himself.

"It looks like a seduction." He forced the words out of his very dry throat.

"You said once that you could make me want things I didn't even know existed yet. I want you to prove it." She slipped her hands out from under his and slid them up under his T-shirt instead, smoothed them over the planes of his abdomen. Patrick's entire gut clenched with unthinkable pleasure, and he trembled with the effort it took to step away.

"And I'd love to. I'd really, *really* love to. But, Liz, why?"

She stepped forward, coy invitation curling her lips, a hint of irritation in those revealing eyes. Patrick latched on to the irritation. He wasn't falling in as easily with her plan as she'd hoped. That was good. Wasn't it? His head thought so, but his body was more of the opinion that he was a raving lunatic.

"Because I want you to," she said. God, was she *pouting*? That mouth was killing him. "Isn't that enough?"

"Normally, yes." Patrick forced himself to take another step back. "But not from you. A week ago you weren't even prepared to be my colleague, and now you want to be my lover? I don't think so, Liz. Especially not when you've got *master plan* written all over your face. Somehow, sleeping with me has become an asset in your twisted little mind. I don't know why, I don't know how, and trust me on this, I'm sorely tempted not to care and just toss you onto the nearest flat surface and stop thinking for the next twelve hours or so. But I'm not going to. Not until you tell me what the hell happened."

She banded her arms over her waist, her face going rigid and blank. "Nothing happened."

"Bullshit."

"I had a hard day and wanted a good fuck, all right?" She cocked a hip and glared. "You were here, you were handy, you've expressed an interest. Simple as that."

He stared at her, taken aback. "A hard day?"

She shoved past him. "Listen, I'm offering you the chance to get busy on that revenge fuck you've been after since, oh, the minute you arrived in town, all right? If you don't want it, just say so. But will you please make up your mind? Because I'm in no mood for conversation."

"I don't do sex without conversation. It's a little quirk of mine."

She glared at him. "Go home."

Patrick stared after her as she stalked down the hallway to her bedroom and slammed the door. Liz was a damn good liar. The innocent face, the diminutive stature, the aura of earnest justice seeker that surrounded her like a heavenly glow. But Patrick was a good liar, too. That's how he'd learned to recognize another.

Everything Liz had just said was one big lie. That was the easy part. The hard part was going to be figuring out why.

HALF AN hour later, Patrick walked into Mara's kitchen just in time to see his niece streak through it, bare-ass naked and soaking wet. She disappeared around a corner, cackling wildly.

"Huh." He headed to the fridge for a beer.

He twisted off the cap and pushed through the French doors onto the balcony. The dark wrapped around him like a comfortable blanket as he lowered himself into one of the rattan chairs. He sipped the beer and tried not to think for just a minute. He'd been thinking for days now and just wanted to turn it off. Wondering if Liz knew that he knew that Villanueva was in town—along with why the bastard might be playing hard to get—was making him crazy.

The temptation to lay all his cards on the table and let Liz make sense of them was nearly overwhelming, but so far he'd resisted. This was no time to play by the book and Liz didn't seem to know any other way to play.

Or so he'd thought. Patrick slouched farther into his seat and scowled into the night. What the hell had gotten into Liz tonight?

Evie bolted out onto the balcony, still naked but considerably air-dried, with a piercing shriek. Her father snatched her up, wrestled a nightie on over her head, then dropped her to the ground and backed away, hands aloft like a world-champion calf roper. Evie giggled and bolted back into the house.

Patrick looked at Jonas. "You're back."

Jonas grinned at him. "You, too."

Patrick took a deep pull from the bottle. "Not on purpose, believe me."

"Mara said she'd asked you to visit."

Patrick snorted. "You could say that."

Jonas gave him a friendly thump on the shoulder, the kind that men give one another only after they've come to an understanding with their fists. His brother-in-law had fists like cinder blocks, if Patrick remembered correctly.

"Poor bastard," Jonas said. "Let me get a beer."

In a few minutes, he was sprawled across the chair beside Patrick's, long legs stretched toward the railing, beer in hand, while Patrick gave him the shorthand version of the last two weeks.

"FBI gig, huh?" Jonas shook his head. He wasn't a much bigger fan of law enforcement than Patrick, though his feelings had less to do with a criminal past than growing up as the only Indian kid in the whitest town in Minnesota. "Fuck."

Patrick smiled into the darkness. Women were wonderful and he loved them, but sometimes it was good to talk to another guy. "Yeah. And add in the sexual thing between me and Liz, and it only gets worse."

Jonas sipped his beer as Evie clattered through the kitchen behind them, naked again except for her mother's high heels. "Liz has a problem with it?"

Patrick lifted a shoulder. "Before tonight, I'd have said yes. Big-time."

"What happened tonight?"

"Hell if I know. Girl's got a plan, I guess. A plan that turned *hell, no* into *do me now.*"

"Interesting."

"Well, yeah. But it's not going to happen 'til I know why."

Jonas's eyebrows lifted slowly. "You turned her down?"

"Yeah." Patrick fought the urge to snarl.

Jonas laughed. "Never going to get that offer again," he said. "Poor bastard."

"She spent the last two weeks insisting that she'd never sleep with me. Now she gets to hate me when I oblige her?"

"Well, yeah."

Patrick finished off his beer. "Fuck."

"Amen, brother." Jonas finished off his. They looked out into the deepening night in companionable silence. Evie, nightgown on backward, streaked past them and bounced up to catch the top railing of the banister. Patrick rose and plucked her off without conscious thought. They were three stories up, after all, and everybody knew that a kid shouldn't be monkeying around on a banister railing. He turned toward the open doors, Evie on his hip.

"Mara at work?" he asked.

"Yeah." Jonas stayed seated, plunked his feet onto the railing and tipped his head back on the chair. "I'm on bed-time duty."

Patrick glanced down into Evie's eyes, which gleamed with an unholy amount of energy. He laughed. "Poor bastard," he said, then turned his niece loose in the kitchen.

PATRICK WOKE the next morning to the insistent trill of his cell phone. He groped for it, flipped it open and squinted at his watch. "Hello?"

Christ, it was 5:30 A.M.

"Good morning, Mr. O'Connor," a man said. "I understand you're looking for a little instruction in the art of making money."

He sat up slowly. "Yeah. Is this the Great and Powerful Oz?"

The man laughed delightedly. "It is. Call this number in three hours if you want a little lesson." He reeled off a number and Patrick committed it to memory as the line went dead. He stared for a moment, then dialed Liz.

Chapter

16

PATRICK STRODE into the FBI's Grief Creek Resident Agency later that morning, prepared for an icy reception. He hadn't turned down many women in his day, but he knew enough not to expect hearts and flowers the next morning.

He found Liz in her cubicle, all starched up and buttoned down, her hair twisted up in a silver clip that left the nape of her neck bare. The urge to put his lips just there was nearly overwhelming and he took a moment to marvel at last night's unthinkable self-control. How he had managed to refrain from stripping her bare and worshipping at the shrine of her body until dawn, he hadn't the slightest clue. He must have pissed off some powerful deities this time to deserve such punishment.

She looked up before he had a chance to find his voice and smiled at him.

Smiled. At him.

What the hell?

"You're here," she said briskly. "Great. The sound tech

wired up the phone in the conference room for us. You can make your call to the Great and Powerful Oz from there. It'll ID as your cell, and we're equipped with full recording capabilities."

Patrick frowned. "Where's Goose?"

"She couldn't get away." Liz rose, tucked a pencil into the twist of her hair and nudged him gently back into the hallway and toward the conference room. "She'll meet up with us later to review the tapes."

Patrick followed her into the conference room where he stood next to the chair Liz waved him toward. She was wearing a skirt today rather than her usual pantsuit, and even though the hemline hit a conservative inch or two below her kneecaps, he wondered if it had been an intentional choice—if she was purposely torturing him with the smooth, bare calves and ankles he'd forsaken his chance to touch. He watched helplessly as she rounded the table, slid on a pair of headphones and fiddled with a few dials and switches.

"Okay," she said, looking up with that impenetrable air of professional collegiality that was really starting to bug him. "Ready when you are."

"I'm not ready."

She blinked. "You're not?"

"No." He rounded the table, plucked off her headphones and glared down at her. "You're acting strange."

She folded her hands primly in her lap. Which bugged him even more, because Liz was a lot of things, but prim wasn't on the list. "Strange how?"

"Strange like . . ." He twirled a hand in the air, at a loss for the right word. He hadn't realized how fundamentally his world depended on Liz being sturdy, upright and principled, and it had shaken him, deeply, when she'd suddenly gone rogue. "Like everything is just fine and dandy between us. Like nothing insane happened recently."

She canted her head, peered at him like a scientist with a fascinating and unpredictable specimen under the microscope. "Is this about last night?"

He sank back against the table, pinched the bridge of his nose. "You have to ask?"

She crossed her legs and he could hear the whisper of silky skin sliding over silky skin. He swallowed, prayed it wasn't audible. God, she had him so tangled up.

"I'm sorry," she said simply. "I didn't realize that the idea of having sex with me would disturb you so much. I shouldn't have offered."

He resisted the visions that threatened to swamp his brain. He didn't want to have this conversation while his mind was full of sweaty, tangled sheets and warm peach skin. "Then why did you?"

She made a small, amused noise. "After the effort you put into seducing me this past week or so, I thought you were interested. My mistake."

He kept his eyes closed. "I *am* interested, Liz. You know that."

He heard her rise, smelled her when she leaned into him, felt his entire body go on red alert when she spread her hands on the table on either side of his hips. "Are you?" she murmured, her mouth bare inches from his ear. "Are you really?"

"Yes." He shot to his feet, out of the cage of her arms, and stalked to the opposite end of the room. When he spun to face her, she looked soft, accessible and, God help him, vibrantly touchable. "Christ, Liz, you know I am. Did you really think it was all just a sham to make you uncomfortable?"

"No, of course not," she said, moving toward him with a predatory gleam in her eyes. "There are certain things a man just can't fake." A smile tipped up that full mouth of hers, transformed it into a carnal invitation, and she stopped just shy of touching him. The air between them seemed to vibrate, and Patrick channeled every ounce of his energy into keeping a grip on his self-control.

"So, are we reopening the subject?" she asked.

He stared down at her, at the hint of calculation gleaming in her eyes. "No," he said finally.

She blew out an irritated breath. "For God's sake, why not? You survived an orgy with a dozen Russian supermodels, but doing one Midwestern cop freaks you out?"

"Yes. A girl like you starts inviting reformed felons into her bed, it's a sure sign of the apocalypse." He smiled at her, in spite of the repressed need still pounding through his system. "And you shouldn't believe everything you read in the tabloids. I don't even know a dozen supermodels, Russian or otherwise."

She gazed at him for a long, suspended moment. "You need to make up your mind, Patrick. Either you want me or you don't. But don't kiss me like you're dying for me, then turn me down when I kiss you back." She turned away, but he took her elbow before she could stalk off.

"How many times am I going to have to say this?" he asked, not sure if he was asking her or whatever sadistic deity had put him in this situation. "I do want you, and quite desperately. I don't mind admitting it. But before I take you, I want to know what changed. Because something did. Something important. What was it?"

She frowned at him, then said slowly, "My mind."

"Why?"

"None of your damn business."

Patrick considered her. "You're really not going to tell me?"

"There's nothing to tell."

He gazed at her, then sighed. "Then there's nothing to discuss. Let's make that phone call."

FRIDAY NIGHT found Patrick reliving one of his fonder memories from this latest sojourn in the Midwest, only with a nightmarish twist that sucked out all the fun.

In preparation for his latest meeting with the Great and Powerful Oz, he and Liz were once again alone together in the abandoned brewery adjoining Cargo. Goose was off tinkering with her radio or something, and he was taking his shirt off at Liz's command. But this time, he wasn't the predator. This time, he was the prey.

Liz smirked at him, her eyes going hot and vividly blue. "Shirt," she said. "Off."

He frowned at her. "I think I know the routine by now," he said. "Surely I can wire myself this time?"

She moved toward him, her lips pursed into a moue that did odd things to his pulse. "Nope. This job doesn't come with many perks, but wiring you is one of them." She smiled then, widely. "It's my job and I'm keeping it. Stop whining."

"I'm hardly whining," he said, then caught the pleading note in his own voice. God. He *was* whining. "Fine. Have at it." He made short work of the buttons, dropped his shirt onto the desk and threw his arms wide.

Liz gave a happy sigh and Patrick braced himself against the feel of her small, warm hands moving leisurely over every inch of the skin he'd bared for her. He swallowed down a hum of pleasure at the drift of her fingers over his abdomen, the clean scent of her hair as she bent her head toward his chest to affix the tiny microphone. She circled him, dragging her fingers deliberately over his skin as she did, and he shuddered at the touch, at the waft of her breath against his shoulder blades. Everything in him demanded that he turn, snatch her up in his arms, crush her between his body and the nearest flat surface and claim her in every way a man can claim a woman. Standing on principle suddenly seemed like an extremely bad idea.

She smoothed adhesive tape into the small of his back and nestled the transmitter into place, her hands lingering warmly. His blood heated a few degrees more, and he knew suddenly that he'd reached the absolute limit of his control. He'd wanted Liz for longer than he could remember, wanted her more intensely than he'd ever wanted another woman. Why exactly was he denying himself what he wanted more than anything, what she was so clearly willing to give him?

He turned slowly, his fists clenched and rigid by his sides, but she didn't back away. She swayed into him instead, reached up and threaded her fingers through his hair. Her eyes were heavy lidded and sparkling with that disturbing combination of desire and calculation that had been eating at him for the past few days. Her mouth was close enough to kiss, her breath warm on his lips. He clung with a superhuman strength to one last shred of self-control and didn't close the gap. He held himself immobile, apart. God, it was killing him.

In the end, it was Liz who moved.

"For luck," she said. His own words, he thought, and it was the last thing he thought for some time because then she was kissing him. She kissed him with all the frustration, the need and the raging, edgy want he'd gotten used to living with. Patrick's already tenuous grip on his self-control slipped and he banded his arms around her. He pushed her back onto the desk, boosted her up until he was between her knees, pressing himself mindlessly into the consuming fiery center of her.

Her mouth opened under his, her knees came up to grip his hips and she pulled him even closer. Closer. God, that's all he wanted to be. Closer and closer until there was nothing left between them. No secrets, no space, no history. Nothing that could divide them.

"Liz," he said finally, breaking the kiss. He didn't open his eyes, just leaned his forehead against hers and tried to control his ragged breathing. "You win. I don't care anymore. I want you too much. You can keep your secrets. I'll take whatever you're willing to give me." He pulled back to look into her face. She was flushed, her lips rosy and plump from his kiss. "But one way or another, I'm taking you home tonight and I'm finishing this."

"Thank God," she said with a catlike smile, but there was something else in her face, too. A sort of terrified relief. He tried to focus but it was gone in an instant and she was all business again. All cop.

"You have a meeting," she said, glancing at her watch.

She handed him his shirt. "Do you want to go over the setup again?"

He shoved his arms into the shirt. "Not much to go over. I present myself at the DJ booth as usual, only this time I ask about buying some weed from Oz." He grimaced. "Since I can't avoid sounding like an idiot, I'll at least try not to look like one."

"Yeah." She gave him a sideways smile. "Good luck with that."

"WHAT'S YOUR name, kid?" Patrick asked as he followed the teenaged DJ's very wide shoulders through a steel door marked EMPLOYEES ONLY. The noise level dropped dramatically as it clanged shut behind them, and the kid stopped to scowl at him.

"Do I look like anybody's kid?" he asked.

Patrick made a production of looking him up and down. The guy was a good six feet and solidly built. The lank hair was thick but in desperate need of a wash, he smelled powerfully of cigarettes and his jaw was covered with a very authentic stubble. But the indignation in his eyes over being termed a kid told a different story. Patrick put him at sixteen. Seventeen at the outside.

But all he said was, "Sorry, man." He put just a hint of boredom into his voice. "Habit, I guess. In Hollywood, everybody's looking to shave a few years off."

"Yeah?" An avid curiosity lit his eyes, but he turned away to lead Patrick down a narrow set of stairs lit only by a couple of bare bulbs. "Must be some kind of crazy place."

"Can be."

"You're a big shot, though, huh? A celebrity?"

Patrick chuckled. "You think?"

The kid threaded them through a dank hallway barely wide enough to accommodate his shoulders. "Why else would Oz be looking for you?"

"What makes you think he's looking for me? Maybe I'm looking for him."

"Nobody finds Oz unless he's looking to be found."

"Yeah?"

"Oh, yeah." The kid smirked. "What do you want him for, anyway? You don't look like the dime-bag type."

"I'm writing a new screenplay centered on a rather brilliant counterfeiter. I find my criminal education a bit spotty on the topic," he said lightly. "I need a primary source."

"A what?"

"A real live counterfeiter," he said. "A good one would be nice. A brilliant one would be better. Somebody to walk me through the whole process, from making bills to making a profit. I've heard that Oz is quite good."

The kid paused at a darkened intersection, a door before him, hallways leading into blackness on either side. "Is there good money in being a, what did you call it? Primary source?"

Patrick smiled slightly. "Depends on what you think is good. Better than DJing, probably."

The kid squinted at him in the dim light. "How's the pussy in Hollywood?"

Patrick's smile spread. This kid was all brass balls. Damn if he wasn't starting to like him. "Again, probably better than what you get DJing."

"Fair enough. Well, listen, this is where I get off." He turned and ambled back down the hallway from which they'd come. "Best of luck, dude. Good chat."

Patrick's entire system revved with adrenaline, but he kept his voice smooth when he called after him, "Oz is in here then?"

The kid just lifted a meaty hand in farewell and disappeared around a corner. Two impulses rose up inside Patrick—one counseling rapid and immediate flight versus one that wanted desperately to know what, or who, was on the other side of this ugly door.

He deliberated over his options for the space of two heartbeats. Then all pondering was cut short by the fist that flew out of the darkness to his left and crashed into his jaw like a speeding train. He went down, first to his knees, then to the floor when another punishing blow landed on his cheekbone.

Fuck, he thought as lights flickered in his head and went dim. *Please let Liz have the good sense not to charge in like the cavalry.*

"FUCK!" LIZ leapt up, banged her head on the hollow duct-work in which she crouched. "What the hell was that?" She keyed Goose on the two-way. "You get that?"

Goose crackled back, "Didn't sound good for our boy."

"Shit," Liz said. *Villanueva,* she thought. Had to be. She dropped out of the ductwork onto the dented steel desk in the brewery office and hit the ground running.

She shoved her way through the line outside Cargo, flipped her badge at the indignant bouncer and plowed into the sweaty darkness of the writhing crowd. She was dressed for work this time—sensible shoes, a disposable black suit and a prominent badge but she didn't have Patrick's gift for parting crowds like a hot knife through butter. She made vicious use of her elbows and stomped mercilessly on countless insteps before she arrived at the DJ station, out of breath and out of patience.

She grabbed the guy by his fashionably wrinkled shirt, dragged him over the console and into her face without regard to the fact that he had her by a foot and a good hundred pounds.

"Patrick O'Connor," she snarled, shoving his headset off. "Where did you take him?"

The guy's eyes were wide and wary. "Who?"

"Six feet, black hair, blue eyes, wanted to buy some weed."

He eyed the badge on her belt and licked his lips. "Are you going to arrest me? Because, I swear to God, I've never smoked pot in my life. I just get a phone call so I can tell people where to meet the guy, right? I'm not—"

"I don't give a fuck how you use your anytime minutes, all right? But I'll be happy to put a bug in the DEA's ear about it if you don't tell me everything I want to know in the next two seconds."

"Um, boiler room," he said quickly, pointing toward a set of doors at the back of the cavernous room. "Through there. Down the stairs."

"Hang around. I'll want to talk to you later." Liz gave him a hard look before she released his collar. He nodded quickly and she watched his Adam's apple bob as he swallowed. She fought her way to the doors marked EMPLOYEES ONLY. Goose met her there. They both had their weapons drawn and Goose looked to Liz calmly. "High or low?"

Liz looked her over and said, "You're taller. I'll go low."

"Fine."

Liz kicked through the door, went into a deep crouch and swept the hallway with her weapon and her gaze. She could hear Goose doing the same above her. Nothing. Christ. Her pulse was even, her hands steady, her brain was clicking through procedures on autopilot. But in her chest there was a sucking pit of terror. The kind of numb panic that put cops out of commission.

She pounded down the hallway with Goose on her heels. If anybody had asked what her goal was, she'd have said Villanueva. She wouldn't have hesitated. It was true. She wanted that collar so badly she could taste it. But it wasn't her primary goal.

She needed Patrick. Needed him safe. Needed him whole. Because after two weeks of waiting, after two weeks of agonizing indecision, Liz finally had her answer. This wasn't a friendly overture to renew an old partnership. This was a sneak attack, the opening volley in what could rapidly degenerate into an old-fashioned bloodbath. Patrick's blood.

She shoved back against the panic and ran.

Chapter

17

PATRICK DRIFTED out of the blackness. His jaw ached like a bitch and his cheekbone didn't feel much better, but he didn't open his eyes. Didn't stir, shift or give any indication that he was anything but good and unconscious. He needed a minute to orient himself to this latest development.

An ungentle hand slapped his cheek. "Come on, now, O'Connor. I knew you had a glass jaw, but this is ridiculous."

Villanueva. Christ. Why couldn't his instincts ever be wrong?

He let his eyes drift open slowly, let them stay unfocused for a minute.

"Ah, there you are," Villanueva said. He was crouched over Patrick in the filthy hallway looking as lean and dangerous as a jungle animal. He was older, his skin a few degrees darker and tougher than Patrick remembered and a deep web of lines fanned out from the corner of each eye. All those years in the baking Central American sun,

Patrick supposed. "I was beginning to wonder if you'd gone softer than I'd thought."

Villanueva extended a polite hand, and Patrick took it. He sat up and worked his jaw gingerly back and forth. "Christ, you've got a fist like a brick, Villanueva. And you sucker punched me."

"Well, yes." He smiled, but his eyes remained flat, cold. "I apologize for that, but my time is limited, and I needed to make a point."

Patrick rose lightly to his feet, lifted his brows in question. Villanueva smiled, as if pleased with his former protégé's resilience. "You owe me a great deal," he said, "both monetarily and otherwise. And I'm a dangerous man to owe. Neither you nor your loved ones are entirely safe while you have debts to discharge. It's time to pay up."

Patrick slipped his hands into his pockets, rocked back on his heels and considered him. "I pay my debts," he said finally. "And I know I owe you. Where will I find you when I'm ready to make good?"

Villanueva smiled again, and it was chilling. "Be ready soon. You'll hear from me," he said, then disappeared down the hallway from which he'd first appeared.

Patrick was still standing there, pushing his tongue against a particularly sore spot on his jaw when Liz and Goose came barreling around the corner, hair flying, guns drawn. He smiled at them in spite of everything. One more hot girl cop and they'd be Charlie's Angels.

Liz swept down the left hallway, Goose down the right.

"He's gone," Patrick said helpfully, though they could already see that for themselves. Liz shoved her gun back into its holster. She stalked up to him, grabbed his chin in one hand and jerked his head toward the light. Patrick hissed.

"You're going to have a shiner," she said, then released him. "You want to take him through the debrief?" she asked Goose. "I'm going to clear the building and shoot a description to the local authorities."

Goose shrugged. "Sure." She took Patrick tenderly by the arm. "You feeling up to the stairs, ace?"

Patrick scowled at Liz's retreating back. "I could've been killed," he said. "Is a little sympathy too much to ask?"

"She was very worried about you." Goose chuckled. "The DJ nearly wet his pants when she came after him."

"Yeah?"

"Oh yeah."

Patrick smiled, mollified. "All right, then."

"PLAY IT back again." Liz stalked to the far end of the room as she listened, her hands laced together behind her neck. She couldn't hear Villanueva's voice linger lovingly over his threats and stay still. So she paced.

"Neither you nor your loved ones are entirely safe while you have debts to discharge."

"Got to say, I don't like the sound of that," Goose said when the recording clicked off.

"You know what debt he's talking about?" Liz asked Patrick.

"I assume he's talking about his share of the take from our last job together."

She frowned at him. "There wasn't a take from that job."

"Well, no. Not technically." He spread his hands reasonably. "But that wasn't his fault. That was on me. I chose to spring my sister rather than honor my commitments, and he paid for it with no score and six years on the run. His wife's remarried, their kid probably doesn't even know the guy's not his real father. It's not a stretch for him to decide that somebody owes him something, and I'm the logical choice."

"And you were sure Villanueva was in town when, exactly?" It made her feel ill even to ask, but she forced herself. He might lie to her, but she had to ask. Had to allow him the chance to tell her the truth. To trust her.

"About the time his fist met my face. Until then, I wasn't sure."

"But you suspected."

He inclined his head.

"And yet you didn't share that information with your team."

"I didn't see how it applied to the case," he said simply.

A hot retort was burning on Liz's tongue, but Goose cut her off. "I don't think any of us could have foreseen that a cold case would suddenly go live and intersect with an active like this," she said. "And I think it's counterproductive to dwell on who knew what when. We need to focus on the next steps."

"I agree," Patrick said, sliding a glance at Liz.

She sucked in a breath, shoved back against the panicked fury that had been dogging her ever since she'd heard Patrick hit the floor over her transmitter. "Fine," she said.

In truth, she wasn't anxious to dig too deeply into the subject either. She'd known that Villanueva was back in the country, too, though she'd been under orders not to share the information. Would she have told him if she'd been able? Would she have trusted him that far? Did she trust him now? She didn't know. She only knew what she'd felt when she heard the thud of his unconscious body hitting the floor.

"This thing about your loved ones not being safe, that bugs me," Goose was saying. "What does Villanueva know about your personal life? If he wanted to hurt you by hurting somebody else, who is he most likely to target?"

PATRICK SHRUGGED, but the blood turned to ice in his veins. He forced himself to speak calmly, to not even look at Liz. "My sister, most likely," he said. "Our parents are both dead. Private plane crash, en route to Monte Carlo two years ago. Villanueva never met Mara, but he knew she existed. I'm sure he knows she's why I fucked him."

Goose nodded. "Would he know where to find her? Would he know about her family? Her husband, her children?"

"He must if he's here. But to answer your question, her husband wasn't on the radar when Villanueva left the country. And Evie, Christ, she's only two." He pushed down the sour bile rising in his throat, swallowed the bitter laugh that wanted to bubble up after it. He'd worked so hard for so many years to be unlovable, to discourage friendship, affection, emotional ties of any kind. He'd dropped his guard once—one damn time in thirty years—and look what had happened. He'd turned a man like Villanueva loose on his sister and her innocent child.

"Is there anybody else?" Goose asked gently.

He didn't look at Liz. Didn't dare. She was on Villanueva's radar now, too. All because he'd wanted her. Desperately, hopelessly and, he admitted now, selfishly. He'd gotten complacent, hadn't bothered to hide his desire beneath his usual careful layers of casual detachment. No, he'd let the world see how much he wanted her. He'd let Villanueva see it. And now she was paying for it.

"Liz," he said finally. "He knows about Liz."

Goose just nodded. "I'll see about ordering surveillance for the potential targets," she said.

"It'll be done tonight?" Patrick asked.

"I'll make certain of it."

"Good." He watched as she disappeared through the door, cell phone already to her ear. He turned to find Liz watching him, her eyes dark and intent. "I modified your security system," he said, for lack of anything better to say. There was an apology hovering somewhere in his throat, but he couldn't bring himself to force it out. Because the nasty truth was that he wasn't sorry enough yet. He still wanted her with a raging ache that clawed at him. "You should be safe enough at home."

"You're not coming with me?"

He scrubbed a weary hand over his face. Christ, why didn't she just paint a fucking target on her chest? "No."

She gave him a piercing look, and he did his best to erase any remnants of hunger from his face. "I'm already a target, you know," she said, as if she could read his mind. "Have been for years. I'm used to it." She crossed the room, laid one small hand on the arms that Patrick had crossed over his chest. Something inside him broke and bled at the gentleness of her touch, at the forgiveness in it. Forgiveness he didn't deserve.

"I'm not going home with you, Liz. It was a bad idea."

"You don't want me?" she asked, her face small and serious.

He resisted the urge to close his eyes, to whimper. Instead, he composed his face in the coolest lines he could manage and lied. "No. I don't."

Her hand faltered, then fell away. "I see."

He doubted very much that she did. But he didn't stop her when she walked out the door.

"I BEG your pardon. I had no idea," Liz said into the phone the next morning. "I'm so sorry to have intruded. My condolences on your loss." Shaken, she hung up and peeled off her suit jacket. Summer was a ways off yet, but the weather had taken a capricious turn toward July overnight. The air was so heavy and hot that breathing was like sucking a milk shake through a straw.

She squinted against the sun blasting cheerfully through the meager windows of the FBI's Grief Creek Resident Agency. Her eyes were gritty and tired as she turned this grim new development over in her head, tried to make it fit with the other pieces of the puzzle.

No matter which way she turned it, she didn't like the picture that emerged.

Coffee, she thought, rubbing her eyes. A cup of coffee would blow out the cobwebs and she'd get back to the ugly task of tracking down every last living soul who might have had contact with Villanueva during the past six years, who might be able to provide one clue about what his next likely move might be.

Another agent wandered past her cube, leaned in and said, "Hey, Liz. Gorgeous day, huh?" She gave him a look that had his stupid grin faltering. "Ah, SAC Bernard's looking for you," he said, hastily ducking back into the hallway. "Sounds pissed."

Liz rubbed the wrinkle between her brows, bid a reluctant farewell to that desperately desired cup of coffee. "Great."

Two minutes later, she was standing in front of SAC Grayson Bernard, her face as blank and precise as his desk. "You wanted to see me, sir?"

"I did." Bernard was facing the window, gazing at Main Street like a king surveying his holdings. "I understand there was an unexpected confluence of the Villanueva case and the counterfeiting case last night. Report."

Liz clasped her hands behind her back, kept her eyes level and gave him a terse rundown of last night's events. "There's some phone work I want to do today on the Villanueva case that I'm hoping will provide some clarity on his motives."

"And your counterfeiter?" Bernard hadn't moved from the window, hadn't yet glanced in Liz's direction and it had her nerves stretched piano-wire tight.

"Is as bright as his profile implies. He's been careful never to call from the same phone twice, never to meet in person or in a location where recording devices are of any use. But I'm confident in our plan. The trap's been baited. Now we pit our patience against his ego."

"Patience is an undervalued trait," Bernard said, "and I admire it in an agent, particularly one as young as you. But I don't think it's patience behind your desire to linger over this case."

Liz frowned. "Sir?"

Bernard moved away from the window, his flinty eyes

meeting hers for the first time since she appeared in his office. He walked to the desk, reached into a drawer and removed a folded newspaper with his usual economy of motion. He placed it on the desk facing Liz and slid it toward her with one finger, as if it were something toxic.

She stepped forward, scanned the paper and her gut went to ice water. Because she was looking at a photo of her and Patrick—grainy but exquisitely recognizable—the first time they'd visited Cargo. They were dancing, if you could call it that. She closed her eyes, but the image was burned into her brain. Patrick's hands spread low over her hips, her arms twined lovingly around his neck, the arch of her body as she pressed herself willingly against every available inch of him, the expression of pure and sensual abandon on her own face.

And that frightened her more than anything. In Patrick's arms, she was different, softer. More vulnerable and lost. She'd known that. She just hadn't known it showed so badly.

And she certainly hadn't known it had been recorded and published.

"Is there an explanation for this, Agent Brynn?" Bernard's voice was clipped, expressionless.

Sweat gathered under her heavy ponytail, between her shoulder blades, and she cursed herself for not checking the weather before she'd dressed in a winter-weight suit that morning. She felt wilted and wrinkled from the inside out.

"O'Connor attracts attention," she said simply. "We knew it was possible that the press would trail us. It had to look authentic."

Bernard gave her a penetrating stare, his eyes like granite. "You're good undercover, Brynn," he said, his diction as sharp as the crease in his trousers. He turned the newspaper to face him, tapped one blunt fingertip on the picture of her face. "But not this good. He's gotten to you. Again. And he's using it to screw with your head while he pursues his own agenda." He paused, captured her gaze. "An agenda that's brought Villanueva right into your territory. *My* territory."

Liz clamped her teeth together, sucked a breath in through them. "With respect, sir, I don't believe that's entirely accurate. After conducting extensive interviews with O'Connor, both together and separately, Agent di Guzman and I are of the opinion that he's a target to Villanueva, not an accomplice."

Bernard gazed at her. "Do you deny that your feelings for O'Connor have become personal? That they're affecting your performance in this case?"

Liz's heart thudded to a halt inside her chest. She couldn't give an answer to that. Not to Bernard, not to herself. She simply wasn't prepared.

"He's given me reason to trust him," she said finally. God knew she didn't want to trust him, hadn't meant to, but now that she said the words aloud, she knew they were true. There'd been a brilliant flash of honest pain on his face last night when he'd talked about his niece as one of Villanueva's potential targets. There had been a similar pain in his eyes when he'd lied and said he didn't want her. It meant something, enough to have trust sinking fragile roots into her heart. But was it enough? Trusting the right people had never exactly been her strong suit, after all.

"As of this morning, however, whether I trust O'Connor has become a secondary concern," Liz said.

Bernard lifted a pale brow. "Yes?"

"I attempted to contact Villanueva's ex-wife this morning to find out if she'd had any contact with him since he skipped the country. I spoke to her current husband."

"And?"

"She's dead. She and the son she had with Villanueva were killed three weeks ago, their throats slit while they slept. The boy was seven." Liz's voice wanted to tremble but she held it steady as she reported. "Villanueva's profile shows he has a particular propensity for knives and the psychological ability to delay gratification for years if he deems it necessary. It's my professional opinion that he's pursuing a vendetta, systematically taking out anybody he feels betrayed him. He talks about paying debts, but he doesn't want money. He wants blood."

Bernard's brows came together as he considered this new angle. "I see."

"This is born out by the conversation O'Connor had with him last night, which we do have on tape. Maybe he talked about money, but his fists said something different. I believe, as does Agent di Guzman, that O'Connor is next on Villanueva's hit list."

Bernard turned back to the window, and Liz felt the sweat collect between her shoulder blades as she watched him, waited for his verdict.

"I'm leaving the case in your hands," he said finally. "For now. But bring in that counterfeiter, Brynn, and figure out how the hell he's connected to Villanueva." He glanced at her over his shoulder. "Dismissed."

PATRICK GLANCED in his rearview mirror and sighed. Damn. After last night, he should have known Liz would put a tail on him. He knew it was her job to mistrust him, but the blatant evidence of it stung nonetheless. He pulled into Grief Creek's wretched excuse for a shopping mall and parked.

Twenty minutes later, he emerged. His own clothes were, regrettably, stuffed into a Gap bag and he was wearing a cheap pair of jeans, a tasteless polo shirt, a new pair of dark sunglasses and a Twins ball cap. He stepped into the cab he'd called on his cell and pulled away from the mall entrance while his tail stayed parked in the lot, binoculars trained on the car he'd left behind.

He shook his head. Either Grief Creek's law enforcement left a great deal to be desired, or Liz had purposely selected the most inept tail ever. He liked to think it was the latter but wasn't counting on it.

"Grief Creek Community Bank," he told the cabbie.

THIRTY MINUTES later, Patrick was in a cab speeding back toward Grief Creek's Haven for the Sartorially Disabled, a safe-deposit box's worth of cash nestled among his clothes in the Gap bag. Since his first score, he'd been squirreling away a small percentage of every take in safe-deposit boxes around the country as a sort of insurance policy. For bond, bail, an amazing defense attorney or just a rainy day.

He probably should have eased the funds into legitimate, interest-bearing accounts now that he was reformed, but he liked having access to wads of untraceable cash. It allowed him a certain freedom he found appealing. The freedom to make a large purchase without consulting his financial manager, for example. Or the freedom to apply monetary solutions to old, sticky problems.

Solutions of which the FBI would not approve. Solutions that would make Liz blow a gasket when she found out he'd applied them without her go-ahead. He sighed. No help for that one. Liz wasn't going to understand, so he'd just have to make sure she didn't find out.

His cell phone rang, and he frowned at the unfamiliar number.

"Hello?"

"O'Connor," Oz said. "You still interested?"

"Depends," Patrick said. "Do you have anybody else lined up to jump out of a dark hallway and kick my ass?"

Oz chuckled. "Sorry, man. Dude said you owed him, and you *were* trying to fuck me over. Check that wire shit, and we'll deal."

Patrick paused. "Fine."

"You screw me, and I'll know. You don't want that kind of pain."

Patrick pushed his tongue into his sore jaw. "No, I don't."

"Cargo, tonight, ten o'clock."

He sighed. "I'm starting to dislike that place. Don't you ever go anywhere else?"

"Ask for me at the DJ station." He disconnected before Patrick could agree or object. Cocky bastard. Still, he smiled. The kid reminded him of himself at that age. Ambitious enough to dream big, smart enough to back it up, reckless enough to enjoy it. Patrick was starting to like him. Enough to want to keep his ass out of juvie, anyway.

He paid the cabbie and stepped into the mall to change back into his own clothes. In minutes, he was back out in the sweltering heat—Minnesota was not a habitable climate, he'd decided—where he got back into his car, cranked up the AC and called Liz.

"Thanks for the police escort," he said when she answered. "I feel so much safer."

"I was hoping you would," she said sweetly. "Please don't lose them. My boss would be pissed."

He watched them in his rearview mirror. "They haven't lost sight of my car for an instant," he said.

"Your car?" she asked, her voice instantly wary. He smiled into the phone.

"Oz called. He's ready to show me the ropes. What are you doing tonight?"

Chapter

18

EIGHT HOURS later the whole team assembled in the dimly lit office of the abandoned brewery that adjoined Cargo.

"No wires this time, as requested," Goose said. She handed Patrick a cell phone containing a miniature recording device and a black leather holster to attach it to his belt.

He eyed the holster with distaste. "Do I really have to wear that?"

Goose blinked. "You could just point the phone at the guy the whole time, but that would be a little obvious, don't you think?"

"I suppose so." He leaned back against the dented metal desk and frowned at the holster in his hand. The bass thumped in the club next door, vibrated through the desk under him. "It just seems so . . . desperate."

"Really?"

"Well, yeah." Patrick unfastened his belt and threaded it through the holster, securing the phone to his hip. "You only wear your phone on your hip if you're truly unimportant and desperate to appear otherwise." He glanced down at the phone on his belt, gave a delicate shudder. "This is lowering."

Liz dropped out of the ceiling's exposed ductwork onto the desk, missing Patrick by maybe a foot. Her hair was disheveled and a smear of dirt decorated one smooth, golden cheek. She smirked at him.

Patrick gave her booted feet a significant look. "You could give some warning before you drop out of the sky, you know. Or at least let us turn on the lights so we can see you coming."

Liz gave him a bland stare. "No lights tonight. Whoever owns this place does so through an ungodly tangle of holding companies. Until I can figure out who else besides us might have a key, we're low profile."

He gave her a winsome smile. "Then perhaps you could just clear your throat or something the next time you plan to leap out of the ceiling."

"Poor Patrick. Did I scare you?"

"Bad manners always scare me. It's the hallmark of a civilization in decline."

Liz rolled her eyes. "The decline of civilization isn't our big problem tonight, Patrick. We're more interested in shutting down a little counterfeiting operation, and thereby pulling in the guy who tried to dislocate your jaw last night. Remember him?"

He nodded slowly. "Um, yeah. Hard to forget."

"And if Oz stands you up again, I'm sweating the DJ whether you like it or not. That guy gets grilled like a rotisserie chicken, got it?"

"Yes, sir." Patrick gave her a lazy salute. She glared at him.

Goose cleared her throat. "So, are all the receivers in place in the ductwork?"

Liz hopped off the desk with an efficient agility that Patrick appreciated with an automatic eye. God, he wished he could stop noticing the way she moved her body now that he'd never get the chance to explore it.

"Yep," she said. "We should be all set to monitor his location at all times. Unless Oz's supersecret evil lair is hidden in a lead-lined bomb shelter or something."

"Or right in front of a twenty-foot speaker," Patrick muttered, his ears already ringing in anticipation.

"Fine," Goose said. She patted Patrick's arm. "You're only enabled for recording—audio and visual, though we don't expect much from the visual. We won't have a live feed this time, but I'm going to monitor your location. There's a tracking device embedded in the phone that'll talk to the receivers Liz just placed." She turned to Liz. "I'm going to the van. It's in the alley behind the fire exit. I'm on the two-way if you need me."

Then she was gone, and Patrick was exquisitely aware that he and Liz were alone in a room that had been the scene of a few of their better kisses. Not that she'd ever given him an average one.

"You should go," Liz said, her voice suspiciously neutral, her gaze determinedly elsewhere.

Looked like he wasn't the only one taking a hot, sweaty little trip down memory lane.

He was going to have to fix this, he thought with a mental sigh. Lord knew he didn't want to. He wanted her aware of him, as achingly, exquisitely conscious of him as he was of her. But he couldn't ask that of her, no matter how sweet a balm to his ego. He'd tangled her into this wretched disaster of thwarted passion and impending doom; he'd be the one to cut her loose.

"Liz," he said, leaning lazily on the vowel. "Darling." Drawing a cloak of breezy superiority over his true self was usually as easy as breathing. Why was it so hard tonight? He forced himself to saunter over to her, to flick a careless finger over the curve of her down-turned cheek. "Aren't you going to kiss me?"

She looked up at him, and he realized that he'd miscalculated, badly. Because her eyes weren't snapping with temper, as he'd intended. Instead, they were a dark, serious blue, and he fell helplessly into them. He didn't move, couldn't move, as she reached up with slow, deliberate intent and threaded her fingers through the hair at the nape of his neck. She laid her lips against his with a sweetness that all but shattered his heart. It certainly cracked his control.

When she drew back, he tried to breathe again but found that his lungs had gone temporarily off the job. He stared at her. God, how did she *do* that? Make each kiss an unexpected revelation?

"Why?" he asked. It was all he could manage.

"I wanted to," she said with a lopsided smile that put the finishing touches on the wreck of his heart. "Plus I figured you should know what you're saying no to."

He shook his head slowly. "What we are, the two of us, it just can't happen. You know that, don't you? We're too different. The proverbial oil and water." He felt his lips twist into a ghastly approximation of a smile. "It's like howling for the moon, Liz. We want, but it's no good. Taking would be suicide, for both of us."

"Oh, please. I asked you to sleep with me, not marry me." A hot spark snapped in her voice and temptation roared up inside him to meet it. "It was a very nice offer, if I do say so myself. An offer you refused. Unless you've changed your mind?"

For an endless, suspended moment, he wavered. Wanted.

"No," he said finally. "I haven't." He turned on his heel and headed for the door.

LIZ HUNKERED down in the ductwork that reverberated with the thump of the music next door, two-way radio in hand, ready to move any and all transmitters upon Goose's instruction. She tried desperately to focus on the work, but it would take Patrick a few minutes to fight his way through the crowd, and until then, she was left with nothing to occupy her but the bottomless well of sorrow that had opened up in her chest the instant she realized that she'd kissed Patrick O'Connor for the last time.

Not that losing him was a shock. That had been the plan all along, hadn't it? She couldn't keep him. Of course she couldn't. She'd never even considered it. But until she'd been blindsided by this towering sorrow, she'd never stopped to ask herself why not. Turned out, it wasn't because of what he'd done or who he was. It wasn't even because of her job, or how laughably their careers would combine.

It was because she was afraid.

She was willing to give him her body without restraint, but her body wasn't enough. No, he wanted more. He wanted her to fling open her mind to him, too. He wanted to touch her thoughts, know her emotions, see her heart, and the very idea opened a yawning pit of terror inside her. She'd worked too hard and too long to untwist whatever her father had twisted in her to risk handing her heart to another dangerous man.

But she'd allowed herself one last kiss. Something to remember. And she'd paid for it. The bleak, dazzled wonder in his fallen-angel face would haunt her for the rest of her life.

She squeezed her eyes shut, forced herself to focus on the work. Work would save her. Heal her. Just like always.

FOR THE second time in as many days, Patrick found himself being led deep into the thumping bowels of a dance club by a fledgling criminal mastermind posing as a disc jockey. The same kid, he reminded himself, who'd opened negotiations by allowing the most dangerous man of Patrick's acquaintance to beat him unconscious. What the hell was he doing here?

A smile twisted his lips that was part self-mockery, part startled discovery.

He was here because the two women he loved—his sister and Liz—had asked it of him. Simple as that. Apparently, that's how love worked. He shook his head, as if to settle the awkward realization better into place. He knew he loved Mara—she was his sister, for crying out loud. But Liz? He loved Liz?

Of course he did, he thought bitterly. He'd uprooted it and flung it aside time and again, but whatever he felt for her had refused to die. In his experience, only love—and hate—were so remarkably persistent.

"Here we are," the kid said, pushing through a battered door into a tiny, dank office. A bare bulb hung down from the ceiling, but it was unlit. The glow from three different computer monitors provided enough light for Patrick to follow the kid inside and wedge himself between a laser printer and a scanner while the door creaked closed behind him. The kid reached up and screwed in the bulb, bathing the tiny space in a harsh, yellow glow.

There was nobody in the room but the two of them. This was it, Patrick knew. Every job had a similar moment, the point from which there could be no veering from the set course. The second this kid acknowledged on tape that he was the counterfeiter, the card had been played. There was no taking it back. Patrick would just have to find a way to convince Liz to use the knowledge in the kid's best interest.

He was too much a pro to hesitate over the moment. He stepped calmly into the scenario he'd planned, tossed the DJ a skeptical look and cocked a brow. "Oz, I presume?"

Oz treated him to an ironic little bow. "At your service."

"Wonderful." Patrick let his tone sour. "Just wonderful. You'd better be as good as I've heard. Because if I bring a sixteen-year-old DJ to the set and he's not a fucking counterfeiting wunderkind? Well, let's just say it'll be unpleasant."

Oz's face darkened, and he took a quick step toward Patrick. His massive shoulders blotted out at least two of the computer monitors. "First of all, I'm better than you've heard. Better than you've ever seen or can imagine. And second, I'm not sixteen."

For an instant, Patrick didn't move. He stayed slouched casually back against a desk, let the kid loom over him, his face like a thundercloud, his fists clenched with adolescent temper. Then he leaned into the kid's face and said with quiet menace, "I know exactly what you are. You look like a man, but you're just a boy who thinks that a great big brain and a set of brass balls makes you a hardened criminal. You think I don't recognize you?" He laughed lightly. "Please. I *was* you." He gave the kid a critical once-over. "Fifteen?"

The kid's shoulders slumped. "God. Seventeen."

Patrick nodded philosophically. "Okay. It's not ideal, but by the time we hit production, you'll probably be eighteen. I can work around it if what you show me is worth the hassle." He glanced at the jumble of high-tech equipment crammed into the tiny space, then back at the kid. "Feel free to dazzle me."

Oz's face brightened, and he suddenly looked exactly like the teenager he was in spite of the man-stubble on his jaw and the unholy breadth of his shoulders.

"Yeah, okay," he said. He rustled around in one of the myriad stacks of junk that littered every available surface. "It's all about the paper."

Patrick nodded as if he'd never heard it before and settled in for the show.

TWO HOURS later, Patrick held an extremely convincing hundred-dollar bill in his hand. He snapped it just to hear the crisp sound of new money. The kid was good. Goose would wet herself.

"It's not bad," he said. "Not half bad." He glanced around the cramped space. "But surely this isn't where you usually work. You hardly fit through the doorway."

Oz grinned at him, shoved a handful of unwashed hair out of his eyes. "No, this is a great workspace. Nobody comes down here and the club's noisy enough to cover up any racket I make."

"Still. You can hardly keep all your supplies here, and if

you were operating on a larger scale, you'd need a place to assemble the bills, to dry them."

"This is a big building. Plus, the owner likes me."

"You know the owner?"

"Sure. Interesting guy. I pay cash for office space and he looks the other way when I need to spread out my product." Oz glanced at the humming printer. "This is a good batch," he said. "You wanna hang around and get some more hands-on experience?"

Patrick laughed. "I don't think so. You want an assistant, you'll have to hire yourself one. I don't work cheap."

Oz grinned. "I already spotted you a hundred."

"Consider it an investment in your future," Patrick said, and Oz laughed delightedly. He probably wouldn't be so thrilled if he realized that the future Patrick was steering him toward was quite a bit different than the one he'd planned for himself.

"You up for phase two tomorrow?" Oz asked as Patrick stuffed the hundred into his pocket.

"I'm always up for a learning experience."

"We're going shopping." He looked up from his work to cast an assessing eye over Patrick's imported Egyptian-cotton shirt and custom-tailored trousers. "For cheap and tacky shit. You going to be able to handle the stress?"

"Punk," Patrick said mildly.

Oz laughed. "It'll be worth it, trust me. The first time you buy twenty bucks' worth of junk with a fake hundred and pick up eighty untraceable, genuine American dollars in change, you'll thank God for cheap and tacky shit." He grinned. "I'll pick you up at Brightwater's, ten o'clock."

Patrick let himself into the hallway and threaded his way back through the labyrinth of corridors, leaving Oz to tinker happily with his latest batch. Nostalgia warred with guilt. If he'd been bounced out of the life at seventeen by some rich asshole, he wouldn't have thanked the guy, Patrick knew. Not at the time. He might now, though. A few years, a few close calls, a few ugly dents in his stone-cold heart changed a guy's perspective.

But nobody had stepped in, and there was no changing history, was there? He could only work with the present as it stood. And right now, things weren't looking too bad. He was making serious progress toward solving Mara's counterfeiting problem and closing Liz's case. He'd pay off Villanueva next, hopefully before Liz dragged him into custody and pissed him off some more. Then he could get back to the safety of sunny California. Forgetting Liz always seemed easier there, somehow.

He reentered the nightclub, where the crowd was still writhing to the endless mix Oz had left thumping. He negotiated the dance floor with only a few minor inconveniences, mostly of the groping variety, and let himself out the rear exit and back into the brewery. He could have gone right to the van and let Goose raise Liz on the two-way, but he wanted to see her again. Wanted to explain a few things before the information stored in the recorder on his hip was officially downloaded in FBI and Secret Service files.

PATRICK WAS safe. Liz knew the instant he'd hit the club doors because Goose had raised her on the two-way, given her the okay to gather up the receivers. Liz shoved aside the ridiculously powerful surge of relief and started the long dirty crawl through a couple hundred yards of ductwork. There were about a dozen receivers to retrieve, receivers that had kept Patrick safe under the FBI's watchful gaze that evening. She'd just snagged the last one when Goose had tagged her again.

"Our boy's coming your way, Brynn. Debrief and upload the audio to the network, will you? Good luck. I'm out."

The two-way was clipped to the back of her jeans and she didn't bother to reply. Goose didn't seem to care what designation SAC Bernard gave Patrick—in her mind, he was Liz's source and she left him in her hands whenever possible. Liz cursed softly and shimmied her way back through the ductwork to the open vent on top of the desk. She landed with a muffled thud about six inches from Patrick's hip.

"Still working in the dark?" he asked.

She climbed off the desk and put a few more feet between them. "Yep. Law-abiding citizens don't do paper trails like this one."

"Liz." He clucked gently. "So suspicious."

She let that go with a shrug. She *was* suspicious. So what? Being suspicious was her job, and she was damn good at it. She swiped at the cobweb that trailed from her hair and resisted the urge to flip on the lights. She wanted to see him, to assure herself that he was undamaged. It was a weakness she had no intention of indulging. "No sign of Villanueva?"

She heard the desk creak as he eased off it. He was nothing more than a vague impression of motion in the dark, but she could feel his approach. The air went supercharged, her skin supremely sensitive to every current and drift. "No," he said. "Oz seemed to think that letting him beat the crap out of me once was enough to discourage any further attempts to wire up."

Liz snorted. "Cocky."

"No, just young. Listen, Liz, about that—" He broke off abruptly, and Liz froze. She'd felt it, too. A whisper of air swirled around them, the back draft from an opening door somewhere nearby.

"Christ," she muttered, and grabbed Patrick by the elbow. She didn't even wonder that she knew exactly where to grab to get it, either. At this point, she was so finely attuned to his body, she could probably lay her hands on him blindfolded in the middle of an open field. She hauled him across the tiny office and onto the wide open factory floor.

"Uh, Liz? Where are you—"

She yanked open the door to the thermostat control room she'd spotted earlier and shoved him inside. Liz had scoped it out for herself, and she could squeeze in pretty comfortably, but Patrick was about twice her size. *Fuck it,* she thought, and jammed herself in after him.

Chapter

19

THERE WAS a moment of expectant silence in which Liz strained her ears for any signs of motion outside their door and tried like hell to ignore the fact that her butt was planted firmly against Patrick's crotch. He threaded his arms around her waist, nestled himself more comfortably into the curve of her behind and whispered into her ear, his voice barely more than a breath, "You couldn't find any place smaller?"

She stiffened, but it only pushed her more firmly against the unmistakable evidence of his growing arousal. *Small is not your problem, buddy,* she thought helplessly as a wave of heat crashed over her, tempting her to melt and soften for him. Only for him.

She shoved temptation aside, forced herself to summon up all those years of training. "Shut up," she hissed. He nodded against her hair, but the arm around her waist held her firmly against the solid wall of his chest, her thighs riding intimately against his, her butt cozied up to his impressive erection. God.

Then a dull light filtered in through the doorjamb and somebody started whistling tunelessly and moving about the factory floor.

"Oz," Patrick mouthed in her ear. She didn't know how she could possibly hear him when the word was no more than heat and texture against her skin, but she nodded. "I was going to tell you. He has some kind of arrangement with the owner."

Liz twisted slowly against him, tried to put her mouth in the vicinity of his ear. She could feel as much as hear Patrick's breath catch at the friction. She knew how he felt. She'd brushed one breast against his arm and thought she was going to spontaneously combust. She kept her voice several degrees under a whisper. "How much did he print?" she asked. "How long is this going to take?"

"Not much." She felt him shrug. "Half an hour maybe?"

She sagged against him. Christ. How was she going to survive half an hour of this? Her heart thudded into double-time when he wriggled a hand between his stomach and her back. Her indrawn breath hissed between her teeth.

"Radio," he said softly, and her cheeks burned in the darkness. He'd been reaching to switch off her radio so it didn't give them away, and she'd jumped like a virgin at an orgy. He eased the radio from her waist, clicked it off and set it aside. Then his hand came up and smoothed down the hair above her ear. He was probably breathing it in, she thought. It and all the dust she'd accumulated during her travels through the ductwork. God, what if he sneezed?

But his hand didn't stop at pushing the stray hairs away from his face. It continued down the length of her hair, slid under the heavy weight of it, lifted it away from her neck. Suddenly, his mouth was there against the vulnerable curve of her shoulder, hot, open, avid. She froze, a million messages bombarding her nervous system—surprise first, then heat, need and an indescribably powerful pleasure. It flowed into her blood like warm honey, loosening her bones, softening her resolve. A noise crept into her throat, but she was worried that it was more moan than reprimand so she swallowed it down.

His tongue touched her skin, unleashing a devastating shock wave that rippled under every inch of her skin, and the last of her resistance crumbled. She tipped her head to the side, and his mouth trailed slowly up the side of her neck to her ear. He took her lobe between his teeth and bit with exquisite delicacy. She felt it all the way into her belly, low and hot. His wide, warm hands crept up her abdomen, cupping her breasts through her T-shirt and bra, his thumbs brushing over the aching points with a lazy deliberation that had her edging toward madness.

It had to be madness, because she couldn't find any other explanation for this new certainty that she would die without his hands on her body. Everywhere on her body.

He pulled his hands away from her breasts and a tiny moan escaped her. Nearly inaudible, but desperate and strangled nonetheless. She felt his hands tremble against her at the sound of it. She wanted to turn around, to press herself against him until every angle, every curve and every hot, secret place was open to his touch. But then he pulled her shirt free of her jeans, and those hands slid like liquid fire against the smooth skin of her midriff, streaked up to capture her breasts.

This time the heat was so intense, so immediate, that her head simply lolled back, found a beautiful cradle against the hard curve of his shoulder. The front clasp of her bra gave way and suddenly his hands were against her skin, the hard prod of her nipples between his fingers. She rolled her hips back into him, strangled back a cry of need as he answered her with a roll of his own hips, and then he raked his teeth lightly up the edge of her throat.

She wanted his mouth on hers, she realized dimly. His hands were clever—hell, they were magical as far as she was concerned—but she wanted his mouth. She twisted against him, struggling to turn in the cruelly limited space, and he loosened his grip to allow it.

Then her breasts were crushed against his chest, the

fabric of his shirt an expensive and exquisite friction, while his mouth came down to claim hers with a savage desperation. She answered the kiss with all the edgy need raging through her veins, opened her mouth to him, danced her tongue across his. He rocked his hips against hers in a maddeningly constricted motion that had want pooling hot and heavy between her legs.

And then something was missing.

The whistling. The light? Which had stopped first? She couldn't say. All she knew was that they were alone again. She could feel it in every fiber of her incredibly sensitized body. Patrick had also gone utterly still. After three long heartbeats, he let her go, easing his hands away from the curve of her bottom.

The desire pounding through her veins cooled slightly, drifted toward shame. She put her clothing back together in swift silence, then reached for the doorknob with a trembling hand. She didn't flip on the lights, didn't even turn to look at him. She concentrated instead on the makeshift clotheslines stretching across the warehouse floor, strung with an impressive amount of counterfeit cash.

"Guess you were right," she said softly. She checked the doors with shaking hands. Locked, all of them. "Guy has a key. Looks like I'm going to have to get to the bottom of that paper trail after all."

"Liz," he said, his voice dark and steady. "What just happened here?" There was no hint of reproach in the question, but she felt wretched anyway.

"You started it," she snapped. "You tell me." She was cranky, horny and teetering on the ugly edge of heartbreak, and suddenly she'd had enough.

"What are you trying to do here, Patrick?" she demanded. "Really. What is it you want exactly? You come to town acting like somebody blackmailed you into being here, get yourself embroiled in not one but two of my active cases, and then when I'm not appropriately thrilled to be working with you, you threaten to seduce me. And *then*, when I'm too damn knotted up over you to think straight, you decide no, tragically, we're just too different for sex to be an option. But you take the first opportunity to feel me up in a closet. Why are you doing this?" The words tumbled out on a reckless surge of anger. "Why are you screwing with my life this way? Why can't you just do the job and leave me alone?"

"What do you want me to say, Liz? That I can't resist you? That you draw me in and I'm helpless against it?"

She gazed at him, shock and hope pooling inside her. "Are you?" she asked softly. His silence was answer enough, and it was truly all she'd expected. Even so, it sent a hot surge of anger through her that he'd been cruel enough to make her hope.

"God, of course you aren't." She laughed bitterly. "Even if it were true, you'd never say so. It would be too foolish, too vulnerable. It would make you a real flesh and blood man, and you'd never risk that, would you?"

His face went absolutely blank and she knew she'd hurt him. She was sorry for it, but at the same time, something hot and joyful and furious rose up inside her. She'd broken through. Finally. The mask was coming off.

"What do you know about risk, Liz?" he asked. "What the hell do you know about taking a real chance? You, with your boarding school education, your riding lessons and debutante balls. How the hell does somebody like you talk risk to somebody like me?"

"This isn't about me."

"The hell it isn't." Those black brows had lowered into a single, ominous line, and Liz felt her own temper rush to meet his.

"Fine. Then tell me just because I want to know. Tell me why you're here."

"Liz." He pushed his hands through his hair again and blew out a sharp breath, struggling visibly to regain control. Liz would be damned if she'd let that happen now. Not when she was so far beyond control herself. "It's almost over," he said wearily. "I've already been here longer than

I planned and I'll be gone inside a week. Why does it even matter anymore what this thing is between us?"

"Because!" she yelled, throwing out her arms in frustration. "I'm in love with you!" She sucked in a breath that didn't seem to contain enough oxygen. "Christ knows I don't want to be, and I've done everything I can think of to get out of it, not that you've been any help, Mr. Do The Right Thing. So if you're not going to sleep with me, I'd consider it a personal favor if you'd really make an effort to stay out of my life. Starting with avoiding any FBI investigations in the future. You want to do something nice for your sister, maybe you could send flowers. That's what most brothers do."

He stared at her, shock written plainly on his beautiful face. "Oh, for God's sake," Liz snapped. "Don't look like that. It isn't a death sentence, you know. I love you. I'll get over it, whether you fuck me or not. Just make up your mind so I can settle on a strategy, okay?"

"And what if I do?" he asked slowly. "Sleep with you. How exactly are you going to handle that? I mean it's not exactly in your best interests, careerwise."

She jerked her shoulders. "I'm not asking for a permanent arrangement, Patrick. Given your cooperation and unlimited use of my bed, we can be on the other side of this in a couple days. A week, tops." She left out the part about the unlimited wear and tear on her heart, but surely he didn't need to know about that. "Love's not one of those lasting things."

He snorted. "And your superiors? Have they okayed your plan to screw the daylights out of a former thief?"

Liz stiffened. "The FBI doesn't choose who I sleep with."

"The hell it doesn't," he said. "Letting me into your bed, however temporarily, puts your badge on the line, Liz. Maybe not in any official way, but anybody finds out and your career path dead-ends."

"That's not going to happen."

"Why shouldn't it?" He leaned in, dark and knowing. "Tell me you love me more than your badge, Liz. Tell me you're willing to risk everything you've worked for to get this thing out of your system."

She folded her arms and gave him a defiant glare. The very idea of losing her badge set loose a slithering terror in her chest but she pushed it back. It was either risk her career or spend the rest of her stupid life miserably in love with him. And as much as she needed her badge, she needed her heart back more.

"What do you care?" she said. "Isn't it your plan to have your wicked way with me anyway? Don't you want your sweet revenge?"

He gazed at her for a long, tense moment. "Not at any price," he said. "Not at this one, anyway. I'll take you home."

HE HELD out his hand when they reached Liz's front door and she handed over her keys without an argument. Progress, he thought.

"You want my gun?" she asked.

He curled his lip into a sneer that probably made them both feel a little more normal. "I'd rather not. Guns are so . . . obvious."

"True. But they're darn handy for shooting armed intruders." She sneered back, and Patrick felt things settle a bit in his gut. He liked Liz sneering at him. He *expected* Liz to sneer at him. He did *not* expect declarations of love. Though now that he considered it, the style had suited her completely. Both reluctant and defiant, straightforward and pissed. He wondered if there had ever been a problem she hadn't tackled just so.

"Stay here," he said, and eased into her darkened house. Five minutes later, he returned to the porch, found her leaning against the railing, her gun in hand. "Come on in," he said. "You're clear."

"Great." She sailed past him in a cloud of temper and

pride, that lovely back stiff, those eyes still blazing blue fire. "Thanks for everything. I'll be in touch should we require your service again as pertains to this case, but I don't anticipate that. Good-bye."

Good-bye. The word struck him like a physical blow. One second he was enveloped in the hot, clean scent of her as she passed under his nose, the next she was shoving him out of her house and out of her life. Suddenly it was more loss than he could bear. He moved before he could even think it over.

"What? No kiss good night?" He had her wrist before she could snatch it back, shouldered past her door and captured the other one. He backed her up against the wall of her little foyer, her wrists pinned on either side of her startled face, and settled his weight right into all those tidy, compact curves. God, he loved the way her body fit him.

Temper chased the shock right out of her eyes and he nearly laughed at the sweetness of it, the ridiculous rush of satisfaction he got from fighting with this woman. She opened her mouth, presumably to singe his hide with some well-chosen words, but he kissed her before she could wrap that gorgeous mouth around any of them. Her words were always so hard but her mouth was so damn soft, and he fell into it with something like relief. God, he wished he could keep her like this. Just like this—startled, then open, yielding, melting—forever. Was that possible? Her tongue touched his, and he was suddenly inclined to find out.

He pulled back, looked into her determined little face so full of frustrated desire and reluctant love. His heart thudded to a halt, then broke wide open. She loved him. *Him.* And he loved her right back. Maybe he couldn't give her the words, but he could give her this. One night to stamp his love on every inch of her beautiful skin. One night to worship her with his body, his hands, his lips.

"So this is what you want?" he asked softly. "This, your bed and the next couple days?"

"Yeah," she said her eyes burning and clear. "That's it."

He moved in again, pressed the entire length of his body

to hers. He wanted to moan at the perfection of the fit. "I think we can work something out."

"Thanks be to God," she said. She wrapped her hands into the front of his shirt, kicked the door shut and pulled him into that wanton, willing mouth.

Chapter

20

SHE DIDN'T bother with the lights, just kept kissing him as they groped their way down the short hall to her bedroom. She didn't want to open her eyes, didn't want to know what he looked like in this moment. She'd have a hard enough time forgetting how he felt under her greedy hands, how *she* felt with his hands racing over her body, setting off minor earthquakes in their wake. She didn't want to have to forget his face, too.

She fumbled blindly with the buttons on his shirt, keeping her mouth fused to his as they finally popped free under her trembling fingers. Then her hands were on him, streaking over smooth golden skin, over muscle and bone. It wasn't enough, she thought wildly. Not nearly enough. Desire spiked with bright panic whipped through her in a wicked, rising tide. What if she couldn't ever get enough? What if this burning thirst to touch him couldn't ever be slaked, no matter how deeply she drank of him? How was she ever going to be free?

A noise of distress escaped her, and her hands faltered

against his chest. "I can't," she whispered. "This isn't going to work."

He stilled against her. "Liz. Darling." He turned her in his arms, put her back against his stomach and rocked her in his arms, slow and soothing. He laid his mouth into the crook of her shoulder and spoke against her skin, his voice sliding over her like honey. "It'll work just fine. Relax."

His hand slipped under her shirt to draw slow circles low on her belly. He pressed himself into the curve of her behind and she could feel him there, hot, hard and demanding. Even so, his hands stayed lazy, playing against her stomach, tracing circle upon circle, each one reaching just the tiniest bit higher than the last.

Her breath caught in her chest and she found herself swaying with him, allowing him to comfort her even while her breasts swelled and tingled with anticipation. His thumbs finally brushed the lower swell of her breast and she stopped breathing altogether. Her nipples hardened to tight straining points and his hands slid up to cup the aching weight in his palms. His thumbs feathered over her nipples with slow deliberation, and the shock of it ripped through her, shoved the air from her lungs and all rational thought from her mind. She arched into his hands with a throaty cry of surrender while those clever hands of his dealt with the front clasp of her bra.

In that moment, she stopped worrying about what would happen to her if she went through with this. She was more concerned about how she'd survive if she didn't. When he urged her arms over her head, she raised them without conscious thought. He pulled her shirt over her head and tossed it away.

"Open your eyes, Liz," he murmured, rubbing his jaw lightly against her cheek. "You're beautiful."

She'd been lost in the dark haze of desire he'd woven around her, but her eyes flew open at his words. Beautiful? Even the men who'd claimed to be in love with her had never tried that one. But then she focused on what he was showing her, and she stared. She'd never seen such a thing.

God, she'd been right to keep her eyes shut. She'd never erase this image from her brain.

Moonlight streamed through her bedroom window, brushing everything with a silvery glow. They were reflected together in the mirror above her dresser, both naked to the waist. She looked soft, she thought wonderingly. Curvy and ivory white against the darker gold of his arms. He loomed behind her like a fallen angel come to lead her into sin, his hands splayed possessively over each breast, her nipples jutting wantonly through those long, clever fingers. He plucked and rolled them while she watched, and the sight sent a nervy desire crashing through her. Her eyes drifted shut and he nipped at her jaw.

"No, darling. Stay with me. Watch what I do to you. What you do to me."

"No." She couldn't. Not if she wanted to come through this intact. She wrenched herself free, spun in his arms and took his mouth with a fierce kiss that had him stumbling back a step. He came up short against the bed and she toppled him onto it, then leaned over to plant her hands on either side of his face.

"You've had your turn at the wheel," she said. "Now I want to drive."

He blinked up at her, then a wicked smile tipped up that elegant mouth of his. He reached up, filled his hands with her. "By all means," he said, brushing a kiss over the upper swell of each breast. "Take the wheel."

She trailed a finger along the groove running down the center of his abdomen, flicked open the button of his khakis and slid down the zipper. "I will, thanks," she said.

She found him hot, hard and ready. Renewed need rocked her when he hissed in an appreciative breath at her touch. She was empty, aching, and she wouldn't ever be full until she was closer. Until she'd covered herself with all that lovely heat, drawn that hardness deep inside.

But what about after? a voice whispered in her head. *Will you still be warm after, or will everything just seem colder because he's gone?*

She shoved the thought aside and released him long enough to strip off the last of his clothing, the last of hers. Then she straddled him, shared with him the moist heat that pooled between her own legs, and he rocked up into that melting center. She accommodated him with a smooth little twist of her hips and had the indescribable pleasure of watching those cool, controlled eyes of his go hot and blind. His hands went to her hips, clutched there, stilled her.

"Liz," he said. "Wait. Slow down."

She smiled down at him, wondered if it looked as fierce as it felt. "Hell no," she said. Another quick twist of her hips and she'd taken the very tip of him inside her body. *Taken,* she thought, latching onto the word, focusing on it with grim determination. She had to remember that this was taking.

She slid down onto her elbows, the silky friction of his chest against her skin sending ripples of pleasure straight to her core. He jerked against her and she took him deeper.

Putting her mouth to his ear, she took the lobe between her teeth and bit gently. "I want this, Patrick. Hard. Fast. Sweaty. Give it to me. Now."

He groaned and took her hips in his hands, plunged into her with one swift, sure motion. She gasped, arched back as profound satisfaction shot through her, coupled with a bolt of pure terror. He was in her now, heart, brain and body. She was no longer even a separate being. He'd invaded her very self, and God help her, she craved more. She drove herself down upon him, pulled him deeper even as her brain sputtered and panicked.

She rode him with fierce determination, set a viciously demanding rhythm, but he matched it, rising to meet her in perfect countertempo. He took what she offered, but at the same time stretched her, filled her, fit her so perfectly that a sob rose up and took her completely by surprise. She muffled it against his chest, but he stilled immediately.

"Oh God, Liz." He was hard and aggressive inside her but his voice was gentle, his hands incredibly delicate as they spanned her waist. "What is it?"

She kept her face buried in his shoulder, shook her head silently as she bowed up then sank back down on him. He slid into her as if he'd been custom designed for her body, and she shuddered at the exquisite friction.

"Nothing," she said, and repeated it inside her head like a mantra. Nothing, nothing, nothing. There was nothing here but his body and hers and the primal urge to drive herself onto him until the world shattered out from under her. "It's nothing. Just let me do this. I need it."

"Liz, please." He gasped the words into her mouth. "Are you sure?"

"Yes," she said, and levered herself upright. She reared back, her body a bright flame of pure sensation as she pushed herself higher and harder. His fingers danced over her stomach, delved lower, seeking her most intimate center, but she brushed his hand aside. Whatever she needed, she would take. She couldn't allow him to give it to her.

She drove herself onto him until their bodies were slick with sweat and everything in her tensed and pitched, then went impossibly tight. Her heart stuttered, her body jerked, then she exploded in a shattering instant of pure pleasure. He bowed up under her on a broken cry and followed.

FOR LONG moments, Patrick's world consisted of nothing but his own heartbeat and Liz's ragged breathing. He came slowly back to himself, found that she'd propped her hands against his chest, her elbows locked to keep him at arm's length, her head drooping forward like a wilted daisy.

He slid his fingers up either side of her spine, reveling in the subtle, feminine muscle under the satin of her skin. He speared his fingers deep into the damp heat of her hair, lifted it and watched through narrowed eyes as it sifted slowly back down to settle around her shoulders. She shuddered once and he curled an arm around her.

"Come here," he murmured. She stiffened for a split second and he thought she might refuse, but then she relaxed.

She melted onto him like warm wax, her lips against his throat, one hand laid directly over his heart. A rush of emotion swamped him, so powerful that he had to close his eyes against it. He wrapped his arms around her, brushed his mouth over her hair and drew the hot, sweet scent of her deep into his lungs.

Just for a minute, he told himself, letting his eyes close as he held her. He drifted, let the feelings wash over him as they came. There was love like he'd never imagined—buoyant, sweet and almost painful in its purity. But there was fear, too. Fear, regret, anger, all mixing uneasily with satisfaction and a growing desire to do it all again.

He'd have to sort it out eventually, but for now, for this one moment, he just wanted to savor the trusting weight of her body curled on top of his and the indescribable peace of being inside her.

"Patrick?" Her voice was sleepy and satisfied, and he smiled into the darkness.

"Yeah?"

"My butt's asleep."

He slid his hands down to the curve of her behind, ran a questing finger along the cleft to the place where they were joined. "Feel anything?"

She paused. "No, but that doesn't mean you should stop. I could get feeling back any minute, and I don't think I want to miss this."

He laughed, amazed at how good it felt. He'd always known that sex between them would be explosive, but he hadn't anticipated this easiness afterward. A shred of pain darted through him at the thought of breaking it, but he had to. Soon.

He slapped a hand lightly against her rump and said, "Up for round two, are you?"

She lifted her head, a speculative gleam in her eye. "I am if you are," she murmured with a testing rock of her hips. A shot of pure pleasure cruised through him and she smiled silkily. "Is that a yes?"

He grabbed for her hips, lifted her bodily off him and set her onto the bed next to him. "I wish," he said, sitting up so she couldn't crawl back on and blow his willpower all to hell.

Her eyes wandered down his body. "Looks like more than wishing to me."

"Yeah, well, the flesh is willing, but the conscience says no."

"You don't have a conscience." She shoved lazily at the curtain of rumpled hair in her face. "I'd have noticed it when I arrested you."

"Hey. I turned myself in, didn't I?"

She curled onto her side like a sleek cat and watched him with those sleepy blue eyes. "It's a technicality, but I'll give it to you. I'm feeling generous just now."

Her moonlight-bathed skin was more than he could resist, and he reached out to smooth a palm down the elegant line of her hip. "Yeah? How generous?"

"Want to find out?" She reached for him, but he caught her hand before she could touch him. He'd be lost if she touched him again.

"Yes," he said, bringing her hand to his lips and kissing each knuckle. "God, yes. But I'm not going to. I have to leave."

"What?" She sat up, shoved her hair back, and all that crackling energy dropping back into place around her. "You're leaving? Why?"

"Because Villanueva is somewhere out there painting targets on anybody he thinks I might dislike losing." He rose from the bed, located his pants and stepped into them. "Believe me, Liz, there's nothing I'd rather do than spend all night with my mouth on every inch of your body, but it would be like throwing gasoline on the fire. It's bad enough that I was here this long, that we did what we did with the windows wide open."

Not that he could ever regret the sight of Liz wearing nothing but moonlight, he thought as he buttoned his shirt.

That was something he'd never expected to see and would cherish for the rest of his life.

Her gaze flew to the open window, to the darkened woods beyond, and color crept faintly into her cheeks. She drew up her knees and banded her arms around them.

"What we did here tonight was dangerous to you," he said. "God knows I tried to avoid it."

She regarded him gravely. "You regret it?"

"No." He gave her a lopsided smile in the darkness and shrugged. "God, how could I? I wanted you too much. I still do. But it was reckless and irresponsible nonetheless. I put you at risk when I agreed to work with you. I'm having a hard enough time living with that. I won't make it worse by letting Villanueva guess that we're lovers now, too."

She frowned over that, but she let her knees drop back onto the bed, rested her hands on them. The moonlight worshipped her body and Patrick swallowed hard. Where the hell were his shoes? He had to get out of here. Now. He dropped to his knees and groped under the bed.

"Maybe that wouldn't be such a bad thing," she said slowly.

He froze, head under the bed. "What?"

"Letting Villanueva guess we're lovers. It would piss him off, wouldn't it? That he's been living in exile while you're fucking the woman who put him there? You think it would be enough to force his hand?"

He sat up with exquisite control, because rage was suddenly pumping through him in quick, savage bursts. "You slept with me because you thought it would move your case along faster?"

She drew back as if slapped. "No. I slept with you because I thought it might cure me."

Patrick sat back on his heels, the rage giving way to astonishment. "Cure you of what?"

"Whatever this is that I'm feeling." She didn't look at him. "I told you that."

"I know, but . . ." He gaped at her. "You really thought having sex would cure being in love?"

"Well yeah. Familiarity breeding contempt and all that."

He shook his head, smiled at her in the dark. "Were you even *there* when I was kissing you these past few weeks? How could you have thought that would work?"

She hunched her shoulders. "I was kind of hoping it would be like that time in college when I worked in a pizza parlor. Free pizza, up to my elbows in mozzarella every day. Dream job, right?" She lifted a shoulder. "It never occurred to me that I could OD on pizza. To this day, I can't look a pepperoni in the eye."

Patrick shoved his foot into one shoe, groped under the bed for the other. "So you thought you could OD? On me?"

"Yes, and you should know something," she said. He finally dragged out his other shoe and looked up to find her lying on her stomach across the bed, those pretty breasts pillowed on her crossed arms, her forget-me-not eyes hot and wicked on his.

"What's that?"

"I'm not even close yet."

Blood surged fast and hot through his veins, and his hands itched to touch. He clamped back on the need. "Villanueva—" he began.

"—Is coming after somebody," she finished for him. "Maybe you. Maybe me. Maybe Mara." She didn't mention Evie, Patrick noticed. A small kindness, but he was grateful for it. "Why not bump your sister and her family down the list a little? Make him focus on us. I'm trained for this kind of thing."

"What about me?"

"You seem to have a natural talent for it."

Patrick sat there on his heels for a long moment, staring at her, his shoe forgotten in his hand. She laid there, her skin glowing like she'd been carved from the purest marble, that delicate face alight with the joy at the idea of presenting herself to Jorge Villanueva as bait.

It was madness. He could hardly believe she'd even

proposed it, then reminded himself that she'd also thought it reasonable to fall out of love by ODing on really hot sex.

"Come on," she said now, rising up on her knees to lay a hand against his chest. "He's coming after somebody. Unless you have a better idea—"

"In fact, I do." He shoved his foot into the shoe and stood, backed carefully away from her touch. He couldn't think straight when she was touching him. Hell, he couldn't think straight when she was naked either, and here she was doing both. "I could just pay the guy what I owe him."

"What?"

"I could pay him the money," he said. "His half of the take I screwed him out of, plus a reasonable amount of interest and a bonus for having to live in Central America for six years. It actually comes to a nice little figure. I could have it transferred to a numbered Swiss account, easy as pie. All he needs to do to access it is present himself at the bank. In Zurich."

"You think that's all it's going to take?" She snatched up a robe from the foot of the bed and shoved her arms into it as she stalked the length of the room, her hands raking through her hair. "For God's sake, Patrick, the guy gave up six years of his life. Abandoned his wife and baby. His son, for crying out loud. What makes you think this is about the money?"

Patrick frowned at her. "It's always about money with Villanueva," he said. "He'd never love anything else. It was like his personal mantra."

Liz snorted. "And then you sold him out for the love of your screwup sister."

"Yeah, he probably didn't like that."

She turned to him, her hands balled into fists in the pockets of her robe. "This is a stupid idea, Patrick. He's not after the money. He wants blood."

He went to her, pulled her rigid body into his arms and brushed his lips over that pale golden hair. "Come on, Liz. This isn't the movies, you know. In real life, criminals who can't separate the personal from the professional don't last

very long. You run around offing everybody who screws
you—"

"He killed his ex-wife," she said.

Patrick went utterly still. "What?"

Chapter

21

"THE SON, too," Liz said, her voice threaded with fury. "He slit their throats. Three weeks ago. I spoke to the widower. Guy was a mess still."

"You're sure it was Villanueva?" Patrick asked, a cold ball of dread growing in his lungs, pushing out all the oxygen.

"You know anybody else with motive and a thing for knife work?" She pulled out of his arms. "You can pay him all the money in the world and it's not going to do a damn bit of good. He's taking what he's owed all right, but he doesn't care about the money. He cares about the pain, the betrayal. He wants an eye for an eye. His pound of freaking flesh. Christ." She turned from him again, hands in fists on her hips, her head bowed.

Patrick felt his brain click into motion, automatically processing all the angles, the details that he couldn't consciously focus on over the riot in his heart. "Why would he kill his wife and the boy? Why not kill the new husband, take back what was his?"

"She betrayed him," Liz said softly. "She should have waited for him, raised her son to worship his lost daddy. But she remarried within the year, let the guy claim the boy as his own. She gave away his son, don't you see? But he made her pay. The coroner's report said that the son's time of death was a good two hours before the ex-wife's."

"He killed the boy in front of her," Patrick said slowly.

"That would be my guess, yes." Her voice was cool now, steady, but Patrick still heard the undercurrent of rage in it.

"And now he's here. To collect his debt from me."

"That's right," Liz said. "And since you betrayed him for a woman, smart money says he'll come after the most important woman in your life. He'll want to make you bleed that way first. He'll plan to kill you eventually. That'll be the pièce de résistance but also his little act of mercy. You won't want to live after what he'll make you watch."

The words dried up in his throat and Patrick struggled against a rising tide of fear and anger. "How long have you known about this?"

"About Villanueva offing his family? Or about him looking at you with bloody revenge in his eyes?"

"Either. Both. Jesus, Liz, *how long*?" He grabbed her by the shoulders, spun her to face him. He hauled her up onto her toes, hideous visions of Mara and Evie at the mercy of a madman with a knife dancing through his mind. "You knew this was happening," he said. "You knew he was stalking my family and you didn't *say* anything. You put a higher premium on your fucking badge than the life of an innocent woman and child. What kind of person are you?"

"I'M A cop," she snapped. "That's the kind of person I am. I put surveillance on their house right after their break-in, and added personal security for them both after I found out about Villanueva's wife and kid. Which was this morning, by the way. I didn't leave them twisting in the wind, Patrick. I just didn't tell you what I was doing."

"Why the hell not?" He was nearly shouting, she realized with fascination. She'd never seen such a thing, not from Patrick O'Connor, the king of self-contained cool. "There's no way I'd have stayed here if I'd known I was the reason they were in danger."

"How was I to know that? How was I supposed to know you weren't hooking up with Villanueva for a new job?" she demanded irritably.

"You think I'd do that? Throw away everything I've worked for these past six years?" There was genuine distress in his voice, in the tense lines of his body. At least it looked pretty genuine to Liz. But he could put on any number of emotions, she reminded herself. She'd seen him do it time and again. Still, she didn't like the guilty shame that was starting to crowd in on her logic.

"Of course I thought it! God, who wouldn't? Look at it from my perspective, will you?" she said. "The jewel thief I forced into reluctant retirement arrives in town supposedly to rescue his sister. Only the problem he's rescuing her from is inconsequential at best. Plus he hasn't spoken to her in three years. And, well, they're both from one of America's most notorious criminal families. But, hey, they've been clean a long time. There's no reason to think one or both of them are coming out of retirement, is there? Maybe it's nothing.

"But wait, then the fugitive ex-partner—who's been MIA for the past six years, by the way—turns up in the very same small town the very same week and sets off a rash of minor B and E reports. Coincidence? Okay, now we're stretching it a little bit."

She folded her arms and glared at him. "But wait, it gets better. Because then the jewel thief—sorry the *ex*-jewel thief—talks his way onto the FBI payroll, onto *my* caseload, and instead of sharing his suspicions about his ex-partner and what's really going on, tries like hell to divide my attention by launching an improbable but convenient seduction campaign out of the blue. So tell me, Patrick, where did my logic go wrong? Did I miss the part where you did or said something that would inspire me to trust you? The part where *you* shared information instead of just demanding that I tell you everything and get nothing in return?"

She twitched her shoulders in a bad-tempered shrug. "You gave me absolutely no reason to trust you, so I didn't. I won't apologize for that."

She spit the words at him but shame was a choking mass in her throat. It was all true, of course, but that didn't mean she was right. And it didn't mean he was wrong.

"You really believe I'd do that?" he asked again, his voice hard, his eyes glacial. "You think I'd let a monster like Villanueva within a hundred miles of my sister for any reason, let alone a score?" He shook his head. "You're not in love with me, Liz. You don't even know what the word means if you think I could do that."

She held herself perfectly still, not even daring to breathe for fear she'd splinter like glass. He was right, of course. She didn't know how to love anybody, not in any healthy way. That part of her heart had been broken years ago. The place in her soul where she'd imagined love lay empty. It had been nothing but an illusion, a wish. She could see that now. The hole in her chest ached and spread until her limbs were dead weight, her body a block of ice.

"But this wasn't about me at all, was it?" he went on, and she felt each word like a separate blow. "This was about you, your badge and your ambition. Well, congratulations. You played this one like a pro. Not that I'm complaining. I've been used before, but never so enjoyably." He glanced pointedly at his watch. "You know, I have a few minutes after all. I could stay. We could do it again." He reached for her. "We can leave the windows open, too. In case Villa-nueva missed your screaming my name the first time."

She shook her head and backed away from him, her stomach clenching with each vicious word. Rage pumped off him in tangible waves, but she couldn't look away from the awful beauty of his face.

"I'm sorry," she whispered. "I made a mistake. I'm so sorry."

"Liz. Darling." The drawl was back, but it only sharpened the cutting edges of his words. "I think I liked you better ruthless. At least it was honest."

He turned from her then, walked out of the bedroom as if loathe to share even air with her. The desire rose up strong and urgent to run after him, to explain. To beg, if necessary. She'd try harder. She'd be better. She'd prove to him that she was worth a second chance.

She'd actually taken two faltering steps toward the door with the intention of doing just that when cold realization finally broke through the shame.

He'd manipulated her, she realized on a sudden flash of fury. He'd played her masterfully. The bastard.

She flew into motion without conscious thought, caught up to him in the foyer. She snagged a handful of his ridiculously expensive shirt and jerked him back, shoved him against the wall where he'd kissed her senseless just an hour before.

"How dare you talk to me about honesty?" she spat. He came off the wall with a snarl and she knocked him back with the heel of her hand. To her fierce satisfaction, he stayed put. "You, the virtuoso manipulator. You set me up with consummate skill, I'll give you that. Drawing the seduction out over long, aching days until I was so lost to reason I couldn't tell the difference between love and lust, until I was all but begging you to sleep with me. You must have loved that. Well, now you've won. You fucked the woman who fucked you all those years ago. Did it make you happy to dismiss me? Reject me? It must have been sweet to render judgment like that, to find me so morally deficient that even you couldn't stomach my company."

"Liz, I didn't manipulate—"

"The hell you didn't." The words were boiling out of her now without any conscious thought, carried on a pent-up stream of hurt and fury. "I almost ran out here and begged you to forgive me. Can you believe that? *You* brought this ugliness to Mara's house and *I'm* running after *you*, crying apologies for not protecting her better. But you knew

I would. You wanted that. God, you'd think I'd learn, but no. Here I am again, some brilliant amoral bastard using my own heart against me until I'm nothing but a trick pony. But I'm not that little girl anymore, Patrick. No matter how good you are, I cut my teeth on better. I'm not responsible for somebody else's acts of viciousness. I'm sworn to protect and serve, and I save who I can, but not at any cost. I'm nobody's victim. Not anymore. And I won't be yours now."

"Liz." Patrick stuffed his hands into his pockets, and she could see anger fighting with confusion in every taut line of his body. "What are you talking about? Did somebody hurt you?"

"I want you to go." She forced her spine to stay rigid as the anger ebbed, leaving her limp and exhausted. She'd probably regret every word she'd just hurled at him in five minutes, but right now, all she wanted was to be alone. "I'm sure you'll want to judge for yourself whether the security I put on Mara this morning is up to your exacting standards."

He stared at her for a long, brittle moment, his face blank and remote. "Fine."

It wasn't until the door closed behind him that she realized she hadn't collected the recording device clipped to his belt. God, they hadn't even verbally debriefed. She'd been too busy devouring his body. Heated memory washed over her—his lips on her skin, the taste of his kiss, those clever hands on her body—followed by a punishing shock of loss. It was amazing how quickly and completely she'd accomplished her original goal. Without much effort, too.

Heartbreak achieved. Good for her. She must have a natural aptitude for it.

She shook off the hurt and forced herself to think about how pissed Goose would be when she logged on in the morning and there was no new data. But she'd be damned if she'd run after him now, because she'd just realized something else.

He'd walked out her door without a word about her alarm.

Since he'd been back in town he'd never once left her house without either setting the alarm himself or reminding her to do it. It had become something of a ritual between them and she'd gotten used to the luxury of his concern. But he hadn't checked tonight, and she knew why.

Keeping her safe was no longer a priority with Patrick O'Connor.

She set the system with clumsy fingers, then walked slowly to the bathroom. She brushed her teeth and washed her face as she always did, then straightened her sheets with automatic motions.

She crawled into her bed only to discover that while her heart was utterly numb, her body was not. It was a glorious symphony of aches and twinges, as if Patrick had branded her with every touch, every kiss.

She stared at the ceiling for a long time. Then in the still, quiet hour before dawn, she curled into an anguished knot and wept.

LIZ'S CELL phone twinkled merrily from the floor, and she sat up, blinking in the early morning light. Shoving a tangled mass of hair from her eyes, she stumbled out of bed and began pawing through the twisted mass of clothing strung out between the foot of her bed and her front door. The memory of Patrick stripping it all off her brought a rush of pain that knocked her back onto her heels, but she breathed through it.

This had been the plan, she reminded herself sternly. Trigger the heartbreak, survive it, maybe gain some sort of immunity for the future.

Cold comfort, she decided. Damn cold.

The phone rang again and she found it under her jeans.

"Liz Brynn," she croaked.

"Good morning," Goose chirped. "I didn't wake you, did I?"

Liz glared at her bedside clock. It was 6:12 A.M. "At this

hour? Lord, no. I've already had breakfast and milked the cows."

Goose laughed. "Oh, good. Then you won't mind that I'm on your front porch."

Liz shoved herself into her robe, shuffled into her front room and drew aside the curtain. Goose was standing right there on the porch, looking fresh, pressed and polished. *As always,* Liz thought bitterly. Goose flipped her cell phone shut with her chin, displayed two large to-go cups of coffee and wiggled one finger in an apologetic little wave. Liz sighed and disengaged the alarm.

"Good morning, sunshine," Goose sang as she sailed into Liz's living room. Liz started to snarl, but Goose pressed a coffee into her hand and said, "Drink. We don't have time for a mood this morning."

Liz lifted it to her nose, inhaled deeply. Even the fumes had a nice little punch. She peeled off the lid and sipped cautiously. Hot as lava, black as tar. Just the way she liked it.

Goose watched her go at the coffee with an alarming combination of amusement and sympathy. "It's a double depth charge," she said. "I figured you'd need the hit."

"Why's that?" Liz asked slowly. Her brain was beginning to clear and she didn't like the implications here. An early-morning house call from a female agent, hot designer coffee and a face that all but screamed *sorry you fucked the wrong guy.*

"Patrick called me last night," Goose said.

"Oh Christ."

"He only said that you and he hadn't had time for a decent debrief," Goose said, her eyes sharp, her face carefully neutral. "And that Oz is picking him up to pass the new hundreds this morning."

Liz fumbled the coffee. "What? God, what time?"

"Easy there," Goose said, plucking the sloshing cup from her fingers. "We have a few minutes. I wasn't as concerned with what he said as what he didn't." Her dark eyes were warm and full of that awful sympathy again. "Oh, honey, I was kind of pulling for you. But you gave in, didn't you?"

Liz arranged her face into a blank. "What do you mean?"

Goose sighed. "You slept with him. And don't bother to deny it. I can see the trail of clothes leading to your bedroom. And not to be rude, but honey, you sure don't look like you had a great night's sex."

Liz frowned. "The sex was great."

Goose pursed up her red lips and considered. "Just not the rest of the night?"

"Something like that."

She handed Liz the coffee again. "Drink up, honey. Oz is picking Patrick up at ten at Brightwater's. We have to go wheedle an unmarked car with surveillance capabilities out of maintenance." She cast a critical eye over Liz's robe. "Is that Burberry?"

Liz ignored her, took the coffee into her bedroom. Why the hell was everybody so hung up on her bathrobe? "Give me a minute to get dressed," she called over her shoulder.

"Take your time," Goose called back as Liz dove into her closet. "And do something about those bags under your eyes, will you? Have a little pride."

FOUR HOURS later, Liz was balancing a laptop on her knees while Goose flew along the two-lane highway, a modest couple of cars behind the old Volvo station wagon that Patrick had stepped into ten minutes earlier. Liz frowned at the screen, poked a few keys and let out a triumphant "Ha." She'd accessed last night's recording that Patrick had finally handed over half an hour earlier. Neither of them had seen it yet. "Okay, it's downloading."

"Good. Turn up the volume so I can hear it, too." Goose tapped the brakes as a rusty pickup in front of them pulled onto the shoulder and turned onto a dirt road. "Oh, damn. There goes one of my lead cars." She paused a moment. "Well, shit, there go the other two."

Liz glanced up at the stretch of empty road between them and the Volvo. "Just maintain your distance," she said, then turned her attention back to the laptop. "Okay, here we go."

The video was dark and grainy, but the audio was pretty clear. She could hear the DJ leading Patrick off the dance floor and into the twisting hallways of the club's basement. And then they stepped into a pool of harsh light and the DJ's scruffy smirk filled the screen.

"Oz, I presume?" she heard Patrick ask.

"At your service."

"Oh, hell," Liz said.

"What?" Goose shot her a quick look. "What?"

"Wonderful." Patrick's voice filled the car, impatient and pissed. *"Just wonderful. You'd better be as good as I've heard. If I bring a sixteen-year-old DJ to the set and he's not a fucking counterfeiting wunderkind? Well, let's just say it'll be unpleasant."*

Goose whistled through her teeth. "Oz is the DJ?"

"Looks that way." Liz pressed balled fists to her weary eyes. "Donald S. Brady. High school junior, excellent fake ID."

"No way is this guy in high school. He's twenty-five, easy."

". . . and second, I'm not sixteen."

"See?" Goose smiled at the road, her eyes glued to the Volvo cruising ahead of them at a conservative five over.

"I ran him after he let Villanueva jump Patrick in the basement," Liz said. "He's seriously still in high school."

"You think I don't recognize you? Please. I was you. Fifteen?"

"God. Seventeen."

"See?" Liz paused the playback and leaned back to stare at the stained fabric of the unmarked car's ceiling. "I was going to bust him this morning. Well, maybe not bust him per se, but maybe make a little house call to see if his folks knew he was moonlighting as a twenty-five-year-old DJ and a counterfeiter's errand boy." She rocked her head back and forth as if the motion could shake loose a new plan. "This complicates things a bit."

"Holy shit!" Goose yelped and punched the gas. "Somebody else is in the car. And I don't think Oz knew about it. Must've been in the backseat or something."

Liz jerked upright and sure enough, there was a third figure silhouetted between Oz and Patrick in the Volvo. The car swerved wildly and then corrected, the driver clearly agitated.

"Oh Christ, what's this now?" Liz muttered. She snapped the laptop shut and grabbed up the binoculars between the seats. Goose closed the distance between the cars as Liz focused.

"It's Villanueva," she announced. Her voice was grim, but her heart was pounding out a wild, fear-laced rhythm. "I think he's holding a knife on Patrick."

Liz watched as Patrick handed something slowly over the seat to Villanueva's free hand, then a passenger-side window rolled down. Something small and black flew past Liz's window. "There go our eyes."

"Well, shit," Goose said. "I loved that cell phone camera."

I love him, Liz thought, then blinked as the words almost came out of her mouth. It had been an automatic, unconscious response, rising up from the deepest place in her heart. God, it must be true. She hadn't known what to think after last night, but this certainly clarified things. When it came down to it, she'd rather Patrick not actually die just yet.

She reached for the radio.

Chapter

22

"WHAT THE fuck?" Oz craned his neck to look into the backseat where Villanueva had appeared. "Listen, man, we made a deal—I set up a few meetings for you with Mr. Hollywood here and you let me rotate my operation through the brewery. Nobody said anything about you fucking killing the guy in my car, okay?"

Patrick glanced at Oz. "This is your landlord?"

"Yeah. He owns the whole building. Cargo, the brewery. Everything." His smile was wan. "Reasonable rates."

Patrick glanced in the rearview mirror at Villanueva. "That's a lot of investment for a little revenge."

"It pays to be thorough." Villanueva smiled thinly, then shifted his attention to Oz. "Lose the cops, please," he said, his voice obscenely mild for a guy holding a seven-inch combat blade to Patrick's throat.

"Cops?" Oz glared at Patrick.

"In the white sedan, maybe a hundred yards back. Speaking of which, let's have the wire, O'Connor."

Patrick didn't demur. He handed the cell phone to

Villanueva, who buzzed down his window, flicked the cell phone out onto the highway and conscientiously buzzed the window back up.

"Jesus, O'Connor," Oz said with great disgust. "What did I tell you about wires?"

"Oz," Villanueva said again. "The cops. Lose them."

"Whatever you say, dude." He spun the wheel like a stunt driver and hit the brakes. The car lurched into a deep skid that had Patrick's gut dropping into his knees. As if he wasn't in quite enough mortal peril. Jesus.

The rear bypassed the hood, then the car squealed to a halt in the passing lane, facing the wrong direction. Patrick could see Liz's face as she and Goose shot by in the unmarked car. Her eyes were huge, her expression grim. He managed a weak little wave.

Oz punched the gas and the car bucked forward, heading back toward Grief Creek.

"Turn here," Villanueva said, and Oz jerked the wheel to the right. They skidded onto a gravel farm road, the car fishtailing wildly and then correcting. They took a curve in the road on what felt like two wheels and Patrick swallowed hard.

"So, Patrick," Villanueva said. "Are you ready to settle up?"

"I've already arranged for payment," Patrick said. "Your half of the take I screwed you out of at a nice interest rate, plus a substantial bonus for your years in sunny Central America. It's all waiting for you."

The knife remained steady at his throat while Oz negotiated another curve at a heart-stopping speed. Villanueva tapped the fingers of his free hand against Patrick's headrest. "How accommodating of you," he said. "Waiting for me where?"

"Zurich. There's a one-way ticket being held for you at LAX." Patrick set his jaw, willing his face to remain utterly impassive. Villanueva had always been a ruthless bastard. If he suspected even for an instant that Patrick's intense desire to continue breathing stemmed solely from a need to protect his loved ones, he wouldn't hesitate to slit his throat right here. He'd probably force Oz to bury his body in one of the farm fields whipping past the windows.

"Not that it hasn't been lovely seeing you again," Patrick murmured politely. "It's just that you're a rather uncomfortable acquaintance to acknowledge at this particular juncture."

Villanueva laughed and the sound sent an ugly ripple up Patrick's spine. "So you *are* fucking the little blond cop."

"It's a goal," Patrick managed, keeping his voice light and careless. "And your presence in town hasn't exactly favored my cause."

"Then I'll just get out of your hair," Villanueva said, leaning close to Patrick's ear. He smelled like sour sweat and years of rage. "But I'll leave you with a little something for your generous cooperation. A parting gift, as it were."

"Oh?" Patrick met Villanueva's eyes in the rearview mirror. They were black and burning with hatred in a tanned, sharp-boned face.

"Pull over," Villanueva said to Oz, who complied with alacrity. The car skidded to a halt and the sudden stillness was awful and charged. Villanueva pressed the knife to Patrick's skin until a thin, warm dribble of blood ran down the column of his throat. Patrick forced his breathing to remain steady even as he lifted one questioning brow at Villanueva's reflection.

God, I'm sorry, Liz, he thought. There was so much more he wanted to say. That he loved her. That he had for years. That he wanted so many more years to keep loving her, to spend exactly as he'd spent the night before—in her arms, in her heart.

But if he could protect her from this evil, he'd gamble with whatever was necessary. Even his life.

He waited for Villanueva to jerk the knife to the left, to finish him. But he didn't. Instead, he leaned forward and dropped a manila envelope onto Patrick's lap.

"I think you'll find this interesting," he said. "A little light reading. Enjoy it. I know I did."

He sheathed the knife, slapped the back of Patrick's

headrest and slipped out the door. He disappeared into a wooded field before Patrick had sucked in his first full breath.

Patrick and Oz sat in silence, both staring straight out the dusty windshield for what seemed like an eternity. Then Oz reached slowly across Patrick, clicked open the glove box and handed him a paper napkin.

"You're bleeding," he said quietly.

Patrick took the napkin, dabbed it against the shallow cut in his throat. His hands were trembling, he noticed. Christ, his entire body was vibrating under the twin assaults of relief and adrenaline. A helicopter buzzed overhead and Patrick could feel it in every oversensitized pore.

"What should we do now?" Oz asked.

"Sit tight and put both hands on the wheel," Patrick said. "Nice and high."

Oz frowned but complied. "Why?"

"Because the cops are about to arrest you, and they get nervous if they can't see your hands."

His face went white, and he suddenly looked exactly like the kid he was. "Wait, what now?"

Patrick only tapped one ear with his finger and cocked his head. Sirens wailed in the distance, getting louder and closer. The helicopter buzzed by again, lower this time.

"Fuck that." Oz tried to jerk out of the seat, but he was still belted in. He started fumbling with the clasp as the sirens approached. "I have five thousand in fake hundreds in my wallet."

"I know," Patrick said. "I was looking forward to watching you pass them, too."

The first cop car screeched around the bend in the road behind them and Patrick shrugged. "Well, here we go."

Oz laid his head against the steering wheel. "Shit."

"Yeah."

LIZ'S STOMACH was sour, her eyes burning with fatigue as she slipped out of Interview Room Two, leaving Goose to referee while Oz's parents berated each other with discouraging gusto. It was no more than she'd expected. She doubted they'd voluntarily been in the same room since finalizing their divorce. Which probably hadn't been a bad parenting decision, judging from their current behavior. They'd turned on each other like rabid dogs the minute Liz had informed them of their son's extracurricular activities.

She slipped into the observation room and her heart stuttered to a halt when she spotted Patrick there, lounged elegantly over the gimpy folding chair that faced the one-way glass. A small white bandage stood out in stark relief against the tanned column of his throat, and her knees went watery at the reminder of how very close he'd come to dying today. She recovered her stride just before he turned those glacial eyes her way.

"You caught the show?" she asked as she fed the Coke machine a few quarters. She belted back the sugar and caffeine with the exhausted desperation of an addict.

"Yeah," Patrick said. "Nice touch, turning them on each other like that when their son needs their full attention. They teach you that in cop school?"

The fog enveloping her brain surrendered to the caffeine just in time for her to catch the thread of disgust in his voice. She shrugged and pressed the cold can first to one eye, then the other. It was too late to change his opinion of her. Truth be told, she didn't even want to. What would be the point? So he'd think well of her from his separate future across the country? It was enough that he was alive to have a future of any sort.

She'd just have to pray that her tenuous grip on all the pieces of her heart held long enough for her to arrest Villanueva and get Patrick out of town.

She watched Goose exit the interview room through the one-way glass. The Bradys barely noticed.

"God." Goose shuddered as she slipped into the observation room. "That poor kid."

"Yeah," Liz said. "Have either of them asked to see him yet?"

"Nope. Too busy divvying up the blame."

Liz shook her head, her heart somehow finding room for another ache at the memory of being seventeen herself and searching desperately for a life that made sense of her gifts. With the kind of moral guidance these two had provided, it was a wonder Oz—Donald, she corrected herself—hadn't decided to go into arson. "The kid must have been conceived in a moment of wild optimism."

"Or an alcoholic stupor."

"Yeah, that's probably more the case." They stood in silence for another few moments while Liz finished her Coke and tossed the can into the recycling bin. Patrick watched the Bradys fling accusations at each other with increasing vitriol through the one-way glass.

"Listen," Liz said, drawing Goose toward the far wall and lowering her voice. "I know this is technically a Secret Service collar and I don't want to step on your toes, but can I make a suggestion?"

At Goose's nod, she said, "Recommend counseling, reparations and community service in lieu of a formal charge. I know he could be tried as an adult, but—"

"Yeah, I was thinking that myself." Goose smiled, but it was a little crumpled around the edges. "He's well old enough. It won't be an easy sell with the DA."

"I'll do whatever I can to help out."

"I'll set up a meeting with the DA and invite the whole family. That ought to go a long way toward generating some sympathy for the kid." Goose glanced at the bickering couple on the other side of the glass and sighed. "Let those two wear themselves out a few minutes more, then cut them loose. I'm going to make some phone calls, see what I can do."

"Thanks," Liz said. Goose patted Patrick's shoulder on her way out and he reached up to touch the back of her hand, flashing her the sweetest smile Liz had ever seen. She closed her eyes against a punishing wave of jealousy and hurt. She'd never seen such honest and uncomplicated affection in his face and it was a revelation. Had she really thought he wasn't capable of that sort of emotion? Why had it never occurred to her that he just wasn't interested in bestowing any of it on her? God, she was screwed up.

"So what's on tap for our young friend now, Liz?" Patrick's voice was smooth and urbane as always, but she could still hear the thin sliver of disgust in it.

She forced her face into a cool mask. "It's out of my hands. He's in the system now."

"The system, huh?" Patrick turned those piercingly blue eyes on her. "You think the system will do any better by him than it did by you?"

Her heart stopped, swelled painfully against her ribs, then shrank down into a hard, black nugget. He knew. He knew who she was. What she'd been. She should have known he'd find out sooner or later. She'd said too much last night, and he'd opted for sooner.

"The system saved my life," she said carefully.

"No, Liz. Your grandmother saved your life when she pulled you out of it." He regarded her with hard eyes. "Mrs. Lacey Brynn Chambers. Socialite, heiress and the unlikely savior of one damaged little girl the system couldn't have cared less about."

She stared at him blindly. "What are you talking about?" she asked, even though she knew it was pointless to pretend she didn't know.

"I'm talking about before, Liz. Before you were rescued. Before your granny plucked you out of your precious system. Before you had your trust fund, your education, your fresh start. Before you became super-agent Liz Brynn."

Liz shook her head in silent plea, but Patrick went on.

"Come on, Liz, this is history we're talking about. You were the most famous face in America for a while there. You were on the cover of *Time, Newsweek, People, The New York Times, The Washington Post.*"

"How did you find this out?" Liz asked, hating the tremble in her voice. "Nobody's ever made this connection before. My grandmother made sure of it."

He smiled at her. "A parting gift from Villanueva, who

asked me to tell you the FBI database isn't quite as well secured as it could be." His smile died. "It is, however, extremely thorough. I was shocked to see how much the two of us have in common."

"Were you?"

He inclined his head and studied her with unfriendly eyes. "Tell me, Liz, from one child of crime to another, how does the daughter of the country's most famous criminal grow into a woman who'd throw the book at a neglected child?"

Chapter

23

"IT WASN'T easy." She smiled faintly, or tried to. It might not have worked. She couldn't tell from his face. She couldn't tell anything from his face. "Getting from there to here. I could have just wallowed in my victimhood for the rest of my life, I suppose. Being a victim is pretty damned seductive. Just ask my father. He built an empire around it."

"Your father was no victim."

"Did I say he was?" Liz rolled her eyes. "Please. Pay attention here, Patrick. I'm not going to go over this more than once. My father was a cult leader. He capitalized on other people's victimhood. He gathered up all the broken, sad, disenfranchised people he could find and recast them as martyrs. Victims. God's chosen ones, enduring the slings and arrows of the secular world in exchange for eternal glory." She shrugged, the past shrinking in on her like an ill-fitting jacket. "If life is going to suck, it's so much more satisfying to think it sucks for a reason, you know? They spoon-fed it to us with our mother's milk. We were different. Special. We were The Chosen, handpicked by God to live by the sacred law as He revealed it. Funny thing, though. God only ever talked to my father. Which might explain, if you were the skeptical sort, why God was so concerned with his flock's sexual practices. But hey, it made sense, right? God wanted his prophets to have lots of wives so they could have lots of children. Strength in numbers, you see?"

Patrick didn't say anything, only continued regarding her with those still, unreadable eyes. Liz rolled her shoulders and plowed on.

"Sometimes a brother or sister left us, and we mourned them as if they had died. Even though we saw them in town with their hair cut short and their legs and arms showing, we knew their souls were condemned to the fiery depths of an eternal burning hell. And we were more afraid of hell than of anything, except maybe my father. Because to us, he *was* God. He interpreted the scripture, he received the revelations. He blessed us, he baptized us, he banished us."

She stopped, unable to go on.

"And he gave away little girls as wives to anybody who had the power to line his pockets or advance his ambitions," Patrick said, a bubbling river of rage in his voice. "As if he hadn't already stolen enough money from his congregations. Christ, Liz, you were a *child*. Your wedding dress was all ribbons and bows, like you'd been fucking gift wrapped for some sick old man."

"I know," Liz said, bile rising up in her throat. She'd never forget that day. Her wedding day. The scent of dust and blood, the foreign pop of gunfire interrupting the ceremony, the heat and noise and confusion. FBI agents in black flak jackets swarming through the makeshift church like locusts, trampling her flowers, staining her dress. "But it didn't happen. Not to me."

"That was an accident of timing," Patrick said softly. "If the FBI had scheduled their raid one day later, that lucky photographer would have captured you as innocence shattered rather than innocence saved."

"Is that what you think you saw?" She looked at him, startled. "Innocence saved? Is that what America found in that photo?"

"Hell, yes. It was a pretty powerful image, Liz. A young girl teetering on the edge of womanhood, young enough to burrow down into the arms of that agent and cry, woman enough to know what that virginal white dress she was wearing meant. You knew exactly what that agent was saving you from, Liz. It was written all over your face. That's what America responded to."

"I guess I never thought about it that way. I only knew what I saw when I looked at it." She laughed softly, bitterly. "You see, I'd been taught that my only value to God was in fulfilling my sacred duty to marry as He directed," she said. "By preventing my marriage, I thought those agents were sentencing me to hell."

"What?"

"They stopped me from obeying God's will for me. They made me sinful. Unclean."

"Bullshit," Patrick said roughly.

Liz shook her head. "When that agent picked me up, I clung to him because he was huge and scary and strong, and I thought maybe the devil wouldn't come for me if I stayed in his arms. That famous picture wasn't of a little girl weeping over a near miss with polygamy. It was a picture of a little girl weeping over the eternity she'd have to spend in hell. It took years to understand I'd been saved, not damned."

She gave him a lopsided smile. "Saved, Patrick. By the system that you're so fond of denigrating. If it hadn't been for the system, I'd have lived in uneducated poverty with a dozen or so sister wives, pumping out as many babies as possible to pave my way to heaven. If it hadn't been for the system, I'd never have understood that what I'd been taught was God's will was nothing but the ruthless ambition of a sociopathic abuser and I doubt I'd have even survived.

"But that raid produced a photograph that put my face in front of every influential person in the country, including my grandmother. Not that she was instantly filled with grandmotherly love for a kid she'd never even met. Losing her daughter—my mother—to a cult had broken her heart too badly for that sort of nonsense. But whatever she lacked in love, she made up for in responsibility and duty. She gave me a home, a name, a top-notch education and the anonymity to live as normal a life as possible. She also gave me that ridiculously expensive bathrobe you like so much. And it's all because of the system you hate.

"I'm not saying it's perfect, because God knows it's not. But it's the only thing that stands between abusers and the people who are too vulnerable to protect themselves. I wouldn't call Donald Brady abused, not by any stretch. But he's still a child, a badly neglected child, who deserves everything the system can provide in terms of the guidance and discipline his parents failed to give him. He needs to pay for what he did. That's right and just. But he shouldn't pay with blood, nor with his future. I'll do everything I can to see to that."

Patrick stared at her for a long moment. "You really believe you can make that happen?"

She returned his gaze, unflinching. "I can't promise anything. But I'll exhaust every avenue open to me on his behalf."

He shook his head slowly. "How can you still be this innocent after everything you've lived through? Everything you've seen? You charge that kid and he's going to jail. And all he's going to learn there is how to be a better criminal."

"But letting him skip out on any formal consequences of his actions isn't going to teach him how to be a better citizen, either," Liz said. "He needs to face this. The system needs to work."

"Christ." Patrick raked both hands through his hair and turned from her, stalked to the one-way glass where the Bradys were now disregarding each other in icy silence. "You're acting like God himself carved the U.S. legal system on stone tablets and handed it down from on high. I don't think you really ever recovered from that extremist childhood of yours, Liz. You still can't understand shades of gray. You just transferred all that blind faith from God to the FBI."

Liz stared at him, stunned. She wanted to dismiss him, to scoff at the very idea, but something inside her vibrated like a struck bell. Could that be true? Had she somehow managed to devote herself just as rigidly to FBI policy and procedure as she had to her childhood religion?

Her phone buzzed at her hip, and she moved carefully so as not to shatter. She felt as fragile as spun glass all of a sudden.

"Liz Brynn," she said into the phone.

Thirty seconds later, she slowly closed the phone.

"SAC Bernard wants us in his office," she told Patrick. "Now."

PATRICK FOLLOWED Liz's rigid shoulders down the narrow aisle between cubicles and into SAC Bernard's office. It was spotless, as usual. If the man actually worked in this space, he hid it well.

An invisible and efficient admin clicked the door shut behind them, and Patrick instinctively put himself next to Liz, who was standing at attention in front of Bernard's massive desk. Regardless of any argument he had with her philosophy on crime and punishment, whatever she was going to face here was on him, too. No matter what he'd just said, no matter how true it turned out to be, he admired what she'd done with her life. Hell, he marveled at it.

But everybody had their limit. He'd be damned if he'd stand back and let Liz reach hers alone.

"Have a seat," Bernard said with a nod at the stiff-backed chairs behind them.

Liz looked briefly startled, but she sat. Patrick followed suit. "Villanueva was in the car with you and Donald Brady for approximately eight minutes after he discarded the recording device," Bernard said to Patrick. "This is your one opportunity to tell us what was arranged during that time."

Liz frowned. "I've already interviewed Mr. O'Connor on this matter," she said. "He stated that Villanueva neither made new demands nor indicated a time or place for further meetings. He simply reiterated his demand for payment."

Bernard ignored Liz and kept those cold gray eyes trained on Patrick. "Information was exchanged," he repeated. "Information Villanueva wanted to remain private, a desire with which you readily complied. I'm giving you a chance here, O'Connor. We've always dealt fairly with you. Give us what we're after, and we can protect you. You haven't done anything you can't recover from so far, but you're perilously close to the line."

"What are you implying?" Patrick asked. He always liked to see his opponent's cards, and sometimes all you had to do was ask, especially with the truly unimaginative.

"I want to know what you're partnering with Villanueva on." Bernard spoke without inflection. "I'm prepared to deal leniently with you if you can provide what we need to put him away."

Patrick let his brows rise in lazy surprise. "I'll admit the upstanding life hasn't always been my cup of tea, but I don't think I've backslid to a degree quite that significant. Surely you can't imagine that this entire stalking business Villanueva's been engaging in—the break-ins at Liz's and my sister's, the surprise left hook in a dance club basement, the armed carjacking—has all been a tricky ruse to throw you off the trail?" Patrick let a mocking smile curve his lips. "I write movies. I don't live them. Criminals are simple people, SAC Bernard. You of all people should know that. Villanueva just wants the money."

Bernard gazed at him for long, tense moments, those granite eyes of his suddenly sharp and weary. "Think about it," he said finally. "You pursue your own ends any further, and I can't sanction your activities as undercover work. You'll be off the reservation."

Patrick held his gaze and wondered for a moment exactly how much Bernard knew. Was he really warning him away from another heist with his long-lost partner, or had he somehow connected the dots and realized that Patrick was running his own little sting operation counter to the FBI's long-standing desire to put Villanueva in jail? Did Bernard somehow know about the Swiss account with enough cash in it to persuade crazier bastards than Villanueva to put down thoughts of revenge forever? Did he suspect Patrick's plans to finish off Villanueva himself if the cash didn't do the trick?

All he said was, "With all due respect, I've never really been *on* the reservation. The FBI and I? We make deals, not alliances. That said, however, rest assured that I quite enjoy my life as it stands. I have no plans to jeopardize it by pulling one last job with a violent thug I left behind years ago."

It was all true. Each and every word. The problem was in what he hadn't said. A lie of omission was still a lie, after all. And while he didn't mind lying to SAC Bernard one bit, it pained him to mislead Liz. But what else could he do? If she knew he'd moved beyond considering making a deal with Villanueva, if she knew that he'd already decided to deal with Villanueva himself rather than let the FBI try to arrest him, she'd only be doubly determined to catch him with her own bare hands. That was the problem with idealists. They were so damned extreme.

Bernard let a few uncomfortable seconds tick by, then said, "In that case, I'll simply thank you for your assistance in the Donald Brady matter. You'll forgive me if I suggest that you return to California as soon as possible? In the unfortunate event that Villanueva does engage in any further illegal activity, you'd be wise to learn of it from across the country."

"I would indeed," Patrick said, flashing him a look he hoped was full of humble gratitude.

"If you'll excuse us, Mr. O'Connor, I need to have a word with Agent Brynn."

"Certainly," Patrick said, rising and taking the man's offered hand. He wanted to turn and walk out, just make the break and live with it. But in the end, he couldn't do it quite so coldly. No matter how much he paid Villanueva, he couldn't ever see Liz again. It wouldn't be safe for her, and if he were perfectly honest with himself, he would admit that he didn't know how many more of these partings his heart could take. He ought to walk right out that door and leave her behind—safely behind—once and for all.

But he couldn't abide the thought of not touching her just once more.

He turned and extended his hand to her, as if it was a professional courtesy and not a soul-deep hunger to feel the press of her skin against his. "It was a pleasure working with you, Agent Brynn."

She came to her feet and frowned at him but took his hand. She gave it a brisk pump, and Patrick couldn't help smiling. It was so very Liz, he thought. After everything he'd put her through these past two weeks she should have refused to suffer his touch. But she didn't shrink from the difficult and she didn't give in to pettiness. She simply stood up and put her hand in his.

He knew the memory would have to last him, so he lingered over it just a shade longer than professionally acceptable, letting the feel of that small capable hand carve itself on his brain.

It put one final dent in his heart to be the one to pull away. She just stood there, frowning at him, a wealth of confusion and wariness in those forget-me-not eyes.

"Good-bye, Liz," he said, and left.

LIZ STARED at the door Patrick had just clicked shut behind him. There had been something chillingly final in that casual little good-bye, and it had arrowed straight into the depths of her soul. What had just happened there?

"I want twenty-four-hour surveillance on O'Connor," Bernard said, breaking abruptly into Liz's reverie.

"What?" she asked. Her brain wasn't firing on all synapses today. If Patrick had planned to dull her reflexes—and she couldn't say for certain that he hadn't—he couldn't have done a better job than stringing together the events of the past twenty-four hours. Between the sex, the sleepless night, the heartbreak, the fear of Villanueva slitting Patrick's throat on the highway, and this new nagging feeling that she'd lost him just as permanently this very minute, Liz didn't know which end was up. But she forced herself to focus on Bernard.

"I want twenty-four-hour surveillance on O'Connor," Bernard said again. "He's planning something. Guys like that don't change."

The caution that had been Liz's governing impulse her entire life suddenly failed her. She wasn't interested in listening right now to how people didn't change. She hadn't worked for the past twenty years to put the past behind her only to have everybody from her ill-chosen lover to the gatekeeper of her career tell her that it couldn't be done. It was the final straw that pushed her beyond control.

"Guys like what?" she snapped. "To the best of my knowledge, Patrick O'Connor is one of a kind. If all thieves came just like him, we'd be shit out of luck as an agency because we'd never catch a one."

"You forget yourself, Agent Brynn." Bernard didn't raise his voice, but the temperature dropped several warning degrees.

"No, I just remembered myself," Liz shot back. "O'Connor's a source, an independent consultant. Not a criminal, not a prisoner, not even a formal suspect of any kind. If he's willing to help us work the angles of the Villanueva case, fine. Great. If not, he's subject to prosecution for any criminal acts he might engage in, just like anybody else. But it's his decision, and I won't order surveillance on him just because you don't like his type. It's wrong."

"I could insist," Bernard said, watching her thoughtfully. The rational part of Liz's brain wondered what he was seeing, but the rest of her didn't much care.

"Then you'll have to take the case out of my hands, because I won't insult a cooperative and valuable source this way."

Bernard leaned back in his leather chair, pressed his palms together and regarded her over his fingers. "I could have your badge over it."

Liz felt her lungs constrict of their own volition, and a panic rose up in her at the idea of losing her badge. It was the only tangible proof she had of what she'd made of herself, of how much distance she'd been able to put between the woman she was now and the defenseless little girl she'd been, the one America had embraced all those years ago.

And that was her problem. The realization hit her like a bolt of lightning, electrifying her, lifting her up and transforming her in ways she couldn't ever undo. She *was* that little girl. It didn't matter what kind of woman she'd made of herself, that little girl would always be the foundation from which that woman grew. The more distance she insisted on between herself and that child, the more precarious her balance.

"You could have my badge over it," she said, marveling at the cool authority in her voice. "That's a problem, isn't it? That justice succumbs to bureaucracy so easily and so often. Is that what's happening here?"

Bernard looked at her, no sign of temper, nerves or insulted ego visible in that stony face. "Not today," he said finally. "But be on your guard, Brynn. You're not objective anymore."

She nodded tightly.

"Dismissed."

TWO HOURS later, Liz did the unthinkable. Something she'd never done before in the history of her professional career. She took the afternoon off.

She was heartsick and weary, and there was a cavern inside her chest that wouldn't stop echoing no matter how much or how fast she talked. Something the job used to fill was empty suddenly. Maybe it had always been empty and it had taken Patrick walking out the door and her boss putting politics ahead of ethics to make her realize it.

She drove to a park and found a lonely, splintery wooden railing. She sat on it and stared out over the Mississippi River Valley until the sky was a great flaming lake of oranges and yellows at her back, and when she made a decision, she knew it was the right one because her soul quieted somewhat.

Her badge was a huge part of who she was, but it wasn't all of her. She was finally ready for the three pieces of her life—her past, her present and her future—to hang together with some kind of integrity. And Patrick O'Connor was one of the only threads that ran through all three. At least she hoped he was. She didn't care what he thought he'd said to her. She wasn't going to let it be good-bye.

She angled her sedan toward home, cranked up the radio and drummed her fingers to the beat of the music and her rising anxiety. What did a girl wear to ambush a guy like Patrick? She mentally flipped through her closet for a dress that would bring him to his knees. The blue tulle? The rose satin? And shoes. God, which *shoes*?

Her house was in shadows when she pulled up, but she wasn't so distracted that she didn't notice her door hanging just slightly askew. Relief and joy rushed through her entire body in a single electrifying shock.

Patrick. It was her first thought. Her only thought. He hadn't left. He cared for her. Of course he did. Why else would he keep breaking into her house? She could take care of herself just fine, of course, but there was something really touching and lovely about his obsession with her safety.

She all but ran up the front steps, an irrepressible smile breaking free and plastering itself all over her face.

"Patrick?" she called as she pushed through the front door. She was damn glad he wasn't in the habit of arming himself or she'd be more worried about surprising him. "Are you still breaking into my house, or can I turn on the lights?"

"Oh, I'm about done."

Not Patrick. Oh Christ, not Patrick.

Her blood froze in her veins and every nerve snapped to exquisite attention. One hand went for her weapon, the other for the light switch, but she wasn't as fast as Villanueva.

She caught just a glimpse of him—sleek, compact and lethally graceful—before a shattering pain crashed through her temple. Her world tilted sideways, blurred and faded, but not before she caught the brilliant flash of the streetlights on a knife blade.

.

Chapter
24

PATRICK FOLDED a slate gray merino wool sweater and laid it carefully in his suitcase while his sister glared flaming holes into his back.

"I can't believe you're leaving," Mara said, and Patrick turned to give her his best patient face.

"I've already been here longer than I'd planned," he said mildly. "But your counterfeiter is finally in custody and Villanueva is en route to Switzerland as we speak." Or so reliable sources had indicated. "My work here is done."

"This isn't about that, and you know it," Mara snapped. "You finally have a shot at a normal, decent life and you're throwing it away because the FBI isn't serving it up to you on a silver platter. God."

She threw her hands up in disgust and Patrick hoped she might just walk away for a while. She'd been at him all afternoon and it didn't look like she was planning to take the evening off. He wondered if his ears were bleeding yet. She stalked into the room and plopped herself down on a pile of Patrick's freshly pressed shirts. He tried not to wince.

"I don't know what you're talking about, Mara," he said. "Most people with normal, decent lives daydream about moving to California and living *my* life. I'm not feeling particularly abused here."

"Oh, shut up. You are so."

"I am?" He let his brows elevate with the cool mockery that always made her crazy. He *was* feeling kind of raw. Enough to take a petty pleasure in pissing her off, anyway.

She didn't take the bait. "Yes. When the hell are you going to *get* it? You're my brother. I love you. I want you to be happy. And you know what makes you happy?"

He gave up folding and just pinched the bridge of his nose. "If I let you tell me, will you go away so I can pack in peace?"

"Liz. Liz makes you happy."

He closed his eyes for a moment. Lying used to be so easy. Why was it turning into such an act of superhuman endurance? "Lots of women make me happy."

Mara let that bit of ridiculousness pass unremarked. He had to assume that it sounded as pathetic to her as it did to him. "The good things in life aren't free, Patrick," she said. "You know that better than anybody. Look at what you paid so I could have my chance at a few of them."

"This whole Patrick-as-guardian-angel business is getting really stale, Mara."

"I'm almost done. I'm just saying. Good things are expensive. But they don't always cost money. Sometimes all they cost is trust and risk and love and faith. Those are things you've never anted up, Patrick. And if you want my opinion—"

"I don't."

"—I'd say Liz is a damn good bet for you. But you're walking away from the table without ever laying down your cards to see if you could win. You're pretending that the FBI scares you or something so you can skip town and do God knows what in your customary solitude. And I think that sucks."

She rose slowly, came to him and laid a hand against his cheek. He didn't dare meet her eyes. For once, he didn't know exactly what might be in his own.

"Just please consider it," she said. "Trust, risk, love and faith. Is that so expensive?"

Not to give, he thought. *But to ask?* They were a hell of a lot more expensive than he could ever in good conscience ask of a woman. Especially a woman like Liz.

AN HOUR later, Patrick loaded his suitcase into the trunk of his sporty little car. He could be at the airport in under two hours, depending on traffic. He'd hit the Twin Cities in the heart of rush hour, but he didn't want to wait until morning to go. He didn't know if his willpower would sustain him through one more night separated from Liz by nothing but a few miles and some sincere convictions.

The agents tailing him were pitifully easy to make. Patrick slammed the trunk and walked directly to the driver's window of their car, keeping his hands in plain sight at all times. He'd lived most of his life among some of the more dangerous creatures the human race had to offer, but nothing was less predictable than a nervous cop.

He tapped on the glass and offered a benign smile. The cop in the driver's seat glanced at his partner, who shrugged, then buzzed down the window.

"Evening, officers." Patrick widened the smile. "I just wanted to make things easy on you by offering up the night's itinerary. I've booked myself on the midnight flight out of Minneapolis to LAX. I'll be driving myself in that little car right there." He hooked a thumb over his shoulder. "It's pretty distinctive so I doubt you'll lose me, but I wanted you to be aware of my plans in case you wanted to get in touch with your California counterparts to arrange continuing surveillance."

The driver's side cop blinked up at him. "Uh, thanks."

"No problem," Patrick said, though it stung to be polite to the tangible evidence of Liz's distrust. "Hope you nail your guy."

That was a bald-faced lie. Every source he'd been able to tap said Villanueva was already en route to Switzerland. But he gave the door a hearty slap. "All right then. Let's drive."

He sauntered back to his car, gave a casual little wave to Mara. She was on the front porch, flanked by her husband and daughter, glowering at him like a thunderhead. She didn't wave back.

He pointed the little car toward 35 North and watched while the ugly beige sedan fell in behind him. His cell phone jumped on the passenger seat, vibrating itself around in a mad jig to be answered. He frowned at it but didn't recognize the number. It wasn't Mara, and it wasn't Liz, that much he knew.

What the hell. He could use the distraction. He answered. "O'Connor."

"Patrick?" Liz's voice trembled out of the earpiece and hit him like a bullet.

"Liz?" He tried to keep his voice light, but every nerve he had jangled in warning. "Did your cops check in already? I hope they told you I was being extremely cooperative."

"I need you, Patrick." Her voice was stiff, reluctant. Patrick's gut clenched. Something was very, very wrong here. "I'm with Villanueva. He says it's time to pay up."

"Are you all right?" Patrick gripped the phone with slippery fingers, his heartbeat thudding audibly in his head. "Did he hurt you? Christ, Liz, where are you?"

The phone rattled as it switched hands; then Patrick's ear was full of Villanueva's oily voice. "Hello, Patrick."

"What do you want?" Patrick forced the words through gritted teeth. *Just tell me where you are,* he thought. *That's all I need.* He wasn't a violent person by nature, but if this man had laid one hand on Liz, he was going to beat the living shit out of him. And then he'd get nasty. The FBI could have the leftovers.

"Just what you owe me," Villanueva said, his voice nearly pleasant. Patrick flexed his hands on the wheel, consciously relaxing his grip before he snapped the damn thing in half.

"What I owe you is sitting in a very exclusive Swiss bank," Patrick reminded him.

"What you think you owe me," Villanueva corrected. "It's not quite what I want from you."

"And what might that be?"

"A new identity."

Patrick frowned. "That'll take time. Who are you looking to be?"

"You're in the fiction business," Villanueva said. "I'll leave that up to you. But I want it all—passport, driver's license, birth certificate, social security card—along with two-point-five million in cash by tomorrow noon."

"Where?"

"Oz's little basement workshop in the dance club will be fine," he said. "If you're there by noon tomorrow and the goods meet my approval, your Agent Brynn can live."

Patrick closed his eyes, forced back the terror and fury until he could speak dispassionately. "And if I don't? Or if the goods are substandard?"

"Well, killing her *does* serve a certain kind of justice."

Patrick bit down on the inside of his cheek until he tasted blood. The pain helped clarify his thinking, if only slightly.

"Put Liz back on," he said. "I'm not running all over hell and back to get your documentation unless I'm convinced she's healthy and whole."

"As you wish."

The phone rustled again and Liz's voice came over the line. "Patrick?"

"Liz." Relief washed through him, smoothed out the jagged edges. "God, Liz, are you all right? Has he hurt you?"

"Not really. But I didn't give you enough credit the other night. He has a fist like a wrecking ball." She gave a shaky

laugh and Patrick bit back a bitter curse at the idea of Liz
having any idea what Villanueva's fist felt like.

"I'll be there by noon tomorrow," Patrick told her. "Do
whatever it takes to stay safe between now and then."

"You, too," she whispered. He could hear Villanueva's
muffled voice telling her to hang up. "I have to go."

"Listen, Liz—" A greasy desperation rolled through
him at the thought of breaking this tenuous connection
with her.

"Don't worry, Patrick. He's not going to hurt me," she
said.

Not until you're here to watch. The words were unspo-
ken, but Patrick heard them all the same. Knew in his heart
they were true.

"Patrick? Are you there?"

He cleared his throat of the awful emotion. "Yeah."

"I love you, Patrick. I do."

The phone went dead before he could answer.

"God. I love you, too."

And he did. That was the crazy thing. He'd always loved
her but had simply chosen not to ask for her love in return.
It was his little sacrifice, he thought with a bitter chuckle.
His way of infusing life with some of the balance that the
universe habitually failed to provide. Life needed balance,
didn't it? Good guys and bad guys? White hats and black
hats? Last time he'd looked, his hat sure wasn't white and
that meant he had no business asking any woman worth
loving to share his life.

But what kind of fucked-up universe pulled this shit?
Liz's childhood could easily have sent any rational person around the bend, but had she fallen apart? No, not
Liz. She'd turned it into a platform from which to launch
a crusade against abusers. And the fates went ahead and
dropped her into the hands of a knife-happy revenge seeker
just because she had the very bad luck to be in love with
the wrong guy?

He'd spent his life beating back the chaos, trying to
impose some kind of order on a life that wasn't fair or

orderly or rational. He'd denied himself everything he'd ever secretly longed for, from college to love, in an effort to balance scales that were inherently and perpetually unbalanced. It was time to stop fighting.

He was going to save Liz. But not because it was his job as appointed by fate and his sins to be her bulldog. No, he'd save her for himself this time. And he'd be damned if he let anything—her stubbornness, his unworthiness or a half-demented criminal he'd had the misfortune to piss off years ago—stand in his way.

He glanced in his rearview mirror, then jerked the wheel to the left. The sporty little two-seater skidded happily into the U-turn. Patrick lifted a casual hand to the startled agents as they went flying past in their ugly unmarked car.

He punched the accelerator to the floor and sped back toward Grief Creek.

IT WAS well past five, but Patrick was betting that SAC Bernard was still at the office. He barreled into the lot behind the Grief Creek Resident Agency and smiled grimly at the light glowing from Bernard's office window. He wasn't a world-class gambler for nothing, now was he?

He angled into a parking spot in a shower of flying gravel and was out of the car and into Bernard's office before most of it hit the ground.

Bernard looked up from the paperwork on his desk. "Brynn was right," he said. "We really need to do something about our security."

"Villanueva has her," Patrick said.

Bernard's brows shot up in the first display of honest emotion Patrick had ever seen cross the man's stony face. "What?"

"I just got the call on my cell. Suffice it to say that I now have a new commitment to seeing the bastard swing. You can have him. I'll serve him up on a fucking platter."

Bernard pulled a fresh sheet of paper toward him and picked up a gold pen. "Talk."

"Oh, no," Patrick said. "You'll get what you want only after I get what I want."

Bernard tapped the pen thoughtfully on the paper and Patrick watched as the mask of cool remoteness dropped back over him. "And what might that be?"

"I go in first and I go in alone," he said. "No wires, no ambush. You'll get your arrest, but I have a few things I need to make extremely clear to Villanueva as to how our relationship will work henceforth."

Bernard brought the pen to his lips. "I see."

"In addition, I want Oz released into my custody. As it turns out, Villanueva has a few demands after all, and they mesh quite nicely with Oz's area of expertise."

Quite a few of them, actually, he thought. Not one more legal than another. But he didn't share that with Bernard. He held the man's gaze steadily, let him see without a shred of uncertainty that Patrick meant exactly what he said.

"When and where is the meet?"

Patrick shrugged and lied without blinking. "Tomorrow, but I don't know when or where. He said he'd be in touch."

After what felt like an eternity, Bernard shifted in his chair, came forward to drill Patrick with a direct look. "Brynn is one of mine," he said. "I protect what's mine."

"So do I."

"Ah." Bernard leaned back again, considered this. "I was afraid this would happen."

Patrick gave him a sour look. "Yeah, so was I."

Bernard barked out what might have been a laugh. "You have until noon," he said. "I want instant notification when you hear from Villanueva, and you don't so much as think about moving without my okay. You go in first, you go in alone, but you'll have backup, or I'll shoot your ass myself."

"Done."

OZ—HE *so* didn't look like a Donald—slouched in the passenger seat of Patrick's car, exuding surly teenage attitude in big, fat waves. His hair hung down over his jaw in a greasy curtain, hiding everything but the sullen set of his mouth.

"You're pretty pissy for a guy who just got sprung from jail," Patrick said.

"You're the guy who put me in there in the first place," Oz snapped. "What do you want, a parade?"

"Hey, you put yourself there with the illegal extracurriculars," Patrick said. "I just happened to be the guy that caught you doing it."

"Great, fine." Oz slouched deeper into the seat. "So this is like your hobby or something? Putting kids in jail, then busting them out again?"

"No." Patrick slowed to scan street signs, then jerked the wheel to the right and rocketed into a residential neighborhood. "This is a special occasion."

"Yeah?" Oz stuffed a handful of hair behind his ear. "Happy fucking birthday."

"Shut up," Patrick said mildly. "I'm about to do you the biggest favor in the history of the known universe. A little gratitude wouldn't be amiss." He shot into a darkened driveway and halted mere inches from the bumper of a government-issue sedan.

"Cop." Oz glared at Patrick from the passenger seat. "Nice favor."

Patrick sighed and walked around the hood of the car. He opened the passenger door and grabbed Oz by the collar. "Trust me," he said, yanking him out of the car. "You're going to like this."

He marched Oz up the front steps, then held the doorbell down until the door opened and Goose appeared.

"For Christ's sake, *what*?" she snapped, her hair hanging over one shoulder in a lopsided ponytail and sheet marks on her cheek.

Patrick gave Goose a grim smile. "You law enforcement types," he said. "Don't you ever check the peephole?"

She shoved a hand into the mess on top of her head, pulled her robe higher on one shoulder and stepped back from the door.

"What's happened?" she asked, her eyes already clearing.

It was a nice counterpoint to Oz's growing daze. In spite of everything, Patrick nearly grinned. Seventeen was so simple. The sulk on his face faded into slack-jawed wonderment as he took in Goose's nearly six feet of female charm.

"Donald Brady, meet Maria di Guzman. Secret Service."

"Pleasure," Oz whispered, awestruck.

"Likewise." Goose turned back to him and frowned. "Patrick?"

"Villanueva has Liz," he said. "I'm getting her back, but I need your help."

God bless her, Goose never blinked. "What can I do?"

"I need two-point-five million in really good fake bills by noon," he said. "Along with a few other items."

Goose nodded, looked back at Oz. "This is my apprentice?"

"Consider him an intern. If things go well, he can count the hours toward his community service sentence."

Goose gave Oz a close once-over. "You'd better impress me, kid."

Oz nodded quickly, apparently having lost the power of speech in the face of Goose's beauty.

Patrick shook his head. "I also need some papers—social security, birth certificate, driver's license, passport, the works—for Villanueva's approximate height, weight and coloring."

"I'll wake a few people up," Goose said. "Let's get started."

"There's one more thing," Patrick said. "And I think Oz will be waking up a few people for this one."

Chapter
25

PATRICK LET himself into Mara's apartment as the sun was rising. He put on a pot of coffee to brew, sat down at the island counter and waited for the aroma to pull his sister out of bed. He resisted the urge to rub at his gritty eyes. He couldn't afford to be tired.

Patrick was pouring himself a very large mug of industrial-strength coffee when Mara stumbled into the kitchen ten minutes later. She squinted at him and said, "You're back."

"Looks like." Patrick poured a second cup and shoved it under her nose. She plunked onto the stool beside him, wrapped both hands around the mug and inhaled greedily.

"What's the occasion? You come to your senses?" she asked, eyes closed as she took her first, testing sip. "God, that's good."

He filled her in with short, succinct phrases that got to the point as quickly as possible. No wasted words, no editorial. No wasted time.

"I need your help, Mara," he finally said. "If I let the FBI handle this and Villanueva slides, nobody who cares about my sorry ass will ever be safe again. I need the time and space to make him understand exactly how things are going to be between us from here on out. Liz's boss is making all the right noises, but he doesn't trust me. He wants to do this his way and he'll screw me without thinking twice."

Mara pushed away from the counter and took the coffee with her as she paced the length of her kitchen. She stopped to stare out the French doors into the lightening sky. "Would you do it differently?" she asked. "If it meant keeping one of your people safe?"

"Hell, no." Patrick refilled his own mug, slugged back a scalding mouthful. "That's exactly what I'm doing in my own way. But I'm not a moron. I'm not planning to tackle the guy without backup. I just need ten, maybe twenty minutes under the radar. Can you give it to me?"

She turned from the window. "Why are you doing this, Patrick?"

He shrugged jerkily, unable to summon up even an ounce of the silky assurance that used to be second nature.

"Liz," he said simply. "I love her. I love you, too. And I refuse to let that damage either of you." He glanced over his shoulder down the darkened hallway where Mara's husband and child were still sleeping. "Or your families."

Mara followed his glance and when her eyes returned to his, they were grim, determined. "Bet your ass," she said. "What do you need?"

She listened in silence while he explained what he wanted.

"Bernard's going to be pissed," she said when he'd finished.

"Yeah. I'll spring for renovations if he trashes the place."

She came to him, laid a hand on his cheek. "I'll hold you to that, you know."

Patrick smiled for the first time in what felt like years. "I know you will."

He refilled his mug again and headed for the door. "I'll be in touch," he said.

"Better be," she said. "Hey, and Patrick?"

"What?"

"I love you, too. Try not to get killed, hmmm?"

"Right."

IT TOOK a little longer to spot the tail this time. Patrick pulled up at one of Grief Creek's only stoplights and checked his rear view. Still there. Either Bernard had requested a better caliber of cop this time around or Liz had been giving him a free ride when she'd picked out the last ones. He kind of suspected the latter, and it pained him now to think how he'd taken having a tail at all as ultimate proof of Liz's distrust.

After he let them follow him to the bank, the hardware store, and the local pawnshop, Patrick phoned Goose.

"Ready?"

"Yeah," she said. "Kid does good work, Patrick. Really, really good work." She paused. "And he knows some scary people."

"You want some free advice? Recruit him. Teach him how to use his powers for good instead of evil. You don't want this kid on the wrong side of the law when he comes into his own."

"Truer words." Goose sighed. "Where do you want us?"

"Mara's. Eleven thirty. Bring bags, but leave the goods at your place."

There was a moment of uncomprehending silence, then, "You got it."

"And Goose? Make sure they see you coming."

"Right. High profile."

"Thanks."

SAC GRAYSON Bernard watched from a surveillance van in Brightwater's side lot as an undercover agent in a Softee Loaf Bread Company shirt hefted a pallet of dinner rolls onto his shoulder and disappeared into the service entrance of the restaurant.

"I have a visual on Agent di Guzman," the agent muttered into a concealed microphone in his collar. "She's making contact with a white male—black hair, six feet, maybe one-eighty."

O'Connor. Bernard checked his watch. The guy had all of twelve minutes left before his noon deadline for making contact with the FBI, but Bernard had no intention of waiting for O'Connor to come to him. One of his agents' lives hung in the balance. Now wasn't the time for trust.

The service doors opened again, and the agent wheeled his now empty dolly back toward the bread truck. "Conversation between di Guzman and subject indicates that a meeting will take place in Brightwater's restaurant at noon sharp. Agent di Guzman passed subject a briefcase and stated her desire to meet with the subject afterward."

Bernard's hand tightened on the radio. That was what he'd been waiting for. Confirmation of what his gut had always known: O'Connor had no intention of working with the FBI on Brynn's rescue. He'd officially screwed them. The only surprise was that di Guzman appeared to be screwing them, too.

Bernard keyed the main frequency, spoke to all the agents scattered in and around the restaurant. "O'Connor is in the building. Who has a visual?"

"Got him," one of the agents buzzed back. "I think. My angle's for crap, but I have a white male taking a seat in the rear corner of the restaurant. No visual on the face, but he's approximately six feet tall, dark hair, briefcase in hand."

"Is the rest of the table visible?" Bernard asked.

"Yeah, I got a real nice look at the empty seat across from him."

"Anybody joins him, I want to hear it," Bernard said. "Agents on the ready. Go on my signal." The blood began to pump now. It was close. He could feel it. He was going to take down Villanueva and O'Connor the way they should've been taken down six years ago: together.

He cinched down the straps on his flak jacket and pulled on the FBI windbreaker. He checked his watch. Four minutes.

"White male sitting down at O'Connor's table, maybe six feet, dark coloring, possibly Hispanic."

"Go." Bernard gave the order, then came out of the van in time to see his agents surging toward the casino restaurant like a swarm of hornets, converging on windows and doors, covering all the angles. Pride warred with caution as Bernard drew his weapon and followed the first wave through the door.

He was just in time to see his agents take down Jonas Brightwater and Donald Brady.

Bernard holstered his weapon and closed his eyes for a brief moment. He was going to have O'Connor's ass over this.

When he opened his eyes, Agent di Guzman was on her feet, badge out, murmuring something soothing to the adrenaline-charged agent still holding his weapon on Patrick O'Connor's brother-in-law. Who happened to be, Bernard noticed for the first time, approximately O'Connor's height, build and coloring. Except for the fact that O'Connor was a blue-eyed Irishman while Jonas Brightwater was at least partly Native American and had a furious wife who was busily berating the agent who'd taken him down.

"To the best of my knowledge, having coffee with a counterfeiter isn't a federal crime," Mara Brightwater spat at the flustered agent. "Now get your fucking knee out of my husband's back."

The young agent's face went deeply red and he looked around uncertainly. He'd taken down a six-foot, well-muscled man without blinking, but five feet nothing of furious temper wrapped in a huge white apron was like kryptonite, apparently. Bernard shook his head. Lapse of training. He'd have to address that.

"Stand down, Agent Jacoby," Bernard said, striding into the melee. "You have the wrong man."

The agent released Brightwater immediately, and the man stood.

"Well," Brightwater said. "Been a while since I've had that particular pleasure. I was just having a professional chat with Donald here. I thought he could provide some advice on how to better protect my operation from counterfeiters. Agent di Guzman set up the meeting and provided samples of his work." He offered a broadly innocent smile. "Is there a problem with that?"

"I don't give two shits about what you do with your business," Bernard said. "But I have a real problem with obstruction of justice, which is what you'll all be charged with if Agent Brynn isn't back in my custody within the half hour. Now where is O'Connor?"

Brightwater's eyebrows shot up, and he glanced over at his wife. "Mara? You have anything you'd like to share with the nice officer?"

"What do I look like, a babysitter?" She put a protective hand on her husband's arm and glared daggers at Bernard. "How the hell should I know where my brother is?"

Bernard returned her hot glare with an icy one of his own. "Any ideas would be welcome, Mrs. Brightwater."

"Christ." She rolled her eyes. "For the past two weeks, he was either here, at Liz's place or at that dance club he's so fond of. Over in the warehouse district. Cargo?"

Bernard cut his eyes to Agent di Guzman. "Is there any reason to suspect O'Connor would go back there?"

"He'd go anywhere he thought he'd find Villanueva."

He paused to get a firmer grip on his patience, then asked with careful precision, "Would he think Villanueva's there?"

"Sure," Donald spoke up. "Villanueva, like, owns the place."

Di Guzman nodded confirmation of this astounding fact.

"Of course he does," Bernard muttered sourly.

IT WAS still three minutes shy of noon when Patrick arrived at the dank little basement door where Villanueva had punched his lights out a week earlier. The briefcase he'd

picked up from Goose's house was heavy in his hands—
heavy enough to contain the whole two point five million,
although he hadn't dared open it for a precise count.

He lifted a hand, steadied it with a conscious effort,
then rapped his knuckles against the door. It swung open
immediately, and Villanueva smiled at him.

"O'Connor," the man said. "So punctual."

Patrick lifted his shoulders. "There's rarely a good
excuse for poor manners."

Villanueva's smiled broadened and he backed away
from the door, swept a hand toward the dim interior of the
room.

"Please," he said. "Welcome to my humble abode."

Patrick stepped inside, searching the shadows until he
discovered Liz sitting in the corner. She was tied hand and
foot, and her lip was split, but she was alive and conscious.
Relief washed through him. She was dinged up a little but
not seriously hurt. And not scared either. If her expression
was anything to go by, Liz was good and pissed.

God, he loved this woman.

Villanueva laid a hand on Patrick's sleeve. "I'm just
going to pat you down now. Merely a formality. I have my
standards, too."

Patrick shrugged. "Suit yourself." He laid the bag at his
feet and put his hands on the wall while Villanueva con-
ducted a thorough search of his person.

"You never change." Villanueva laughed softly in Patrick's ear. "No weapon. Are you truly that arrogant?"

Patrick lifted one lazy shoulder. "Guns are so . . .
crude."

Villanueva tipped his head in agreement. "They serve
a purpose," he said. Then he drew a wicked-looking blade
from the sheath at his waist and ran a testing thumb over its
edge. "But knives. What do you have against knives? They
seem like such an ideal fit for you. Subtle, elegant. Almost
poetic, if used properly. I could show you a few things."

Villanueva caressed the knife with a reverence that put
a sucking hole in Patrick's gut. His face was soft, like a

lover's, but his eyes were utterly mad. What the hell was he remembering, Patrick wondered? What had he and that knife done to put that look on his face?

He was damn sure he didn't want to find out.

"Maybe later," he said. "We have business first." Patrick inclined his head toward the briefcase at his feet.

Villanueva sheathed the knife and said, "Excellent. Bring it into the light."

The FBI had left behind a small table when they'd raided Oz's basement workshop, empty now but for a raggedy stuffed bunny. Evie's bunny, Patrick knew with an icy shock. The one Mara hadn't been able to find after Villanueva had tossed her house. Proof that Villanueva had considered Patrick's niece as a target before settling on Liz.

Rage twisted inside him but he stuffed it down and laid the briefcase on the table with steady hands. He clicked open the latches, opened the case, then stood back so Villanueva could inspect the contents.

"Do you mind if I ask why you demanded all this?" Patrick asked as Villanueva picked up a banded stack of crisp one-hundred-dollar bills and flipped through them to make certain they were all the same denomination. "Surely your exit strategy didn't depend on this kind of last-minute work?"

"Of course not." Villanueva selected another stack from a different part of the briefcase and did the same. "But how else to make you hope?"

"Hope? For what?"

"For victory." Villanueva shrugged as he reached into the inside pocket and withdrew the paperwork. "After all, where's the glory in defeating an opponent who believes he can't win?" He scrutinized each item, and Patrick took another step away from him and closer to Liz. She was watching them both carefully, those blue eyes of hers intensely alert.

"Oh, I believe I can win. Rest easy on that point," Patrick said. "But now that you've verified my end of the bargain, I'll just make certain that you've kept up yours."

Villanueva turned to him. "My end of the bargain?"

Patrick nodded toward Liz and lifted his eyebrows in lofty reminder.

"Oh, yes, the girl." Villanueva gave him a little moue of apology and fingered the knife at his waist. "She's fine, of course. But I'd rather you didn't get any closer."

Patrick blew out a purposefully impatient breath. "I don't have even fingernail clippers on me and you know it," he said. "What do you think I'm going to do, chew through the ropes like a beaver?"

Villanueva drew the knife from the sheath slowly, seemed to savor the low hiss of metal sliding over leather. "I'm afraid I just don't trust you, O'Connor. You've proven yourself rather unreliable in the past."

"You didn't trust me long before I screwed you in Vegas," Patrick said. "If you'd trusted me back then, you wouldn't have bolted like a scared rabbit at the first sign of trouble. I had a little family emergency to take care of, but I would never have sold you out entirely. If you'd trusted me just a few more hours, I'd have cut you into the deal. You'd have spent the last six years enjoying a nice little golden parachute out of the criminal life, just like I did."

"Family emergency," Villanueva spat. "Your sister was a fuckup. She deserved to be caught. But you, you were something special. You had promise, or so I thought. I went out of my way to free you up from your ridiculous sense of responsibility to your incompetent sister, and how do you repay me? By turning yourself in to the FBI?"

Patrick narrowed his eyes at Villanueva. "It *was* you," he said slowly. "You turned Mara in that night."

"Christ, yes," Villanueva said. "She was dragging you down. I did what I thought necessary to open your eyes, to force a choice. But I never thought in a million years that you lacked the intelligence to make the right choice. And as a result of your stupidity, I lost my wife and child."

He went eerily still then, and Patrick felt the impact all the way through his body.

"Justice demands, therefore, that I take what's most important to you," Villanueva said. "I'll kill you, too, of course. But first I'm going to kill her." He waved the knife in Liz's direction and Patrick's mouth went utterly dry. "And you're going to watch."

Chapter
26

LIZ WORKED the ropes binding her wrists back and forth as much as she was able and watched as Patrick ignored the knife in Villanueva's hand.

"Surely your wife and child were worth more than one ex-criminal and a dinged-up FBI agent?" he asked with a dismissive sangfroid that had Liz blinking. Was he *baiting* the guy?

The ropes binding her wrists tore at her skin, but she twisted against them with a little more urgency. Why the hell couldn't Patrick have done what any sane, rational person would have done and armed himself? Or arrived with a SWAT team? Or even a dozen or so of Liz's colleagues? That would have done the trick.

But no. The bad guy was armed to the teeth and teetering on the edge of madness, and Patrick decided to go in with the verbal attack. Christ.

"I thought they were worth that and much more," Villanueva said. "Once. They proved otherwise, but still. They might have had the opportunity to outgrow such weakness had it not been for you. You forced my hand, and that debt is yours to pay." Villanueva shifted to smile at Liz, and it was the cold, slippery smile of a reptile. "I've been waiting some time for satisfactory payment. This is going to be sweet indeed."

He shifted his grip on the knife to something a bit more purposeful and all the breath left Liz's body as she watched Patrick roll up onto the balls of his feet, his entire lanky body coming to the ready. Oh Lord, was he going to *fight*?

In the eight years she'd been following his career, she'd never known him to even carry a weapon, much less throw a punch. And now he was going hand-to-hand? Unarmed? Against a guy with a seven-inch blade?

Villanueva released a rich chuckle. "Oh, this is wonderful. Please, defend yourself at will. It'll be all the sweeter for me to kill her in front of you if you really try to fight me first."

Patrick smiled back, and it was as sharp as the blade flashing in Villanueva's hand. "I'll do what I can."

Liz closed her eyes and a low moan escaped her as what was left of her heart broke and bled. She couldn't watch this.

"Liz." Patrick's voice was mild and just a little indignant. "A bit of faith might be in order."

"I do hope you've improved over the years," Villanueva said. "Or this is going to be very anticlimactic."

She opened her eyes in time to watch Patrick shrug. "I'll try not to disappoint."

Villanueva moved like a snake striking, sudden and lethal, the knife making a swift slashing stroke toward Patrick's midsection. Liz couldn't stop the thin scream that tore itself from her throat as Patrick sidestepped nimbly and put what looked like half an inch between his liver and Villanueva's knife.

He backed toward Liz, gave her a reassuring glance over his shoulder. She closed her eyes again, unable to accept the message of love and reassurance in all that glacial blue. He was going to die for her. She couldn't let that happen.

She forced her eyes open and started in on the rope with her teeth.

"You're still quick," Villanueva commented as he circled Patrick assessingly.

Patrick nodded. "It's a gift."

Villanueva feinted toward Patrick's shoulder this time, a deliberately testing move. Liz gnawed desperately at the ropes binding her wrists as Patrick twisted away from the blade and danced a little closer to Liz. There was a subtle flash and ping, and Liz frowned at the ground next to her knee.

A razor blade. God damn, he'd just dropped her a fucking razor blade. Where the hell had he stashed a razor blade that Villanueva could possibly have missed it? That search had been damn thorough. She didn't waste any time speculating. Patrick O'Connor had secrets and gifts she would never understand and she was done forcing herself to figure them out before she accepted them.

She edged herself over to the blade, scooped it up and went to work on the ropes around her wrists while Patrick continued to hang on to his life by centimeters. Her fingers shook and she dropped the blade, scrambled to her hands and knees to claw it up again. She didn't care if Villanueva saw her. She could only pray it distracted him before he removed something vital from Patrick's anatomy.

The rope was down to threads now and Liz sawed desperately at them with the dulling blade. Villanueva circled to his left with a deadly grace that had Liz's blood running cold. He lashed out with the knife at the same time he hooked a booted foot in the opposite direction, mere inches from Liz's knees. Patrick moved with a boxer's nimble grace, dancing out of the blade's reach, but the step he needed to keep his balance took him directly onto Villanueva's boot. He stumbled, one arm flailing for balance even as his body twisted toward all that sharpened steel.

The ropes at her wrists fell away and Liz shoved to her bound feet with a cry of fury and terror as Villanueva threw his entire weight into the thrust, following the path of the blade toward Patrick's body. It was a killing blow and he knew it, put his entire energy into driving it home. A ghastly smile stretched his lips and his eyes glowed with an insane anticipation. Liz was moving before she even fully understood her intent.

She saw Patrick drop to the ground as if he'd suddenly gone boneless, nothing but a sliver of air between him and the blade, but her focus was entirely on Villanueva and his slow-motion dance with murder. They were nearly on top of her now, and as Villanueva dropped his guard to deal Patrick that killing blow, Liz cocked back her arm and drove her fist into his jaw with enough force to send shards of pain splintering all the way up into her shoulder.

But he didn't go down. She'd deflected his aim just enough to save Patrick's skin, but with her feet still bound, she hadn't managed enough stopping power. All she'd done was remind him of her presence, and that he wanted to kill her, too.

Now they would both die, she thought. Together. She'd gambled with both their lives and lost.

The momentum of the swing had dropped her to her hands and knees at Villanueva's feet, and she was sprawled nearly on top of Patrick's still form. She covered him with her body as best she could and braced for the blow she knew was coming.

Patrick's arms came around her and she thought, *Okay.* If she was going to die, this was the way she wanted to go. In Patrick's arms, doing what she knew she was meant for. Standing between the innocent and the evil.

Because she knew—had always known, really—that regardless of what Patrick had done, regardless of what his parents had made him, of what he thought he'd been made for, he wasn't evil. In his own way, he was a force for good in the world, same as she was. She'd done nothing but use and judge him since he'd smashed into her carefully constructed world, and yet he'd still been willing to lay down his life for hers. She would die protecting him with her body, and it was right. He deserved at least that final act of love from her.

But then everything went topsy-turvy, because Patrick didn't stop with embracing her. He all but bench-pressed her, shoving her up and over his head, tossing her away from him. He used the momentum to roll away from the blade meant to skewer him to the ground.

A snarl of pure rage escaped Villanueva when his knife sparked off the concrete floor instead of spilling Patrick's guts. In that sliver of vulnerability, while Villanueva's arm was outstretched and his guard down, Patrick gained his feet and his balance. From the advantage of both height and position, he delivered the punch that Liz had been aiming for—a vicious, short-armed blow that drove Villanueva to one knee.

She didn't have time to admire it or even to speculate on where he'd learned to do such a thing. Violence always seemed so antithetical to Patrick's whole being, and yet here he was doling it out with a grim-eyed determination that had her mouth hanging open.

His next shot put Villanueva's second knee on the floor. Patrick's elbow was cocked back to deliver a third blow, his beautiful lips peeled back in a snarl that Liz had never imagined when her instinct and training kicked in.

Villanueva had dropped to his knees not two feet from where she was still sprawled on her back, and she recognized an opportunity when she saw one. She coiled herself and jackhammered out with both feet, landing her boots squarely in the man's crotch. He went down like a flour sack, the knife clattering to the floor. Patrick scooped it up before Liz could kick it clear and he went down on one knee beside Villanueva's crumpled form.

He grabbed a handful of dark greasy hair and jerked the man's head back until Liz could see the jugular vein pumping fast and vulnerable in his throat. Patrick laid the knife against it, pressed hard enough that a thin line of blood appeared under the blade when Villanueva's throat worked in convulsive swallows.

"Do I have your attention now, Villanueva?" he asked, his voice soft and deadly pleasant.

"Fuck you," Villanueva muttered. The words were slurred, his eyes vague, but hate rang unmistakably in every syllable. "You're not going to kill me, you pussy. You don't have the guts." The man's eyelids drifted to half-mast and Patrick pressed the blade more firmly against his throat until he opened his eyes and focused with apparent effort.

Liz had gained her hands and knees, and she dragged herself over to Patrick's side. "He's altered," she said, putting a restraining hand on his elbow. "How hard did you hit him?"

Patrick ignored her, shook off her hand. "You're right, Villanueva. You know me so well. I probably won't kill you."

In a lightning-quick maneuver that Liz would think about later, he'd moved the knife from Villanueva's throat and placed it against the thumb of the man's knife hand. "But I won't hesitate to put an end to your days of knife play forever."

Villanueva's eyes fluttered open and Patrick smiled. "Oh, good. You're awake. Pay attention, now, Villanueva, because I'm only going to say this once. If you ever come after me or my family again, if you make even one move I don't like in the general direction of anybody connected to me, I will hunt you down like the animal you are. I will take you apart piece by worthless piece and feed your guts to stray dogs."

Villanueva curled his lips into a mocking snarl. "Fucking nancy. You don't have the balls to put your sister in jail and you're going to feed my guts to the dogs? Be a man for once in your pathetic life and just slit my throat."

For one horrible moment, Patrick looked beyond tempted. Liz stood frozen beside him, knowing she should stop him, knowing she had a duty to stand between Villanueva and whatever Patrick was ready to deal out. But she couldn't even open her mouth against the incandescent fury that had transformed him into some kind of dark angel of vengeance. She watched in helpless fascination as Patrick drove the knife through the meaty flesh at the base of Villanueva's thumb without an ounce of effort or regret.

A terrible noise hissed through Villanueva's clenched teeth as Patrick gave the blade a tiny twist. "Do we understand one another?" He could have been inquiring about the weather, so cool and detached was his voice. "That was your radial nerve. You won't lose your thumb, but you'll never have quite the same dexterity or range of motion in that hand. I'm considering it a public service. I missed the artery by a wish but I could try again. I'm fully prepared to continue in this vein—so to speak—until you're quite clear on what I'd like from you. Shall I go on?"

"Finish it, O'Connor." Villanueva was sprawled on the floor, hair sticking to the sheen of sweat on his forehead. His lips peeled back in a fierce snarl but Liz saw pain and something new—fear?—slide into his eyes. "Grow up and finish this."

"You know, I find myself tempted," Patrick said softly, almost to himself. As if he were musing over the pros and cons of a reasonable suggestion. "I'm actually quite tempted to do just that. Liz? Darling? What do you think?" He could have been asking if she'd like her drink refreshed, there was so little feeling in his voice, in his face when he turned to her.

But the breath caught in her throat when she looked at him. Really looked at him. Because while his body was absolutely relaxed and easy, his eyes were blazingly hot, alive with rage and temptation and barely leashed vengeance. He wanted to kill this man, she knew it with every cell in her body. He wanted it quite desperately, but had disciplined that desire, chained it down. And the more it ate at him, the more remote he became, the more he retreated behind the smooth sophistication Liz had never quite forced herself to look past before.

She'd been wrong about so much, she realized now. The money, the clothes, the manners, they weren't any part of him at all. They weren't what he felt or who he was. They were simply a way for him to hide when he was feeling more than he deemed wise to feel.

But she knew him now, with her heart instead of her eyes, and she didn't see a man who could casually deal out torture and death. He crouched before her, one hand on the hilt of the knife protruding from Villanueva's hand, the desire to avenge and protect practically pulsing in the air around him, but he was offering her his sword. His obedience.

She put one hand over his on the knife, staying it. She put the other on his cheek in a gesture that both gave and sought forgiveness.

"Patrick," she said softly, rubbing her thumb lightly over the sharp curve of his jaw. "It's done now. Please."

He smiled at her, though it was tight and edgy, then turned to Villanueva. "The lady is merciful," he told him. "Your lucky day." He glanced back at Liz. "He's out."

She leaned over his shoulder to look at Villanueva's unconscious face. "We should call for backup," she said. "We're putting him in prison for life; we ought to make sure it's a long time. I'd hate to have him pop off from a brain bleed before he gets to see the inside of his cage."

"He's fine. This is just a flesh wound—" Patrick yanked the knife free from Villanueva's hand, wiped it on the man's pants then sliced through the ropes still binding Liz's ankles. "And he didn't hit his head when he went down."

"No?" Liz rubbed carefully at her screaming feet. "Then why's he out like a frat boy at Mardi Gras?"

"Because I drugged him."

Chapter

27

"YOU *DRUGGED* him?" She stared at him, astonished. After the past twenty-four hours, she hadn't thought she could be surprised by anything. She'd been wrong.

Patrick gave her an impatient look as he rubbed briskly at her feet. "What? You wanted a fair fight?"

"Well, no, but . . ." She trailed off, moaned against the vicious return of sensation to her feet. "You really drugged him?"

"Of course I did. I'm not an idiot, Liz. I've got nothing against a good brawl, but the guy'd been honing his knife skills in Central America for the past six years, dreaming of nothing but slicing me into ribbons. Did you really expect me to ante up without making sure the odds were in my favor?" He smiled at her then, but it was self-deprecating and just a little bitter. "I'm not above cheating, Liz. Particularly with your life on the line."

She ignored that. "How?"

"How did I drug him?"

She limited herself to a nod. It had been a very disorienting twenty-four hours and she didn't trust herself to speak. God knows what she might ask.

"The money," Patrick said, helping her to her feet as the blood surged back into them. "While Oz and Goose were printing it up—"

Liz blinked. "Wait, you have more money than God and you paid my ransom with *fake bills*?"

"Well of course. What did you expect?"

"I'm not entirely sure. I think I might be insulted. I'll let you know." She took an experimental step, stifled an involuntary curse. "So while Oz and Goose were printing up the fake money . . . ?"

"I had Oz add a little something extra."

"Like what?"

"A date-rape drug. Oz has some predictable connections, given his choice of hobbies."

Liz frowned at him. "Every date-rape drug I've heard of needs to be ingested somehow. How did you get it into him? I was distracted, I'll admit, but I'd have noticed him eating a C-note."

"Your war on drugs sucks. You know that, right?" Patrick smiled, but it was still tight and violent. "As it happens, there's a new variant of Special K making the rounds. Absorbed right through the skin. Doesn't knock you out, really. Unless you get punched in the face, of course." He smiled down at Villanueva. "It just slows you down, makes you a little more suggestible than usual."

"So." Liz spoke slowly, trying to take it all in. "A knife-wielding maniac kidnaps me and instead of breaking down the door with the SWAT team like any normal person, you decide to drug him instead. With a date rape drug that you solicited from the juvenile delinquent we just busted, whom you also hit up for enough fake money to pay the ransom."

"That's about it," Patrick said. "How are your feet?"

She ignored him. Emotion ran up in a sudden wave, crashing over her head and tightening her throat. She forced herself to speak anyway. He'd protected her with his life. She owed it to him to reveal at least this much of herself.

"I don't think I could have survived watching you die," she said quietly. "I just don't think I could, and I can't believe you almost made me do it. Do you really hate me that much?"

"Liz, darling." He took her hands in his. "I don't hate you."

"Then why did you do that?" She felt raw, exposed and completely incapable of dissembling. "I love you, Patrick. It would kill me to see you hurt. What were you trying to *do*?"

"Protect what's mine."

She glanced at the mangy stuffed bunny still sitting on the table by the briefcase. Evie's. She'd guessed as much. His hands were large and warm and incredibly dear, and Liz could feel her own trembling inside them. Her throat ached with unshed tears and the effort to keep them that way.

"Your sister and her family would have been just as safe if you'd gone the SWAT team route, you know," she said, pulling one hand free and swiping it under her nose. "You didn't have to go hand-to-hand with a violent criminal to protect them."

"But I did," Patrick said. "Villanueva's operating on a pretty primitive world order. You can lock him in a cage, but the instant he gets out, he'll dedicate himself to hunting down and destroying any enemies who haven't proven themselves too costly to engage. A show of strength was the only way to protect the people I love." His hands closed tighter over hers and she looked up to find his eyes on her, intense and wildly blue. "And despite what you think of me, I am capable of love, Liz."

She smiled at that. "I've never doubted it," she said. "Nobody sacrifices what you did for your sister without knowing what love is."

He shook his head. "That's not what I'm talking about. I'm trying to say—"

The door crashed open under a furious assault from the outside and Liz found herself crushed between Patrick's body and the wall. He'd shoved himself between her and whatever threat was pouring through the door, she realized. Protecting her again. Love and relief poured through her battered soul like a healing balm. She rested her forehead between his shoulder blades, felt rather than saw him relax.

"Looks like you got your wish after all," he said, that old-money drawl back in his voice. "The SWAT team has arrived."

Liz looked around him to see the room swarming with agents in navy windbreakers with FBI emblazoned across the backs in bold gold letters, guns drawn, shouting to one another in the verbal shorthand that had become like a second language to her.

Then SAC Bernard was there, his face lined with responsibility and a fair amount of temper. He glanced at Patrick with what looked like animosity, then turned to Liz. "What's your condition, Brynn?"

"I'm fine."

Patrick spoke over her. "She needs to see an EMT. She was bound for several hours and her circulation may have been impaired." He pushed a lock of hair away from her cheek with a casual flick of a finger. "Somebody ought to take a look at that shiner of hers, too."

Liz reached up and fingered her cheekbone. Jesus, it felt like somebody'd driven a truck over her face.

"He had a decent swing," she said. "But I'm fine. Really. If I were concussed or something, I'd have had symptoms overnight, but—"

This time SAC Bernard spoke over her. "I want you checked out. And I want your report on my desk by tomorrow, noon."

Liz looked at his hard face and decided not to argue. "Yes, sir," she said.

An EMT appeared at her elbow and she allowed him to draw her toward a quiet corner.

"I still want to talk to you," she yelled over the noise to Patrick, who waved a reassuring hand at her and turned back to accept his dressing-down from her boss.

"Pipe down, will you?" The EMT frowned at her over his blood pressure cuff. "You want to stay out of the hospital tonight, you'll make a serious effort to relax. Your pressure's through the roof."

Liz sighed, leaned her head against the cinder-block wall at her back and concentrated on breathing in some kind of normal pattern.

SAC BERNARD watched him with stony eyes and Patrick looked back without a shred of remorse.

"You fucked me," Bernard said, his lips barely moving.

Patrick nodded. It was beside the point to mention that Bernard had been trying to fuck him. They both knew he had. He tipped his head, considered the man in front of him.

"Tell me, Bernard. What if it had been your wife? Your kids? You come across a lot of dangerous people in your line of work, you know that sometimes violence is the only language spoken or understood. Would you really have let the system stand for your family, or would you have sent a message yourself?"

Bernard was still for a long, tense moment; then he said, "I can't answer that."

Patrick accepted that with a shrug. "Of course you can't. But you understand."

"Yeah. I do." He blew out a breath, and all that solid squareness seemed to sag for a moment. "But I can't condone it. And I can't condone the rest of it, either."

"The rest of it?" Patrick's spine tried to stiffen, but he forced it to slouch instead. Forced himself to laze into the arrogant posture that had been his home for so long.

"You'll kill her career," Bernard said simply. He didn't look away from Patrick, didn't shift his gaze or shuffle his feet. There was regret in his face, but no uncertainty. "She's talented, she's driven and she's passionate about what she does. Agents like Brynn aren't easy to come by and she has a future with us. A damn bright one. Before you go any further with this, you need to know that you'll cost her that future."

Patrick didn't say anything. Couldn't. It was the truth, a truth he'd always known in some piece of his heart. He'd gotten momentarily caught up, he supposed. In the romance of the moment, in the adrenaline of victory. He'd almost told her everything. That he loved her, that he wanted her. Not just for a night or for a dozen nights, but for the rest of his life, in whatever capacity she'd allow him.

Christ, he'd almost begged. And wouldn't that have put her in an awful position? He didn't doubt that she loved him. Even if he hadn't trusted what he'd heard in her voice, seen in her eyes, he'd go to his grave feeling the press of her body against his, shielding him from a madman's knife.

What kind of man would force her to choose between the two things she loved most in the world?

Patrick met Bernard's eyes, found an unexpected compassion in them. It made it easier somehow to muster up the nonchalant smile he'd perfected all those years ago. "I fear you've misunderstood my interest in Agent Brynn," he said lightly.

Bernard nodded. "I must have," he said. "I assumed you were planning to stay in town."

"No. I'll be flying back to California tonight."

"I see." Bernard extended a hand. "The FBI appreciates your service."

Patrick took his hand, shook it. "My pleasure."

He glanced over the man's shoulder, saw Liz shake off the EMT and stalk over to her team. Bruises stood out starkly against that gorgeous, creamy skin, but her eyes were clear, and every line of her body exuded purpose and calm authority. She was doing what she'd been made for, he knew. His heart swelled with pride, then broke with regret.

He slipped out the door before she could turn back to him.

Chapter
28

One month later

Patrick stood in his darkened living room and considered fate's elegant way with a backhand while he gazed out the window. The view was spectacular—black, rolling hills stretching out toward the twinkling lights of a distant city, all of it neatly framed by an entire wall of glass. He'd worked damn hard for this sprawling almost-castle in the desert. He couldn't have cared less about the house; it was the view he'd wanted. Needed. The feeling of space, of isolation, of miles and miles of empty air between him and the world.

It soothed something restless in his soul to stand in front of this window night after night drinking in the view, but tonight he didn't even see it. Tonight, he was watching the window itself, and the reflection it showed him of the surveillance monitor embedded in the opposite wall. He didn't turn to study the monitor itself; he didn't need to. He'd have recognized her anywhere, his little housebreaker.

The irony of it made him smile. Liz Brynn, of all the damned people, was blowing through his security system with a panache that would have made better thieves than he propose without a prenup. His heart leapt painfully, joyfully at the sight of her, and he gave a self-deprecating chuckle.

Had he really deluded himself so badly? Had he really thought that just because he couldn't say with exact certainty how many days it had been since he'd left her in that dank little basement room that he was making progress? That his heart wasn't quite as broken?

He tossed back a mouthful of whiskey with a brief, violent motion. What the hell was she doing here? He watched while her reflection made short work of his intricate security system.

She was good, he thought wryly, powering down the monitors. But then she always had been. Wasn't that just the problem?

The monitors sank back into the wall and polished maple panels, complete with original if incomprehensible oil paintings, slid silently into place over them. He heard her enter the room—she made no apparent effort to muffle the click of her high heels against his gleaming wood floors—but he didn't turn. She wore heels for breaking and entering, he thought a little wildly. He took another sip of whiskey, let it burn down his throat and reached for self-control.

"You're slipping, Patrick," she said, and he could hear the smug grin in her voice. "Your security system is for crap."

He took a moment to study her reflection in the window, to prepare himself. She wore sky-high heels and a knee-length trench coat, and from her wasp-waisted silhouette, he'd lay decent odds that the coat covered up some amazing, vintage dress. He told himself he didn't want to know which one.

He pulled in a breath, then turned to face her.

"Liz," he said, infusing the single syllable of her name with just the right degree of polite reserve, as if she'd crashed a cocktail party rather than broken into his house.

As if it hadn't been a viciously painful month since they'd last spoken. "How delightful to see you. Care for a drink?" He tilted his glass toward the Waterford decanter on the sideboard.

Her eyes stayed sober and dark, but her voice was airy when she said, "Don't mind if I do."

She stepped into the room like the seasoned debutante she was, running her gaze lightly over him, then over the surroundings. "Quite a place you have here."

Patrick lifted an eyebrow at the noncompliment. "A bit modern for your taste, I imagine."

"Mmmm." She skirted the sharp edge of a low glass table, then paused to study a canvas full of the slashing blacks and reds his obscenely expensive decorator seemed to favor. She threw him a pitying glance over her shoulder. "It's a bit modern for *your* taste, if I recall. When are you going to let yourself settle down, Patrick?"

"I *am* settled," he said easily. "I even know where the nearest Home Depot is. Not that I've ever been in it." He moved toward the sideboard to pour her a drink. Refreshing his own held a certain appeal, as did turning his back on the full impact of her gaze.

"Patrick," she said, drawing his name out into a verbal eye roll. "You know what I mean. This place is gorgeous, but it's generic. You could sell it tomorrow. This isn't a home, it's an investment."

Patrick dropped ice cubes into a crystal glass, and splashed an inch of aged, single-malt whiskey over them. Her footsteps rang hollowly as she wandered farther into the room, and as he crossed to her with the glass, he took a moment to memorize the sight of her in his house. Had he imagined her here? He hadn't meant to.

"Darling, naïve little Liz," he said, patting her arm. "A house is always an investment. Didn't your trust fund manager teach you anything?"

She ignored him with admirable aplomb. "All this house," she mused as she sipped her whiskey, "and still no home for Patrick. It's sad. It really is."

He didn't say anything, just watched her and waited. She'd get where she was going eventually, and he didn't intend to indulge her apparent desire to detour into his psyche.

"Can I ask you a question?" she said finally, turning those sharp, lavishly blue eyes on him again.

"Can I stop you?" Patrick asked. He looked carefully away from the smooth expanse of calf and ankle displayed under the hem of her trench coat, away from those gloriously sexy shoes of hers. He'd give an indecent sum of money to see what she was wearing to go with them.

She smiled. "No."

"Then by all means, ask away."

"Do you love me, Patrick?"

"No." He didn't even hesitate over the lie. He just ripped it out like a weed from a garden. It left a bleeding hole behind, but how could he regret it? "You flew all the way to California and broke into my house just to ask me that?"

"Oh, no. I already knew what you'd say." She wandered into the room, touching edges and curves with one fingertip. "Flying here and breaking in, that was just my little love letter to you. I thought you'd like watching me blow through your security." She threw him a little smile over her shoulder. "Come on, Patrick, admit it. You watched every second of my little performance out there, I know you did. You could have stopped me whenever you wanted to, but you just watched. It kind of turned you on, didn't it?"

He sighed, as if despairing for her lost decorum. He'd die before admitting how very right she was. Even now, his palms itched to touch, to plunder, to gorge themselves on greedy handfuls of her before she disappeared again.

"Liz, please. If you don't mind, it's been a long day and I don't care to play games. This has been a lovely little trip down memory lane, truly, but unless there's something else . . . ?"

She turned to him, leaned back against the arm of the sofa, and rolled the rim of her tumbler against her chest. "Since you asked so nicely, there is." He sighed again, and she sent him a winning smile in return. "You see, I don't believe you."

He put his shoulder blades to the wall, lounged there as if his entire system hadn't just gone into panicked damage-control mode. "Beg your pardon?"

"I don't believe you," she said again. "You're lying to me."

"No, I really am tired." He gave her a polite smile. "Is this going to take much longer?"

She stepped up into his face, left mere inches between their bodies, inches that heated and vibrated with want. "Don't," she said softly. She reached up and put one of those small, strong hands against his cheek. "Don't do this. Don't disappear behind all that bored sophistication. Stay with me. I need you."

He couldn't move for a full three heartbeats, just stood there like a rooted tree and absorbed the incredible warmth of her palm against his skin, the sheer rightness of being inside the circle of her affection and approval.

"Liz," he said. It was all he could manage, and he'd meant for it to be a reproach but it came out more like a prayer. "Liz, please. Why are you doing this?"

"Don't you want to know why I'm here?" she asked softly, and when he opened his eyes, there was nothing but her face. Nothing but her. He nodded helplessly.

"I'm here for you. I'm not satisfied with how we left things last month. Or, should I say, how *you* left things."

That warm hand dropped away from his cheek, and he felt the loss intensely. Her eyes narrowed on his, and she tipped her head to the side to look him over. "Because I didn't actually get a chance to participate in the decision, did I? You just left. Abandoned me, like what I wanted or thought or felt didn't matter. You bestowed me on the FBI like a gift and walked away, all smug and righteous and pure. I was always worried that I'd fall for a man like my father, and it looks like I had good cause to worry."

The bottom dropped out of his stomach and he stared. Shook his head slowly. "God, Liz. It wasn't like that."

She smiled at him, the anger falling away with disorienting suddenness. "I know. At least I do now. I thought it over, and while I may be a bit paranoid, I'm not stupid. You *played* God. My father thought he *was* God. There's a difference. He wanted the power. You just wanted to spare me some pain by taking it all on yourself. Because you love me." She shook her head fondly. "You're a little bent, Patrick."

He nodded. On this, at least, they agreed.

"Even so," she said, "I love you right back and I've decided that I'm not ready to accept this ridiculous idea that you're in charge of whether or not I get what I want." She moved forward with exactly the kind of resolve and purpose he'd come to expect from her, as if she had right and justice unquestionably on her side, and kissed him. Her mouth was hot and sweet and open, and he felt it all the way through his bones.

And just like that, his self-control snapped. Desires he'd chained down with the ruthless efficiency of long habit broke free and surged to the surface. The drink he'd had dangling from languid fingers crashed to the floor and he seized her up like a drowning man snatching at a life preserver.

"Fuck it," he said roughly, tumbling her back onto the ugly modern sofa his decorator had picked out. It was hard and uncomfortable, but Patrick didn't care. He'd burn it in the morning. He'd burn the rest now. "I wanted to be better than this, Liz. God knows I tried. But I love you." He rested his forehead against hers, felt her arms come around him, heard her soft noise of triumph. "I know the FBI and I can't coexist and I know you loved them first. I know I'll come second to that and I'm willing to be whatever you need me to be for this to work. But I love you and I'll have you, as long as it lasts."

He didn't say *forever*, but the word trembled on his lips, in his heart. "I'm not afraid to lose you, Liz. But I've been so damn afraid that I'll never have you."

"I came to you," she whispered, her mouth hot against

his ear. She was running wet little kisses along the line of his throat. "I'm here. You have me. You've always had me. Now I want you to take me."

HER HEART thudding in her ears, she watched those glacial eyes catch fire. He lowered his mouth to hers and she lifted herself to meet him. For the first time, she kissed him with everything in her—all her fear, her love, her soul, her desire. She didn't hold anything back, just laid it all out where he could see it, where it was his to accept or reject.

He made a noise she couldn't identify, but it had her heart leaping with joy, her body shimmering onto another level of awareness. Those clever hands were at her waist, tugging at the tie of her trench coat, then stripping it off her.

"Oh God, the green," Patrick said, his eyes blazing down at the pool of emerald chiffon enveloping her. "I almost took this off you once."

She smiled at him, lifted her arms. "I know. I wanted to give you another chance. I wanted another chance myself."

He pulled her to her feet, stood up and moved behind her. She could see their reflection in that wall of glass, watched as he slowly lowered the zipper at her back. She heard the hiss as it released, and the air was cool against her bare skin as the fabric parted. Then his mouth was there, burning a trail down her spine, even as his busy hands pushed the dress off her shoulders. It floated to the floor, leaving her there in nothing but stockings and high heels.

"God," he said reverently, like it was a prayer. His hands streaked over her body, capturing her breasts. He brushed long fingers over her nipples and she arched into his touch with a cry of abandon. She let her eyes drift half shut, glorying in the wild whip of desire through her veins, the solid wall of his body framing hers. She leaned back into him, rubbed against him like a lazy kitten. He was hard against the curve of her bottom, and she pleased herself with a slow roll against the length of him.

He turned her in his arms, tunneled his fingers through her hair and captured her mouth with a certainty that sent shock waves pulsing over every inch of skin she possessed. Want pooled hot and moist between her legs, and she rose up on her toes to meet him, to tangle her tongue with his.

She yanked at the buttons on his shirt until they either popped open or shot off, and then that lovely, smooth chest was hers. Her hands roved greedily over it, learning each curve, each edge until she knew it blind. And it was a good thing, too, because at that moment, he slid one hand down the plane of her belly and into the center of her body, penetrating all her heat and want with one long finger.

She didn't think, didn't even try to hold back, just let him shoot her directly over that towering edge with a ruthless speed. She cried out, her knees going to water even as he caught her.

"Again," he said, his voice dark and rich. He scooped her into his arms, and she drifted on the echoing pulses of pleasure until he laid her onto the cool, smooth sheets of his bed. She opened her eyes, found him stripping himself and her with a determined purpose that had renewed heat lapping at the edges of her satisfaction. Then he laid himself beside her, the hard length of him hot and demanding against her hip.

She smiled at him, feline and silky, took him in her hand and said, "I want more." She rolled up on her side until her nipples rubbed against the plane of his chest and the breath shuddered out of her involuntarily. She watched as he closed those wildly blue eyes to savor her touch, and it sent tiny tongues of fire licking over her.

"I'll give it to you," he said, his voice hoarse and thick with need. He reached for her, took the curve of her hips in those big, warm hands, fastened his hot mouth over one nipple. She moaned and tumbled herself into his arms, sprawled over his chest. Her hair was a curtain on either side of them, narrowing the world down to only what was between them, the heat of their breath, the sweet pull of their lips, the small noises of want and need.

"No," she said, nipping at his lower lip. God, it was gorgeous. How had she lived without this? Without him? "I'm going to give it to you this time."

With a swift tip and roll of her hips, she had him exactly where she wanted him, all that lean strength coiled under her, ready and aching for what she would give with her body, with her heart. She kissed him as she sank down and took him deep inside. The moan could have been hers, could have been his. She only knew that she'd never in her life felt anything like it, the peace, the completion, the rightness, all alongside a raging hunger to be closer. She lifted and plunged, and he cried out, seized at her hips.

"Show me," she said. "Show me how to please you. I want to please you."

"You're doing fine," he said, his fingers twitching on her skin.

She rose up like a flame, twisting and leaping, his hands on her guiding, supporting, exploring. She reveled in each touch, each stroke, each layer of intimacy, until there was nothing hidden from him. Everything she was, heart, body and soul, was laid bare to his hands, his eyes, his desires. She was his without reservation, and when he rose up under her, his body bowed and trembling, she arched into him with a cry of pure satisfaction.

She drove him over the edge and flung herself after him, leaving nothing behind but the empty shell of her fear.

IT COULD have been minutes or hours later when Liz propped her chin on his chest and said, "I want more."

Patrick opened one eye and said, "Really?" A smile spread across his face and one hand curved around her hip.

Liz stretched languidly against his side and said, "Well, that, too, but that's not what I meant."

Patrick lifted an eyebrow and pushed a hand into all that tangled blond hair. It was warm and alive against his skin and he savored the feel of it between his fingers. "What did you mean?"

"You made me an offer earlier, a very nice one." Those earnest eyes of hers were very serious. "But it didn't go quite far enough. I want more. I want you. Forever."

His hand froze in her hair, and he sat up slowly. She curled into a lazy C at his knees and he couldn't resist the urge to slide a palm into the lovely curve of her waist even as alarm bells started to clang in his head. "You want what?"

"I want forever," she said simply. "I want the whole deal. A ring, a dog, a fixer-upper house and a charge account at Home Depot. Maybe even a kid someday, if we're ever really in the mood for a gamble. There are some oddball genes between the two of us."

Tell me about it, he thought. The very idea of a child with his father's black heart froze something deep inside him that had just started to thaw. "What the hell are you talking about? Didn't anything I said to you earlier sink in?"

"Well, yeah," Liz said. "But it was all predicated on the idea that the FBI was the first love of my life, and it isn't."

"No." He shoved himself out of the bed. "I won't let you do this. I saw you work, Liz. I know exactly what it meant to you to do that job. You were meant for it. You were designed for it, and believe me, the world can't afford to lose somebody like you doing what they were meant to do."

She rolled onto her back, stretched with every appearance of perfect ease. "I quit."

He went still, shock waves radiating from the center of his body outward in electric ripples. "What?"

"I quit," she said again, this time with a sunny smile. "You were right."

"About what?" he snapped. He couldn't have this conversation naked. He scrounged for his pants, found them in a crumpled heap at the foot of the bed and shook them out.

"You said that I hadn't left my extremist upbringing behind, I'd just switched gods—my father for the FBI. And you were right. I hadn't searched my soul at all for what I thought was right or good. I just adopted a new bible. I outsourced my moral code." She rolled onto one side, propped herself on her elbow. Patrick practically dove to his knees to look for his shirt. He couldn't look at all that gorgeous skin and think straight.

"I've spent this past month wondering how to fix that," she continued. "How to let go of all the rules and regulations I've let define me and figure out who I'm supposed to be. Who I *want* to be, and how I can have everything I need, you included. I think I've come up with a pretty good solution." She rolled off the bed and strolled to the living room, casually and spectacularly nude. He gaped after her. She returned a moment later, dress in hand. She eyed it critically. "A little wrinkled, but hell, it's chiffon. Nobody'll notice."

Patrick scrubbed his hands over his face, utterly at sea, hope warring with despair in his gut. "Liz." He dropped his hands and looked at her. "What are you talking about?"

She smiled at him. "I finally got in touch with the woman I want to be, and as it turns out, the FBI is a little stifling for her. Not enough room to explore those shades of gray that mean the difference between cutting a troubled kid a break and upholding the law. So I finally tapped in to that trust fund of mine. I started a foundation. Advocating for underage victims of criminal neglect and abuse. You're looking at the CEO."

Patrick felt his mouth drop open as this new piece of information tumbled around on the sea of conflicting emotions inside him. He waited for the regret, for the sense of wrongness or injustice, but it didn't come. Her face was bright and open, peaceful and optimistic. This was something he'd never considered. His avenging angel could work without a badge. Could possibly be happier that way.

"You quit the FBI." He kept circling back to that. "When?"

"A week after you left," she said, wriggling into her dress. He watched with some regret as all that beautiful skin disappeared into the chiffon. "When you left, I knew the badge had finally cost me too much. But I also knew you wouldn't have me until I proved to you that I had something else, something that filled those empty spaces inside."

She crossed to him, kissed him with a sweetness, a knowledge and affection that undid him. His heart all but shattered and fell around his feet. "You're so damn honorable, Patrick. So damn good. You're subtle, and I missed it for a long time, but I'm on to you. You're good all the way through, and I love you. More than anything. Please come with me."

"Anywhere." The word was out before he knew he was saying it, but it was true. Truer than anything he'd ever said. "I love you, Liz. I'll go anywhere you want me."

Love sparkled in her eyes, along with a few tears. "I was hoping you'd say that. You want to start with a fund-raiser? I'm kind of mixing business and pleasure here."

He drew back and stared at her. Then he laughed. "There's a fund-raiser for your new foundation?" he asked. "Here in Palm Springs?"

She gave him a sheepish smile. "Well, yeah. Have you ever known me to be without a backup plan? If you rejected me, I didn't want to wallow. So I'm scheduled. Will you come with me?"

He pulled her into his arms, right off her feet and swooped her into a joyous circle. God, he loved this woman.

"Anywhere," he said again. "Anywhere at all."

"You'd better mean that. 'Cause I really do want the dog, the ring and that little fixer-upper. Not necessarily in that order, either."

He dropped his chin into the sweet curve of her neck and closed his eyes against the unexpected and mortifying sting of tears. It was everything he'd never let himself want, and she was not only giving it to him, but acting as if it were all her idea. What had he ever done to deserve such a woman? He drew back, looked into her eyes and was startled to find something uncertain and yearning buried deep under the bravado.

"You'd do that?" he asked slowly. "Marry me?"

"God, yes. What have I been saying all this time?" She rolled her eyes, but he didn't miss the way joy started to edge out the nerves in them. "Do I have to ask you again?"

"No," he said. He could feel a goofy smile breaking free and spreading across his face, but he didn't care. She loved him. The real him. The man he'd tried so damn hard not to be all his life. And she wanted to marry him. "I'll do the asking this time."

He let her slide through his arms until her feet were safely back on the floor. Then he dropped to his knee in front of her and took her hands in his. When he looked up, she was beaming down at him, love and laughter warming her eyes, the beginning of tears sparkling on those long, long lashes.

"Marry me, Liz. Marry me and I'll give you everything you ever wanted. The house, the ring. Hell, you can even have the dog, as long as it doesn't shed or drool."

She dropped to her knees and threw her arms around him. The scent of her was sweet and familiar, the weight of her in his arms was precious, and he knew suddenly that this was home. Anywhere, everywhere. Just in her arms.

"All dogs shed and drool," she told him, though her voice was thick with tears.

"Seriously?"

She nodded. "So do men."

"We do not."

"You do." She swiped a hand at the tears running down her cheeks. "I love you anyway. I want to share my life with you."

Patrick smiled at her. "Is that a yes?"

"Can we negotiate on the dog?" She sniffled inelegantly. He kissed her.

"We'll negotiate on the dog."

"I'm thinking Saint Bernard."

"Oh my Lord."

She smiled at him. "You want me to sweeten the deal? I'll let you burn all my work suits."

"Liz. Darling. Polyester doesn't burn. It melts."

"Whatever. Do we have a deal?"

He kissed her again, and this time it was a promise. "Yes."

Keep reading for a special preview of

the next romance by Susan Sey

Money Shot

Coming soon from Berkley Sensation!

Chapter

I

BELLS JINGLED merrily as Mishkwa Island Park Ranger Rush Guthrie pushed through the jaunty red door of Mother Lila's Tea Shop.

"Coming!" Lila sang out in that wavery soprano of hers.

Rush slid into the room, his back to the wall, his fingers hooked casually into the custom-sewn pocket in his jacket that concealed his Sig Sauer. He scanned the cozy, doily-splattered sitting space of his aunt's tea shop with the calm, flat eyes of the professional killer he used to be. He'd come a long way since he'd landed on this island nearly two years ago, but not so far that he could walk into a room—any room—without performing at least a basic threat assessment. He wondered if he ever would.

His cousin Yarrow sat behind the register. (Second cousin? Third, maybe? A couple of times removed? Rush never could figure that stuff out.) But she sat there, her chin propped on the flat of her hand, her black-painted finger-nails flicking idly at a silver hoop that went clean through her eyebrow. Her *eyebrow*. That was another thing Rush couldn't figure out. Why a kid with a perfectly service-able face would want to perforate it? Between that hoop, the little stud in her nose, and the hardware dangling from her ears, the kid had a half-dozen extra holes in her head, easy.

Yarrow looked up from the paperback she had open on the counter and yelled, "It's just Rush, Grandma!" She gave him a smirk as he finished up his visual sweep. "So, any terrorists lurking in the tea shop today, Ranger Rush?"

"Nope."

She lifted the lid off the teapot at her elbow and peered gravely inside. "All clear here, too."

The urge to smile took him by surprise. The kid was flipping him crap. How about that? It wasn't so long ago that she wouldn't have dared. Nobody would have.

"Too bad." He put on a frown. "I haven't shot anybody all day."

Her eyes went round as lollipops, and she stared at him in shocked silence. "Did you just make a joke?"

This was the part where he should have smiled, or even laughed. But normal conversation had a rhythm, a beat pat-tern. It went fast and if you missed your mark, the moment was lost. Rush's timing was terrible. Had been for the last, oh, ten years. Give or take.

He pulled off his knit cap and stuffed it into his pocket. The one that didn't have a gun in it. "So, Lila called me?"

His aunt glided into the room, tall and handsome as a ship in full sail with scarves and skirts swirling, her long gray braid swinging. Yarrow said, "Grandma. Rush made a joke."

Lila clasped her pretty, ringed hands together and beamed. "He did?"

"It was about shooting people, but it was definitely a joke." She quirked a brow his way. "Wasn't it?"

"I don't talk about shooting when I'm serious," he said. "It spoils the surprise."

Lila's mouth fell open. "Good Lord, he did it again."

They both gazed at him in wonder, then Yarrow leaned toward Lila and dropped her voice to a stage whisper. "I'm scared, Grammy," she said. "Is this the apocalypse?"

"No, dear. Of course not." Lila patted Yarrow's shoulder absently while she continued to study him. "It'll rain frogs first."

A tiny trickle of unfamiliar warmth bubbled up in Rush's chest as he stood in front of these laughing women. Together they constituted a full two-thirds of his family, and for just a moment the gift of them pierced his soul, sweet and sharp. The urge to laugh with them kicked in but as usual the moment had already passed.

Yarrow broke the circle first, deliberately shifting out from under Lila's hand, as if she'd just noticed it resting on her shoulder. The rejection sent a wisp of grief over Lila's face but by the time she turned to Rush it was gone. "So," she said brightly, "what are you doing here besides being unusually amusing?"

"I have no idea. You called me, remember?"

"Oh yes." Lila came around the counter, slid a confidential hand into Rush's elbow. He tensed automatically, then forced himself to relax. *Jesus, Rush,* he thought. *She's your beloved aunt. She's not going to stick a knife between your ribs.* "It seems my dear neighbor Mr. Barnes has his shorts in a knot over the compost again."

Rush glanced automatically toward Ben Barnes's place next door. Midsixties with the build and endurance of a guy thirty years younger, Ben ran Mishkwa Island Outfitters in the summers and built birch bark canoes by hand in the winters. A pretty straightforward guy for the most part, but not overly patient with Lila's kookier endeavors. Probably didn't help neighborly relations at all that Lila had the *kooky* market pretty well cornered.

"Ben doesn't like your compost?"

"Evidently not."

"He thinks it's attracting Sir Humpalot," Yarrow said.

"Sir Humpalot?"

She arched the brow without the ring. "Sure. Seven,

maybe eight feet tall? Long brown beard, big rack?" She put her free hand to her head, thumb against her scalp, fingers fanned out, miming antlers. "Unsuccessfully humping the Dumpsters since September?"

Rush blinked at her. The kid had nicknamed a rogue bull moose with sexual identity issues Sir Humpalot.

He frowned down at Lila. "This kid needs to go back to normal school."

"Normal school. Pah." Lila fluttered her fingers in the air. "She joined your little ski team, didn't she? That's plenty of interaction with her peers."

"More than," Yarrow muttered. Rush felt for her. He'd spent years being the scariest bastard on the block, but even he was scared of teenagers. All those churning appetites and no sense of mortality to curb them. Dangerous as fuck. But Lila had determined they both required more human interaction, so suddenly Yarrow was sweating it out with the high school ski team on the mainland. And Rush? Rush was coaching it. Jesus.

"As for her schooling," Lila went on, "the child reads incessantly." She smiled her earth-mother smile at Yarrow. "Don't you, dear?"

"You bet, Grandma." Yarrow smirked at Rush and tipped up her paperback so he could see a half-naked couple on the cover clinched together in a swirl of purple smoke. There might have been a unicorn rearing up behind them in a phallic reference Rush didn't want to contemplate in relation to his sixteen-year-old cousin.

"I don't know that romance novels count as mind-improving literature, Lila."

Lila smiled at him, her imperious face gentle. "Love improves everything, Rush. The mind included. You should try it sometime."

"What, romance novels?" Rush shrugged. "Not my thing."

"I mean love, and you know it," Lila said. "You want to talk about people who ought to reengage with their peer group—"

"Hey, that's true," Yarrow said, her eyes dancing with wicked glee. "Sir Humpalot gets more action than you."

Rush experienced a pang of nostalgia for the good old days when nobody dared screw with him. "I don't date Dumpsters."

"You don't date anybody," Lila said.

"Nobody to date. It's December, in case you hadn't noticed. Single women aren't exactly thick on the ground this time of year."

"You didn't date when it was July and the pretty hikers were all faking sun stroke and sprained ankles to get your attention," Yarrow pointed out helpfully.

"You didn't get here till September, Cuz," Rush said.

"Doesn't mean I don't hear things." Yarrow lifted her thin shoulders. "People talk."

"About stuff that's none of their damn business." Rush turned to Lila, who was peering at him with a disconcerting intensity in those bird-bright eyes. He snapped his mouth shut. His misanthropy was showing, damn it. And he'd been doing such a good job today. Now he was in for it.

"Rush. People aren't talking about you out of malice. They're talking about you out of love." She rubbed her palm briskly up and down his arm. "They want you to be happy. We all do."

"I *am* happy." His aunt gazed at him skeptically. "Happy enough, anyway." She didn't blink; she only arched one pale brow. "Okay, maybe not *tra-la-la, baby-ducks-and-chicks* happy but I'm doing okay. Honest."

And he was. Compared to the condition he'd been in when he'd arrived on Mishkwa the spring before last, he was doing fucking great. At least his brain wasn't buzzing anymore. At least he didn't wake up angry and leashed and whipcord tight anymore, his trigger finger ready for a quick day's work. Something about putting a couple miles of cold, clean space between him and the next beating heart had dulled his sharper edges. Quieted the static that had lived inside his head so long he'd forgotten how blessed silence could be.

Now if only he could find the inner voice that used to speak into that silence, he'd be set.

"He did make a joke, Grandma," Yarrow said, unexpectedly switching allegiances. Kid was a pot stirrer, no question.

"He did, didn't he?"

"Tried to, anyway." Yarrow turned to Rush. "Work really hard and the next one might be funny."

Lila gave his elbow a final pat. "It was his first try," she said to Yarrow. "Let's cut him a break."

Yarrow shrugged and went back to her book. Lila turned to straighten the sugar bowl and the honey bear sitting on the counter next to a blue-glazed vase full of wooden stir sticks and a fat little pot of creamer. Rush stood uncertainly in the middle of this hotbed of femininity and tried to remember what he was supposed to be doing.

"So." He cleared his throat and drew a battered notepad from his jacket pocket. "About Ben Barnes and the compost. Moose been around lately?"

"Not here more than any other place in town." Lila flipped the end of her long, gray braid over her shoulder. "Ben objects to me more than my garbage and we all know it, so let's not get all legal about it."

Rush paused. "So then what am I doing here?"

"We wanted to see you." Lila gave him a lofty look down the length of her nose. "What, you had a more pressing engagement?"

He ducked his head to look out the window at the fat, gray clouds tumbling down from Canada. Clouds that looked likely to steam straight across Mishkwa on their way to Wisconsin. "Weather's coming," he said. "Thought I'd turn that deadfall up on the ridge trail into firewood before it gets here."

Lila curled her lip. "Another lovely afternoon of battling nature into submission?"

"Well, sure." Rush liked his job for a lot of reasons but foremost among them was the number of days he spent working up a good, honest sweat with nobody for company but his chain saw. Plus, he got firewood. It was always nice when a huge amount of effort yielded a tangible reward. Unlike this endless interview with his aunt.

"Rush." Lila pinned him with eyes entirely too sharp for the soft curve of her smile. "First of all, you can't fight nature. But second? You spend too much time alone."

"Oh. Oh, no." He held up his hands and backed toward the door. "Whatever it is, I'm not doing it."

Lila followed him. "You haven't even heard what I want yet," she said, her voice dangerously reasonable.

"The last time we had this conversation, I ended up coaching a high school ski team." He groped behind him for the doorknob, unwilling to take his eyes off his aunt when she was in this particular mood. "The time before that, it was supervising a meeting of the Young Anarchists of America."

"That was the Young Politicos."

"Whatever. I signed my name to stuff. I'm probably on a half-dozen watch lists by now."

"Don't be ridiculous, Rush. They're children. Harmless."

Yarrow snorted and Rush wholeheartedly agreed. Lila ignored them both.

"The point is, you have a duty to take your place in this community. The place that's been waiting for you."

"What place might that be?"

"There's a full moon next week," she said. "The coven is gathering here for esbat, social hour to follow. I think you should come."

He frowned at her. Stripping away all the traditional language of his childhood religion, this was essentially a request for him to come to church. "That's it?"

"That's it." She treated him to her warmest smile. "Think it over, Rush. Surely you can squeeze some pondering into your busy schedule of hiking and chopping things up."

Yarrow swallowed a chuckle, though when he looked her way she was reading her book with studied innocence.

"Okay," he said. "Sure." His hand finally landed on the knob, thank you, Jesus. "I'll think about it."

"Thank you, dear."

Then the knob twisted under his hand—from the outside—and years of training so rigorous it had replaced instinct took over. Lila leaned in to kiss his cheek, and Rush lifted her clean off her feet. In the space of half a heartbeat, he'd moved her three long strides to the counter where he could put both her and Yarrow behind him. By the time the door flew open with a sweep of wind and the frantic tinkle of sleigh bells, Rush had the women covered and his hand wrapped around the butt of his gun in his pocket. He'd domesticated himself enough not to actually draw the gun, but not so much that he wasn't prepared to blow a hole clean through his new jacket.

And whoever came through the door.

Chapter

2

EINAR OLSEN ambled through the door like an earth-bound Apollo, all golden curls and chiseled cheekbones rubbed ruddy by the raw winter wind. He poked lazy hands toward the ceiling.

"Dude," he said, his blue eyes twinkling with wicked laughter. "I surrender. Don't shoot."

Rush eased his finger off the trigger and willed his body to stop mainlining adrenaline. One of these days, his cousin was going to figure out that sneaking up on him wasn't as funny—or as safe—as it had been when they were kids. Rush sincerely hoped that blessed day came before he shot the guy's ass off. Lila would kill him.

"Honestly, Rush," Lila said from behind him. "Was that really necessary?"

He gave Einar a hard look. "Yes."

She delivered a sharp poke to his kidneys, which he took as an invitation to stop squashing her against the counter. He stepped aside and she huffed out an exasperated breath. "You see now why I want you at esbat? I swear, you're

barely housebroken. You need to get used to people again."
She patted at the soft gray wings of hair over her ears and
leaned around him. "Hello, Einar."

"Hey, Auntie." Einar scooped Lila into his arms, delivered a smacking kiss to her cheek, then set her back on her
feet. "You're looking exquisite as always."

She swatted his arm. "Oh, go on. Sweet-talker."

"Hey, Einar," Yarrow said, her eyes huge and adoring
on their mutual cousin. Poor kid. He'd be worried about
her if the entire female half of his ski team weren't in love
with Einar, too. It was going around, apparently. Like the
stomach flu or something.

Einar tossed her an absent grin. "Hey, little girl."

Rush winced. Even he knew better than to call a sixteen-
year-old nursing a raging crush a *little girl*. Yarrow's smile
went brittle, but Einar had already shifted his attention
back to Rush.

"What's this now?" he asked, his eyes still laughing
at Rush's stiff shoulders. "You're coming to esbat this
month?"

Rush jerked one of those shoulders. "Maybe."

"Yes," Lila said at the same time. "High time, too. Mishkwa Coven is one of the only blood-bonded covens left on
the continent. You two are the last of our line. Attending
services is the least you can do."

"Services." Einar made a rude noise. "You want to
ensure the future of the coven? We should be doing a hell
of a lot more than holding services, if you ask me."

Lila sighed. "I'm not asking you."

"That's because you're stubborn and you lack vision.
The lunar standstill only happens once every eighteen
years, you know. And thanks to you we missed the last
one." He threw out his hands. "The Stone Altar is a gold
mine, Lila, and I don't understand why you won't at least
consider tapping in to it."

"Because it's not a gold mine. It's a death trap. And I'm
not going to have this argument again. If you want to turn

this island into a theme park, you'll have to wait until I'm dead and gone."

"I hope you're planning to kick the bucket before the next lunar standstill, then."

Lila drew back sharply.

"What? You have fourteen more years."

She continued to stare at him in offended silence until he sighed and rolled his eyes. "It was a joke, Lila."

"Rush made a joke today," Yarrow said suddenly. "He was all 'I haven't shot anybody for days' and we were all 'What?' and then it was all 'Where are the raining frogs' . . ." She stopped, eagerness dissolving into embarrassment as Einar waited politely for the funny part. Her cheeks went bright.

"I guess you had to be there," Einar said. He turned back to Rush. "So you're coming, then? To esbat?"

"You know what? Sure." Rush smiled—right on time for once—into the sudden chill in Einar's blue eyes. He didn't know why Einar didn't want him showing up at the pagan ceremony to celebrate the full moon. He didn't really care. All he knew was that when a grown man embarrassed a child and insulted an elder all within the space of two sentences, he deserved not to get what he wanted. "I'll be there."

Lila clapped her hands. "Wonderful!"

"Yeah," Einar said, his smile almost convincing. "Great."

The sleigh bells at the door jangled again. Rush automatically put himself in front of the women, though he didn't reach for his gun this time. Baby steps.

"Easy, trigger," Einar said, his voice low and mocking. "I'll get this one."

Then the door opened, and in walked that rarest of all commodities on Mishkwa in December—a stranger.

And not just any stranger, either. Lord, no. This stranger was about six feet of long-legged, dark-eyed woman, all smooth hair and golden skin, with a let's-be-friends smile lighting up an extraordinary face.

Not a pretty face, exactly, but certainly one that deserved a second look. The discerning man might go back for a third. It was all those sharp edges and uncompromising slants against the lush oasis of that mouth, he thought. The contrast or something. It made a guy want to do stupid things. Rash things. Hot, wet, sweaty things, for sure.

"Hoo, boy," Einar said. "Dibs."

Fuck, Rush thought. For a guy who never stood when he could sit—or hell, lie down—Einar could move when it counted.

GOOSE HAD hardly cleared the door of the little tea shop when Rush Guthrie himself—because who else could it be?—strode forward and engulfed her hand in a hearty grip.

"Welcome to Mishkwa," he boomed, his voice radio-announcer cheerful, his eyes Caribbean blue. Goose blinked. Good Lord. His file hadn't included a recent photo—a convention designed to protect behind-enemy-lines types against intel leaks—but it had included a basic physical description: Six-three, blue/blonde, approximately 190. Based on that, she'd been ready for the Captain American type, but this guy was a recruiting poster come to life. She wondered if the military was still kicking itself over losing him.

"Can I help you?" he asked.

"Well now, that depends." She gave him a smile with just a hint of flirt around the edges. Based on the smug interest in those clear blue eyes, Ranger Guthrie sort of dug the glamazon type. Maybe not as much as he dug himself, but enough. A surprising number of men did. But yard-wide shoulders, thick hair the color of fresh butter, and a jaw that could make Superman himself feel weak-chinned did not necessarily translate into the confidence to deal well with the double whammy of a tall girl and her badge. Thus the little bit of flirt-insurance. Flattery worked on everybody.

"On?"

"I'm looking for somebody," she said.

He stepped just close enough to edge into her personal space, and grinned down at her with very white teeth. "Dare I hope you've found him?"

Goose kept her smile on high beam. Okay, this guy's confidence wasn't going to be a problem. Stomaching him long enough to determine if he had the brains and the connections to run supernotes, however? That might be an issue.

"Depends." She freed her hand from his and produced the badge she'd stashed in the Prada purse she'd treated herself to last Christmas. "Special Agent Maria di Guzman," she said. "Secret Service. Ranger Rush Guthrie?"

Captain America shook his head and stepped closer yet. Close enough that she could smell his breath mint and the chewing tobacco it was trying to cover. "Now what would you want with my cousin when all the man you need is right here?"

She tipped her head and gave him a curious look. "You're one of those guys who likes getting arrested by girl cops, aren't you?"

He gave her a lingering once-over. "I'd try anything once."

She patted his arm. "I bet you would." She tried hard to make it sound like a compliment. "You could start by directing me to Ranger Guthrie."

"I'm Ranger Guthrie."

She looked past Captain America for the first time and met a pair of eyes so pale she couldn't tell if they were blue or gray. The color hardly mattered. Not compared to the intense attention in them, and the wary spark it sent dancing all the way down her body to her half-frozen toes. If she hadn't been purposely holding her ground against his cousin's hokey moves, the impact might have knocked her back a step. Possibly two.

She glanced between the men. Ranger Guthrie was maybe two or three inches taller than Captain America, but a good twenty pounds lighter. Not that he was skinny.

Hardly. He just had the lean, wiry build of a distance runner rather than his cousin's gym-toned muscle mass. He lacked his cousin's classic looks, too, with hair clipped so brutally short she could only speculate about its color. It was a fashion choice that did nothing to soften the bones pressing harsh and sharp against wind-touched skin.

But where his pretty cousin had sailed forward with supreme confidence toward the stranger at the door, this guy had put his body in front of the only other occupants of the shop—women, Goose suspected. And unless she was dreadfully mistaken—which she almost never was—his fingers were hooked casually into a pocket that held a weapon.

Sound and fury, she thought looking back at Captain America. *No mistaking which cousin was which.*

"Good afternoon, Ranger Guthrie," she said. She sent him a friendly smile but didn't move in for the handshake. She wasn't about to crowd a guy with his particular skill set.

"Agent di Guzman."

"Can I speak with you?"

"Regarding?"

God, that voice. It was low, slow and a little rusty, like he'd just woken up, or maybe hadn't used it in a while. She'd bet on the second scenario, though it was the first that caught her imagination. An image of him waking up hijacked her mind's eye—all those efficient muscles and long limbs tangled up in some plain white sheets, the sleep in his gray eyes giving way to that powerful focus.

Another spark shot through her body, but this one wasn't wary. It was all heat, and it didn't make it to her toes. It detoured to places best left unmentioned and set up a nice little glow there instead. A bolt of fear, pure and reflexive, chased it down. Snuffed it out before it did anything stupid, like bloom into an actual desire.

Because desire, Goose knew, was not her friend. It ran through her character like a fault line—thin, deep and potentially catastrophic. It could lay dormant for years but then, out of nowhere, she would simply *want*. Want with a passion that drove her beyond reason, limits or perspective. A passion that left her heedless. Unpredictable. Uncontrolled.

Dangerous.

She'd indulged that passion exactly once, and though she'd survived, others had not. The experience had marked her. Defined her. At this point, resisting desire was no harder than putting on her badge, firing up her laptop, or straightening her hair. Just one more thing she did every day that made her who she was.

Which was not a woman who indulged her weaknesses. Not here, not now, not with this man. Not ever.

She put a hand to the smooth sweep of her hair. The calm, orderly fall of it reassured her.

"I'd rather speak with you in private," she finally said.

Guthrie jumped as if pinched, then stepped aside to reveal a tall woman in her midsixties. She favored vibrant jewel tones, a choice Goose approved given the dramatic silver of her hair. A startlingly sweet smile transformed the patrician sternness of her face as she stepped forward.

"Agent di Guzman, is it?"

"Yes, ma'am," Goose said.

"I'm Lila."

"As in Mother Lila's Tea Shop?"

"The very one." Lila threaded her arm through Ranger Guthrie's and beamed at Goose. "You'll have to forgive my nephew here. His job keeps him from civilization most of the winter. He's lost the habit of polite conversation." She took Goose's elbow in her other hand and turned them both toward a little wire-legged table in the bay window that framed a heartbreaking sweep of Lake Superior's jagged beauty. "You just have a seat right here. Yarrow will bring you a nice hot cup of tea and Rush"—she nudged the silent ranger into the chair opposite her—"will remember his manners shortly, I'm sure."

Lila bustled toward the counter, snapping her ringed fingers at the teenage Goth queen Goose was startled to find sitting at the register. *Good Lord*, she thought. *How many people had Guthrie been hiding behind those broad shoulders?*

"Yarrow!" Lila sang out. "Two cups of Lady Grey at table five, please!"

Captain America stopped at the table's edge on his way to the door. "See you around, Maria."

She sincerely hoped not but sent him a smile anyway. "Nice meeting you."

He turned to his cousin. "I'm out of pocket for a few days starting tomorrow morning," he said. "Some fat cats from Duluth are having a conference down on Mackinac and can't be bothered to drive. Keep an eye on the girls, will you?"

"Feed still in the kitchen?"

"Yep."

"Will do."

Goose watched him saunter out the door, jacket unzipped, curls dancing on the bitter wind. "Your cousin, was it?"

"Einar."

"Guy's going to freeze to death going out like that." She sent Guthrie an amused half smile. "Look pretty doing it, though."

He shot a dubious glance at her cranberry wool beret. "Guess you'd know."

Okay, so no common ground poking fun at the ridiculous cousin. She touched her hat—her *adorable* hat—and gave a self-deprecating chuckle. "I would, actually. It if gets much colder than this, I might have to consider earflaps." She shuddered dramatically.

"It does."

She paused, backtracked. "Does what?"

"Get colder."

"Oh." She looked into those pale eyes, saw not a hint of humor. She tried again. "Surely that's not possible. It's already ridiculous out there. I think I freezer-burned my lungs just walking here from the ferry dock. How much colder could it get?"

He gave her a long, steady look. "Much."

Irritation pressed in on her. What, was there some kind of word rationing in effect on Mishkwa she hadn't been informed of? A law against small talk? Or had Guthrie simply ceded his lifetime supply of words to his chatty cousin? She swallowed a few acidic words of her own—sure to give her heartburn later—and summoned up her best look of laughing chagrin.

"So. Earflaps? Really?"

Pause. "Depends."

"On?" She smiled around gritted teeth.

"You."

She sighed. "Not one for small talk, are you, Ranger Guthrie?"

"I suck at it."

She shook her head solemnly. "Surely not."

A corner of his mouth flickered, like maybe he wanted to smile but didn't quite remember how. "So how about we skip it and you just tell me what you're doing here?"

"Fair enough." She swung her legs to the side—no room for them under this teeny table, of course—and crossed them. She took a moment to admire the supple leather boots that encased her calves like a butter-soft second skin until they disappeared into the dark wool of her plaid wrap skirt. So, she noted with a sharp satisfaction, did Ranger Guthrie. Maybe he hated her hat but didn't mind her boots so much. Or the legs inside them.

"How about you tell me why a guy with a gun in his pocket would want to stab a sitting governor with a flaming pitchfork?"

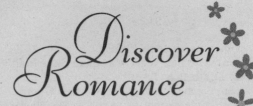